CW01391556

The Last Days of Summer

Sarra Manning has been a voracious reader for over forty years and a prolific author and journalist for thirty.

Her novels, which have been translated into numerous languages, include *Rescue Me* and *London, With Love*. Sarra has also written a number of YA novels, and several light-hearted romantic comedies under a pseudonym.

She started her writing career on *Melody Maker* and *Just Seventeen* and has written for the *Guardian*, the *Sunday Times*, the *Telegraph*, *ELLE*, *Grazia*, *Stylist*, *You* Magazine and *Harper's Bazaar*. She is currently the Literary Editor of *Red* Magazine.

Sarra lives in London surrounded by piles and piles of books.

Also by Sarra Manning

Unsticky
You Don't Have to Say You Love Me
Nine Uses for an Ex-Boyfriend
It Felt Like a Kiss
After the Last Dance
The House of Secrets
The Rise and Fall of Becky Sharp
Rescue Me
London, With Love
The Man of Her Dreams

Sarra Manning

The Last Days of Summer

HODDER &
STOUGHTON

First published in Great Britain in 2025 by Hodder & Stoughton Limited
An Hachette UK company

The authorised representative in the EEA is Hachette Ireland,
8 Castlecourt Centre, Dublin 15, D15 XTP3, Ireland
(email: info@hbgi.ie)

1

Copyright © Sarra Manning 2025

The right of Sarra Manning to be identified as the Author of the Work has
been asserted by her in accordance with the Copyright, Designs and
Patents Act 1988.

All rights reserved. No part of this publication may be reproduced, stored
in a retrieval system, or transmitted, in any form or by any means without
the prior written permission of the publisher, nor be otherwise circulated
in any form of binding or cover other than that in which it is published and
without a similar condition being imposed on the subsequent purchaser.

All characters in this publication are fictitious and any resemblance to real
persons, living or dead, is purely coincidental.

A CIP catalogue record for this title is available from the British Library

Hardback ISBN 978 1 399 70788 6
Trade Paperback ISBN 978 1 399 70789 3
Ebook ISBN 978 1 399 70790 9

Typeset in Plantin Light by Manipal Technologies Limited

Printed and bound in Great Britain by Clays Ltd, Elcograf S.p.A.

Hodder & Stoughton policy is to use papers that are natural, renewable
and recyclable products and made from wood grown in sustainable forests.
The logging and manufacturing processes are expected to conform to the
environmental regulations of the country of origin.

Hodder & Stoughton Limited
Carmelite House
50 Victoria Embankment
London EC4Y 0DZ

www.hodder.co.uk

I'm twenty years into this book-writing thing and I realise that I've never dedicated a book to the people that I do this for, the people without whom I'm nothing; the people who read these stories that I love to tell. Whether you've been here since the J-17 days of Diary of a Crush *or still think that* Unsticky *is my best novel or even if this is the first time you've picked up one of my books, this one is for you.*

Thank you from the bottom of my grateful little heart.

Even amidst fierce flames
The golden lotus can be planted
— the *Bhagavad Gita,* or
Monkey, attrib. Wu Cheng'en

I

As Cassie Scott stepped out of Finsbury Park station and into the light, she had no idea that she was about to have one of the worst evenings of her life.

After all, bad things should only ever happen in November.

November was miserable enough. A little more misery couldn't hurt on top of those damp grey hours that gave way to darkness by four o'clock. Besides, there was always the promise of Christmas just around the corner with its glitter and presents and huge tins of Quality Street.

Yes, let November fold the bad things into the fabric of its bleak thirty days.

Bad things should never happen on a fiercely sunny Friday evening at the beginning of July when there were blue skies and the endless possibility of the long summer ahead.

Cassie was hot, sticky and bedraggled. Her loose, sleeveless maxi dress with its graphic black and white pattern had looked crisp and on trend that morning but was now clinging damply to her. Her feet in white Birkenstocks had collected a lot of city grime over the course of the day and though she'd washed and tonged her long, brown hair that morning to make the most of some very expensive honey-toned highlights, the loose waves hadn't survived the tube journey into town. Her hair was now twisted in two space buns, secured with bright yellow scrunchies, while her thoughts were firmly fixed on the evening to come.

Truthfully, there was a small but very insistent part of her that would have quite liked to go straight home, shower, then sit in her pants in her tiny little garden with a Calippo for dinner, but it would be rude to cancel now. Also, there had been an email summons, which had been a slightly odd and formal way of arranging things. Cassie had even replied, 'Could this email have been a WhatsApp?'

For one moment, almost as if she had an inkling of what was to come, Cassie stood motionless and in the path of the sweaty, irritated people who were trying to enter and exit the tube. But she was only wondering whether she should buy a bottle of wine. Instead she bought a large bag of cherries and a couple of punnets of nectarines from the fruit seller outside the station. Then she eyed up the long queue for the W3 bus, which was doubling back on itself.

She was the last person to squeeze onboard. It was standing room only and Cassie could feel the last of her make-up sliding off. She was just as grateful to get off the bus as she had been to get off the tube. Then it was a short walk along streets full of the imposing three-storey redbrick Edwardian houses that this part of north London did so well. The streets became narrower, the houses smaller until Cassie finally reached a terraced row of Victorian cottages that edged along the bottom of Alexandra Park. She could just make out the splendour of Alexandra Palace and the spindly radio-transmitter tower in the distance as she ambled slowly along the street.

Cassie was still preoccupied with the week that had just been. Fashioning work grievances into amusing anecdotes and wondering if it was even worth mentioning the Hinge date that had lasted only ten minutes.

She unlatched the gate and walked up the tiled path to the front door, which was painted a cheery egg-yolk yellow. The sight of it, and the memories of all the good times she'd had once she'd stepped through the door, never failed to lift Cassie's spirits.

She rang the bell and waited for the sound of footsteps, a shadowy figure appearing in the door's frosted-glass panels, but all was silent.

'I'm here and melting on your doorstep,' she messaged and when there was no response, Cassie messaged the other occupants of the house.

It was the law that a teenage girl could never ignore the ping of her phone. Not even a minute later, the door was opened by Joni and Fleur, fifteen and thirteen respectively. All gangly limbs, long hair and braces.

Cassie smiled in delight and, no matter that she was hot and unpleasantly moist, she opened her arms wide.

'Bring it in, ladies,' she said and the two girls launched themselves at her, the force of their connection almost rocking Cassie off her feet.

'I'm so glad you're here,' Joni mumbled into Cassie's neck. There had been a time, not that long ago, when hugs had meant that the girls grabbed Cassie around the waist, but now Joni was so tall that she could rest her chin on the top of Cassie's head. Fleur was also shooting up at an alarming rate and always insisted that they stood back to back so she could see if she'd overtaken Cassie's five feet four inches.

'Tall enough to join the police,' Cassie said when the girls called her pocket-sized.

'Why would you want to join the Feds?' Fleur would ask, like she'd been brought up in a rough neighbourhood in South Central LA and not in a very leafy enclave of north London which local estate agents referred to as 'between the parks'.

It was a very clingy hug and they seemed quite subdued compared to the last time that Cassie had seen them a couple of weeks before, when she'd taken them and her baby brother Ryan to see Taylor Swift at Wembley. It was undoubtedly the greatest work blag Cassie had ever pulled off, and the four of them had scream-sung to every song. For the rest of the week Cassie had sounded like she smoked thirty a day.

'OK, you can let me go now,' she said at last, but still had to disentangle Joni's arms from around her neck. 'Everything all right?'

Joni shrugged and Fleur gave a choked cry, then they disappeared up the stairs. Being a teenage girl was hard. Cassie would never want to relive her own adolescence. MySpace and Bebo had been bad enough; Instagram, TikTok and boys addicted to violent pornography were much, much worse.

She followed the same red and black tiles that had lined the garden path along the hall to the big open-plan kitchen at the back of the house, the patio doors open to the garden.

The door of the cream Smeg fridge was also open, obscuring Cassie from view as she looked around the kitchen at all the little details she loved: the rose-gold splashback and matching taps and handles, the bespoke cabinetry painted in Farrow & Ball's Sulking Room Pink. They'd gone through tester pot after tester pot of muddy pink colours that all looked much the same – though Cassie had refrained from pointing that out; it had been a very stressful time.

But it wasn't just the colour scheme and the striking features in the kitchen that Cassie coveted. It was also the wall painted in blackboard paint with reminders about who was meant to be where and when and a list of things to be added to the supermarket order. It was the huge blown-up pic of the four of them, Fleur and Joni tiny, dressed up as KISS for Halloween. All the trappings of family life. Of someone finding their person. Of choosing them from all the other people in the world and creating something magical and everlasting with the love they had for each other.

The fridge door suddenly closed and both Cassie and her best friend Lucy gave a start to see the other one standing there.

Lucy ran a hand through her long blonde hair. She always said that she wished she was an ashy blonde rather than a yellow blonde, but Lucy wasn't a cool-toned, ashy person. She was far more exuberant than that. 'I was miles away. Didn't even hear the doorbell.'

'The girls let me in, then I was perving at your kitchen as per usual,' Cassie said sheepishly.

'Feel free to perv away.' Lucy smiled and took a step towards Cassie, then stilled. There was something off with her. Like she was moving underwater. Everything about her slow and clumsy as she held up a bottle of wine. 'Rosé?'

'Rose, yay!'

Lucy smiled tightly at the very weak pun and Cassie felt a little ping of panic twang in her solar plexus.

Had she done something to piss Lucy off? Was that why she'd cancelled their Saturday plans two weeks in a row at very short notice? Was that the reason for a summons by email on Monday instead of their usual WhatsApps?

But they were sisters from different misters (a phrase that they both hated). They told each other everything.

It was a friendship of sixteen years which had started off in unlikely circumstances and flourished. At the tender age of twenty, after three years as office junior rising to office manager at a funeral director's on the Holloway Road, Cassie was ready for a change. She'd signed up with a temping agency in the West End and her first assignment had been as illness cover for the assistant to the commercial director of an aspirational fashion and lifestyle magazine called *Skirt*.

After three years of having to wear a neat blouse and skirt, court shoes and her hair pulled back in a ponytail, Cassie had been lowkey terrified of the sophisticated, glossy women on the *Skirt* ad team. They all wore sleek black trouser suits and high heels, which they'd switch up to an evening look with the addition of a sparkly going-out top. Not that they were in the office much; they were usually out wooing clients at chic breakfast meetings and expensive lunches. When they did return to HQ, it was to have long shouty conversations on their company BlackBerries about double-page spreads, gatefold covers and the rate card.

It was a glimpse of another world. A world that Cassie desperately wanted to be a part of. Even though her out-of-work look was more indie sleaze than ad exec, she bought a black trouser suit in the Jane Norman sale and when the commercial director's assistant didn't return, Cassie had all but refused to leave. It helped that she could type eighty-five words per minute and survive on the tiny salary because she was still living at home.

Lucy was one of the ad girls. That is to say she was among them but not of them. Lucy didn't wear sleek black trouser suits but flowery dresses and plimsolls, before flowery dresses and plimsolls were a thing. She rarely shouted on her BlackBerry because she tended to either lose it or drop it down the loo. In her first month at *Skirt*, Cassie had had to order Lucy not one, not two, but three replacement BlackBerries. Each one came with an increasingly dire warning about what would happen if Lucy lost or damaged the replacement.

Lucy would nod obediently and blink her big cornflower-blue eyes as if she was on the verge of tears. Then a week later, she'd sidle up to Tamara, the commercial director, and say, 'Please don't shout at me, Tammy, but my BlackBerry has had a little accident,' in a voice that always managed to be both gravelly and squeaky at the same time.

Lucy rarely got a bollocking because she was the personality hire. She'd never once closed a deal, but she was instrumental in getting the deals in the first place. Her talent was for establishing a quick and easy rapport with even the most fearsome of account directors. Lucy was always losing things but she was great at remembering people's birthdays and their favourite restaurants and the names of their children.

Now her innate super-connector skills were put to much better use in the charity sector where Lucy matched girls and women from disadvantaged backgrounds with mentors in the creative industries.

But back then, life on the ad floor wouldn't have been quite so much fun without Lucy. Her spot on the big bank of ad girls' desks was nearest to Cassie's solitary one in front of Tamara's glass-walled office. When everyone else was on appointments and it was just Cassie and Lucy in the office, Lucy could always be relied upon to disrupt Cassie's contractually obligated duties.

'Cassie, would you rather have your toes as fingers or your ears where your eyes should be?'

'Cassie, Chandler, Joey and Ross. Shag, marry or kill?'

Then at five on the dot every afternoon: 'Cassie, what are you having for dinner? It's Thursday, isn't it? Is that sausage casserole night?'

Cassie would try not to be distracted, but it was hard. The only distractions at the funeral director's had been very sad, incredibly upsetting distractions like when relatives came to view the deceased.

'I'm really busy, Lucy,' she'd say very sternly.

'I'm sorry,' Lucy would say very sorrowfully.

Cassie would always relent. 'Give me fifteen minutes to finish doing these expense forms then we'll have five minutes to muck around, OK?'

The mucking around involved throwing Maltesers at each other and trying to catch them in their mouths, or sticking a song on and grooving at their desks. 'I Don't Feel Like Dancin'' had been a particular favourite.

Somehow mucking about in the office had turned into getting lunch together every week. Then a semi-regular cinema date. When the ad team hit their Q3 targets a fortnight ahead of schedule, they cemented their friendship during the mandatory team celebration at a Soho club that the ad girls loved because they served pitchers of Cosmopolitans and low-carb bar snacks. It was sparkly going-out tops a gogo.

Cassie drank so many Cosmos that Lucy had to hold her hair back as she threw up, then she took Cassie back to the Primrose Hill flat she shared with her fiancé (an academic away on a field trip) because she was too pissed to go home. She'd even phoned Cassie's nan to say that they were having a sleepover and not to wait up. Though she ruined it somewhat by giggling, 'She's absolutely not drunk. I can't stress that enough.'

They had been best friends ever since. Even though Lucy had grown up on a farm in Hampshire and Cassie had grown up on a sprawling council estate on the Caledonian Road that overlooked Pentonville Prison. Lucy had belonged to the Pony Club, while Cassie had been thrilled to get a My Little Pony for Christmas one year. Lucy had been going out with Russell, currently completing his PhD, who she'd met at Fresher's Night during her first week at Durham University, for seven years and was now engaged. Cassie was dating a Polish plumber called Bogdan and even though they'd been seeing each other for six months, he still didn't want to say that they were exclusive.

Despite the fact that they'd always had very different lives and very different life milestones, they'd remained best friends. Through all the drama and the drudgery, from dirty nappies and baby-led weaning to work catastrophes and broken hearts, their friendship had changed shape and weathered storms but it was absolute.

So Cassie was ninety-nine per cent sure that whatever was wrong with Lucy, it didn't have anything to do with her.

'Look, is everything all right?' she asked, genuine concern in her voice. 'The girls seemed upset. Did something happen at school?'

Lucy shook her head. Then she put the bottle down so she could hug Cassie. Or rather she slumped against Cassie until Cassie put her arms round her friend. Lucy was half a head taller than Cassie, but reed slim, so Cassie always felt that there was something insubstantial and fragile about her friend whenever they hugged. Then she'd remember that Lucy was one of the strongest people she knew. Not just mentally; she could hold a plank for over two minutes.

'It's been a long week,' Lucy muttered.

'Tell me about it,' Cassie said with great feeling, pulling away from her friend and noting the shadows under her eyes, the tight lines of her normally cheery face. 'I brought you something. It's nothing, really, but the cherries won't be in season for much longer and I know you love them.'

Cassie delved into her tote bag for the fruit, which Lucy received with barely a flicker of a reaction and dumped them on the counter. It was then that Cassie realised that usually when she came for dinner, she was greeted by the smell of something delicious cooking. Not this evening.

'Too hot to cook?' Cassie ventured. 'Or is Russell going to fire up the barbecue?'

'I suppose I could order a takeaway,' Lucy said vaguely with an even vaguer shrug. After a brief pause during which Cassie looked at her friend with increasing consternation and Lucy gazed into the middle distance, Lucy came to and retrieved two wine glasses from the cupboard next to her. 'We're in the garden.'

Cassie thought that was a collective 'we', as in the three of them; she, Lucy and Russell – but as they stepped through the open doors, she saw that she wasn't the only guest.

Sitting in one of the curved rattan chairs was the archest of all her nemeses, Marc Lacourt.

2

Cassie stiffened immediately like a cat who'd had its fur brushed the wrong way then, for good measure, its tail pulled too.

Of course, Marc was sitting there like he owned the place. Like someone who didn't work a fifty-hour week then feel like a wrung-out dishcloth by Friday evening. Like a white, heterosexual man in his forties who'd grown up amid great wealth and privilege. The world was built by men like him for men like him.

Just one brief glance was all Cassie needed to reaffirm her intense dislike for Russell's best friend. He was tall, even seated, and had a tan that came courtesy of exotic foreign locations rather than out of a bottle and smelling of biscuits. His brown hair, just a little too long, had been lightened by the sun and yes, objectively he was handsome with his absurd cheekbones, his green eyes (typical of him to have green eyes) and his forearms. Cassie had to concede that he had really good forearms. But subjectively, Cassie would rather look at fish guts than have to look at Marc Lacourt.

He was wearing jeans, a black T-shirt that fitted as if it had been tailored for him – in fact it probably had – and because she worked in fashion, or at least a fashion-adjacent industry, Cassie recognised the black suede Malone Souliers trainers. It was a simple outfit, which had probably cost more than Cassie earned in a month. Not that she held that against Marc. No, she had other entirely valid reasons for the thin smile that it killed her to give him.

He didn't get up, just lifted a hand in greeting as if even that was more effort than Cassie warranted.

'Marc.'

'Nice hair,' he said and accompanied the subtle put-down with his ever-present and very tiresome smirk.

Her space buns were suddenly ridiculous. She was ridiculous.

At least Russell looked pleased to see her. He was a big blond bear of a man who quickly got up so he could fold Cassie into his arms and kiss her sweaty forehead. 'Hello, lovely. So good to see you.'

He was the only member of the family who was behaving as Cassie would have expected. Unlike Lucy, who had put the bottle of rosé down on the weather-beaten wooden garden table and was now staring at it blankly.

'Oh! I forgot glasses.' She promptly disappeared back into the kitchen.

'I'll see if I can scare up some nibbles,' Russell said and followed her.

Then it was just the two of them. Cassie could feel Marc's eyes on her as she sat down and plucked at her dress so she had something to do with her hands.

Marc would sit there quite happily in a spiky silence but Cassie wasn't built that way.

'You're well?' she asked, her tone entirely uninterested.

'Very well,' he said in his stupid drawly voice like he was always amused at a joke that Cassie didn't get and was probably at her expense anyway.

She sighed and wondered just how long it took to bring out two glasses and maybe a bag of Kettle Chips.

'Have you been away this summer?' She persisted even though she already knew from Lucy that he'd been to Santorini for the wedding of a friend. Like Marc, some financial tech entrepreneur who was rich enough to be able to afford a destination wedding to one of the most expensive Greek islands.

'Here and there.' He was absolutely determined not to give Cassie anything to work with.

There was a bottle of lager from a local microbrewery on the table in front of him. He picked it up and tapped a finger against the neck of the bottle. Then he raised it to his mouth, there was a flash of tongue, and Cassie had to look away.

God, it had been sixteen years and the memory still made her quiver then want to die . . .

'Sorry about that. We're all at sixes and sevens today!'

Cassie looked up gratefully as their hosts returned. Lucy was a woman who'd yet to meet a tiny decorative bowl she didn't like, and she lived for a charcuterie board, but now she dumped a load of items, still in their wrappings and containers, on the table: olives, crackers, half a salami.

Russell placed another bottle of lager in front of Marc, who was perfectly capable of smiling and saying, 'Thanks, mate,' to people who weren't Cassie. 'But I said I was only having the one. I'm driving, remember?'

'So you did, so you did,' Russell said, rubbing his hands together. 'Mind like a sieve.'

Lucy poured herself and Cassie glasses of rosé that were up to the brim.

'Steady on! Are you trying to get me drunk?'

'Jesus Christ, I wish I was drunk,' Lucy said, picking up her glass with a shaking hand.

There had never been a time during their forced acquaintance when Cassie had ever felt any kind of kinship with Marc, but now as she glanced over at him, it was to share a fleeting, anxious look because something was clearly wrong.

'You're not moving, are you?' Cassie asked suspiciously. She'd lost count of the number of her friends who'd left London, even when they'd sworn that life outside the capital with its sandy beaches and rolling green open countryside and much cheaper housing stock held no temptation for them. 'Oh my God, are you moving to Whitstable? *Everyone* has moved to Whitstable!'

'Not Whitstable,' Lucy snapped, which was very unlike her. 'Fuck Whitstable!'

'Bit harsh on Whitstable.' Marc put down his now empty bottle and looked like he was regretting his decision to drive over so he could only have one lager.

Russell cleared his throat. 'OK, there's no easy way to say this, I'm just going to hit you with the headlines.' There was a pause. Whatever Russell was going to say, Cassie didn't want to hear it. She suddenly knew, with a deep certainty, that there was a before and after bookending this pause and that her life, all their lives, were about to change.

She made an indistinct noise of protest, which made Russell glance over, but it wasn't enough to stop him.

'I've got stage four cancer,' he said, each word like a bullet. 'Metastatic hepatocellular carcinoma. Liver. Lymph nodes too, unfortunately. Not curable. Not really treatable. I'm hoping to hang on until Christmas. We're not telling anyone else for now.' He looked at Lucy, who shook her head. 'I think that just about covers it.'

Cassie felt herself grow hot. Hotter. As if she was boiling where she sat. She wanted to speak but couldn't think of a single word to say so instead she gasped and put a hand to her chest. She could hardly breathe; it was as if there was a crushing weight bearing down on her; her face collapsing . . .

'No, Cass,' Lucy said sharply, again so unlike her. 'You can't cry. I can't deal with that.'

So the four of them sat there in stunned silence. Even Russell and Lucy, as if neither of them could believe it either. The diagnosis. The prognosis. It couldn't be true. Someone, somewhere, must have made a terrible mistake. Maybe some blood samples had been swapped around. A computer error. A human error. These things happened all the time.

'Is this why you suddenly pulled out of the marathon?' Marc asked, just as Cassie was wondering if they might sit there without talking for the rest of the night .

It was their thing, Russell and Marc, running marathons together, something that had started when they were at Oxford. They ran the London Marathon every year, as well as a second marathon somewhere else; Paris, New York, Rome. Because Russell was sporty. Fit. Oozing ruddy good health – except this year, he'd cried off the London Marathon with just a week's notice. Something about an injury . . . Cassie really hadn't paid much attention – though she'd missed cheering Russell on as he emerged from the underpass at Blackfriars – but she'd forgotten about it until now.

'In a roundabout way,' Russell was saying. 'You know I had that shortness of breath on our training runs . . .'

Marc nodded. 'You thought you'd sprained a muscle in your back. You were going to get it checked out.'

'Well, the pulled muscle turned out to be cancer,' Russell said. Cassie didn't even know how he could say the word or muster up a smile. 'Don't you hate it when that happens?'

'Obviously you've had a second opinion?' Marc didn't wait for Russell to reply. 'What does not really treatable mean? Are you having chemo? Radiotherapy? Have you looked into having a liver transplant? Obviously, you've had a second opinion.' He had his phone out and was busy scrolling. 'There's no harm in getting a third opinion. You know, I've been diversifying into MedTech so I've got quite a few contacts. I'll get you in front of the best person. Whatever it costs. You don't even have to ask.'

Lucy and Russell shared another look. A despairing look that made Cassie want to cry again.

'That's really kind of you, mate, but we won't be doing any of that,' Russell said very gently.

'We've decided . . .' Lucy's voice cracked. She took a large gulp of wine. 'We've decided that Russell's quality of life is the most important thing.'

'The time that I've got left I want to spend with Lucy and the girls. Not in hospitals and doctors' offices,' Russell said in his firmest voice, which was still light and laced with good humour. In all the time that Cassie had known him, sixteen years, she'd never heard him shout. If she were him, she'd be shouting to the fucking heavens right about now. 'It's not a decision that we've taken lightly, but our minds are made up.'

Cassie didn't even realise she was clutching hold of the arm of her chair in a white-knuckled grip until Lucy prised Cassie's hand free and threaded their fingers together. She tried to think of the right things to say, but there was nothing right about this and Cassie couldn't trust herself to speak because she knew she'd cry. Instead she held hands with Lucy and let the conversation, Marc now firing questions about proton therapy, float above her head.

Eventually the girls drifted into the garden, Fleur sitting curled on Cassie's lap like she'd done when she was littler and much lighter. Cassie didn't mind the elbow in her ribs or Fleur's sweaty stranglehold around her neck, her damp, shallow breaths against Cassie's skin. Even the discomfort felt like a privilege.

They ordered Lebanese food for dinner. Normally Cassie would dip falafels into the hummus until she'd eaten so much that she felt sick, but even the act of putting food in her mouth, chewing, then swallowing was too much effort. She stroked Fleur's hair and only spoke when she was spoken to, as Joni and Russell did a valiant job of making sure that they didn't all lapse into another painful silence.

As soon as it was nine, the sun sinking and the shadows lengthening, though it was still hot and muggy, Cassie found her voice. 'It's getting late,' she said, though she'd stayed much later before. So late that in the end she'd crash in the spare room. Not tonight, though. 'I should be going.'

There weren't the usual protests to have one more glass for the road. As Cassie stood up, her thighs practically numb from Fleur using her as a chair, Marc got to his feet too.

Cassie sighed with relief when the front door shut behind them. Usually the goodbye was protracted and featured a lot of hugging, but she couldn't even look at Russell, let alone touch him.

She hurried down the garden path, Marc at her heels. He followed her a few metres down the road until Cassie stopped, turned around and took a deep breath. Her heart was pounding like she'd just done some heavy cardio, which she would *never*.

Marc watched as Cassie put a hand to her breastbone and pressed down with her fingers to will her heart to slow down, to quieten her shuddering breaths.

It wasn't until Cassie was able to exist at a normal volume and a normal heart rate that Marc pointed at her with his key fob as if she was as biddable as his fancy electric car. 'Want a lift?'

Never, but especially not now. 'No, thank you. I'm going to walk,' Cassie said. 'I need to clear my head.'

'Suit yourself.' Marc stepped past her without another word. A second later, she heard the smooth purr of his car door opening.

The fact that, even after the world had tilted off its axis, he could still be a condescending dick was actually a small crumb of comfort.

3

In the time it took Marc to drive off, Cassie realised that she didn't want to walk home.

It had nothing to do with the hill – it was impossible to go anywhere in their part of north London without encountering a really steep hill – or the fact that it was now too dark to safely cut through the park.

It had everything to do with Cassie not wanting to be alone with her thoughts. The main road was still humming with activity as she walked towards the bus stop. The bus wasn't crowded but there were enough people on it, enough life, to distract Cassie, but all too soon she was getting off and it was a short walk home to a little crescent behind Muswell Hill Broadway.

The flat was empty. Her flatmate Savita was back home in Manchester with her wife for the weekend so she wasn't there to take a perceptive look at Cassie's frozen face and say, 'You look like you need a drink. Also, I've made brownies.'

Cassie had had three huge glasses of rosé on an empty stomach and the thought of more alcohol . . . absolutely not.

It wasn't even nine thirty. Too early for bed when Cassie felt so restless. Far better to be productive and deep clean the kitchen.

It wasn't as if she and Savita were slobs. They were professional women in their late thirties who always did the washing-up after dinner, then ran a damp cloth over the worktop and cooker. Still, Cassie was undaunted.

She even emptied the toaster's crumb tray and took all the shelves out of the fridge to wash them in the sink, but the deep clean really didn't take that long. The kitchen, like everything else about the flat, was very small. There was a sink, cooker and fridge along one wall, and some very shallow cabinets attached to the opposite wall. Two people couldn't fit in the sliver in the middle unless they stood side by side.

Cassie moved on to the bathroom with her bucket of cleaning supplies. The bathroom was marginally bigger than the kitchen, though not big enough for an actual bath. Cassie knew a brief moment of joy when she lifted up the shower drain cover and, with a special implement bought for this exact purpose, hooked up a long, slimy, matted hank of hair. Mostly her hair. Cassie didn't believe in guilty pleasures – if something gave you pleasure, Christ, why feel guilty about it? But even she had to admit that if they did exist, then cleaning her own gunky strands of hair out of the shower was the guiltiest pleasure of them all.

Once the bathroom was gleaming, it was still only eleven o'clock. Cassie had a shower, then decided to do her full ten-step skin routine with a lot of the little sample products that were always cluttering up the bathroom cabinet, much to Savita's annoyance. It was one of the few things that they bickered about.

Working with high-end fashion and beauty brands and having had free access to a fully stocked beauty cupboard for most of her adult life meant that Cassie had the product stash and skincare regime of a much, much wealthier woman. By the time she'd finished with the hot-cloth cleansers and the retinol and the serums and the facial oil that cost more per ounce than gold, she couldn't put it off any longer.

Her room had enough space for a double bed (not even a king-size) pushed up against the wall, a skinny bedside table on the other side, a couple of free-floating shelves above the bed and that was it – or almost it. Because Savita had the biggest bedroom, they'd agreed that Cassie could have the hall cupboard where she kept her clothes and accessories, and though she could have spent a good hour editing and decluttering in there, she really had to stop procrastinating.

Cassie lay down on her bed even though she had absolutely no intention of sleeping. Her heart was still slightly racing and as soon as her head hit the pillow, her mind geared up for its usual night-time sprint.

It was time for The Fear. Because Cassie was thirty-seven and no one loved her. Or rather, people *did* love her – she wasn't entirely loveless or unlovable: her family loved her, despite Cassie's complicated place within its branches; her friends loved her – not all of them, of course, but the majority of them liked her a lot; so, familial love, platonic love, great. But romantic love? Nope. Nada. Zilch. There wasn't even the prospect of finding a man, another person, who wanted to throw their lot in with Cassie.

Every time Cassie fired up the apps – Tinder, Bumble, Hinge – she felt nothing but a grinding despair at the thought of trying to find a connection with men who were always shorter, older, balder and much angrier than they'd seemed on her phone screen. Not that they thought Cassie was much of a catch herself.

Which meant that Cassie now transitioned seamlessly from contemplating her loveless state to wondering what was wrong with her. Objectively, she was attractive, thanks to the premium beauty products and being old enough to be mostly comfortable in her own skin. She loved her thick, long hair, which she kept in a state of relative glossiness, again thanks to premium products. It was a rich brown, which she tended to titivate with lighter-coloured highlights when she could afford them. She liked the natural arch of her eyebrows and her big, brown eyes, and she knew she was lucky to have been blessed with full lips and equally full breasts, which were still fairly perky. There were other bits that Cassie liked less but she didn't dwell on them as she had done when she was younger and believed her life would be infinitely better if she was taller, thinner and didn't have such a high forehead.

So, looks, OK. Personality, also OK. Cassie tried to be a good friend, a good granddaughter, a good niece, a good aunt. She wasn't a great daughter but Alison wasn't a great mother and they'd both made their peace with that. Cassie hoped that she was kind, loyal, funny, caring.

She also knew she had many flaws and toxic traits. Her ability to bear a grudge was positively elephantine but that didn't make her a bad person.

This was now Cassie's cue to think about all the bad people she knew and how quite a large number of them had life partners. Lucy's sister, Heather, was a monster but she'd managed to get married. Although as Lucy said, 'It's not so much that *even* Heather is married, but more that the only person who wanted to marry her was Davy.'

Cassie definitely didn't want to be married to a mansplaining, manspreading, handsy man like Davy, but time was marching on relentlessly. Thirty-seven was edging into dangerous territory. Being in your late thirties, even early forties, was a frantic merry-go-round, and many of Cassie's friends had blindly jumped onboard because they didn't want to miss the ride.

Cassie wasn't even sure that she wanted children. She appreciated her friends' and relatives' babies in much the same way that she appreciated Henry Cavill. She was happy that he made other people happy but he did absolutely nothing for her.

If she was with someone, and that mystery someone wanted children, then Cassie might decide that she wanted them too. Perhaps she didn't want children because she wasn't with someone and circumstances were making the decision for her.

Maybe Cassie would get to forty or forty-five, even fifty, and regret all the roads not taken. Especially the road that led to Jojo Maman Bébé, soft-play centres and a whole other world that she'd forever be denied access to because she'd left it too late.

Then, as now, to lessen the panic and the fluttering in her stomach, Cassie tried to focus on all the rich experiences that she could have because she didn't have a partner, children. The career opportunities. The travel. The adventures! But that simply made The Fear intensify.

There was no money for travel or adventures. At thirty-seven, Cassie was living in precarious rented accommodation – every penny she'd saved up to buy her own place had gone when her corporate event-planning business imploded during the pandemic. She was still paying off the loan she'd taken out so she could give her staff redundancy payments.

To the casual observer, Cassie had a glamorous, well-paid job. She was the 'Director of Experience' at a well-respected boutique PR agency with a roster of fashion and beauty clients. Cassie headed up the team who organised product launches and influencer lunches, press events and parties. So many parties. It was a demanding job but the perks were phenomenal, like the bathroom cabinet full of premium beauty products and Taylor Swift tickets. But even earning a decent salary, with her debts and the cost of living crisis, every month Cassie was forced to live leaner and leaner. Then there was the surcharge you had to pay, mostly to Transport for London, for daring to even *exist* in the capital.

Round and round it went in her head. With detours for the time that she'd been engaged to a man who owned his own house. If she hadn't broken things off, she'd be married now with at least two children and even though her breasts would no longer be quite so perky, she'd probably have her name on the deeds to the house.

There were so many different lives that Cassie could have lived but tonight, serenaded by the creak of her fan, she thought about the life that she did have. In a variety of ways, both very bad and very good, it wasn't the life she'd expected. But she loved and she was loved, and she had a job that she adored, and she no longer had to pay VAT and business rates which was a huge bonus, and every day was full of small and precious joys.

The problems that kept her awake at night, even The Fear, were an indulgence. To worry that her life wasn't quite right in a variety of ways when Cassie had the luxury of, hopefully, years and decades to come to achieve the life she wanted. To simply live.

Secretly, deep down, she'd always been envious of Lucy and Russell. Mostly because of the depth of love they had for each other but also because they'd both led such charmed lives. They'd grown up nestled in the wealthy cushion of the upper middle classes; prep school and public school and riding lessons, and long holidays where they always stayed with godparents or relatives who had houses in sunny locations like Cornwall or Corsica. They'd started dating at university, got married soon after that, established careers with comparative ease, and their lives had continued to follow the same safe, comfortable pattern.

Cassie loved both of them, loved Fleur and Joni. She'd never begrudged them their good fortune because they were good people – warm-hearted, caring, generous – but she'd also wished that her life could be charmed too. A little less full of rejections and scrimping and working so hard all the time. It had taken her years before she finally realised that working really fucking hard didn't guarantee success if you didn't have the right accent or you hadn't been to the right school and you didn't have parents who would pay the deposit on a flat.

As Cassie lay there in the sweltering darkness, occasionally sitting up to turn her pillow over, she realised none of that was important right now. Because Russell, who filled up every room he was in with his relentlessly sunny nature and his terrible jokes, was . . . Cassie couldn't even say the word in her head.

Not Russell. It was impossible. Unthinkable. Cassie couldn't even let her thoughts wander in that terrible direction. She'd much rather think about how she wasn't at all where she expected to be at the age of thirty-seven. And, really, genuinely, what was to become of her?

Sleep was absolutely not a thing that was going to happen. Cassie had been in bed for nearly an hour now and was staring wide-eyed and dry-eyed into the darkness when there were several loud thumps at the window.

She sighed. 'Oh my God, it's open enough for you to wriggle through, you fat lump.'

A plaintive meow was the only reply.

Cassie scrambled to her knees so she could haul up the sash window.

Still yowling indignantly, Koita jumped from the window-sill to Cassie's bed. He was a truly magnificent tuxedo cat, all black apart from his white bib and paws, who was named after a Malian footballer. Cassie wasn't sure which one – she'd tried googling but it turned out there were quite a few footballers from Mali with the same surname.

She left the bedroom, Koita winding through her legs, in danger both of getting stepped on and of knocking Cassie off her feet. 'Yes, yes, I'm going to feed you,' she complained. 'It's not like you're starving. You could live off your fat deposits for a good few weeks.'

Koita begged to differ. He kept up his meowing as Cassie opened a tin of gourmet cat food into his bowl and made sure he had fresh water. After all, it was in her best interests to make sure that Koita was kept in the bougie style to which he was accustomed. It was because of Koita that she and Savita paid well below the market rate in rent. All the way through the cost of living crisis, when Cassie's friends who were still renting had almost universally experienced massive rent hikes and sudden evictions, Cassie had been spared.

The flat and Koita had originally belonged to the late Mr Sidibe. When he'd died in early 2021, his son, a private chef in New York, and his daughter, an academic living in Australia, had wanted to keep the flat in case either of them relocated back to the UK. They'd also wanted to keep Koita, who their father had doted on.

So when Cassie was looking for a flat, along with her friend Beth, another old colleague from *Skirt*, their references from previous landlords weren't as important as how well they got on with Koita.

Cassie was not a cat person. She'd been bitten by a neighbour's Siamese when she was little and had never warmed to the species after that. Beth, however, had grown up in a feline-ruled house, which sounded like it had been covered in cat hair and reeked of cat piss. They'd even joked that maybe Beth should secrete a few Dreamies in her pockets to get the cat onside.

Of course at their interview with Mr Sidibe's son, Roman, and the estate agent, Koita had ignored Beth in favour of climbing onto Cassie's lap with legs akimbo, until she gingerly petted his tummy. Typical bloody cat.

Once she'd been anointed as Koita's designated slave, the tenancy agreement was signed and now a generous amount was deposited into Cassie's bank account every month for Koita's food, pet insurance and miscellaneous items including his catnip supply and toys. Cassie couldn't quite believe her luck. Whenever anything broke in the flat, rather than contacting either of the Sidibe siblings, in case they were suddenly reminded that they should increase the rent, she either replaced or repaired it herself. Her finest moment had been re-enamelling a small chip in the shower tray.

Or rather her finest moment was the three years that she'd kept Koita alive. He wasn't just surviving but thriving, even though he was very much an outdoor cat and Cassie had conniptions any time he was late home from tarting about the neighbourhood.

When Beth had moved out and Savita, another so-called cat person, had moved in, Koita still preferred to lavish his attention on Cassie. She suspected that it was because she was always the one who fed him, and the hand that controlled the Dreamies supply was the hand that ruled Koita's world.

Though Cassie would never be a cat lover, it did make her feel quite special that Koita had singled her out as his person. She had grown quite *fond* of him.

Now she watched as he ate, washed up his bowl as soon as he was done then picked him up and carried him back to her room.

'You can sleep *on* the bed, but no touching,' she told him sternly, something that she'd said to other males on other occasions.

Of course as soon as she lay down, Koita padded over to Cassie and draped himself over her chest.

'Please no, it's too hot,' she whimpered, but he was already making biscuits on her tummy and purring, because she really was Koita's person and he had an unerring knack for sensing when she was down.

And somehow, against all the odds, Cassie fell asleep.

4

When Cassie woke up, and managed to haul herself out of bed several long minutes after that, she was fit for nothing. She felt as if she'd downed a bottle of meths rather than three large glasses of rosé. How she wished that last night had never happened and Russell was . . . he wasn't . . . that everything was going to be fine.

On Saturday mornings she and Lucy took a yoga class in the park. One of the very last things that Cassie felt like doing was yoga. With Lucy. Or doing anything with Lucy.

She typed out a message. 'Are we yoga-ing this morning? No worries if not! xxx'

Was that enough? What else could Cassie possibly add? 'Btw, I'm sorry your husband is . . .'

No, she still couldn't even think it. Cassie sent the message and hated herself a little bit for the relief when Lucy replied immediately.

Lucy: Can't make yoga. Sorry. x

The relief was short-lived.

Lucy: But can do brunch. Usual place? 10.30?
Cassie: Cool. See you then. x

There was no point in avoiding Lucy. However awful Cassie was feeling, Lucy had to be feeling a thousand times worse.

She did think about skiving off yoga in favour of wallowing in her own misery for a couple of hours, but then there
was another ping from her phone. A message from Castiel
(probably not his government name) the yoga instructor,
reminding Cassie that she'd promised to lend him her copy
of *The Green Roasting Tin* because he was hoping to impress
a second date by cooking for her tomorrow.

It was the universe's way of telling Cassie that she really
would feel much better for getting out into nature, seeing
friends and exercising. Also, Castiel was a lovely young man
and who was Cassie to thwart his romantic plans?

Even so, she wasn't particularly looking forward to a
sweaty session of al fresco yoga. It wasn't even eight thirty
and she was already moist as she yanked on her tight-fitting
yoga vest and leggings. That was a workout in itself.

Two hours later, as she walked back along Muswell Hill
Broadway with her yoga mat tucked under her arm, Cassie
did feel better and also a lot more bendy.

As she neared the café that was their favourite brunch
spot, Cassie saw Lucy waiting outside. She was looking at
her phone, her face drawn and serious despite the cheery
turquoise drapey top she was wearing with white jeans.

The closer she got, the more Cassie felt inexplicably shy
and awkward, as if she'd forgotten how to speak to her best
friend. Then Lucy looked up from her phone and waved.
'Here she is!'

It was easy enough to say 'Hi,' even if Cassie knew that her
smile was forced. She held out her arms for their usual hug,
but Lucy shied away. 'I'm sorry, Cass, but I can't because it
will make me cry. And you're not to cry either . . .'

'I'm not going to cry,' Cassie protested even though her eyes were already throbbing.

'I just can't, Cass. I need things, I need you, to be normal.'

Cassie nodded as she held her face very still until the threat of tears had gone. 'I can do normal but I really need food first. I'm starving. Castiel made us do that open-legged squat thing . . .'

'Garland pose,' Lucy said as she held the café door open for Cassie.

'I was terrified I was going to fart,' she muttered, which made Lucy smile, and that felt like a win.

Even though it was that busy stretch on a Saturday morning when a late breakfast became brunch, they were seated immediately.

'I can't wait for all these people to go on their summer holidays,' Cassie said, because in a week or so, Muswell Hill would be virtually deserted as its more well-heeled citizens decamped for what felt like the whole of summer. 'Are you still going to France after the girls have broken up?'

Lucy's parents owned a farmhouse just outside Nantes. The whole extended family spent their summers there. Cassie had been invited a couple of times and it was always blissful. Mornings spent buying fresh baguettes and pastries from the local *boulangeries*, and visiting *brocantes*, then long, lazy afternoons around the pool.

'Only for a couple of weeks,' Lucy said. 'We can't disappear for the whole summer. Not when . . . there's a lot to organise and Russell . . . he can't be away from his doctor for so long because, you know . . .'

Lucy's voice was catching again and Cassie had never been so pleased to greet the server who was bearing down on them.

After they'd given their order and fussed with menus and the bottle of cold, mint-infused water that had appeared, Cassie took a deep breath and looked Lucy straight in the eye.

'Do you want to talk about it?' she asked.

Lucy shook her head. 'No.' She took a long gulp of water. 'You know how we have this pact that I won't treat you like the kooky single friend and live vicariously through tales of your dating life . . .'

'And we don't want to have conversations that wouldn't pass the Bechdel test,' Cassie reminded her.

'Absolutely but God, Cass, I could really do with some light conversation about your latest date.' Lucy bared her teeth in an approximation of a smile. 'Please say that you've been on a date recently.'

Even if she hadn't, Cassie would have made something up, but there was no need to because, 'On Wednesday night I met some guy I'd matched with on Hinge,' she said as Lucy settled back in her chair. 'He works round the corner from me so we agreed to meet for a quick drink. No pressure. No expectations.'

'No point in chatting for weeks on end until it all fizzles out,' Lucy agreed. She'd never had to brave the dating apps herself but had indeed lived vicariously through many tales of Cassie's adventures in dating.

'So we meet and he actually looks quite like his pictures. Definitely not over six foot as he claimed but I was happy to let that one go. Added bonus, he didn't flee in horror when I approached him.'

'I should think not,' Lucy said indignantly. 'You're gorgeous.'

'Thank you for the validation.' Gorgeous was maybe pushing it. Even if Cassie had looked like a supermodel, but a *relatable* supermodel, on the dating apps she was regarded as too old, too desperate and too likely to have a very high body count. None of which had seemed to bother Kevin.

'Kevin? I can't imagine groaning "Kevin" in the throes of passion,' Lucy said with a genuine giggle as their food arrived.

'That's not going to be an issue,' Cassie said, piercing her poached egg with her fork so the golden yolk oozed obligingly over the smashed avocado on her sourdough toast. 'He asked if I wanted a drink and I said I'd just have a tonic water because you remember that I've stopped drinking alcohol during the week? Anyway, he kept pressing me to have a cocktail, said it would loosen me up, which I thought was very optimistic of him, so I said I had a couple of big projects on at work and I needed a clear head in the morning.' Cassie paused to take a gigantic bite of loaded toast because her body had been denied sustenance for far too long.

'Which is entirely reasonable,' Lucy interjected, following her remit as a best friend to weigh in like a simpatico Greek chorus.

'Right. Then he asked me what I did and I told him and he . . .' Another pause, another bite of toast.

'And he?' prompted Lucy because as distractions went, this tale of what was soon to become woe was proving to be a winner.

Cassie held her hand up as she chewed, then swallowed. 'And he said, "Well, it's not like you're splitting the atom, is it, dear?"'

'He didn't?' This was worthy of Lucy putting down her knife and fork. 'What did you say?'

'Oh, he did. And I didn't say anything, I just raised my eyebrows . . .'

'Never a good sign when you do that . . .'

'Then at least twenty very awkward seconds passed until he said, "That was a bit harsh, wasn't it?" and we decided that it was probably best to cut our losses and end things right there.'

Lucy reached across the table to pat Cassie's arm. 'God, that's brutal.'

'Not my most successful date ever but also, not the worst. Not even close,' Cassie said, and she had to laugh, but it was quite a hollow laugh.

'One day you're going to find someone amazing who will worship you like the queen you are.'

'Well, I wish he'd bloody hurry up.'

There was a brief intermission as they finished eating, then ordered another coffee each.

'Emma says that I should think about dating divorced men.' Cassie didn't think much of her aunt's theory but it was worth floating to Lucy as another distraction. 'They've already been whipped into shape by another woman and I might as well benefit from all her hard work.'

'Unless they got divorced because they can't keep it in their pants,' Lucy pointed out.

Cassie had been of the same opinion, and added, 'Also, very likely to be quite bitter, and to want to date younger. A lot younger – plus I might end up being a wicked stepmother to a whole brood of resentful stepchildren.'

'Not wicked,' Lucy said. Then she smiled.

Despite having to shoulder her own considerable burdens, which had to be responsible for the purple shadows and the little furrow in her forehead, she still looked so much like the chaotic young woman that Cassie had met all those years ago. She was a lot less chaotic now, but her hair was still a glorious buttery yellow, and although there were fine lines creeping into the corners of her eyes and mouth, when she smiled, the years, the burdens, were suddenly erased and she could have been that twenty-three-year-old personality hire determined to stop Cassie from getting through her own work. 'We both know someone who is divorced, definitely doesn't have any children and, as far as I'm aware, has been dating in an appropriate age bracket. Just saying . . .'

'Don't say that and don't smile like that, it's very creepy.' Cassie's shoulders stiffened. She was genuinely alarmed at the unpleasant turn this conversation had suddenly taken. 'Yes, he's Russell's best friend, but Marc and I are nothing more than mutuals. Also, hello! You and Russell were very quick to warn me off him at your wedding.'

'That was sixteen years ago. The divorce has softened him. Did I mention that he's absolutely loaded?' Lucy's smile was now pure mischief.

'Would you like me to list all the ways that this is never going to happen?' Marc was also a sarcastic, condescending man. Getting divorced and even losing some of his considerable wealth thanks to the pandemic hadn't humbled or softened him in the slightest. Besides, he and Cassie had burned several bridges within twenty-four hours of first meeting and there was no coming back from that bruising introduction.

Not that Cassie could say this to Lucy. She and Russell didn't have a clue about what had really happened at their wedding. She was relieved to hear several pings from her phone.

'Emma,' she explained to Lucy as she opened the messages from her aunt, who was only eight years older than her and more of a big sister. 'We're going out tonight. Nothing fancy – just her local Italian.'

'Give her my love,' Lucy said as she made the universal sign language for 'can we get the bill?' at their server.

'You're welcome to come along,' Cassie said, because Emma, like her whole family, loved Lucy almost as much as she did.

'I'd love to but Joni's having a sleepover so I need to stick around to make sure that they don't get high on bubble tea and pick 'n' mix and wreck the place.' Lucy pulled a face. 'I do love an Italian, though. Maybe we can go to that new small-plates place in Crouch End for my birthday.'

'But it's your fortieth. You don't want to do something more exciting?' Cassie asked delicately.

'Russell was going to plan something but that isn't important any more.'

The mood had shifted again.

Much as Cassie wished they could really pretend that it wasn't happening, she waited until they were about to say their goodbyes.

Next to them there was a long line of mopeds and delivery drivers lined up in a parking bay. The beep of the pedestrian crossing. A woman with a pushchair carrying a silver helium

'Happy Birthday' balloon from the toy shop across the road. All of it normal. Mundane. Ordinary.

It was a scene the two of them had played out a thousand times.

But now saying goodbye to Lucy felt extraordinary. It was hard to find the right words in the right order for what Cassie wanted to say. She took hold of Lucy's hand. 'I know you don't want to talk about it, I get that, but I love you. Whatever you need, whenever you need it, I'm here.'

Lucy squeezed Cassie's fingers. 'I . . . we don't need anything. Not yet.' Her sigh said everything. 'God, Cass, I don't know what life is going to look like even a month from now, two months.'

'Whatever it looks like, I'll be right there with you,' Cassie said and they parted with the unspoken acknowledgement that they'd be WhatsApping within the hour.

Two minutes later, Cassie hadn't even made it home when she felt her phone vibrate. But the message wasn't from Lucy. It was from Russell.

Russell: We need to talk. Tuesday? Usual time, usual place?

5

Ordinarily, Cassie would have worked through her lunch break on Tuesday. London Fashion Week was in September, but unfortunately many of her clients' big cheeses, the decision-making, final-sign-off cheeses, were away for the whole of August, so July was always hectic.

It meant that Cassie and her team were currently run ragged trying to finalise details for all the breakfasts, lunches, high teas and dinners taking place between fashion shows. The current bane of her work life was a late supper she was organising for a luxe cashmere brand launching a new range of loungewear. She'd had to go all 'as per my last five emails' on their marketing director that morning. She didn't really have the time for what would inevitably be a long lunch at Manzi's, which was something of a Soho institution.

Both she and Russell loved how glamorously kitsch the restaurant was, from the huge, truly bonkers seascape mural inspired by Ernest Hemingway's *The Old Man and the Sea* to the turquoise mermaid figurines holding up the gantry of the upstairs bar. The restaurant harked back to an older, wilder Soho when the Colony Room and the Coach and Horses were full of reprobates who never went back to their offices after extended, mostly liquid lunches. Also, Manzi's did a really good fish-finger sandwich.

Russell was already waiting for her. He'd snagged a window table and looked as he usually did: glowing with vitality as he was haloed by the sun streaming in. He smiled as Cassie approached and stood up so he could wrap her in a hug as soon as she reached him.

It was a patented Russell bear hug. Solid and dependable, smelling of crisp cotton and Old Spice because when the girls were younger they'd buy him Old Spice for every birthday, Christmas and Father's Day and he now had a never-ending supply of it. Cassie felt overwhelmed with love for him. She and Russell had a deep friendship which existed independently from her relationship with Lucy and her relationship with them as LucyandRussell, two people but very much one unit.

Yet when Lucy had first mooted the idea that Cassie, her brand-new friend, should meet her fiancé, she hadn't expected to like Russell at all.

For starters, it seemed as if Russell was posh. Proper posh. Cassie was wary of the posh; even the very, very middle class made her feel as if she was nothing better than a street urchin.

Russell had grown up in a beautiful old manor house in Surrey. Lucy said that there was a *suit of armour* in the hall. In the halls of Cassie's friends, if they even had a hall and the front door didn't open straight into the lounge, there was maybe a coat rack and very definitely a chaotic row of shoes and trainers which had been toed off upon entering.

Russell had gone to Harrow, then Oxford, before doing his MA at Durham where he and Lucy had met. Now he was finishing up his PhD, teaching at University College and writing a book. Cassie had never met anyone who'd written a book before. In his spare time, he ran marathons and belonged to a backgammon club. So posh! Besides, Russell was twenty-seven. Seven years older than Cassie. Back then, seven years' difference when you were a chippy girl barely out of your teens felt like seventy years.

By then, Cassie had been going out with Bogdan for nearly a year, and only recently had he finally – reluctantly – agreed to make the relationship official and exclusive. Bod, as she called him (to his mates, he was affectionately known as Bodge), lived with three friends in cheerful squalor in a two-bedroom flat in Archway. The kitchen was so filthy that Cassie wouldn't even make a cup of tea on the rare occasions that she went round there.

Lucy had suggested that they double date: Cassie and Bod, Lucy and her posho boyfriend. He was bound to be a ruddy-faced rugger bugger who'd treat Cassie as if she were Eliza Doolittle in *My Fair Lady* before her Henry Higgins makeover.

Russell hadn't been like that at all. He *was* kind of ruddy-faced, but that was the only correct part of Cassie's pre-match character assassination.

Because Russell . . . Russell . . . was a golden retriever in human form. He was so excited to meet Cassie that when she and Bod walked into the Camden pub where they'd arranged to meet, he was out of his chair and halfway across the room to greet them before Lucy even noticed their arrival.

'Cassie? It is Cassie, isn't it?' he'd confirmed and when Cassie had nodded, Russell had beamed. His smile seemed to have its own force field. 'I feel like I already know you.

Lucy doesn't stop talking about you. Look, I'm a hugger but if you're not . . .'

Cassie was not a hugger but she found herself nodding and was instantly wrapped in Russell's arms for a brief but heartfelt hug. Then the four of them had sat down, a bottle of Pinot Grigio for Cassie and Lucy, pints for Bod and Russell, and Cassie found all her prejudices melting away.

There was something so engaging about Russell that it was impossible not to warm to him. He had such a genuine curiosity about the world and the people in it, that later when the book he was writing became a surprise bestseller and a career in radio and TV beckoned, Cassie wasn't at all surprised. Within half an hour of meeting him, she'd been utterly besotted.

First, Russell asked Cassie about what it was like to have lived in London all her life 'because it's quite rare to meet a native Londoner'. Then she found herself telling Russell things that she didn't normally tell new work colleagues because she thought they'd look down on her. That her grandad had been born within the sound of Bow Bells. How she'd learned to swim at Hornsey Road Baths, with its iconic 1930s neon sign of the diving woman. About working at the funeral director's, and the send-off for a legendary gangster and associate of the Kray twins. 'A proper East End funeral with the horses with the black feathers. Brought the traffic in Hackney to a standstill.'

Then she'd asked Russell about running marathons. Instead of talking about his training or his run times, he'd instinctively thought of a way to talk about the subject so that Cassie, very much not a runner, would find it interesting.

He became so impassioned about Kathrine Switzer, the first woman to run a marathon in 1967 in Boston, even though race officials tried to physically drag her off the course, that he actually cried a little bit. Cassie still teased him about it although Russell always insisted that they'd been very manly tears.

Russell had main character energy and Cassie, like so many people who knew and loved Russell, was happy to have a supporting role in his life.

But none of that was important now, because Russell was supposedly dying. Which was ridiculous when he was in her arms, so solid, so real.

Russell tried to step back but Cassie tightened her grip.

'This is getting kind of awkward, Cass,' he said, his smile evident in his voice. 'Put me down. You don't know where I've been.'

Then there was another voice. A voice that always made Cassie wince when she heard it unexpectedly, like nails running down a blackboard or someone crunching ice cubes. 'Am I interrupting something? Do you two need to be alone?'

Cassie set Russell free in an instant so she could turn around and glare at Marc, who'd turned up yet again like the baddest of pennies. He was wearing a slim-cut, cream-coloured lightweight suit with a black shirt. It was a stylish and understated look, which, for some reason, enraged Cassie even more. Or maybe it was because of the smirk. Yes, it was definitely the smirk. 'What are *you* doing here?' She turned back to Russell, who quaked at the furious expression on her face. 'What is he doing here?'

Russell's smile did nothing to placate Cassie. 'I asked him because I need to fill him in on the little secret we've been keeping . . .'

Marc paused from sliding into the booth, though if Cassie had her way he wouldn't be staying long. 'What little secret?' His gaze flickered from Russell to land disapprovingly on Cassie. 'Are you two having an affair?'

Cassie glared even harder. 'Typical that *you* would think that.'

'Now now, children,' Russell said equably, because while Cassie and Marc employed a thin veneer of civility in company, especially if that company was Lucy's or their mutual friends, Russell was different. It was hard to dissemble with Russell because he was always so candidly himself. 'Sit down, Cass.'

She slid into the booth, opposite Marc. She was wearing one of her favourite summer outfits, a black, sleeveless, waisted jumpsuit. It was ridiculously flattering, edgy but professional, and cool enough for the hot weather and commuting on the Northern Line. It was the holy grail of jumpsuits. But when Marc gave Cassie his usual dismissive up and down, she felt like ripping the jumpsuit off and burning it at the first opportunity. She flicked back her heavy plait with annoyance.

'I don't know why he's here,' Cassie said to Russell. 'I knew what you wanted to talk about as soon as I got your message. I'd been wondering the same thing. Obviously we're going to cancel now. Not much chance of getting the deposit back . . .'

Russell shook his head. 'No, we're not cancelling. Quite the opposite. We're going hard until it's time to go home.'

'Will one of you tell me what's going on?' Marc asked. He'd slipped off his jacket and was now rolling up his shirtsleeves to reveal the corded muscles of his tanned forearms.

What was about it forearms, even the forearms of a man she disliked intensely, that was so hot?

Cassie decided that it was best to ignore Marc. She took out her laptop and opened it up so he was blocked from her view. Then she turned her attention back to Russell. 'Are you sure? It won't be too much for you?'

'I'm going to get laughing boy here to step up . . .' Russell said, gesturing across the table to where Marc was staring at them both like they were talking in tongues.

'Oh no, you don't have to do that,' Cassie said quickly, horror rising up in her like a sudden bout of heatstroke. 'I've got this under control.'

'For the second time, will one of you tell me what is going on?' Marc bit out.

Cassie and Russell exchanged an exasperated look. Cassie even allowed herself a small, weary sigh, which made Marc's jaw tighten.

'You've already saved the date, mate,' Russell said. 'You're in the WhatsApp group. August bank holiday weekend.'

'Yes, we're going away somewhere, I was waiting for you to firm up the details . . .'

'It's a four-day celebration for Lucy's fortieth, but she doesn't know about it,' Russell reminded him. 'We're talking Whitehall levels of secrecy. My grandparents used to live in this lovely little village outside of Brighton, on the South Downs. Lucy and I honeymooned there. Anyway, they had friends who lived in the manor house, which I've rented for the weekend. It's got a swimming pool, tennis courts, its own beach. Lucy will love it.'

'And I'm on top of everything,' Cassie said as firmly as she could. 'I hate to break it to you, Russell, but I can manage perfectly well without you.'

As soon as the words left her mouth, Cassie realised what she'd said. She couldn't even look at Russell and turned her face away from him even though he put his hand on her shoulder.

Marc, thankfully, resisted the temptation to point-score and tell Cassie off for her horrible, terrible, awful faux pas. The three of them sat there in silence, and it seemed to Cassie that each of them was alone in their own private hell.

Then the server, a startlingly attractive young man, came to take their order. After a brief look at their frozen faces, he swiftly departed with a murmured, 'I'll be back in ten.'

Cassie took a couple of deep breaths as she made a determined effort to get her emotions, her body language, her tear ducts under control. Russell would hate it if she cried. 'I'm sorry.'

'You're allowed to feel sad. I'm sad too,' Russell said with a deprecating snort because Cassie could tell that, like her, like Lucy, even Russell found it impossible to put *this* into words.

Marc, who'd been the quietest, the most still of the three of them, reached across the table to take Russell's hand and, after a few long seconds of mutual hesitation, Cassie's hand too. Cassie stared down at his long fingers clasped tightly around hers. She was surprised to discover that there was something comforting about the warmth of Marc's hand, the strength of his grip.

Then he broke the spell. 'I've been doing some research,' he said, releasing Russell's hand and when Cassie tried to break free too, Marc held on to her, his thumb lightly brushing the back of her fingers, which made her shiver despite the heat of the day. 'There's a guy in California who's been having a lot of success with stem-cell therapy to boost immunity in liver cancer patients. I'll sort everything, fly you out – you don't have to worry about the expense . . .'

'I'm not going to do that,' Russell said patiently. 'I already told you. I don't want to spend what time I've got left blasted by treatments that are going to prolong the inevitable by a few months at best. Months when I'm going to feel like shit. I don't want Lucy and the girls—' He broke off. 'This way is better. We can enjoy what time I've got, make memories that will last . . .'

Marc's grip on her hand tightened so much that Cassie almost squeaked. He looked down as if he was surprised to see that her fingers still rested in his. Then he set her free. 'You can fight this. If I were you . . .'

'But you're not me, so let it go,' Russell said firmly but with finality, a steeliness to his tone that Cassie had rarely heard. 'Lucy and I are decided. So, we're going to throw her the best fortieth birthday we can muster, right?'

'Right!' Cassie agreed, trying to sound her very peppiest and perkiest. 'Four days of all of Lucy's favourite things. Tennis, swimming, yoga, karaoke, fancy dress, maybe a scavenger hunt, fish and chips on the beach on Friday night, a barbecue on Saturday then a massive roast with all the trimmings on the Sunday. Lots of carbs, lots of Aperol Spritz, lots of enforced exercise. That's basically the highlights.'

Lucy and Russell were both very sporty, which Cassie admired but she didn't like to get too involved. Lucy was always telling her that she should do more cardio to elevate her heart rate, 'because good things happen when your heart rate gets elevated'. However Cassie liked her heart rate to maintain a very steady rhythm. But they were also very into food, which was more her thing, and as for . . .

'Karaoke? Fancy dress?' Marc repeated scathingly, his top lip curled. 'Remind me again why you married this woman?'

Cassie would have bristled but she knew that, despite his many faults, Marc adored Lucy and she seemed to rather like him too. Now all the difficult emotions had sunk below the surface, predictably Marc and Russell would resort to some mild banter to restore a semblance of normality.

'You're talking about the love of my life,' Russell said. 'Even though she made me do karaoke on our first date. Once she heard me murder "Bohemian Rhapsody" I'm amazed she agreed to a second date.'

Marc shrugged. 'No accounting for taste.'

'Still can't quite believe that I landed such a hottie.' He turned to Cassie. 'Look, it's a very packed schedule for the weekend and I really can't dump it all on you, Cass, so Marc will step up, right?'

Up until then, Russell had been quite happy to dump it all on Cassie. He was more of the ideas man and she was the person who made those ideas happen. The weekend played to her very specific skill set. If you needed someone to source a karaoke system, an artisanal birthday cake and tennis trophies for a bank holiday weekend, then Cassie was your woman.

So even though there were still seven weeks to go, she had everything under control. In fact, she'd been about to email the itinerary and final details to the guests. 'Honestly, it's all good. I do this for a living, remember?'

'It doesn't hurt to have another pair of eyes. Or hands,' Russell insisted.

Once again Cassie was forced to look at the hands in question. She had a quick and sensory flashback to how those hands, on a night a long time ago, had . . .

Cassie looked up, away from those hands, those devastating fingers, only to catch Marc's eye. She could feel the flush of her cheeks and maybe he was remembering too because he shot her a small, sly smile, that on that night she'd found irresistible. Now, she wanted to tear it off his face.

'OK, Russ. It does sound like too much for one person.' The small, sly smile had upgraded to a shit-eating grin. 'I'm in.'

'No, you're out! I can do this on my own. I *want* to do this on my own,' Cassie insisted stridently and very shrilly.

'It's far too much to do on your own. You're making me feel so guilty,' Russell said, so Cassie immediately felt like a worthless wretch. Russell had enough going on without her adding to his worries.

'Well, I mean . . .' She sighed. 'I really can manage myself, but if you think that another pair of eyes might be helpful . . .'

'That's settled then,' Russell said very firmly and with a twitch of his lips to hide his smile like he couldn't quite believe that Cassie had let herself be played so easily. 'Marc, you're going to help Cass but not be a dick about it. Cass, you're going to be your most gracious self and accept Marc's help. Great – I love it when a plan comes together.'

'I can't wait,' Marc said, his smile positively gleeful.

She was saved from doing anything drastic like throwing her glass of water in Marc's face by the server returning to take their orders.

Cassie really didn't feel like eating. Since the previous Friday night, her appetite had waxed and waned. Her stomach was either tied in knots, or furious and growling that she'd been denying it food because of those knots.

Marc and Russell didn't have that problem. They shared a dozen oysters as a starter, then both had the lobster Thermidor, which seemed very decadent for a Tuesday lunchtime.

Even if Cassie couldn't really eat, apparently she could still talk. Boy, could she talk!

She asked Russell about the family's upcoming holiday, although they went to the same place every year so there wasn't anything new that Russell had to impart on the subject.

Then Cassie decided to give them a blow-by-blow account of the recent outing to the Taylor Swift concert, including the friendship bracelets that Fleur and Joni had made for Cassie and her little brother, Ryan, the elderly man wearing a 'Grand Swiftie' T-shirt sitting in front of them with his granddaughters, and every song that she could remember from the setlist.

Cassie knew that she was talking too much, all of it entirely uninteresting unless you were a hardcore Swiftie, which neither Marc nor Russell was, but she couldn't talk about the stuff she really wanted to talk about. God, she hadn't even told either Russell or Lucy how sorry she was. Also, she knew what Marc was like. He wasn't going to drop it with his experimental therapies with proton beams or what have you, so best that there weren't any gaps in the conversation.

Russell was taking her word vomit with his usual good humour, smiling and nodding in the right places, but Marc kept shooting her these loaded glances, which Cassie ignored. She'd known Marc for sixteen years, so that was sixteen years of knowing that she irritated him. Yet here she was, at her most irritating. She was even irritating herself.

Thankfully no one wanted pudding or coffee. Marc and Russell tussled over who was paying but when Cassie suggested that they go thirds, even though her fish-finger sandwich had cost far less than their oysters and lobster, both of them (even Russell) frowned her into silence.

Marc won the battle of the bill, of course, and just as Cassie was about to slide out of the booth, Russell put a hand on her arm.

'Just one more thing. Promise you won't be cross with me.'

Oh God, what now?

Cassie managed to summon up the faintest of smiles. 'Depends. I can't really handle any more bombshells.'

Russell waved an airy hand. 'Oh, it's nothing. It's just . . . we're going to have to add two more people to the guest list. Don't be angry.'

The sinking feeling must have been exactly what the *Titanic* experienced when it hit the iceberg. 'Who?'

'Heather and *her hubby*,' Russell said, flinching as if Cassie's ferocious scowl had struck him a blow. 'Don't look at me like that, Cass. She suspected that something was up and she said if I didn't tell her she'd ask Lucy, and Lucy's been through enough and I didn't want to tell her what was really wrong. Then I might just as well take out a full-page ad in *The Times*. So I told her about the surprise fortieth birthday weekend and had to pretend she was invited all along.'

Cassie's mind was immediately besieged with all the problems this would throw up. The lack of a room for Lucy's toxic sister Heather and her husband, self-styled cheeky chappy Davy, for one thing. The fact that they were a pair of tight-fisted freeloaders even though Davy worked in finance. Their smug, performative coupledom. Even worse, Heather couldn't handle her drink and was a hysterical, meltdown-having drunk.

'Oh, for *fuck's* sake, Russell!' Cassie snapped. 'This is going to be like Lucy's hen weekend all over again.'

Russell held his hands up. 'I know. I know. If I wasn't dying anyway, you'd kill me.'

'It's a bit soon to be making jokes about that,' Marc said sharply from the other side of the table.

'It's always going to be too soon to make jokes about that,' Cassie added with a sigh. 'You know what? It's impossible for me to be angry with you right now. I'll sort things out with bloody Heather.'

When they stepped out onto a blisteringly sunny street, Russell was the first to take his leave. He seemed to shrug off the carefree man he'd been during lunch; his posture suddenly seemed defeated and his face drooped. 'I really have to go,' he said, leaning down to brush Cassie's cheek with his lips. 'I've got an appointment with my solicitor. You wouldn't believe how much admin there is to deal with.'

Marc lightly touched Russell's arm. 'If there's anything I can do.'

Russell shook his head. 'I've got it all covered. Thank God you bullied me into estate planning and taking out life insurance after Joni was born.' He gave the two of them a half-hearted salute. 'Anyway, I'll see you both soon.'

Cassie watched Russell walk away, still with that loose-limbed stride as if he was strolling onto a cricket pitch, his shoulders broad in his white shirt. You'd never know to look at him that he was . . .

'. . . Are you even listening to me?'

No, no she wasn't. She turned to Marc, who was standing there with the harsh expression he always brought to the surface when it was just the two of them. Like he could hardly bear to even look at her.

'I don't need any help with this birthday weekend.' Cassie smiled in the smarmiest way she knew how. 'It's all right. I know how busy you are.'

He rewarded her with a fake smile of his own, all white teeth and insincerity. 'Russell wants me onboard, so I'm onboard. Don't send out the itinerary until I've had a look at it. Then I'll be in touch with my suggestions.'

Cassie put her hands on her hips, her chin tilting up. 'I don't need your suggestions.'

Marc slipped on his sunglasses and flashed his teeth again. 'Tough. You're getting them.'

Then he walked away, leaving Cassie bristling but miserable all at the same time.

God, how she hated him.

6

LUCY'S NAUGHTY FORTY BIRTHDAY WEEKEND EXTRAVAGANZA!

Cassie: Guys, I'm going to have to create a new chat for this group as Lucy's sister, Heather, and her husband, Davy, have been invited (by Russell. Not me). We need to pretend that this is a new chat and she was invited all along. Sorry for the confusion.

Marc: Also, I'm taking over Russell's organisational duties, so the final details can be a surprise for him too.

Cassie: But I'm still in charge. Otherwise it just gets too complicated.

Marc: We're all intelligent people. I don't think there's anything complicated about having me oversee things, instead of Russell.

Cassie: Like I said, guys, I'm looking after all this AS PER USUAL. Now, I'm going to add you all to the new group chat.

Cassie hissed in sheer annoyance as she hunched over her phone and almost sprained a finger as she set up a new chat group with stabby motions.

'Everything all right, Cass?' asked Savita, her flatmate, who was waiting patiently for Cassie to be done so they could catch up on *The Real Housewives of Salt Lake City*.

Cassie and Savita tried to have one evening together each week before Savita, a Monday-morning-to-Friday-afternoon Londoner, returned to her proper home in Manchester. They'd make something delicious for dinner and catch up with each other's news and, more importantly, on their favourite reality TV. Naomi, Savita's wife who'd moved them up north when her job at the BBC relocated to Salford, wouldn't have it on in the house. Though Cassie and Savita both tried to live lean, their annual subscription to Hayu was a non-negotiable, along with quilted loo rolls.

'Just some absolute power-crazed arsehole trying to wave his dick about,' Cassie explained with great feeling.

'Oh my God, which dating app are you on now?' Savita asked as she delicately selected a prawn from its bowl with her chopsticks. She was small, slight and precise, from her razor-straight, razor-sharp dark bob to her perfectly arched size three feet. A scientist by trade and a baker when stressed, she gave off very self-contained vibes.

Initially her main appeal as a flatmate had been that she wouldn't be there weekends. However, they'd quickly bonded over *Below Deck* and Savita's tahini brownies. It was also good to have a friend who was entirely separate from Cassie's work life or other social circles. It made the flat feel more like a sanctuary. And was why their little dusky-blue living room (Cassie had been influenced by many Instagram renovations accounts that all perpetuated the myth that small rooms felt larger if you painted the walls and ceiling one colour. Not true) with its sagging two-seater sofa and armchair covered in throws and cushions, and framed vintage Chanel No 5 prints on the walls, was definitely one of Cassie's favourite places.

In summer, the sun slanted in through the windows and in winter, with thick velvet curtains keeping out the draughts from those same windows, which rattled in inclement weather, it was very cosy.

Savita was small enough to stretch out on the sofa while Cassie sat cross-legged with her back against the armchair, a hardworking fan stirring the stuffy air, a Thai feast courtesy of a supermarket 'Dine In' promotion spread out on the coffee table. Castiel, of Saturday-morning yoga fame, swore by the benefits of sitting cross-legged to encourage better breathing, digestion and pelvic-floor function.

'Not a dating app, a group chat for that birthday weekend I was telling you about,' Cassie said as she paused from her rage-typing to rage-eat a pork and bamboo-shoot dumpling. 'Russell . . . he's taking a step back . . .'

'Again, I'm so sorry, Cass. I can't believe that Russell is . . . I still can't get my head around it.' Even though Savita was a scientist, all about logic and facts, even she couldn't say the words out loud. 'He's one of those special people that you don't meet very often . . .'

'He really is,' Cassie sighed. 'The definition of good people. His one flaw is his best friend, Marc. With a "c". Because he's half French. Whatever. He's a horrible man. Now he seems to think that he's going to take over the weekend that I've been organising because organising parties is *literally* my job and—'

She paused as her phone pinged.

Marc: I'm still waiting for the itinerary.

'And now he has the audacity to side-chat me with his demands.' Cassie couldn't handle her phone and her chopsticks at the same time.

'Ugh, I hate it when people do that – unless it's to bitch about someone in the group chat, then I'm down with it.' Savita picked up the remote. 'So, shall we stick on *Housewives* now?'

'Hang on.' Cassie was now distracted by a distant thump. 'I can hear Koita at my bedroom window.'

'I'll go.' Savita was already on her feet. 'It's amazing how he always knows when there's food about.'

Cassie made several attempts at her icily dismissive reply to Marc as she heard Savita fill Koita's water bowl and Koita's increasingly shrill demands. 'It's all very well yelling at me but we both know you won't eat your own food when we've got far more interesting things on our plates.'

Koita slunk into the room, back straight, tail up, golden eyes gleaming at the sight of the coffee-table buffet. 'You can have one prawn,' Cassie said, holding one aloft in her chopsticks. 'Just one.'

The prawn didn't even touch the sides. Koita curled up in Cassie's lap. Not affectionately but so he could swipe her hand with a paw each time she tried to manoeuvre a morsel of food in the direction of her mouth.

Savita had cued up the latest episode of *The Real House-wives of Salt Lake City* and Cassie was still working on her reply to Marc's imperious demand when she realised the best response was no response.

Much like Koita making short work of his third prawn, let Marc chew on that.

On a sultry evening one week later, Cassie was walking through Lincoln's Inn Fields on her way to yet another 'Christmas in July' event. She always suggested to clients who had to launch Christmas products in summer to allow for press lead times that *maybe* they could do something that wasn't 'Christmas in July'. It was a plea that was more often than not ignored.

They weren't even halfway through July and Cassie was already over mulled wine, mince pies and stuffing balls. This latest festive hurrah, even though the temperature was edging towards thirty degrees, was for the launch of a premium beauty website's advent calendar. A sit-down Christmas dinner for seventy people. Just kill her now and be quick about it.

Cassie had used the catering firm numerous times before and they were always on point. The guest list was a great mix of press, influencers and even a couple of celebrities, but her clients were having conniptions, as clients were wont to do, about the scented candles both perfuming the air of the event and in the goody bags.

'They're the candles that are going in the actual advent calendar. It feels like we've ruined the surprise,' someone in the marketing department had pointed out.

'OK, I hear what you're saying, but the candle *is* included in the list of contents printed on the back of the box and in

all the promo material, so is it really that much of a surprise?'
Cassie had countered.

There had been many emails, so many emails, back and
forth, about whether to substitute the winter berry and fig
candle with another festive-themed candle that wasn't in the
advent calendar. Maybe the winter spices and rose one?

No decision had been made and the event was due to start
in two hours, but to be on the safe side, Cassie had ordered
a hundred of the plan B candles from the company's ware-
house. They were meant to have arrived yesterday but had
only just been delivered to the venue.

Everything was going to be fine. There were always problems before, during and after events and the wrong scented
candle was a very minor issue, but with the venue in sight,
Cassie sat down on a bench to take five minutes to gather
herself. Her job was stressful, but it wasn't the kind of stress
that kept her up at night. Which was just as well, because
what with her usual existential dread and Russell's terrible
news, everything just felt like *a lot*. Maybe even too much.

Cassie bowed her head so that whatever breeze there was
might brush the back of her neck, which was feeling quite
sticky. She was wearing a red maxi dress, so she'd be easy to
spot in the crowd for when something inevitably went wrong
and she'd have to sort it out, but she really didn't feel she was
in a red dress kind of mood.

And then her phone rang.

And then Marc's name flashed on the screen.

And then it felt like her stomach had plunged all the way
down to the soles of her New Balance trainers.

Cassie could just do what she'd done this past week with his WhatsApp messages and, more recently, his emails: ignore them. But you didn't just phone someone, in a non-work way, unless it was something really important. Something, God forbid, concerning Russell. Though he'd looked fine last Tuesday and that had only been a week ago.

She was going to have to answer this. Speak to him.

'Hi. Is everything all right?' Cassie asked on a nervous intake of breath, which almost made her choke.

'I don't know. You tell me,' Marc said in a bland voice so it was impossible to know if she should start panicking.

'Is everything all right with Russell, I mean?'

'He's fine. I just spoke to him.' He sounded softer, kinder. 'That's not why I'm calling.' That last sentence didn't sound soft or kind at all.

Cassie lifted up her hair to get more of that faint breeze on the back of her neck. 'Couldn't this call be an email?'

'You don't reply to my emails, or my messages, so you leave me with no other option.' His voice was positively wintry now. 'Maybe I should try carrier pigeon. Or a letter, witnessed by a notary, then hand delivered.'

'I get the message,' Cassie said wearily. 'I'm in the middle of a work th—'

'I want that itinerary,' he said. Or rather ordered. 'Russell has already forwarded me a huge Google document that makes very little sense without the itinerary.'

'You don't need the itinerary. I have everything under control,' Cassie insisted. 'I don't know why Russell expected you to get involved.'

'Well, he did and so I am. We're just going to have to get along, for Russell's sake. Now send me the itinerary.'

'It's not "getting along" when you're issuing demands like some two-bit dictator . . .'

'The itinerary. Now!'

'Or I could just turn my phone off and block your number?' Cassie suggested sweetly, which actually seemed like quite a good idea.

'I don't want to have to go to Russell with this when he's dealing with so much awful stuff. He hasn't got time to jolly you out of this childish little temper tantrum you're having.'

Cassie gasped in genuine outrage. Was she really having a very immature and unwarranted hissy fit, or was Marc being his usual arrogant, high-handed self? Possibly, and she hated to admit this, it was a bit of both.

'Fine,' she said thinly. 'I'll send you the itinerary but only for reference. I don't need you—'

But she was talking to dead air – Marc had already terminated the call.

It was quite hard to be the unflappable, never-knowingly-fazed Director of Experience at one of your most prestigious client's events when you were absolutely fucking fuming.

It wasn't until hours later, when Cassie emerged from a successful event with a surfeit of winter spices and rose candles and said goodbye to her team, that she was able to check her phone.

There were the usual messages in the family chat – currently they were all absolutely obsessed with *The Traitors*

Australia. Savita had had a trying day being a scientist and had stress-baked a raspberry layer cake. There were several memes from Fleur and Joni, and a message from Lucy including links to three swimsuits. And – Cassie checked again to make sure her eyes weren't deceiving her – twenty-three messages from Marc.

They ranged from the high-handed ('Must substitute something else for this very poor quality champagne') to the helpful if Cassie hadn't already thought of it first and anyway, everyone had satnav ('You'll need to provide detailed directions') to the autocratic and completely overstepping ('Let's scrap the scavenger hunt altogether').

Because she'd been working late and she had four boxes of candles with her, Cassie got an account car home. Was eleven too late to message Marc back?

When she'd first heard of him from Lucy and Russell, they'd described him in ways that had yet to enter the mainstream. He was a 'disruptor' and an 'agitator' who'd made a mint 'investing in cryptocurrency'. Now, those descriptors were a sure-fire way of sniffing out a complete wanker, but back then they'd seemed edgy and cool.

It stood to reason that Marc was still one of those finance/tech bros who probably went to bed early so he could get up at four o'clock in the morning to spend an hour in a cryogenic chamber before running a couple of Iron Man marathons, then drinking a specially blended smoothie made from the tears of all the women he'd wronged.

Just the thought of Marc smugly asleep made Cassie want to fire off twenty-three messages of her own and wake him up. Then she saw sense. It was never a good idea to message when angry and also, by this time of night he'd have his phone set to Do Not Disturb. Instead she'd go home, eat too much raspberry layer cake, then be too wired to sleep.

The next morning, bleary-eyed after yet another fitful, restless night when Cassie had done more catastrophising then sleeping, she did five minutes' stretching on her yoga mat and a five-minute meditation to clear her head and focus her mind.

Then she was just about to type out an absolute rocket of an email when she realised that she'd been sent yet another missive from Marc.

Or rather, she'd had an email from someone called Marie-France Vartan, who was apparently Marc's executive assistant.

To: CassieScott@CopperMedia.com
From: MarieFrance@LacourtInvestments.com
Subject: Urgent action needed!

Greetings Ms Scott,
Marc asked me to coordinate on this project.
Please see the attached document, which requires
your immediate response.
All best
MFV

Cassie could actually feel her blood pressure rising. She wouldn't have been surprised if she had a stress-related heart attack before she even opened the attachment.

It was a work plan. Very similar to the work plans that Cassie and her team used for planning events.

Three columns to a page. The first column contained the task objective, such as 'Source a better brand of champagne'.

The next column along was so that Cassie could show her working, then the last column was where Cassie would place a tick once she'd completed the task.

Fifty-seven tasks on the work plan. Fifty bloody seven.

Cassie forgot that she had an early meeting. She forgot that she was meant to take the bins out. She forgot that she never sent out emails when she was angry.

> To: Marc@LacourtInvestments.com
> Cc: MarieFrance@LacourtInvestments.com
> From: CassieScott@CopperMedia.com
> Subject: Are you fucking kidding me?
>
> Marc
> I repeat, ARE YOU FUCKING KIDDING ME?
> Regards
> Cassie Scott

She was so angry that she didn't even sign off with 'kind regards' as usual. Let that be a lesson to him. And to Ms Marie-France Vartan too.

Then Cassie heard the rumble and thud of the refuse collection lorry and had to grab the food recycling bin and run outside with it.

Three minutes later, she had a message from Marc.

> **Marc:** These messages and emails should probably be a meeting. I have a window at noon on Sunday.
> **Cassie:** I don't have a window.
> **Marc:** The quicker we sort this out, the quicker we can send out details and stop leaving people hanging.

The delay in sending out the finalised schedule and information for the weekend wasn't Cassie's fault. Russell had been incapable of making any firm decisions, which was understandable given the circumstances. If Cassie had been left to her own devices, she'd have sent everyone the trip details ages ago. Now, for whatever reason – probably because he enjoyed making her life a misery – Marc had decided to get his sticky hands all over *her* finely tuned plans. He wasn't going to fade away into the background, but when had he ever?

Cassie: I can do 11 on Sunday.

(She could actually do noon, but she wasn't letting him have all the power.)

Marc: I could come to you?

She didn't want Marc in her neighbourhood, ruining her favourite coffee shops and hangouts for evermore. Cassie knew that she was being incredibly petty, but knowing wasn't the same as being able to do anything about it.

Cassie: No need. I'll come to you.
Marc: I'll drop you a location pin.
Cassie: Fine.
Marc: Great.

But it wasn't fine and it certainly wasn't great.

7

Marc lived in Hampstead, which wasn't far from Muswell Hill as the crow flies but Cassie wasn't a crow. She was a woman who had to take the bus to Highgate tube station then change at Camden Town *on a Sunday* when every person in the western hemisphere aged between twelve and twenty-five was converging on Camden.

Still, Cassie was eager to have a good nose around Marc's place. Of course she'd looked up his address and the old rental listing for it on Rightmove, Zoopla *and* Prime Location. She'd already cast her judgement on the open slatted glass spiral staircase (perilous and impractical), the décor (minimalist bland) and the angular bathtub in the ensuite of the main bedroom (very uncomfortable).

Marc was also paying more in ground rent and service charges per month than Cassie was (or could afford) for her annual rent.

It was a far cry from his last place. Or the last place of his that Cassie had been to several years ago. Under duress. Russell had been away on a book tour and Lucy had refused to go to Marc's engagement party on her own.

'He's getting married to a model. Camille is bound to have invited loads of her glamorous pals,' Lucy had said when Cassie had tried to wriggle out of it. 'The girl code clearly states that friends don't let their friends go unaccompanied to parties full of models! Please! Have a heart!'

A party that was going to be wall-to-wall beautiful women wasn't at all tempting. It was also very inappropriate to rock up as a plus-one to Marc's engagement party, given their unfortunate history. Cassie had tried to think of an excuse that was fairly close to the truth. 'It will be too awkward. I never invited him to my engagement party and anyway, Marc is much more your friend than my friend.'

'You'll barely have to talk to Marc.' Lucy was in no mood for Cassie's feeble excuses. 'And we've been through this so many times. Honestly, Marc is lovely once you get to know him.'

By then Cassie had known Marc for over ten years and he was very far from lovely. On the other hand, she was desperate to have a snoop around his fancy apartment and to gawp at his fancy fiancée in the flesh, rather than just on Instagram and in the pages of fashion magazines. So with a cheap bottle of wine and a belly full of butterflies, Cassie had accompanied Lucy to Marc's huge penthouse in Battersea, right on the river, with incredible wraparound views.

It had been an imposing space full of quite imposing people but Cassie was delighted to bump into an old friend from their *Skirt* days. When Cassie had been the assistant to the commercial director, Grace had been assistant to the fashion director and confined mostly to the fashion cupboard. They'd been sisters in lowly assistant solidarity.

Some twelve years later, Grace had acquired a very terrifying, very rich art-dealer husband and the confidence, connections and cachet that came when a very terrifying, very rich man clearly worshipped you. She now dressed several A-list clients, styled and shot for a variety of both luxury and edgy fashion brands and was the creative director of a small but highly revered British luggage and accessories label.

But she was still the same Grace who'd used to dye her hair black, let Cassie 'borrow' clothes from the fashion cupboard and loved a good gossip. So when Cassie and Lucy bumped into Grace in the guest cloakroom and Cassie expressed her surprise at the lack of models, Grace rolled her eyes.

'Camille not a girl's girl. Doesn't like any competition,' she revealed in a fierce whisper.

'Oh, but I hope she's nice though,' Lucy whispered back. 'Marc deserves someone nice. It's been such a whirlwind engagement, so they must love each other very much.'

Clearly Lucy had never googled Camille. Cassie had, even before she'd been roped into attending the other woman's engagement party.

'Oh, sweet summer child,' she said gently.

Lucy paused from reapplying her lipstick. 'What? What?'

'Camille's on the rebound. She was dating that Formula One boss for *years*,' Grace explained.

'Which one? The little one? I thought he was married.'

'No, the French one. He's old. In his sixties,' Cassie said, because also unlike Lucy, she was no stranger to the *Daily Mail*'s sidebar of shame. 'He's quite the larger gentleman but super rich. A billionaire.'

'He has big dick energy,' Grace added. 'I mean, I wouldn't, obviously, but he is very charming, very charismatic. He absolutely refused to put a ring on it when Camille issued him with an ultimatum.'

'When was that?' Lucy demanded.

It hadn't even been a year. 'Not so long ago,' Cassie muttered.

'Marc might not be a billionaire but he—'

'He has big dick energy too,' said a new voice with a husky French accent. They'd been so busy gossiping that the three of them hadn't even noticed someone come into the powder room.

A very beautiful, very sexy someone with a sultry face and a body to match. Tawny blonde hair that was the right kind of dishevelled, as if it had been tangled in a lover's hand. Cassie had never been this close to a Victoria's Secret model before and all she could do was stare, embarrassment staining her cheeks red.

'Marc is lovely,' Lucy said again. 'He really is.'

Camille shrugged and even the shrug of her elegant shoulders was sexy; then she smiled so they could see the trademark gap between her front teeth, which was even more celebrated than her thigh gap. 'And yes, he's very, very rich.' She glanced at herself in the mirror and adjusted her absolutely perfect breasts, showcased in a plunging black dress that had hardly any front or any back. 'A woman has to think about her future.'

'But also, he is lovely,' Lucy persisted but Camille wouldn't be drawn.

She simply smiled again and the three of them filed out so Camille could pee in peace, though Cassie couldn't believe that Camille needed to do something as mundane as have a wee.

'It's probably not very "cool" or "fashionable" to admit that you're in love with someone,' Lucy said, making quote marks with her fingers. She was clearly quite rattled by what had just occurred. 'God, I need a drink.'

'Look, I'm the last person to condemn a woman who marries a man for his money,' Grace said, as they followed Lucy through the vast open-plan living space to the kitchen where the bar had been set up. 'But it's not going to work unless you really love that man. I give it six months, tops.'

Then Grace had crossed the room to where Vaughn, her husband, was talking to Marc. Vaughn put his arm around her and curved her body against him. They fitted together well. And the way Vaughn glanced down at Grace, his austere features softened for a fleeting second, made Cassie wish that she could find a stern-looking man who momentarily turned to mush when he looked at her. It also made her hope that Camille and Marc might really be a love match too.

Cassie didn't like Marc. Not one little bit. But at the same time, getting married to someone who only loved you for your investment portfolio wasn't a fate she wanted for him.

Later, as she was standing on the terrace, watching the lights of the city ripple and reflect on the Thames below, she heard a step behind her and turned round to see Marc standing there.

'Sorry,' Cassie said automatically, reflexively. Maybe she was sorry because she knew this new beginning that they were here to celebrate was doomed. But mostly she was sorry because she knew she shouldn't be there at all. It *was* weird and inappropriate. 'Russell's away. Lucy wanted me to come.'

'Right,' Marc said thinly, like he didn't care why Cassie was there but wished that she wasn't.

'I'll leave you alone.' Cassie couldn't wait to get out of Marc's sightline. He looked so disapproving, as if she was ruining not just his party but his beautiful river views. 'Congratulations, by the way.'

To her ears it sounded insincere and mocking and from the twist of his lips, Marc thought so too.

Cassie was about to brush past him, escape to the sanctuary of a large room filled with his rich, insincere friends, when she paused. Her hand was on Marc's arm before she even realised what she was doing. She could feel the muscles in his forearm, hidden by crisp black cotton, tense under her fingers.

'Seriously, Marc, I'm really happy for you. Lucy says that you'll be moving to Paris. Exciting!'

She'd been excited herself when Lucy told her the news because it meant that there was less chance of having to see Marc and the look on his face whenever he saw her. It was hard to put a finger on what his expression conveyed; contempt, disdain, nothing good.

Much like the way he was staring down at her hand on his arm, like he couldn't believe that she had the fucking audacity to touch him.

'You're happy for me?' Incredulity was etched into every syllable.

'Yes, happy for you . . . and Camille,' Cassie insisted.

For a brief few seconds, Marc's hand covered hers, then he flexed his arm to shake away her touch. 'Thank you,' he said like those two words killed him, and Cassie all but ran to find Lucy and insist that it was time for them to head back to the far more pleasant uplands of north London.

She'd tried not to relive those moments on the balcony. Chalked it down to what it was: yet another hideous encounter with Marc Lacourt, which had once again left Cassie feeling scratchy and unsettled.

Anyway, Grace had been wrong. Marc's marriage had lasted eight months. Then before she even heard it from Lucy, Cassie saw, while once again perusing the sidebar of shame, that Camille was back with her billionaire Formula One boss. They were going to get married as soon as her divorce was finalised.

Marc had sold the penthouse apartment before the wedding because of the relocation to Paris, never expecting to be back in London a short time later, on his own, just in time for lockdown.

Now he was renting in Hampstead in a pretty little mews – gated, of course, to keep out the riff-raff. Cassie tapped in the security code that Marc had sent her, then wobbled over the cobblestones, which were playing havoc with her wedge sandals.

His was the last house in the row. Cassie rang the intercom and wiped her sweaty palms on her jeans. The temperature was in the mid-twenties without the oppressive humidity of the previous couple of weeks, which meant Cassie's clammy hands were due to nerves and not the heat.

She couldn't imagine why she was nervous. It was only Marc.

'Cassie?' His voice floated out from the intercom. 'I'll buzz you in, just give the door a big push.'

Then came the promised buzz and she pushed the heavy wooden door and stepped into the lion's den.

As lion's dens went, this was one pretty spectacular. The slightly twee exterior of the house was deceptive because inside all was white and bright and airy. Also, surprisingly big, which hadn't been apparent from the estate agents' pictures she'd pored over.

The entire back wall of the house, which stretched up three storeys, was made of glass, which flooded the space with light. Cassie heard footsteps above her and looked up to see Marc heading down that treacherous open-slatted, glass spiral staircase which dominated the centre of the open-plan living room and kitchen.

She wiped her hands on her jeans again and straightened her spine.

'Why are you hovering by the door?' Marc asked. He was wearing dark jeans and a grey T-shirt, his feet bare and his hair damp, as if he'd just got out of the shower. He seemed more relaxed than normal, which was ironic because Cassie felt like several of her more fragile and delicate bones might snap from sheer tension.

'I'm hovering because I'm not sure if I'm staying,' she said, because she had a speech planned. When Marc raised his eyebrows and folded his arms so he looked more like his usual sneery, supercilious self, it made it easier to say what had to be said.

He gave a terse nod of the head. 'Go on then.'

'Look, I know I may have been quite territorial about this weekend but I've been planning it for months.' Cassie's voice hardly wavered at. 'I'm going to give you the benefit of the doubt and assume that, like me, you want Lucy to have the best birthday weekend possible, especially now. But everything is pretty much organised and although I *might* be willing to compromise, I have several red lines and you've crossed them all. Also, I'm not your secretary. I'm not staff. For fuck's sake, Marc, you're trying to micromanage the meat content of the weekend. So there's no point in me coming in if you're going to be a dick.'

There was a moment's fraught silence, though really was there ever any other kind of silence between them? Then Marc gave Cassie another terse nod.

'OK, I'll try to dial down the dickishness but perhaps you'll do me the kindness of actually listening to my suggestions instead of automatically dismissing them,' he said.

Maybe there was *some* truth in that. 'I'd be happy to,' Cassie said, with her fingers crossed behind her back.

He stepped aside and gestured with a hand. 'Well, now that we've agreed the terms of our mutual non-aggression pact, would you like to come through to the garden? It's up the stairs.'

Cassie looked up the stairs. Going up them wasn't so bad, but coming down she'd need a rope and a safety harness. She'd always had a problem, almost a phobia, about open staircases. Especially open spiral staircases. An open spiral staircase made of glass was the stuff of actual nightmares.

Marc walked through a big open arch into the kitchen. 'Coffee?'

'Yes, please.' Still she lingered in the entrance, putting off the stairs for a few more moments.

'How do you take it?'

Cassie leaned against one side of the arch. 'Oh, instant is fine.'

'I don't have instant,' Marc said in scandalised tones as if Cassie had just asked him if he had scabies, or last year's iPhone. He was standing in front of a sleek but very complicated-looking coffee machine and ran a possessive hand over one of its attachments. Cassie averted her eyes because she remembered that same possessive hand . . . 'How do you take your coffee?'

She hesitated. This seemed like one of Marc's patented simple but actually very tricky questions. 'Um, with milk?'

'Unless it's a latte, which the Italians only drink for breakfast, coffee's meant to be drunk black,' Marc informed Cassie because she'd forgotten that he was one of those people who'd made coffee part of their personality. 'I mean, what kind of roast do you prefer?'

Cassie was one of those people who actually had a personality, so she didn't know what he was going on about. 'Roast?'

'Do you like a smooth blend or something a bit more punchy?' he explained with faux patience, like he was humouring a toddler on the verge of a meltdown.

'Maybe I'll have a tea instead. Just an ordinary tea. Builder's tea? English breakfast? Am I allowed milk in it?' She didn't even mean to be catty, she just needed some caffeine, but Marc's lips had thinned and oh God, they couldn't even sort out a hot drinks order without it becoming hostile. 'I'm fine. I can just have some water. Still. Or sparkling. Whatever.'

'I can do a builder's,' Marc said, turning his back on her. 'I'll bring it up to the garden.'

8

Cassie was relieved to be dismissed and wind her way up the stairs, clutching tight to the rail on her climb. Once, on an influencer weekend at a restored country estate, she'd had to navigate a spiral staircase whose rail was made of rope and about as much use as an umbrella in a force-ten gale. She'd ended up going back down the stairs on her bottom.

She reached the first floor and stepped out onto a landing: more pale wood, more blinding white walls. The door to the garden was open, revealing a small patio area with a wrought-iron table and chairs. Cassie sat down on one of them and looked at the elevated lawn and flower beds beyond that.

It was a beautiful day; the kind of limitless blue-skied, honeysuckle-scented, fat bumblebee-d kind of English summer's day that poets wrote sonnets about.

With one eye on the back door, she took out her pocket mirror to check that yes, she still looked tired. Dark shadows had made their home under her eyes, which looked muddied rather than their usual deep brown. Thank God for concealer, bronzer and . . . she pulled out the big square-framed Bottega Veneta sunglasses she'd bought in a fashion and beauty sale at *Skirt* over ten years ago for a fiver. Cassie had guarded them with her life ever since. Then she plucked at her top, a white T-shirt with huge black circles on it, from a Marimekko x Uniqlo collaboration, which was probably the best thing that had happened to her in 2020.

She stopped primping just as Marc appeared with a tray. 'One builder's, one glass of still water,' he said in a deadpan voice as if he approved of neither of those choices. He put the tray down on the table and picked up a tiny coffee cup so he could knock back his preferred roast blend like it was a shot of tequila. 'Have you heard from Russell and Lucy?'

Lucy, Russell and the girls were en route to their family-owned farmhouse near Nantes. Usually they got there via the Eurotunnel and a hellish day of driving but this time they were flying from London City Airport then picking up a hire car. 'Less stressful,' Lucy had said. 'We usually end up having the mother of all rows by the time we've reached Compiègne.'

So far it had seemed like business as usual. Now this change to their annual travel plans, and cutting down their month in France to just a fortnight, seemed like a sinister foreshadowing.

'Lucy sent me a pic from the plane of her glass of champagne and I've had several memes from the girls. I hope they have a great holiday.'

'Yeah, me too.' Marc folded his arms, so she guessed the small-talk portion of her visit was over. 'Shall we get started then?'

It wasn't as bad as Cassie had anticipated – but then she'd been anticipating a cross between the Spanish Inquisition and a busy day at Guantanamo Bay. She took out her laptop, Marc connected her to his Wi-Fi, then they worked through the itinerary and all the flashpoints that Cassie had already decided weren't worth fighting about.

If Marc wanted to get a crate of vintage champagne and other assorted drinks from a wine merchant in East Sussex who'd deliver, then fine. 'Because it's Lucy's birthday so let's toast her with the Dom Ruinart 2010. She really deserves the best,' Marc said calmly as if *everyone* knew that the Dom Ruinart 2010 was much better than anything Ocado could offer. 'And I'm really not trying to micromanage the meat but in this day and age it's morally reprehensible to eat meat that isn't organic and free range. Again, Marie-France did some research and there's a great local butcher who'll deliver.'

That was fine too. They also agreed that the breakfast boxes from a local baker stuffed full of delicious pastries and artisanal breads would be great for Saturday morning. Marc even conceded that for everything else, Cassie could just do a massive Ocado order, which would be delivered on the Friday morning.

Then they ran through the room allocation, which again was fine. Cassie suspected that Marc just wanted to make sure that she hadn't stuck him in a dingy attic. In fact, he had a very nice room with a view of the lawn.

'Where will you be sleeping?' he asked.

'I'm on the second floor. It's all sorted,' Cassie said in an offhand way to discourage further questions. She hadn't quite finalised her sleeping arrangements. Her former room was now going to Heather and Davy, even though Heather kept clogging up the group chat with her demands for the self-contained cottage that was in the grounds, which Cassie had earmarked from the start for Lucy and Russell.

'Even before I knew about Russell, I thought he and Lucy would want some privacy,' Cassie said softly. It was only then she realised that finally she was with someone who knew how she was feeling. Marc had to be feeling it too. 'You know, I still can't get my head around it.'

'I'm living with this permanent state of dread and sometimes I forget why, then I remember and it's a shock all over again,' Marc said, running his fingers through his hair, as if he didn't know what to do with his hands. 'It's so fucking unfair.'

'Russell . . . I don't even know how to put this into words but he's, like . . . I mean . . . he always brings so much energy and positivity to everything he does, everyone that he's with.'

'Yeah, he does.' They sat there in what felt like a stunned silence for a few moments until Cassie couldn't help the tiny sniff that escaped.

'Don't cry,' he said sharply. 'There'll be plenty of time for crying later, believe me.'

'I'm not crying,' Cassie huffed. These last couple of weeks she'd been constantly on the verge of tears but couldn't quite commit to it. Not that she thought a good cry would make her feel any better. 'Right, let's get back to the itinerary. What's your objection to the scavenger hunt?'

Just call her Mother Teresa because Cassie agreed they could lose the scavenger hunt as it wasn't conclusively one of Lucy's favourite things.

'Let's chill on Sunday and it will save you having to get up at the crack of dawn to hide all sorts of random shit in the garden that people don't really need,' he said rather brutally as Cassie tried not to take offence.

'It wasn't random shit,' she mumbled. For one thing, she had several boxes of luxury candles to offload. 'OK. So, Digby and Kwame want to cook a big Sunday roast and on Saturday, Iris is happy to sort out a picky-bits lunch . . .'

'Picky bits?' Marc raised an eyebrow and accessorised it with his most punchable smile. 'What are picky bits?'

He knew exactly what picky bits were. 'Cold meats, cheeses, salads, there's even talk of a couple of rustic savoury tarts,' she said. 'I think you'd call it charcuterie in French.'

'Charcuterie actually means—'

'Please, we've been getting on so well. Don't Frenchsplain charcuterie, I beg of you,' Cassie said and Marc's smile became slightly less punchable. Which was good because she was dreading what she had to say next. It hadn't even occurred to her until she'd seen the price of just one bottle of Dom Ruinart 2010 champagne and now Marc wanted to order 'two – no, let's play it safe and say three cases'.

To stall and not just blurt it out in a clumsy rush, Cassie tapped her laptop keyboard. 'This has been a really productive session,' she said.

'And I only wanted to kill you a couple of times,' Marc offered with a lazy grin. His arms were still folded but his posture was no longer stiff and he kept smiling at Cassie, which was nice while it lasted but experience had taught her that it wouldn't be for long.

'I thought about murdering you only once, a personal best,' Cassie said, though her heart wasn't really in it. 'Like I said, this has been really productive but I'm worried that – I haven't had a chance to do the exact costings, but – all this is really going to drive up the price per head.'

Marc shrugged because he wasn't the sort of person who'd ever had to worry about the price per head. 'It's for Lucy and Russell. Whatever it costs, they're worth it.'

'They really are,' Cassie agreed as she frantically did sums in her head. Maths wasn't her strongest subject but a thousand quid each seemed to be the lowest she could come up with. 'It's just this is quite a lot of money for a long weekend, especially when people have already forked out on their summer holidays.'

Cassie hadn't had a summer holiday for a couple of years. Not even a mini-break, and she used to love a mini-break. It was one of the many economies she'd had to make while she was paying off the debts she'd amassed trying to save her business, then wind it down. She couldn't even remember the last time she'd bought a takeout coffee, but she still had thousands to go before she was debt free.

'It's not so much spread out over four days,' Marc said easily and Cassie felt the familiar prickle of tears. What was wrong with her that she couldn't cry about Russell but the thought of extending her already extended overdraft . . .

'The thing is, people might be having to cut back on their personal expenses at the moment,' she said in what she hoped was a delicate manner. Though maybe she should just stomp through what had to be said in the heaviest way possible and then Marc might get it. 'Yes, everyone loves Lucy and Russell, but there is a cost of living crisis so maybe we should agree a budget and stick to it.'

'That won't be necessary,' Marc said, wiggling his toes. Normally Cassie was quite repulsed by other people's bare feet, especially men's bare feet, but Marc's feet were as elegant and as well cared for as the rest of him. Did he have regular pedicures? He could afford them.

'I don't want to argue but a budget is very necessary,' she said quite forcefully because she didn't want to cry any more but did want to throw up at the thought of having to admit in the group chat that her share of the payment for the weekend had been declined by her bank.

'I've been racking my brains trying to think of what to get Lucy for her birthday so I'm going to take the easy way out and pay for the whole weekend,' Marc said easily, as if throwing down at least ten grand on a fortieth birthday present was no big deal. 'I should have said earlier.'

'But I'm sure people are happy to spend—'

'You've already all paid the deposit,' Marc pointed out. 'That's enough. I'll sort out the rest.'

'I wasn't hinting or anything . . .'

'Cass, we've been getting on so well, let's not ruin things now.' Marc stood up.

Cassie began to pack her things up. She felt quite light-headed from sheer relief. 'Thank you. That's really generous. The group chat is going to be very lively tonight.'

'It's nothing,' he said.

'Also, Heather and David haven't paid the deposit.'

'They *still* haven't paid?' Unless he was contradicting everything that Cassie had to say about the weekend, Marc was never that active in the group chat. 'Well, I guess now they don't have to.'

'Oh no, they're paying the deposit,' Cassie vowed. 'It's become a point of principle. Even if I have to take them to the small claims court.'

'I almost feel sorry for them. I've been on your wrong side many times and I don't recommend it,' Marc said, the smirk back on his face now that he'd won on practically every point.

Cassie could be gracious in defeat. But not *that* gracious. 'I expect you'll be on my wrong side again quite soon.'

'I'm counting on it,' he said over his shoulder as he headed for the back door. 'No, stay there for a minute. I need to get something.'

Cassie sat back down. She wouldn't be at all surprised if Marc had already known that he could browbeat her into giving way and Mademoiselle Marie-France Vartan had already drafted a new work plan which he was now going to make her sign *and* initial on every page.

'Here you go!' Marc was back and holding out a credit card. 'Marie-France will be able to handle a lot of things but you'll need this to pay for the grocery order and miscellaneous.'

'Are you sure?'

'You're not the sort of person who's always losing her bank cards, are you?' Marc asked sternly.

'No, I'm not.' Cassie was the kind of person who'd managed not to lose or break her Bottega Veneta sunglasses for over a decade. 'I'm a very responsible person.'

'I'll take your word for it,' Marc said.

An edge was creeping back in because their history was long and troubled and Cassie hadn't been a very responsible person sixteen years ago but then again, neither had he.

'I'm not going to lose it,' Cassie insisted as she tucked the black card into her purse.

'The pin is ten, twelve. Ada Lovelace's birthday,' Marc added. 'Because I'm a feminist.'

He loved to wind her up. But Cassie was perfectly capable of returning the favour. She smiled demurely. 'I can't wait to take this bad boy shopping. I've had my eye on a diamond necklace and bracelet set from . . . what's the name of that really expensive jeweller's?'

Marc shook his head. 'I know where you live.'

'Not when I relocate to Monte Carlo to start my fabulous new life,' Cassie said, standing up and hoisting her tote bag over her shoulder.

'Monte Carlo is very small and I have superior tech skills – I'd find you in seconds,' Marc said mildly, as he ushered Cassie through the back door. He wasn't touching her but he was nearly touching her and she was sure she could feel the heat of him even through cotton and denim. 'Or I could just cancel the card. That would probably be easier.'

'Well, that's . . . oh God!' Cassie came to an abrupt stop at the top of the stairs. She pushed her sunglasses up so she'd actually be able to see the ground rush up to meet her as she tumbled down them.

'Is there something we've forgotten?' Marc asked from behind her, a little bite to his words. 'Surely we've covered everything.'

'Is there a way through the garden that leads me back into the mews?' It was worth a try.

'Why would there be? The house is built in an elevation, the garden is too high to be at street level . . .'

'I'm not good with stairs. Especially an open spiral staircase that's . . . why did the architect think it was a good idea to make the stairs out of glass? Was he a complete sadist who'd never met anyone who suffered from vertigo?' Cassie practically moaned in anticipatory terror. 'I'm going to take my sandals off.'

Marc was silent but Cassie could feel the waves of disapproval emanating from him as she wobbled from one foot to the other while removing her sandals. Then she took a deep breath.

He brushed past her to start going down the stairs, clearly impatient with what he thought of as ridiculous theatrics.

Then he paused.

'Give me your sandals and your bag,' he ordered brusquely and Cassie was in no position to argue. Not when she could now have an unencumbered death grip on the rail. She handed them over and, given the gravity of the situation, it wasn't even funny when Marc put her 'My Other Bag Is A Birkin' tote over his shoulder.

Cassie took another deep breath. 'OK, you got this,' she told herself quietly.

'Give me your hand,' Marc said as Cassie shied away from his touch.

'If I just go down very slowly.' She sighed unhappily. 'Maybe if I sat down.'

'Cassie, just give me your fucking hand!'

When Marc snapped at her like that, it did two things.

It made Cassie angry but it also made her do what he was ordering her to do. Which made her even angrier.

Cassie placed her hand in his and gripped the rail tightly with her other hand.

'Just one step,' Marc said.

For one moment Cassie couldn't quite figure out how to make her legs work. Then she was stepping down onto the first stair and he kept her hand in his firm, sure grip, body-blocking her path so Cassie felt brave enough to take another step down.

'You're doing so well,' Marc murmured, stepping down himself but keeping hold of her hand. 'Come on, let's do the next one.'

That one twisting flight of stairs seemed to go on forever but Cassie was moving down them slowly and steadily, one hand clutching Marc's, the other on the rail.

Then there were only three stairs left.

'You're nearly there, Cass.'

Two stairs.

'You can do it.'

One stair.

'I'm so proud of you.'

Then there were no more stairs and her feet were firmly on the ground. Cassie was still breathing hard and Marc was still holding her hand and looking her right in the eyes.

'Such a good girl,' he said quietly, his voice curling through Cassie, so she felt it deep in her belly and between her thighs, which she pressed together as an urgent pulse beat out a warning rhythm.

Then he let go of her hand and they both stepped back and it was an awkward tense scramble to put her sandals back on and mutter something about emails and the group chat and all the while he just stood there, arms folded again, his face all tight lines and harsh angles.

Cassie had never been so pleased to leave a place, to leave someone, as she stepped out into the sunny Sunday and teetered her way across the cobbles. She was sure that she could feel his eyes piercing a spot between her shoulder blades until she finally heard the door shut behind her.

9

When the weather rarely deviated from the mid-twenties, summer in London could be a real treat. Every weekend, Cassie's friends gathered in tiny gardens and backyards for a barbecue. It was getting to the stage where Cassie expected all her food to be served on a skewer and taste mostly of charcoal.

She'd even had a week away in Cromer, staying at her great aunt's static caravan in a holiday park with her aunt Emma and her two little boys, as her partner Luca couldn't get time off work. It hadn't been relaxing, Rafe and Angelo were at an age (ten and eight respectively) when they were constantly fighting, but the beaches were sandy and as it was the only holiday Cassie could afford, she'd made a determined effort to enjoy herself.

Work was relatively stress-free, which was rare and welcome. Cassie didn't have any events planned for the whole of August because most potential attendees were on their holidays, as were most of her clients.

She even got to work from home a couple of days a week and made sure that she took a proper lunch break, usually walking to Ally Pally to sit on the grass with a sandwich. Being in nature and an hour's walk a day was good for Cassie's emotional wellbeing. But she could spend every waking hour walking in nature and it still wouldn't be enough to counteract the debilitating effects of Heather and Davy in the group chat.

Neither of them had paid the deposit, yet they were still adamant they should have the cottage in the grounds instead of their luxuriously appointed room with ensuite bathroom. In addition, Heather's dietary requirements changed by the hour. At any one time, she was gluten free, dairy free, swerving alliums but could force down the odd tomato as her nutritionist had decreed that nightshades were OK in small quantities. She'd also requested oat milk, then soy milk but was now wanting nut milk. Not even easily sourced almond milk; 'preferably macadamia but I could have cashew if the worst comes to the worst'.

Cassie had worked with celebrities and very demanding fashion people – she'd once organised a sit-down dinner attended by Anna Wintour and Karl Lagerfeld, who'd both made fewer demands than Heather.

Then there was the side chat with Marc. Which had unexpectedly become the friendliest interaction they'd ever had.

> **Marc:** This movie-themed fancy-dress nonsense . . .
> **Cassie:** Lucy ADORES fancy dress. You're not wriggling out of it.
> **Marc:** Have you sorted out your costume?
> **Cassie:** Weeks ago. Have you?
> **Marc:** What if I had a doctor's note saying that I have a medically proven intolerance to fancy dress?
> **Cassie:** Like Heather and her alliums?
> **Marc:** Genuinely the most annoying person I've ever encountered.

Cassie: She's claimed my title?
Marc: Hate to break it to you, sweetheart, but you never even made my top ten.

Cassie was sitting at her desk, the very picture of a diligent and dedicated Director of Experience, but she had to duck behind her laptop screen because the casual 'sweetheart' had thrown her for a loop. Even if she was offended that she hadn't made his top ten of most annoying people. Had all her efforts been in vain? Surely she was in the top five. Maybe even the top three. Clearly, he didn't want to flatter her.

Anyway, she had lots of important things to do rather than side-chatting with Marc Lacourt.

But that evening, as she gave herself a pedicure and tried to keep Koita away from the freshly painted nails on her right foot, her phone chimed.

Marc: You never said what your fancy-dress costume is.

'Honestly, Koita, if you don't get away from my foot there'll be no more Dreamies for you. Ever.'

Koita twitched his tail in annoyance but decided that Cassie's threat was real because he stopped trying to bat her foot with a paw and jumped onto the sofa so he could drape himself over her shoulders. As per Castiel's instructions, Cassie was still mostly sitting cross-legged on the floor, though it continued to play havoc with her hips.

She screwed the top back on her cuticle oil and picked up her phone.

Cassie: It's a surprise.

Surely he was meant to be busy disrupting the status quo, tech bro-ing and whatever else it was that Marc Lacourt did, but his reply was instant.

> **Marc:** Nowhere on the infamous itinerary does it say that the fancy dress is meant to be a surprise.
> **Cassie:** Implied innit?
> **Marc:** Did you really just innit me?
> **Cassie:** Sorry. That's more something someone would do if they were in your top ten of most annoying people.
> **Marc:** Feeling left out?
> **Cassie:** Undermarked. But whatever.
> **Marc:** You've certainly moved up the list in the last five minutes.
> **Cassie:** I should think so too.
> **Marc:** So, fancy dress. Can you give me a hint?

He was definitely in her top three most annoying people, but lately it was more of a good-natured kind of annoying than a 'making her dig her nails into her palms so hard that the little half-moon marks took hours to fade away' kind.

> **Cassie:** Uma Thurman in Pulp Fiction. White shirt, black trousers, Chanel Vamp nail polish, all of which I already own, and a cheapo wig off Amazon. Job done!
> **Marc:** Not sure I can pull off the nail polish and the wig.
> **Cassie:** If you steal my fancy-dress costume, I'll make you wish you'd never been born.

And that really was enough of that. Marc obviously thought so – or, like Koita, he decided that Cassie's threats were real, because though she was twitchy as she waited for her phone to ping again, he'd stopped playing.

There was one solitary ping before Cassie went to bed but it wasn't Marc.

> **Lucy:** Just got in. Plane delayed four hours. Absolutely knackered. Let's talk tomorrow. Maybe come round for dinner? xxx
>
> **Cassie:** That sounds awful. Pleased you're back safely. Dinner would be great but OK if you're too shagged. I'll see you at the weekend instead. Xxx

Then Cassie put her phone under her pillow, even though she knew she should have it in another room while she was asleep. Or tried to sleep.

Cassie had already woken up a couple of times and tried to slow-breathe her way back to slumber when her phone rang.

She groped for it and planned to switch it off because it was most likely to be someone on another continent trying to scam her, but when she glanced down at her screen with bleary, sleep-encrusted eyes, she saw Lucy's number.

'Hello? What's up? Is everything OK?' Cassie asked, the fear, cold and metallic, immediately seizing hold of her.

'No. It's Russell. I phoned triple one and they said to call an ambulance. Oh God, Cass, I don't know what to do.' Lucy's voice was hoarse and panicked. 'Could you . . . I know it's so late but the girls . . .'

Cassie was already out of bed. 'I'll be at yours as soon as I can.' She paused to take a couple of deep breaths. 'It's fine. Will everything be fine?'

'He's got chest pains and he's this awful grey colour. It's all my fault because I said we should fly but . . .'

'It's not your fault.' Cassie stuffed clean underwear and the dress she'd worn that day into her tote bag. 'Have you called the ambulance?'

'Yeah, but is it quicker to drive to A & E . . . Should I cancel the ambulance?'

'I don't know. Maybe.' Cassie tried to keep her voice down so she wouldn't wake Savita. She grabbed Lucy's spare keys from the kitchen drawer then hurried to the bathroom to snatch up the essentials. 'How long did they say it would be?'

Lucy didn't reply but Cassie could hear her talking to someone, then she came back. 'Ambulance is here now.'

'OK, go, go! I'm on my way. I love you.'

'Love you too.'

Luckily, there was only a five-minute wait for an Uber but the quick journey down the hill had never seemed so long. Then they were pulling up outside Lucy and Russell's house, which had all the lights on.

She was hurrying up the path when the door opened and Fleur stood there in pyjamas that were too short on her, her ankles protruding from the flower-adorned cotton. She seemed to have shot up since Cassie had last seen her.

Despite the tan, the extra inches, she looked like a little girl. A scared little girl.

'Mum said not to open the door but when I heard the car I knew it was you . . .'

'It's OK. Let's get inside. We don't want to wake all the neighbours.'

As soon as the door shut, before Cassie could even drop her bag, Fleur was in her arms.

'I'm so scared. What if it's something really bad?' she mumbled into Cassie's neck.

'I'm sure your dad is going to be fine,' Cassie said with a lot more conviction than she felt.

'He's not going to be fine forever,' came a throaty, tearful voice from above and Cassie looked up to see Joni, also in pyjamas, her face red and swollen. 'We googled . . .'

'Nothing good comes from googling medical stuff,' Cassie said quickly. 'You have a sore throat and WebMD convinces you you've got TB.'

'Except Dad really does have—'

'I know, I know.' Cassie couldn't let Fleur finish the sentence. She gently detached Fleur's death grip from around her neck. 'You must both be exhausted, with the travel and everything. Maybe you should try and get some sleep.'

Joni shook her head. During the holiday in France, she'd clearly nagged Lucy to have a couple of colourful purple braids woven into her hair. The rest of her hair was tangled and sticking up. 'There's no way I can sleep.'

'No way,' Fleur echoed. Cassie wasn't going to argue with them.

They raided the kitchen for treats even though they'd been away for two weeks and the pickings were slim. Half a carton of chocolate ice cream, a packet of digestive biscuits and some pretzel thins.

Then Cassie persuaded them that at least they could be *in* bed even if they weren't going to sleep.

The three of them ended up in Joni's bed; even a fifteen-year-old had a bigger bed than she did, Cassie thought despondently, half-heartedly dipping digestives and pretzel thins into the ice cream.

With a girl curled on each side of her, Joni hiccupping out a sob every now and again, in a strange way it was like old times.

When Lucy had unexpectedly got pregnant on her honeymoon, then gave birth to Joni at twenty-four, she was the first of her friend group to have a baby. Unlike Cassie's family and the friends she'd grown up with, privately educated girls with a university degree waited until they were at least thirty before they started a family.

Cassie knew from experience that after Lucy had Joni, their friendship, which had been unlikely right from the start, would dissipate rather than deepen. People who had babies gravitated towards the other new parents they met at their NCT classes or at Tumble Tots.

Cassie had left it four weeks after Joni's arrival before she popped round, as she'd hadn't wanted to intrude before that. At the time, she and Lucy were living around the corner from each other, Cassie in a shared house in Camden, quite the party house, and Lucy and Russell in their small third-floor flat in Primrose Hill.

It had taken long moments before Cassie was buzzed in. She staggered up the stairs with a bag of posh ready meals from M&S.

Lucy had been waiting on the landing, a furious, red-faced, frantically wriggling Joni in her arms, both mother and baby in tears. 'I don't know what to do with her. She never sleeps,' Lucy had sobbed.

Inside, it was as if a bomb had recently ripped through the once-pristine flat. There were piles of laundry, and also piles of dirty clothes. The kitchen looked as if it hadn't been cleaned in months and so did Lucy. She had dark circles under her eyes, her hair was lank and greasy and she was still wearing pyjamas.

'How are you?' Cassie had asked rather redundantly because Lucy was clearly not doing well. She also hadn't left the flat in days, it transpired, because she couldn't get the pram down three flights of stairs.

'Why don't you leave the pram in the hall downstairs and bring the baby to the pram?' Cassie asked.

'Because I'm not cut out for this!' Lucy had wept, wiping a snotty nose on the sleeve of her already stained pyjama top. 'I'm a terrible mother.'

'I'm sure you're not. Have you got a sling for the baby?'

The sling was in the tiny spare room, still in its packaging. Cassie put the sling on, put Joni in the sling and told Lucy to have bath.

Joni did scream for a bit but Cassie kept stroking the top of her downy head, and when she'd calmed down, Cassie was able to put a wash on, tackle the washing-up and was just sterilising the bottles she'd found, when Russell came home.

He looked like a husk of the golden boy he'd been the previous time Cassie had seen him; a week before the birth, when he'd been delightedly listing all the ways he was going to be the world's best dad.

'Hi Cass,' he whispered, with a wary glance at Joni who'd given up trying to stay awake and was now sleeping as Cassie swayed from side to side, sterilising the bottles. 'Is she all right in that thing? Is her neck supported?'

'She's perfectly fine. All swaddled up – babies like to feel secure.' Cassie had turned to face Russell. 'Did you two go to NCT classes?'

'We did but we practised on dolls, not on a real baby.' Russell held up his hands. 'I'm so much bigger than her and I'm so clumsy, Cassie. I'm always breaking cups and glasses. What if I break her?'

'Babies are tougher than they look. As long as you try not to drop her on her head, you should be OK.'

Cassie had come round quite a lot after that. Her mother, Alison, had given birth to Ryan six months earlier and was living up the road in Mornington Crescent. She certainly seemed to have taken to motherhood the second time around, and so, with some trepidation, Cassie had introduced her to Lucy.

It was thanks to Alison that Lucy finally became brave enough to leave the flat for walks in Regent's Park and to attend couple of local mother-and-baby groups. Even now, Alison and Lucy were great friends, which still made Cassie feel a bit . . . conflicted. She felt less conflicted and more delighted that Ryan and Joni had been best friends for their entire lives.

By the time Fleur arrived a couple of years later, Lucy and Russell were veterans of child-rearing but Cassie was still very much in their lives and delighted to have another Hunter to love and spoil.

'So, the three of us cuddling up like this, it reminds me of the little flat in Primrose Hill. You probably don't even remember it.'

Much as she had done as a baby, Joni was fighting to stay awake. She opened her eyes. 'I remember our place before we moved here.'

Lucy and Russell had moved to a larger ground-floor flat in Islington when Joni was three and Fleur was still a baby.

Cassie lifted her right arm, which was tucked around Fleur, to pick up her phone to check for messages. Lucy had texted half an hour before to say that Russell was a lot better. He'd been given oxygen and they were waiting on a chest X-ray and the on-call doctor.

It was gone four in the morning now and Joni was finally asleep, while Fleur was resolutely wide awake.

'Do you feel even a little bit sleepy?'

'I'm too panicky to sleep,' she said forlornly. 'Tell me about the time Mum got rid of that awful man you were engaged to. I love that story.'

'That's because you didn't have to live it,' Cassie muttered, because her friendship with Lucy, and Russell too, wasn't a one-way street where she was constantly going above and beyond. It worked both ways.

Like when, nine years earlier, Cassie had found herself engaged to a man she'd been planning to dump.

She'd met Tom at the very last *Skirt* style awards before the magazine folded. He'd got a freebie ticket because he worked in the marketing department of one of their drinks sponsors. There had been a lot of vodka drunk and Tom was cute. Handsome in a boyish, milk-fed way with his floppy blond hair, though now when Cassie thought about him, she had a hard time remembering the exact details of his face. But she did remember the way he'd blushed that first morning when they'd woken up in Cassie's bed. Not that they'd done anything that night.

Because Tom was an actual nice guy rather than a toxic man who claimed to be a nice guy, he then waited a good five weeks before he ended up in Cassie's bed again.

They dated for a year, went on holiday a couple of times, were happy to see each other two or three times a week, with no expectation of anything more than that. It was a perfectly fine relationship. But Cassie wasn't in love and she really wanted to be in love with someone.

Also, Tom had a huge group of friends who he'd grown up with, most of whom had conveniently coupled up with each other, and he always wanted Cassie to socialise with them, rather than making the effort to meet and form bonds with her friends.

Inevitably, one of those couples got married. In a fancy hotel near where they'd all grown up in Surrey. Cassie had forked out for the hen weekend, then on a dress and a present, even though she always felt slightly excluded from the friend group. After the wedding, she planned to gently but firmly break up with Tom, especially as she suspected that he was actually in love with his pal Sophie who was going out with another outsider, Doug, who was also always slightly excluded.

The wedding was the most wedding-y of all weddings. All of the friends were bridesmaids and groomsmen, apart from Cassie and Doug. There were cute flower girls and pageboys.

The respective mothers cried. There was a choice between salmon, chicken and a mushroom risotto for the vegetarians. The best man's speech was a little too ribald and the first dance was to 'At Last' which then segued into Bruno Mars' 'Marry You'.

So far, so like every other wedding. Until it came time for Harriet, the bride, to throw her bouquet. It was caught by one of her bridesmaids and her boyfriend, one of the groomsmen, promptly went down on one knee and proposed, and she gratefully and tearfully accepted.

Cassie watched all this with a smile. She even wiped a tear away, though if she'd been the bride and two of her wedding party had got engaged and stolen her special-day thunder, she'd have been furious.

Then Harriet took back her bouquet, which seemed odd. She threw it again, which was even odder. It was caught by another bridesmaid and the corresponding groomsman again got down on one knee and pulled out a ring. Twice more it happened. Almost like it had been planned because it *had* been planned.

Cassie couldn't think of anything worse than getting engaged in some twee choreographed mass event at another person's wedding, but tried to smooth out the horrified expression on her face. Jesus, not again, she thought to herself as Harriet once again held her bouquet aloft to big cheers from the assembled guests, even though with the exception of Cassie and Tom, and Sophie and poor Doug, the friend group were now the engaged-to-be-married friend group.

'Then I suddenly get whacked in the face by Harriet's bouquet,' she told Fleur who was giggling now, because she really did love this story.

'Then what happened?' Fleur prompted, though she knew full well that . . .

'Tom got down on one knee and asked me to marry him and well, I could hardly say no in the circumstances, even though I was sure that when it came to saying our wedding vows, he'd accidentally call me Sophie . . .'

'Like in *Friends* when Ross says Rachel instead of Emily.' Fleur had heard this story countless times, so she was well versed in all its many facets.

Except, thank God, they hadn't made it to vows. They had made it to looking around wedding venues while Cassie desperately tried to find the right time to let Tom down gently, By then, wedding fever had seized the whole group and the right time just wouldn't present itself.

Until one fateful Saturday night when Cassie found herself going out with Tom and his seven closest friends plus Doug and, yet again, talk turned to life after the four weddings. Houses, babies, bigger houses, more babies plus a lot of pressure on Cassie to just make a decision about the wedding venue so that she and Tom could pay the deposit on the *twenty-thousand-pound* wedding package.

At eight o'clock the next morning, Cassie was standing outside the very house in which she and Fleur were now not sleeping.

On that Sunday morning all those years ago, Fleur and Joni had been parked in front of *The Little Mermaid*, Russell was out for a run and Lucy was there to provide tea, sympathy and wide-eyed incredulity as Cassie painted a picture of her future as dictated by Tom and his friend group.

'Even though I've got an exciting new job in PR and event planning now that *Skirt* has gone tits up, apparently we're going to start trying for a baby right away. Me and my ovaries aren't getting any younger.'

'You and your ovaries are positively youthful,' Lucy smeared cream cheese on one half of a bagel. 'Do you want smoked salmon?'

'Yes please. Then once I've had the first of what may be two or four children, but not an odd number of children, I'm going to give up work until the youngest is in school.'

'Do you even want children? I thought you were undecided.'

'Still am,' Cassie said, accepting a bagel stuffed with cream cheese and smoked salmon. 'But not to worry, once I've had the first child, Tom is going to add my name to the deeds of his house. The house that we don't even currently live in together.'

Tom owned a house. A whole house! It was in Parsons Green (one of the reasons why Cassie wanted to dump him was the geographical distance and the District Line between them), which had been secured with a hefty deposit courtesy of his parents and an inheritance.

'Cass, you *have* to dump him. This has gone on long enough.' Lucy's expression softened. 'Have you suddenly fallen in love with him?'

'He's nice and yes, we both like Arctic Monkeys, Scandi crime dramas and Wagamama but on the big stuff, the inside stuff, we're worlds apart.'

Cassie took a huge bite of her bagel and ruminated while she masticated as Lucy took a sip of coffee, her gaze fixed on Cassie's face.

Once Cassie had swallowed, Lucy reached across the table to squeeze her hand. 'You can't marry someone – and you especially can't spend twenty grand on a wedding package – just because you don't want to hurt his feelings.'

'Apparently the bride's family pays for the wedding. I told Alison that.'

Lucy raised her eyebrows. 'Oh yeah. What did she have to say?'

'She laughed. Mockingly.' Cassie allowed herself a faint smile as she remembered Alison's offer of 'fifty quid if you catch me on payday'. 'But also, it's not just the big stuff, I . . . I'm just going to say it . . .'

Lucy gestured with a hand. 'The floor is yours . . .'

'I hate his friends,' Cassie said in a guilty rush. 'They're a judgemental bunch of basics who look down on me and Poor Doug because we didn't grow up in Godalming and go to the same minor public school as them.'

Cassie was dimly aware of the front door opening, which meant that Russell was back, but there were very few things she said to Lucy that she wouldn't say to Russell.

'And Tom won't ever go down on me. He says that "it's just not his thing",' Cassie mimed quote marks. 'Like, does he think that giving him a blow job is my favourite activity in the world? He can't just say that it's not his thing like eating pussy is the same as eating oysters . . .'

'I love eating oysters but I'd much rather eat pussy,' said an awful, horrible, familiar voice from behind her.

Cassie couldn't bear to turn around to see Marc's smirking face.

Instead she took another huge bite of her bagel, even though his words had made her stomach churn. She tried not to look at Marc in black running shorts and T-shirt as he then leaned against the kitchen island, his tanned limbs glistening. He even looked good when he was sweaty. He was *so* annoying.

This was the part of the story that she always glossed over when she was telling it to the girls. Just as she skipped over it now.

'And then?' Fleur asked, although her voice was thick and Cassie could tell she was struggling to keep her eyes open.

'I was meant to be meeting Tom and his friends for lunch,' Cassie said (at the time, even perpetually good-natured Russell had snapped, 'God, can't these people even take a shit on their own?'). 'Your mum agreed to come with me for moral support.'

Tom had been sitting next to Sophie, surprise surprise, and kept saying, 'Not now, babe,' as Cassie did her best to separate him from the pack. So, finally, much as the engagement had begun in front of all his friends, that was also how the engagement was ended.

'Tom! I have to tell you something,' Cassie had said urgently. 'It's . . . I'm sorry . . . I don't want to hurt you . . .'

'Can we do this later? Sophie was telling me that her gran is really ill . . .'

On Sophie's other side, Poor Doug shot Cassie a sympathetic look.

'Tom! This can't wait. The longer it goes on, the worse I feel . . .' Tom wasn't even looking at her and when Cassie glanced helplessly at Lucy, her friend pushed her out of the way and tapped the nearest glass with the nearest fork to get the table's attention.

'Cassie has something to say, Tom,' Lucy had said in the most chilling 'I want to speak to the manager' voice. It was a voice that Cassie hadn't even known Lucy possessed.

All eyes turned to look at Cassie. She wilted before their collective judgemental gaze. They'd be pleased. All of them. She'd never been good enough for their precious Tom.

'I . . . I didn't want to do it like this.' Cassie shut her eyes. 'I didn't want to have to do this at all but you blindsided me . . . Oh God, I can't . . .'

'Enough is enough,' Lucy said sharply, and this time she shoved Cassie behind her and stood there with her hands on her hips.

'What is it?' Tom's boyishly handsome face creased only in mild concern.

'Cassie doesn't want to marry you,' Lucy announced. 'She likes you but she doesn't love you and next time you propose don't just do it because all your friends are doing it. Give him back the ring, Cass.'

The table was silent, the collective stare now positively demonic; only Poor Doug seemed to understand Cassie's plight.

Cassie tugged off her ring and placed it in front of Tom, who again only looked faintly disturbed. 'I'm so sorry,' she said.

Then she grabbed Lucy and they pushed their way through the crowded pub. Once they were out on the street, Cassie picked up her pace. It wasn't until they turned the corner, almost falling over three dachshunds being walked on one lead, and Cassie realised that Tom wasn't running after her, she stopped running. She was half crying, half laughing; Lucy too, and it . . .

'It was the greatest thing one best friend has ever done for another,' she told Fleur, whose eyelids were drooping. 'And Tom *did* marry Sophie and Poor Doug ended up with a totally hot Brazilian woman so everyone lived happily ever after.'

'Except you,' Fleur said with a yawn. 'You're still single so you haven't had your happily ever after yet.'

Had all the wisdom Cassie imparted been for nothing? 'You don't need to have a partner to have a happily ever after. I'm perfectly capable of providing my own happy ever after,' she said in a hurt voice, but Fleur was now asleep.

10

Lucy and Russell returned home just before eight that morning.

Fleur and Joni were still asleep but Cassie had been downstairs for over an hour – ever since Lucy had messaged to say that they were waiting to pick up a prescription then they'd be on their way.

As soon as she heard the car pull up, Cassie switched on the kettle, pressed down the knob on the toaster – she'd had four slices of bread ready and waiting – and forced herself not to pounce as soon as they walked in the door.

'Everything all right?' she asked casually as they came into the kitchen, as if they hadn't spent several hours at the Whittington Hospital.

'Had worse nights,' Russell said, leaning heavily on the big kitchen table before sitting down.

'Though I can't remember when,' Lucy added. 'I need industrial amounts of coffee. How are the girls?'

'They're fine. They're sleeping,' Cassie said, as she took three mugs down from a cupboard.

'And you?' Russell asked, with a searching look in Cassie's direction. 'How are you?'

Cassie felt horrible. Everything ached. Even her hair follicles. It felt like someone had taken her skin off, then put it back the wrong way around. 'I'm great,' she insisted brightly. 'Never mind me, how are you?'

Lucy and particularly Russell looked much as you'd expect from two people who'd been awake for twenty-four hours and counting, plus had travelled back from another country during that time as well as the whole hospital business.

'It was something and nothing,' Russell said. 'My airways were a little blocked.'

'That doesn't sound like nothing.' Cassie spooned coffee into the mugs. They had a coffee machine that rivalled Marc's in its hugeness and complexity but it was hardly ever used. Only when there was company – Cassie didn't count as company – and then they'd have to google the instructions.

'Don't fuss, Cass,' Russell said lightly, holding up a bulging white paper bag. 'I've got all sorts of medication in here and an inhaler for if it happens again.'

'Or when it happens again.' Lucy leaned against the island and rubbed her hand over her eyes. 'We're going to see the consultant tomorrow.'

'But you're all right now?' It didn't do any harm to check.

'Yeah, I'm all right now,' Russell confirmed.

If Cassie looked past Russell's grey face, his tired, swollen eyes, he seemed the same as he ever did. Maybe even better because after two weeks in the French sun, he was tanned, his hair blonder than usual.

'I owe you a massive favour,' Lucy said, taking the mug of coffee that Cassie pushed towards her. 'I'm so sorry for—'

'You don't need to finish that sentence. And you don't owe me anything.' Cassie paused to savour the aroma of her coffee as she tried to inhale the caffeine. 'I said I'd be here for you.'

'Well, at least have a shower and crash in the guest room, then we'll do something nice for lunch,' Lucy said.

Cassie shook her head then wished she hadn't because the room seemed to spin. 'I've got to go into work, but we'll definitely do something nice one evening later in the week,' she added as Lucy and Russell both looked at her as if she was mad.

She would have loved to take a mental health day. It was August, after all – her quiet period. Except this would be the one day she had two client meetings that couldn't be postponed, including a dinner with the husband and wife owners of a premium skincare brand which was launching in the UK in October. They were only going to be in London for twenty-four hours, en route to their yacht, which was parked (did one park a yacht? Moor it? Anchor it? Cassie didn't know anyone who owned a yacht who'd be able to solve this quandary) somewhere in Mykonos.

It was such an important dinner that Arlo, her boss, took one look at Cassie when she arrived in the office and told her to go and get her hair done. 'Claim it on expenses,' he said after Cassie haltingly tried to explain the reason why she was an hour late and looked like something that the council wouldn't remove without charging a disposal fee. 'Going forward, if you need to take time off, just let me know. September to December is manic but we'll work something out.'

'Oh, everything is fine now,' Cassie said. She was sure last night had just been a blip and after Russell saw his consultant, the prognosis wouldn't be so grim. Russell had said Christmas, but he was walking and talking and just generally being Russell and Cassie couldn't see how that would drastically change in the next four months. 'But thank you.'

'Got to look after my best girl. Sorry, best woman,' Arlo said with a sheepish smile. He was definitely the best boss. He'd picked Cassie up when she was absolutely defeated after closing her business and acted as if she was doing him a massive favour by agreeing to work for him.

Today, after her first important meeting at eleven, lunch was a limp takeaway salad and more coffee while Cassie was having a quick cut and blow dry.

Then she returned to Copper Media's airy, top-floor offices in Soho Square, the sun pouring in through the picture windows so Cassie had to put her shades on. She'd reached the light-sensitivity stage of sleep deprivation.

'Steady on there, Patsy, shweetie,' said Jan, one of Cassie's team. They were going through the calendar for the next month, but Cassie had to keep pausing to rest her head on the desk.

The events team had a bank of desks at the back of the open-plan office, the furthest away from the glass-walled reception area, but Cassie still had a prime view when a tall, lean man in a cream-coloured suit stepped out of the lift.

The man was talking to Georgii (with two 'i's) on reception as Jan walked them through the schedule for London Fashion Week. A second later, Cassie's phone beeped.

'Bloke here to see you. Surname is something French. Hasn't got an appointment. Shall I tell him to do one?'

'Oh no,' Cassie whimpered. 'Not today, Satan.'

Jan looked up from their shared screen with an offended expression. 'You were the one who told me to book in a third event for the twelfth of September. It's no use moaning about it now.'

'It's not that. It's not you. It's him,' Cassie said, as the bloke with the French surname turned from the reception desk to look down the office. He spotted Cassie immediately, then raised a hand in a very imperious beckoning motion. 'I'd better see what he wants.'

'Well, we're done here anyway,' Jan said, closing his laptop with a soft but emphatic thud. 'I'm going home now. What time's your dinner?'

'Not until seven.' Cassie stood up and tugged at the back of her dress where the cotton was clinging to her legs.

It was one of Lucy's dresses. The dress Cassie had picked up from the floor of her bedroom the previous night had a coffee stain on it.

It was a drapey, deconstructed slate-grey number – Lucy was a big fan of dresses that looked like complicated fabric sculptures on the hanger but worked on her because everything worked on her, whereas Cassie hadn't been sure which was the neck hole and which the arm holes and kept tripping on the lowest point of the asymmetric hem, as she did now, while hurrying down the length of the office.

'What are you doing here?' she demanded of Marc who hadn't taken his eyes off Cassie as she approached.

'Lovely to see you too. I was in the area and I need to talk to you about something, so I thought I'd check if you were free,' he said calmly. As usual, he was the picture of elegant self-assurance in an exquisitely cut suit, expensive sunglasses tucked into the open collar of his black shirt.

Behind him, Georgii pretended to swoon.

'I'm sorry, you caught me off guard.' It was very hard to be diplomatic on an hour's sleep. 'Is this about Lucy's weekend?' She couldn't help but sag. 'Is it very urgent or can it wait?'

'I spoke to Russell. He explained about last night.' Marc turned to the reception desk to retrieve a takeaway cup of coffee and a small box from Maison Bertaux. 'I brought caffeine and sugar. Now can I tempt you away for fifteen minutes? We could find a bench in Soho Square.'

'Is it instant coffee?' Cassie asked with the ghost of a smile though she'd drunk more coffee today than the human body was designed to withstand.

'I'm afraid not,' Marc said gravely. 'I begged the barista to use some desiccated granules from whatever jar she could find but she insisted on freshly ground beans and frothing the milk like its life depended on it.'

'That's a shame. But very kind, thank you,' Cassie said, remembering her manners. She had her phone, she had her sunglasses, she was good to go. 'OK, yeah. I can spare fifteen minutes.'

With a look downwards at Cassie's feet in her ancient just-around-the-office flip-flops and the too-long hem on her dress, Marc ushered her into the lift as if he suspected, quite rightly, that if she tried to take the stairs it wouldn't end well. Or maybe he still hadn't recovered from the last time they'd gone down the stairs together.

Such a good girl.

As they stood shoulder to shoulder in the tiny lift, Cassie was glad that she was wearing her shades indoors, even if it did make her look like a massive media wanker.

Outside the offices, they crossed over the road to the small patch of green where hundreds of people were congregated in the way that Londoners did when it wasn't raining and it was the only grassy surface for a good mile or so. 'We probably won't be able to find a bench,' she warned Marc with a glance towards his pristine cream tailoring.

Cassie often thought of Marc as one of those people who good fortune smiled on, even though he didn't deserve it. Taxis appeared as soon as he stood on a kerb and raised his arm. Restaurant reservations never eluded him and he never got stuck with the early slot and forty-five minutes to order, eat then vacate.

So, inevitably, immediately, two people got up from a bench a little distance away and within a couple of long strides, Marc had claimed it as Cassie scurried after him.

He didn't say anything but handed over the coffee and the cake box, which contained a chocolate éclair.

'Thank you. Did you want to share?' She held up the box but Marc shook his head. 'I'll save it for later,' she said when really she wanted to demolish it in three quick bites. 'So, what was it that you wanted to talk about?'

'I think we've come to a better understanding of each other these last couple of weeks, don't you?' Marc asked, sliding on his own shades, then crossing his long legs. 'Much better to be friends.'

They had a long, *long* history which meant that friends was never going to be an option. 'Friendlier,' Cassie conceded. 'Which is good. I don't like us to . . . be constantly sniping at each other.'

'Really?' It was amazing how Marc could make that humble six-letter word sound so sceptical. 'I was under the impression you enjoyed it.'

'Of course I don't.' Cassie took a huge gulp of coffee to wash away the lie because she always took great satisfaction in seeing her barbs pierce Marc's cool exterior.

'Well, I enjoyed it,' Marc murmured, then shifted position so his body was turned towards Cassie and she could feel the heat of him. The expensive aftershave he wore, notes of suede and amber and something a little sharper. 'Why are you sniffing? Do you have hay fever?'

'No, I'm fine.' Another gulp of coffee. 'Do go on – you were saying how much pleasure you get from being mean to me.'

'As if you don't give as good as you get,' Marc drawled.

Cassie shrugged. 'Coming from you, that's a compliment.'

They might be friend*lier* but there was still an edge that separated them and always would.

'Anyway, as illuminating as this conversation has been, it's not why I'm here,' Marc said. He seemed a little nervous. Usually he was quite still, in a way that always made Cassie think of a panther or some other sleek big cat about to pounce but today, he was jiggling a foot (in a very expensive Tom Ford trainer) and the fingers of one hand were drumming out a tattoo on his knee.

Cassie braced herself for more changes to the party itinerary or a worldwide shortage of champagne driving the price up. 'Don't keep me in suspense. You might as well just come straight out with it.'

'Very well.' Marc adjusted his shirt collar. 'I'm worried about Russell.'

He said it without emotion, but the fact that he was saying it at all, *to her*, made panic rise up in Cassie. She took several large sips of coffee to tamp it down.

'Last night was dramatic,' she said slowly. 'I was worried too; frightened; and the girls, they were very upset.'

'We really do have to think about Fleur and Joni in all this. And Lucy. It's all about Russell but at the same time, it's not just about Russell,' Marc said obliquely.

Usually Cassie wouldn't ask for subtitles. She didn't want him to let out a long-suffering sigh like she wasn't clever enough to understand him. But today she was tired, so bloody tired, and they were friendlier.

'I'm sorry, Marc. I don't understand what you're getting at,' she admitted. 'You're going to have to spell it out.'

He nodded. 'We both want what's best for the four of them, yes?'

'Yes! Of course, yes!'

'And they all adore you,' Marc said softly, which touched Cassie in her fragile state. 'You're not just a close friend. You're practically family.'

His words prompted that familiar prickle of tears that was never far away these days. Cassie rubbed a careful finger under one eye, then the other.

'Don't cry,' Marc ordered, because Cassie wasn't allowed to cry. That's all anyone ever seemed to say to her lately. Lucy, Russell, now Marc. Yet when Cassie was on her own and desperate for a really cathartic cry, she still couldn't squeeze out a single tear.

'I'm not crying,' Cassie muttered. 'But I hope they do love me as much as I love all of them. And I know you love them too. In your way.'

Cassie wasn't sure how Marc felt about anything or anyone. But he and Russell had been friends since prep school.

And Lucy had always had the softest of spots for Marc. Fleur and Joni, well, they certainly loved the way he spoiled them on birthdays and Christmas and sometimes just because.

Marc smiled faintly at Cassie's weak endorsement and then, as if it wasn't strange enough that he'd sought her out today and been *nice* to her, he suddenly took her hand in a firm grip like he wasn't planning to let go anytime soon.

What strange days these were. Everything that Cassie knew or thought she knew had been turned upside down, pulled inside out and off its moorings. It was one of those very rare occasions since the night they'd first met, all those years ago, when she and Marc were alone together. Holding hands again.

'You're beginning to freak me out,' she said bluntly and Marc gave her hand a consoling squeeze.

'We have to be a team now, Cassie,' he said in a soft but compelling voice so Cassie couldn't tear her gaze away from the intent look on his face. 'You and me. We have to present a united front.'

'I know that,' she said, her voice wavering slightly because this was a lot, emotionally, to deal with.

'I don't like to use the word intervention because it's something of a cliché and actually as a method of persuasion it's far from efficacious . . .'

His voice washed over Cassie because again she didn't really understand what Marc was saying, but the way he said it in his deep voice with just that suggestion of a French accent despite all these years in England was quite mesmerising when she let herself just give in to it.

'. . . and I know that I was too heavy-handed before, but it was such a shock. Of course Russell doesn't want to go to LA, but now I've found a team in Zurich, which is much closer, who've had some very promising, positive results for patients with stage four cancer . . .'

That brought Cassie back to full consciousness. 'Russell was very specific about only wanting palliative care,' she reminded him. 'You have to respect that.'

Marc's grip on her hand tightened slightly. 'I don't think Russell is thinking too clearly. Which is understandable. I can't imagine what he's going through . . .'

'Then why are you—'

'If I had what Russell has – a family, people who love him, rely on him – I'd be fighting this battle with everything I had,' Marc continued, still with the handholding, still with his gaze on Cassie and even though they were both wearing sunglasses, to be his sole focus was still unnerving.

'Look, I don't think it's very helpful to use terminology like fight and battle when you're talking about this. Studies actually say—'

'This clinic in Zurich can perform a radical surgery, then once Russell's white blood cell count is up, after a complete blood transfusion, chemo and radiotherapy have a much better chance of working.' Marc gave Cassie's hand a little shake. 'It's worth a try. I know you can get Lucy onboard, then I'm sure Russell will agree too. If it gets him even six more months with the girls, with us, then he has to do it. It could even be years. So, what do you think?'

Cassie had never seen Marc this impassioned about anything or anyone. She'd often wondered why he and Russell were friends when Russell was so caring, so kind, such good company and Marc was . . . none of those things.

But it turned out that Marc really did care for Russell, and by extension, Lucy and the girls. Even so . . .

'I know this is coming from a good place, I know that, but I can't be part of this,' she said gently, patting the hand that was still holding hers. 'It's not what Russell wants. I'm sure he and Lucy have weighed up all the different options available.'

'Have you spoken to them about it, then?' Marc asked sharply.

Cassie shook her head. 'We've more talked around it.' She couldn't even say the c-word and every time she tried, she was told not to start crying.

'If *you* talked to them, they'd listen,' he insisted.

'No, I'm sorry, but I don't think it's the right thing to do.' Cassie longed to free her hand, to stop this awful conversation and escape. Even the prospect of an important work dinner with tricky clients was more welcome than this. 'I really have to be getting back now.'

'If you care for Russell, really care, then you'd do this,' Marc said in a low, urgent voice as he leaned closer to Cassie so she felt as if he were about to swallow her whole.

'Of course I care about Russell . . . it's because I care about him that I'm respecting his wishes.' If she and Marc were closer, if their friendliness went back further than two weeks, then Cassie might have confided in him. Explained why she was going to have nothing to do with any kind of intervention or trying to push Russell onto a path he didn't want to walk.

Marc let go of Cassie's hand. He straightened up, put his shoulders back and as he looked at her, his features tightened in a way that she knew only too well.

'It doesn't seem like you care very much about him at all,' he said. All the warmth was gone from his voice. Now he sounded like a nuclear winter.

It was just as well that Cassie had enough heat for both of them. 'How dare you say that to me! If *you* cared about Russell, you'd listen to what he wanted instead of thinking that you always know best.'

There it was! That curl of his top lip. Cassie really hadn't missed it. 'You always have to get so emotional instead of thinking rationally. Formulating a plan, considering the options, laying the groundwork . . .'

'Oh!' Cassie jumped to her feet so she could loom over Marc for a change. 'I should have known the Mr Nice Guy routine these last few weeks was just an act.'

Marc stood up too because he had the copyright on looming. 'I don't know what you mean.'

'You know *exactly* what I mean,' Cassie said, jabbing a finger at him for emphasis, not quite making contact with his chest. 'I remember only too well just how nice you can be when you want something.'

'What have I ever wanted from you?' he asked with that entirely humourless smile that Cassie wanted to take a sledge-hammer to.

'I'm amazed that this time you even asked me, because before you just took, no questions asked.'

'I didn't need to take what you gave away so freely,' he rapped back at her and even though they never talked about *it*, what had happened between them on that May night, sixteen years ago, they were suddenly talking about it now.

Not even talking but throwing accusations and counter-accusations at each other, but still Cassie couldn't say the words. *You did something awful to me and I've never got over it.*

And she wasn't going to say them now. 'I'm not doing this,' she said instead and walked away from Marc with her shoulders back and her heart on the ground.

11

SIXTEEN YEARS EARLIER

Cassie wasn't particularly looking forward to Lucy and Russell's wedding. Not when she'd lost her plus-one two weeks before the big day. Bod had suddenly announced he was emigrating to Australia where they were desperate for plumbers so he'd easily got the required points on his visa.

It took time and forward planning to emigrate to another country. Yet he'd given Cassie a week's notice of his decision to resign from the position of boyfriend.

Now she was forced to fly solo at the fanciest wedding she'd ever been to. The fanciest anything she'd ever been to.

The wedding was taking place at the church in the village where Lucy had grown up; the reception at a country house hotel several miles away. It was more of a stately home and the room, which Cassie was meant to be sharing, and splitting the costs of, with Bogdan, was more than Cassie had ever spent on anything.

It had really eaten into her dress budget, though Cassie was determined to look as smoking hot as humanly possible. 'There'll be plenty of foxy single men who'll be desperate to dance with you,' Lucy had promised.

Russell was lovely but Cassie doubted that his friends would think she passed muster, and she didn't really like posh boys, but still, she didn't want people to think that she was some grubby charity case that Lucy had befriended as part of a community outreach programme. Also, there had to be one really fit bloke at the wedding. Hopefully, more than one.

Thankfully Grace, the fashion assistant on *Skirt*, had let Cassie borrow a Dolce & Gabbana dress from the fashion cupboard. 'But don't spill anything down it. Maybe don't even dance in it either because if it gets damaged, then we'll both have to leave the country,' Grace had warned, when Cassie had squeezed into it in the office loos.

It was black satin with spaghetti straps, a boned bodice that pushed her breasts up to the heavens and a tight skirt so Cassie had to take tiny steps. As she could hardly walk in the very high, knock-off Christian Louboutins she'd bought on eBay, it didn't really matter. She beehived her hair and went heavy on the eyeliner and red lipstick, like a much classier Amy Winehouse.

Her nan wasn't convinced. 'It's hardly suitable for a church wedding, Cass,' she said with a disapproving face. 'Christ, you could balance a tray of drinks on your boobs.' But there would be mood lighting at the reception and as for the service, no one was going to be paying any attention to Cassie with Lucy looking absolutely gorgeous in her floaty Chloé dress.

Cassie did wear a little black bolero jacket to church to hide her cleavage as she sat with two of the ad girls, Lara and Monique. They were single too and promised Cassie that a wedding was the best place to mend a broken heart. 'The only way to get over someone is to get under someone else,' Monique had hissed as they'd all unashamedly gawped at three men in morning suits who'd just walked into the church. They were broad of shoulder, ruddy of cheek. Not Cassie's type and she suspected that they might share DNA with Russell. She didn't want to snog someone (though she definitely wasn't getting *under* someone) only to discover that he was Russell's brother. Especially if it wasn't good snogging and their paths might cross again.

Just as it seemed all the guests had assembled and Russell was standing at the altar with a couple of groomsmen, there was a late arrival. A tall, lean man in a slim-cut black suit, black Converse and a snowy white shirt which contrasted with his tanned complexion. He had dark brown hair, a little too long, a little too tousled, compared to all those ruddy-cheeked men with ruthlessly short haircuts who'd clearly visited a barber the day before to get themselves wedding-ready.

This man looked as if he didn't really care whether he was wedding-ready. Like that was kind of basic and he was very far from basic. As he walked past their pew, he glanced over at the three young women. Cassie got an impression of green eyes, bone structure as exquisite as his beautifully cut suit and a faint smile that she hoped was appreciative.

'Well fit,' Lara whispered.

'Well *well* fit,' Cassie whispered back and even Monique, who wasn't easily impressed, sighed a little as they craned their necks to watch the man slip into the second pew on Russell's side of the church.

Then came the opening chords of an orchestral arrangement of Fleetwood Mac's 'Songbird' and the bridesmaids began their jaunty walk down the aisle. Cassie forgot all about the handsome man as she watched Lucy and Russell exchange their own personal vows 'to never let the sun go down on an argument' and 'to say "I love you" at least once a day'.

It was so romantic. Cassie couldn't wait to find her special someone. To really know what it meant to love and be loved and not just be good enough for a few months until your boyfriend decided to go halfway round the world to get away from you.

After the service, the guests milled about outside the church while the wedding photos were taken. Cassie leaned against the lichen-encrusted stone wall encircling the graveyard to ease the pain of her shoes, which were already pinching, and hoped she wouldn't get stains on her dress.

The handsome man was talking to Russell's parents while the photographer was busy shooting Lucy with her extended family. Then he sloped off, his stride easy and relaxed, to where a black vintage sports car was parked against a grass verge, got in and drove away. Cassie hoped that he'd be at the reception.

Eventually, the minibuses that had transported them from the country house to the church arrived to transport them back, and half an hour later, Cassie had the first of many delicate flutes of champagne in her hand and was standing in the entrance to a huge marquee on the back lawn, trying to find her name on the seating chart.

She was on one of the singles tables, thankfully with Lara and Monique. Although she'd been greeted affectionately by Lucy's friends Digby and Anita, who she'd met at the hen weekend, she really didn't know anyone else. Apart from Lucy's sister Heather who'd also been at the hen. She'd been rude and patronising to Cassie then disgraced herself by getting really drunk, really mean, really vomit-y and then going home early.

Cassie was seated next to Greg, who'd been at university with Lucy and Russell. He was perfectly nice but they didn't have anything to talk about. On her other side was a man called Nathan, a cousin of Russell's, and he only wanted to talk about his 'fucking crazy' ex-girlfriend.

Cassie stuck a fixed smile on her face and made sure her glass was kept full throughout the starter (smoked salmon and dill fishcakes) and the main course (chicken breast in an asparagus velouté). Then it was the speeches, when her glass was topped up again so she'd have champagne to toast with and also something to do because the speeches were quite boring if you'd only known the bride six months and had only met the groom twice. A high point was Lucy's dad making everyone laugh when he quoted Mr Bennet in *Pride and Prejudice*: 'You are each of you so complying, that nothing will ever be resolved on; so easy, that every servant will cheat you; and so generous, that you will always exceed your income.'

All the wedding moments were ticked off. The cutting of the cake. The first dance to Snow Patrol's 'Chasing Cars'. Everyone taking to the dancefloor for 'Come on Eileen'. Many songs danced to. Many hours passed. Many glasses of champagne. Cassie's shoes long abandoned.

The nuptials were winding down. Lara and Monique were each slow-dancing with a ruddy-cheeked man and Cassie was sitting alone at their table, everyone else gone. Her teeth had gone numb from all the champagne; unfortunately the same couldn't be said of her feet, which throbbed in time to 'Careless Whisper'.

Then she felt the light brush of someone's arm against her shoulder and a voice said, 'You look like you could do with some company.'

With a heavy heart and a fake smile, because she really could not listen to any more stories about Nathan's 'fucking crazy' ex, Cassie glanced behind her – but it wasn't Nathan.

It was the man she'd seen at the church. The well fit man who looked even fitter in the flickering glow of hundreds of tiny tea lights and the fairy lights strung across the support struts of the marquee. He looked a little more tousled than he had before and his smile was wider, very definitely appreciative, as he gestured at the empty chair next to Cassie.

'May I?' he asked in a drawly voice that carried the trace of an accent.

'Yeah, I mean, of course,' Cassie said.

He pushed the chair closer to Cassie so that when he sat down, they were almost touching. Then he rested one arm along the back of her chair so she could feel the heat coming off him, the faint scent of soft leather and spice cut through with something sharper.

'I haven't been able to take my eyes off you all evening,' he said conversationally.

'In a good way or a bad way?' She might have drunk a lot of champagne but Cassie still knew that yawning during the best man's speech and her enthusiastic twerking to 'Bootylicious' had not been her finest moments.

'Oh, in a very good way,' the man assured her.

This close, he was mesmerising. The intent way he looked at her, that half-smile, and the way there seemed to be something dangerous about it. About him.

And then he touched her.

One long finger hooked into the spaghetti strap of Cassie's dress where it had slipped down her arm and adjusted it so it was on her shoulder again, the tip of his finger delving into the dip of her collarbone and causing chaos in her nerve endings.

'God, it's been doing that all night. So annoying,' Cassie muttered, unable to turn away from his face because he was so pleasing, so beautiful, to look at.

'Do you want to know a secret?' he drawled, his finger still creating havoc as he now stroked it up her neck.

Eyes wide, Cassie nodded.

'It's one of the most erotic things I've ever seen. Every time it slipped down, it transformed you from proper to improper.' Then, with his eyes never leaving Cassie's flushed face, he slowly and deliberately pushed the thin loop of black satin off her shoulder again.

That brush of his finger across her skin was certainly the most erotic thing Cassie had ever experienced. Just his finger on her shoulder, the top of her arm, and already her nipples were hard, and a yearning ache had begun deep down in her belly. She hardly knew what to do with herself.

'Are you staying here tonight?' he asked, bending his head so his lips didn't quite make contact with her shoulder but she could feel his breath ghost across her skin. She shivered though she wasn't cold. Quite the opposite.

Again, Cassie nodded.

'Do you want to get out of here?'

'Yeah.' A pause. 'I do.'

His smile curved into something positively sinful. 'Good, so do I.'

12

He waited while Cassie retrieved her shoes. Even the pain when she slid her feet back into them couldn't kill the mood, or the insistent throb between her legs at the warmth of his hand at the small of her back, through the black satin, as he guided her out of the marquee.

There was a small set of stone steps that led up to a terrace. Through huge open doors was a room made entirely of glass, the hotel restaurant, where people were clustered around the bar.

'There's a door at the other end so we can avoid the crowd,' the man said, steering Cassie along the path that ran parallel to the terrace.

'Why are we avoiding the crowd?' Cassie asked as it occurred to her that she hadn't spoken to Lucy or Russell all night. At the very least, she should thank them.

'Because I want you all to myself,' he said, stopping, so Cassie stopped too. They were almost in darkness as he backed Cassie up against the stone wall, then pressed his lips against her shoulder again, his tongue darting out to taste her. 'Now, your room or mine?'

Cassie had never done this. Because she was about to do *this*. To make love to a man she'd only just met.

She couldn't have put a halt to it even if she'd wanted to – and she didn't want to. If he could make her feel like this, every inch of her flesh quivering in anticipation, even though he hadn't even kissed her, then she could only dream of how good it would be in . . .

'My room.' She was about to be reckless and though he was a guest and he knew Russell's parents, still, it was probably better to go back to her room. That seemed like the sensible thing to do.

'And what room is that?'

She fumbled in her tiny clutch bag for the room key. '417. Top floor.'

There was a flash of even white teeth as he grinned. 'The top floor? They put you in the servants' quarters? Well, that's a travesty.'

'It's a really nice room,' Cassie protested, as he took her hand and gently pulled her through a side door which opened onto a long corridor. To their left was a busy kitchen, the sound of laughter, the clink of plates and glasses.

It was the nicest room she'd ever stayed in. Also, it was costing her just shy of two hundred and fifty quid, nearly a week's wages, so Cassie was determined to love every centimetre of its pretty flower-sprigged wallpaper, its sloping ceilings, the big bed plump with pillows. It even had an ensuite bathroom.

'I like any room that has you in it,' he said in that voice that made Cassie almost take leave of her senses. They were hurrying down the corridor, her heels clicking over the parquet. 'We'll take the back stairs.'

'You have an accent?' Cassie asked.

'Barely. I'm half French,' he said as he opened another door to a narrow flight of stairs.

Cassie didn't know what she'd done to attract this handsome, sophisticated man who was half French. It kept getting better and better.

'Say something in French,' she said as they began the long climb up to the fourth floor.

'*J'ai hâte de te baiser,*' he purred. Cassie wanted to melt into a puddle. She'd done German as her language option, which had never once made her limbs turn liquid. '*Peut-être que je vais te faire me sucer d'abord.*'

'What does that mean?'

'I'm just saying how beautiful you are. Let's save our breath now for when we're kissing,' he said, which Cassie was relieved about, because climbing these stairs in these heels . . .

She was out of breath by the time they reached the top floor. Maybe it had nothing to do with all those steps and everything to do with the way he pressed himself against Cassie as she tried to fit the key into the lock. He lifted the hair that had escaped from her beehive to sear kisses along the back of her neck.

Cassie finally managed to turn the stiff key and almost fell into the room as the door opened. His arm around her waist saved her.

'So eager,' he said, closing the door behind him, then pushing Cassie up against it. The wood hard behind her, him hard in front of her, as he took her hands to gently pin them above her head.

The room was in darkness and a part of Cassie couldn't believe that she was doing this. She wasn't that kind of girl, but when he ground his hips into her, she made a noise in the back of her throat that wasn't a moan of protest. It was far needier than that.

It made him smile in the shadowy light.

'What's your name?' Cassie asked, her voice giddy.

He let go of one of her hands and smiled again, when she kept her arms raised. Then he put a finger on her lips. '*Pas des noms. Juste un homme et une femme.*'

He kissed away Cassie's swoony little sigh, his lips demanding, determined, and Cassie obediently opened her mouth so he could deepen the kiss, his tongue licking into her.

She couldn't say how long they kissed for but when he pulled away, the tight skirt of her dress was practically up to her hips and he had one hand tangled in her hair, the other cupping her arse.

'Do you want to show me what else you can do with that mouth?' he asked huskily, one hand now on her shoulder to press down in a gesture that Cassie would have to be an idiot not to understand.

He stepped back and she toed off her shoes and sank to her knees and looked up at him. Her eyes had grown accustomed to the darkness now but she heard rather than saw him undo his belt. The clink of the buckle, the swish of the leather . . .

'You can do the rest,' he assured her in that dark, treacly voice that Cassie couldn't resist. 'Take me out.'

She hadn't done this a lot. Didn't really like to, if she was being honest. Not that she'd been honest about it with Bod or the other two boyfriends she'd slept with who'd demanded blow jobs as standard and had never once returned the favour.

But this man, this sexy sophisticated man, clearly thought that Cassie was sexy and sophisticated too. The kind of woman who loved the illicit thrill of meeting a stranger, no names, then undoing his trousers with hands that shook ever so slightly.

Cassie rose up on her knees to pull down the waistband of his boxer trunks and his cock sprang free to meet her. He was fully hard and he gripped the base of his shaft to nudge the head against Cassie's cheek.

Her tongue darted out to touch the tip and he hummed in approval.

Encouraged, Cassie licked a path down the underside of his dick, along the vein that was throbbing there . . . she'd read about this last month in *Cosmopolitan*, one of those '20 Ways to Drive Your Man Wild in Bed' articles. She never thought she'd be putting it into practice.

But here she was, her hands on his hips as she took him into her mouth.

'That's it. You can take me deeper than that.'

Cassie's eyes were already watering but she tried to relax her throat.

'Such a good girl. *Tu es si belle avec ma bite dans ta bouche.*'

His hands were in Cassie's hair, keeping her head still as he pressed further forward and she was trying to suck him, to take him deep, but then he went in too far and she gagged and had to wrench herself free.

'Oh God, I'm so sorry!' She had a trail of spit hanging from her mouth, which she wiped away with the back of her hand. 'I could try again.'

'You could,' he agreed. 'You were doing so well.'

This time Cassie gripped the base of his cock so she could control the depth and with a lot of enthusiasm but not much finesse she licked and sucked for all she was worth. She hoped he wasn't going to come in her mouth because she really didn't like that but when his cock pulsed and she thought it was game over, he jerked away from her.

'Do you not want . . .' She gestured at his dick, which seemed harder and bigger than before. Cassie wasn't even sure how she'd managed to get so much of it in her mouth. 'I mean, I could . . .'

'You could,' he agreed again. 'But I can't have you doing all the work.'

He helped her to her feet; her thigh muscles were trembling from holding her up on her knees for so long. Once Cassie was standing, he turned her round so he could unzip the back of her dress and slide his hands under the satin to cup her breasts and nuzzle her neck.

Cassie bucked against him as he took her nipples between finger and thumb and applied pressure gently, then not so gently when her head fell back on his shoulder, and she gasped.

'I don't know where to start,' he murmured into her skin. 'I want my mouth on your tits.'

'I'd like that too,' Cassie whimpered, but his hands had already left her breasts to slide down the black satin, the skirt still rucked up so in an instant he was stroking along her inner thighs.

His fingers creeping higher and higher up her legs, his touch warm, her skin even hotter still.

'I bet you're wet for me,' he whispered, biting down on the plumpness of Cassie's earlobe as his fingers slipped under the seam of her knickers and separated her folds. 'You are, aren't you?'

It was a rhetorical question. Cassie had never felt so soaked, so swollen, and as his thumb brushed over her clit again and again, a finger twisting inside her, if he hadn't been holding her up, she thought her legs might give away.

'Oh God,' she yelped, though she'd never been much of a talker before. 'If you keep doing that, then I'm going to come.'

He stopped doing *that* immediately. 'I'd much rather you come on my cock,' he said, pushing her forward towards the bed until Cassie felt the edge of the mattress against her thighs and she put her arms out to brace herself.

He kept one hand between her legs to stroke her clit and the other hand was somewhere else. Cassie heard him swear softly, then the crinkle and tear of foil and a faint squelch, which made her giggle, as he rolled the condom on.

She hadn't even thought to say something about protection and then she wasn't thinking of anything, because he was nudging her foot so she spread her thighs wider, still steadily working her clit.

'Stick your arse out, darling,' he said. That shouldn't have been sexy but it was; then he lined his cock up and was in her with one quick but firm thrust, which surprised a squeak out of Cassie. 'That's my good girl.'

Cassie hadn't realised that it was going to happen like this. If she'd been able to think at all, she'd have expected him to undress her, kiss her some more then lay her down on the bed. Him on top of her. They'd do it like that because that was the way she'd always done it.

Missionary position, her eyes tight shut, because she never liked to see her boyfriends' faces during sex; they looked so ugly, so scrunched up, like they were in pain. Cassie would put her arms around them like she really loved them and try to squeeze them with her muscles so they'd think she was enjoying herself, but really she just wanted it to be over. It didn't hurt, but it never felt that great either.

So she'd never expected *this*. Someone, a man whose name she didn't even know, one hand in her hair, to gently pull her head back, the other hand tight on her hip as he drove into her again and again.

'*T'es si bonne. Ma petite salope.*'

It didn't feel like making love. It didn't even feel like they were having sex. They were fucking, and fucking shouldn't feel this good. Even when he pulled her hair hard enough that she moaned in protest. Though it didn't sound like a protest and if he'd just touch her clit again, then Cassie was sure that she would . . .

'I'm coming,' he groaned and he drove into her even harder and she could feel him spilling into the condom as her arms gave way and she collapsed face down on the bed, him draped over her, still inside her.

Then he pulled his softening cock out of her, levered himself off her and walked across the room and into the bathroom. Cassie pushed herself up to standing. She was wearing her dress like a belt. The satin was completely crushed, Grace was going to kill her.

She pulled up her knickers, which were around her knees, tugged the bodice of the dress up, then tugged the skirt of the dress down.

Now it all felt so sordid.

Cassie sat on the edge of the bed, everything still in darkness, until he walked back into the room.

She didn't know what to say, what the correct etiquette was. Should they exchange numbers? Did he want to see her again? Did she want to see him again?

'That was amazing,' he said, sitting down next to her on the bed. 'Sorry it was rather quick, but you felt so good, I got carried away.'

'It's OK,' Cassie muttered, holding herself back as he reached across her, his arm brushing her breasts, which still felt extraordinarily sensitive, to turn on the bedside lamp. 'No, I thought we were doing lights off.'

She turned her head because fucking someone she didn't know was one thing but having to look at him afterwards was something else entirely.

'You didn't come,' he said matter-of-factly, his hand on her chin to turn her face back to him. She hadn't imagined it. He really was that beautiful. Which made her feel even more awkward as her cheeks burned at his statement.

'No, I did,' she said quickly because that was what she always said. 'Of course I did.'

'Sweetheart, I've just been inside you. I could feel everything . . .' He was wearing that half-smile, although now it wasn't turning Cassie on. She tried to look away but he still had his hand on her chin.

'Yeah, I do remember.' She wanted to sound nonchalant but she knew that she couldn't pull it off.

'Look, I don't mind that you didn't come.' He shrugged, which made him seem more than just half French. 'But it doesn't feel fair. So, we're going to do it again and this time, you're going to do exactly what I tell you.'

'You don't have to do that,' Cassie said, succeeding in freeing herself so she could shake her head. 'I don't. I've never. It's cool.'

'Has anyone even gone down on you before?' he asked, leaning back on his elbows, every inch of him at ease with himself, with the situation, while Cassie would have loved it if a gateway to another dimension suddenly bore a hole into the fancy mattress and swallowed her whole.

'Have they?'

'No,' she said sullenly.

'Well, it's your lucky day, darling, because I *love* dining out.'

'I'm fine without you having to do . . . that,' Cassie said and he laughed.

'God, you're so English. So buttoned up. Even when you're unzipped.'

Cassie hadn't been able to zip herself back up and when he ran the tip of his finger down her spine, she couldn't help but shiver.

'You really don't have to,' she said, as his hands delved into her hair to demolish what was left of her updo. He gently disentangled her Bumpit.

'What the fuck is this?' he asked, giving it a curious look and throwing it over his shoulder, which made Cassie giggle, then wish she hadn't.

'I don't expect you to, you know . . .' She gestured vaguely at her lap.

'I know you don't, but I want to.' He grinned as he stood up, then pulled Cassie, unresisting though still not entirely onboard, to her feet. 'It's my good deed for the day. Let's get you naked then you're going to sit on my face.'

'Oh no, I definitely don't want to do that,' Cassie insisted.

Ten minutes later, she was somehow naked and spread out on the bed like an all-you-can-eat buffet with his head between her legs, his mouth sucking on her clit like he hadn't eaten in days.

She came with a series of moans, which increased in volume, her hips lifting off the bed until he pushed her down with a firm hand.

Then some time after that, once Cassie had *begged* him to fuck her again, he made her straddle him and 'take my dick and slide it into that pretty little cunt of yours'.

She hadn't done that before either. And though she'd been called a cunt a couple of times by angry men when she'd refused their advances, no one had ever called her pussy that. He made it sound like an endearment. So Cassie did what she was told, her bottom lip caught between her teeth as she slowly lowered herself onto his hard, condom-covered cock. Holding her breath until she couldn't go any further. She leaned forward and gasped as she felt him bump a delicious, maddening spot inside of her and her clit grazed against the coarse hair at the base of his dick.

'God, that feels *good* . . .' She let out a shuddering breath and raised her head to see him staring at her with heavy-lidded eyes, glittering green, his tongue snaking out to wet his lips.

She raised herself slowly, then sank back down again and flung her head back as her whole world narrowed down to his cock in her . . . cunt.

'You look so fucking sexy like that,' he said unsteadily. 'Go on, again. Do it again.'

Cassie rose and fell, again and again, faster, until she'd lost all rhythm, chasing her orgasm which was just out of reach until he slipped his hand down to rub his finger right there, where his cock was driving into her. Then he pinched her clit hard, let Cassie grind against him, her hand on his chest, right over his heart as she fell for the last time.

Afterwards, she cuddled into him and he stroked her hair and stole lazy little kisses, until he slapped her gently on the arse.

'I'm parched,' he said. 'Have you got any water?'

Cassie was thirsty too. Thirsty was an understatement.

'Bathroom,' she said.

'Be a love.' He kissed the tip of her nose. 'I can't move. You've shagged me senseless.'

'I think it was the other way round,' she grumbled with a smile. But she got out of bed and although, despite everything, she was embarrassed to walk naked across the room, she managed it.

He probably didn't think that she was quite as sophisticated as she'd let him believe, but she was still the sort of girl who could be blasé about her nakedness as she fetched a drink for her *lover*.

Once she was in the bathroom with the door closed, Cassie ran the tap while she had a wee (*Cosmopolitan* magazine was also evangelical about peeing after sex to ward off UTIs), brushed her teeth and then, with a towel around her, emerged with a toothbrush tumbler full of water and a bright smile.

'One glass of fresh tap water coming up!'

But she was talking to thin air.

The rumpled bed was empty and he had gone.

13

Because she was young and resilient, Cassie woke up . the next day without a hangover despite the copious amounts of champagne she'd drunk.

But as she lay in bed, the sun beaming in from the gaps in the curtains that she hadn't quite closed, slowly regaining full consciousness, she was hurting in all sorts of other places.

A soreness between her legs and a heaviness in her heart because simultaneously she'd had the best and worst sexual experience of her life.

She'd had two powerful orgasms, better than anything she'd ever achieved with her own fingers. That was good.

But every other part of the night, from that first moment when a stranger had sat down next to her, felt very . . . not good. Once again, like so many other occasions in her twenty-one years, Cassie tasted the bitter tang of rejection. What was so wrong with her that everyone upped and left?

She decided that the post-mortem on the events of the night before could wait. She was too fragile to confront the role she'd played in her own downfall. Also, she'd paid two hundred and fifty quid for a hotel room, which included breakfast, and Cassie was determined to get her money's worth.

Showering brought it all back again. The bite marks, the faint bruises, on her breasts, her thighs. There was a condom in the bathroom bin and when Cassie walked back into her room and saw the empty bed, she felt as gut-punched as she had done the previous night when she realised that he'd done a runner.

She was stupid. So fucking stupid.

Because Cassie had expected him to come back. Or rather, she'd hoped he would. She'd told herself that perhaps he'd gone to get his pyjamas although clearly he wasn't the sort of man who slept in pyjamas. But maybe he'd gone to get his washbag.

But he didn't come back, and every reason that Cassie had come up with for his continued disappearance was worse than the last. That she was the worst shag he'd ever had. He'd only slept with her for a bet. Or he already had a girl-friend, or even a wife. A significant other that he'd slipped away from at the reception.

Not that she was blameless. Far from it. She'd willingly taken him back to her room. It had been consensual, at every stage. But it still felt as if he'd taken advantage of her. She'd been seduced by a master of the game while she hadn't even read the instructions on the box.

Cassie stumbled down the stairs, the proper stairs this time, including the grand sweeping staircase that led to the imposing foyer. Not sneaked up the servants' stairs like . . . like . . . like some kind of cheap scrubber. Break-fast was served in the hotel restaurant, which was just off the lobby.

Cassie paused in the entrance, suddenly mortified at the idea that she might come face to face with *him*, as she sur-veyed the many tables dressed with snowy white tablecloths and gleaming silverware. It was very smart and she was wearing her beloved black Juicy Couture tracksuit – a Christmas present from Emma, but it was still a tracksuit. Her hair was scraped back in a ponytail and there wasn't a scrap of make-up on her face. Whereas everyone else looked quite pulled together.

'Cassie! Over here!'

Monique was summoning her with a frantic wave of the hand. Cassie hurried over to the table she was sharing with Lara, who was almost obscured by huge sunglasses and a white pashmina.

'Where did you get to last night, you little tart?' Monique asked affectionately as Cassie sat down.

'Oh, um, I had an early night?' It was more of a suggestion than a lie.

'Was that before or after you got that love bite?' Lara asked in a thick voice, her hand shaking as she tried to lift her coffee cup to her mouth. 'Did you pull?'

Again, Cassie was young and hadn't learned to keep her own counsel. Besides, it was a relief to confess everything (well almost everything) to Lara and Monique, who were an enthralled and receptive audience.

'Then he just left and now I feel kind of weird about it,' Cassie admitted as a server appeared with her full English breakfast. She'd already demolished eight tiny triangles of toast while she'd been waiting.

'There's no point stressing,' Monique advised. 'You got picked up by some hot stranger and had some hot sex. It happens.'

'Chances are you'll never see him again,' Lara added. 'I mean, I got stuck with a guy last night who wouldn't shut up about his – and I quote – 'fucking crazy ex-girlfriend', but he's a young farmer so I know our paths will never cross again.'

'This guy was definitely not a young farmer,' Cassie said. 'He was half French, for one thing.'

'There you go, he probably lives in France,' Lara said. 'He's already left because he had to get the Eurostar or the ferry or whatever.'

Cassie brightened. 'Yeah, you're right.'

'And he showed you a good time, twice, and he used a condom both times, so you're golden,' Monique decided. 'Now, shall we order some more toast?'

Cassie felt much better after a debrief and some complex carbohydrates. She left Monique and Lara at the table and decided to have a head-clearing walk around the grounds before they called a taxi to take them to the station.

As she slipped through the conservatory, out to the terrace, there was Russell, Lucy and . . .

Oh God . . .

Cassie backed up like a nervous filly approaching Becher's Brook but it was too late.

'Hello, sweetie. So sorry not to have had a chance to talk to you yesterday,' Russell said, with a huge smile on his face, like he was pleased to see her.

'Yes, the whole day was a bit of a blur,' Lucy added. She had a radiance about her despite the puffy eyes of a late night and a lot of champagne. Like she was high on pure happiness. 'I'm not even sure that we did actually get married.'

While this exchange was taking place, the tall, lean man they'd been talking to gave Cassie a dismissive once-over, then looked away because he clearly wasn't at all pleased to see her.

'Oh, hey, Lucy, Russell,' Cassie said weakly, with a feeble wave. 'Yeah, you definitely did get married.'

'Well, come and give an old married couple a hug.' Russell was already holding out his arms, Lucy too, because goddamn them, they were both huggers and Cassie didn't have much choice but to walk over, heels dragging, eyes on the ground, for a quick and friendly three-sided hug. 'Have you had a good time?'

'It was lovely.' Cassie nodded enthusiastically, her eyes fixed on Russell's beaming face. 'Lucy, you looked so beautiful. I loved your dress and the speeches were lovely. And everything was just . . . lovely.'

Every word that came out of her mouth made Cassie want to wince.

'And you two know each other already,' Lucy said, with a toothy grin because she was high on love and life.

Cassie steeled herself to glance from Russell and Lucy to their friend, who was looking at her impassively despite the fact that not even ten hours before, he'd had her bent over her bed while he fucked her.

'We haven't met,' he said flatly.

Lucy frowned. 'But I saw you leaving the marquee together last night.'

'I don't think so,' Cassie said, a little desperately, wondering what she must have done in a past life to be punished so much in this one.

'Just as well,' Russell said, his arm looping around Cassie's shoulders. 'Cassie, this is Marc with a c.'

'And Marc, this is Cassie also with a c,' Lucy added.

'But you're to keep away from her because she is far too good and far too young for you,' Russell warned as Cassie wondered whether it was possible to die from sheer embarrassment. Obviously not. 'Cassie, also steer clear because I love Marc like a brother but he eats girls like you up for breakfast.'

'Oh stop!' Lucy punched Russell lightly on the arm. 'Marc isn't *that* bad.'

'Well, I hope I'm not that good either.' Marc held out his hand and Cassie had no choice but to shake it as briefly as she could. When she tried to retreat, he kept a hold of her for a fleeting moment, then let her go.

'It was a pleasure.' He smirked like he wasn't talking about this awkward introduction but what they'd done the night before. Immediately Cassie felt less embarrassed and more furious.

One of the ruddy-cheeked men from the previous day suddenly appeared in the doorway that led back into the restaurant.

'Russ, Luce,' he called out. 'Can I borrow you both?'

'In a sec!' Lucy replied. 'Going to have to love you and leave you. Cass, we'll catch up when we get back from our honeymoon.'

Cassie nodded, even as she wanted to beg Lucy not to abandon her so she'd be stuck with Marc with a c. 'Where are you going again?'

'A little village in Sussex where my grandparents used to live, right on the coast . . .'

'Sorry, guys, but Aunt Hester doesn't want to leave without saying goodbye,' bellowed the ruddy-cheeked man.

Russell and Lucy shared a conspiratorial look, like they were in it together now. Officially a team. 'We haven't had a minute to call our own all weekend,' Russell said sorrowfully, giving Cassie's shoulders a final squeeze before he and Lucy hurried off.

With her human shield now gone, Cassie was left alone with Marc, who gave her another of those head-to-toe inspections, his expression faintly incredulous.

'You looked different last night,' he said at last.

'Because it was a wedding,' Cassie pointed out defensively. 'I was dressed up.'

'You looked older. A lot older.' He sounded quite annoyed about it. 'How old are you anyway?'

Cassie paused. She was tempted to knock a few years off, just to pay him back for last night's vanishing act and the serious attitude he was giving her this morning. People were always commenting on how young she looked without make-up . . . but he was a friend of Russell's and she didn't want to make things even more hideous than they already were.

'I'm twenty-one,' Cassie said and he took a step back.

'Fucking hell!' he exclaimed. 'Thank God for that.'

'Well, how old are you?' Cassie asked pointedly, because Russell was twenty-eight, so he was likely to be a similar age. A seven-year difference between them, give or take, so she didn't know why he was acting like he was a cradle-snatcher and she was jailbait.

His smile didn't reach his eyes. 'Clearly not old enough to know better.'

He'd been so different the previous night. But of course he had been, because he'd wanted something from her, and now he'd got it, he didn't want to know her.

It was the kind of thing that happened to Alison, Cassie's mum, frequently. Because she had the worst taste in men. She'd just got married and Ted seemed like a nice enough bloke but time would tell. Anyway, there was no way that Cassie was going to do what Alison always did and just accept being treated like shit because she didn't think she deserved anything better.

Cassie drew herself up like there was a thread tugging through her spine, though Marc was still a lot taller than her, still looking down at her. She set her features so she knew she was stony-faced and flint-eyed.

'You are rude,' she told him, not like that was a newsflash. 'What you did last night . . .'

'Which part of last night?' he drawled and Cassie was assailed by a sizzle reel of all the highlights. Looking up at him while his dick hit the back of her throat. Her hands clutching at the bedspread to get some purchase as he railed her from behind. Him telling her exactly what to do as she slowly lowered herself onto his cock . . .

She shut her eyes so she wouldn't have to see the amused look on his face like he was enjoying this almost as much as the main event.

Again, she was not her mother's daughter. She had a lot more backbone.

Cassie opened her eyes. 'Look, Martin . . .'

That wiped the supercilious smile off his face. 'It's Marc,' he bit out.

'Whatever,' she said airily. 'Running away was a dick move. We both know it. You're just pissed off because someone's calling you out on it.'

'It is what it is,' he said, the five fallback words of a man who had no way in hell of winning an argument. 'The thing is, you were sitting on a back table so you're obviously not a close friend of the bride or groom and I expect that friendship will peter out soon enough.' He shot another withering glance at Cassie. 'And I live in San Francisco, so I doubt we'll ever have to see each other again.'

'Good,' Cassie snapped, holding her face very still again because his implication, that she was some guttersnipe who'd inveigled her way into Lucy and Russell's affections and would quickly be flung back into the gutter where she belonged, had stung. Also, in her heart of hearts, Cassie knew it would probably turn out to be true.

'Fine,' he snapped back.

There was no way that she was going to let him have the last word. Cassie folded her arms and treated him to a disparaging look of her own.

'Well, go on then, fuck off back to San Francisco.'

14

It was all ancient history now.

As instructed, Marc had fucked off back to San Francisco and Cassie had tried to get over that night. Chalk it down to experience.

But in reality, Marc had ruined her for all other men. After him, whenever she had sex with someone new, whether it was a very occasional one-night stand or something less temporary, she now knew what was going to work and what wasn't. Penetrative sex was great but unless Cassie was getting some clitoral stimulation then what was the point? So, she'd either tell her partner what to do, or, more often than not, do it herself and every time she did, she thought about Marc.

Ruined!

Then, after three years, he came back to London to set up his own investment company, a home, to reconnect with old friends. Old friends being Lucy and Russell, by this time with a two-year-old daughter, Joni, and Fleur on the way, and Cassie, who was now much more than a back-table-at-their-wedding friend.

She, Lucy and even Russell were deeply entrenched in each other's lives. They'd met each other's families. They lived around the corner from each other. There wasn't a week that went by without them seeing each other.

So it was inevitable that, despite their deep and fervent wish for the opposite, Cassie and Marc's paths would cross again. At birthday parties and dinner parties and barbecues.

But Cassie wasn't the same wide-eyed, impressionable girl she'd been when they'd met at the wedding. She was three years older and during those three years, she'd done a lot of growing up. There had been a few boyfriends, one of them semi-serious, and none of them had been allowed to treat Cassie the way Marc had treated her.

At work, she'd moved down two flights of stairs from the sales floor to editorial, where she was now executive assistant to Lorna, *Skirt*'s editor-in-chief, which made Cassie the second most powerful person in the *Skirt* office. The promotion, the entry into another world, the new friends she'd made in that world and yes, the freebie premium beauty products, had given Cassie a healthy dose of self-esteem. She knew her own worth and she wasn't going to let Marc Lacourt treat her like she was a whole ladder's worth of rungs beneath him.

He was still so beautiful to look at, so charming with anyone who wasn't Cassie, especially two-year-old Joni, that seeing him always made her heart ache a little. Just the sight of his mouth quirked upwards when he was talking to Russell, his long fingers caressing the stem of a wine glass, the faintest whiff of the heady leather and amber notes of his aftershave, and Cassie would have to catch her breath.

They never discussed what had happened at the wedding and they certainly never discussed how they were going to move forward. By unspoken agreement, they were civil to each other when other people were around and when, rarely, it was just the two of them for a fleeting moment, they were uncivil to each other.

It had been a pleasant change, these last few weeks, to have had something of a rapprochement, but it hadn't been real. Just Marc being charming because he wanted something and now that Cassie wouldn't give it to him, they were back to only being civil.

Barely even being civil.

As the weeks sped by and the bank holiday weekend drew nearer, their WhatsApp messages grew increasingly hostile. Cassie wished that she hadn't invoked the spectre of that awful, fateful night because now it was all she could think about. That night which, even sixteen years later, was still both the best and worst sexual experience of her life.

However, none of this was really about Marc and the blight he brought to Cassie's life. This was about getting on the train on Friday morning, primed and ready to put all her plans into action to give Lucy and Russell the best bloody weekend they'd ever known.

Marc wouldn't even let her have that. The last flurry of messages a few days before the fateful weekend were a pretty good indication of how bad things had become between them.

Cassie: FYI: I'll be arriving at the house for 11.30 a.m. The first of the deliveries comes an hour after that. I've staggered them at half-hour intervals.
Marc: What time do you want to leave London then?
Cassie: My travel plans aren't any of your business.

Marc: WHAT TIME DO YOU WANT ME TO PICK YOU UP?

Cassie: It's so passive-aggressive to use SHOUTY CAPS and what do you even mean? There is no picking me up. I'm getting a train to Brighton, then an Uber.

Marc: Don't be ridiculous. There's no point in getting the train when I have to drive down anyway.

Cassie: I'm good taking the train. I LIKE taking the train.

Marc: Well, you certainly enjoy acting like some kind of martyr. I'll pick you up at 7.30 a.m. on Friday morning.

Cassie: That's far too early.

Marc: You'd have to leave earlier than that if you were catching the train.

Cassie: You don't even know my address.

Marc: You can behave like an adult and give it to me or I can get it from Russell. Your choice.

Cassie: Fine. I'll see you Friday then.

Marc: Can't wait.

Any joyful expectations that Cassie might have had about the coming bank holiday celebration were now gone. Marc had destroyed them. All Cassie could hope for was to get this weekend over and done with, with maybe fifty per cent of her sanity still intact. Then she'd never have to be in such close contact with Marc ever again. And amen to that.

**LUCY'S NAUGHTY FORTY BIRTHDAY
WEEKEND EXTRAVAGANZA!**

ITINERARY

FRIDAY

3.00 p.m. Arrival at Lullington Cove Manor. Please don't be late. Settle into your gorgeous accommodation.

4.00 p.m. Champagne in the drawing room (see attached floorplan).

4.30 p.m. Lucy and Russell arrive. We jump out and surprise her. Let the good times roll.

7.00 p.m. Fish and chips on the manor's very own beach! (see attached map).

9.00 p.m. Those that want to can stroll to Lullington village and the local pub, The Midnight Bell, though we'll have enough booze in to sink a battleship. But pace yourselves. Saturday is jam-packed and you don't want to do it with a hangover.

15

Cassie was no stranger to getting up early. She'd organised and attended many, *many* breakfast launches and client meetings. She didn't like it (and would inwardly curse any sadist who wanted to meet at the Riding House Café in town at some ungodly hour) but she did it all with good grace.

Having to get up at six thirty for a preposterously early call time not of her own making hit different. Her phone was telling her that sunrise had happened at six minutes past six, but the sky outside was still wearing its pyjamas as Cassie stumbled, befuddled with sleep, to the bathroom.

She'd had an everything shower, where every millimetre of her body had been exfoliated, depilated and moisturised, the night before. She'd just finished a more perfunctory morning shower when her phone chimed.

Marc: Am outside. Are you good to go?

Cassie stared at her phone in disbelief and mounting rage. It was seven o'clock precisely. He'd turned up thirty very passive-aggressive minutes early.

Cassie: We agreed seven thirty.
Marc: I'm here now. I'm at your front door.
Cassie: DON'T RING THE BELL!

Cassie came out of her flat and padded down the hall to wrench open the front door. A very quiet wrenching.

'Why are you so early?' she hissed at Marc, who was standing on the doorstep looking smug and well rested in jeans and a slim-fit navy shirt.

'Are you not ready?' he asked even though Cassie was standing there with a towel clutched around her and her hair still twisted in a pink satin-covered heatless curling rod from the night before.

'Does it look like I'm ready?'

'Well, best get a move on!' he said cheerfully.

Cassie could have quite *cheerfully* murdered him.

'Go and get some coffee and come back in half an hour,' she insisted in the same fierce whisper. 'And keep your voice down, my flatmate is asleep.'

'Can't get coffee, nowhere is open this early,' Marc said, stepping forward so Cassie had no choice but to step back, shrinking away from him, and just like that, he'd breached the perimeter of the communal hallway – though she was damned if she was going to actually let him in . . . 'You through here?'

Cassie could only watch and make a strange growling noise as he stepped through the open door of her flat.

She followed him in. Their hall was so narrow that immediately, they were nose to nose. Marc with his air of smug superiority and Cassie in a towel, her skin glistening with moisturiser that hadn't even had time to sink in.

Scrunching up her face in distaste, she poked Marc on the arm, encountering muscle and the sheer heat that he gave off.

'Go in there.' Another poke, then Cassie jerked her head in the direction of the living room. 'Sit down and don't touch anything.'

'Surely sitting down constitutes touching something,' he said pleasantly. All Cassie could do was growl again and beat a hasty retreat to her bedroom.

Cassie was already packed, because she was a very organised person. She was also a very petty person. So she sat on her bed doing nothing but waiting for her day serum to take for ten minutes, which in her opinion was utterly justified. Also, once you were past the age of thirty-five, an essential part of getting ready was sitting on your bed in a slack-jawed stupor for a while.

She could just imagine Marc's curled lip as he cast a disparaging eye over their little lounge. Cassie thought it was cosy and full of colour, a real sanctuary for Savita and herself. The place where they stuffed their faces, binge-watched utterly irredeemable reality TV and shared many stories and confidences.

But it didn't compare to minimalist penthouses with wraparound river views, or minimalist Hampstead mews houses with death-trap glass staircases. Marc already thought that Cassie was far, far beneath him and now he'd see the rickety windows that rattled in their frames whenever a car drove past, the sofa arm that Koita used as a scratching post, even though Cassie had spent good money on products designed specifically for that purpose.

It was such an invasion of her space. In fact, turning up this early was an act of supreme aggression. It was as if he were declaring war and if that was the case, then Cassie was going to put up one hell of a fight.

So she continued to sit on her bed for another five minutes before she got dressed. Very, very slowly.

Cassie knew that she'd be rushing around all day. Apart from when she was *forced* to spend the next two hours in Marc's car; the man who emitted British thermal units like other people emitted carbon dioxide. It was quite chilly first thing in the morning now that August was nearly done, but Cassie would rather freeze than ask him to put the heating on.

So she dressed for comfort, ease of movement and warmth. Black cuffed joggers (not even chic and cleverly cut joggers from somewhere like Hush or The White Company. These had come in a value pack of two from a supermarket and had gone baggy in the knee) and her oversized 'Slay All Day' black hoodie, a birthday present from her little brother, Ryan. Cassie didn't have time to do anything with her hair so she kept it twisted up in the curling rod but covered it with a knock-off Hermès scarf and hoped she was giving off Rosie The Riveter vibes. Then she put on her ancient and ratty purple and yellow Adidas Gazelles and she was done.

It was one of Cassie's finest man-repelling outfits to date. Certainly when she steeled herself to face Marc, she was ready for his assessing up-and-down stare then the barely raised eyebrows and twist of his lips.

'Almost ready,' she whispered in a jaunty tone. 'I'm just going to make some coffee and toast.'

'We're on a clock,' he snapped, rising from the depths of Cassie's sagging sofa. 'And I can guarantee that anything you make from a jar isn't coffee.' He brushed past Cassie. 'You've wasted enough time.'

'I haven't wasted time. It's seven thirty. The time we actually agreed on,' Cassie pointed out with a saccharine sweet smile.

'Can you load these boxes into your car while I make sure I haven't forgotten anything?'

Marc stared at the three cardboard boxes stacked up in the hall. The hall didn't get a lot of natural light so it was hard to know for sure, but there seemed to be a muscle pounding away in his cheek.

'What are these?' he asked in a tight voice.

'Oh, just the goody bags.' Another saccharine sweet smile. 'Did I not mention the goody bags? Just a few things I pulled together. At work, we have a whole cupboard full of spare . . . I won't go into details; not when we're on a clock.'

Yup, there was definitely a muscle jackhammering away. 'How were you going to get all this on the train?'

'I have a wheeled trolley,' Cassie said, her eyes running down the detailed list she was leaving for Savita and Naomi (who was coming down that evening to spend the weekend), noting Koita's needs. Most of them food-related. It read a lot like the small-plates menu for a Michelin-starred seafood restaurant. Marc was saying something, but Cassie managed to tune most of it out.

'This is what Joni and Fleur mean when they're complaining about someone being extra,' he said, lifting up the first box.

'Thank you. It's one of my best qualities,' Cassie trilled.

It was another five minutes before Cassie locked the street door and came down the garden path to where Marc was leaning against his sleek black car, arms folded and not looking quite so smug now.

'Shall I put these on the back seat?' Cassie asked, holding up her weekend bag, yoga mat and a laden tote bag.

He sighed, then made a huge show of opening the rear door. 'Jesus, can we go now?' he said through gritted teeth.

'Of course. I'm ready when you are,' Cassie said brightly, glancing up the road. 'Oh, hang on.'

'What now?' Marc sounded as if he was about to wring Cassie's neck and later insist that it was justifiable homicide, but she could see Koita slowly strolling down the street then speeding up as he saw her.

He hadn't come home the previous night and Cassie was glad that he was here now. If she was away for a few days and he hadn't realised she was going, he wasn't above peeing on her bedroom rug to show his displeasure.

Now he was meowing pitifully, springing up on the garden wall so he could jump into her arms.

'My dark prince. I'm glad you're here to say goodbye,' Cassie murmured, as he twisted sinuously in her arms. 'I've left a note that you're to have Dreamies on demand.'

Marc was stony-faced. 'Is this your familiar?'

'Something like that,' Cassie agreed, her arms too full of affectionate cat to snipe back. 'I need to let him into the flat.'

'Of course you do,' Marc said as Koita jumped down and wound his way past Marc's legs, tail twitching in annoyance at the implication he was a supporting character in Cassie's life and not the main attraction. He hissed once at Marc, spine arched, then followed Cassie up the path.

Marc was in the car when she came out, fingers drumming on the steering wheel. He started the car before Cassie had even fastened her seat belt.

It was now 7.45 a.m. exactly. Only fifteen minutes later than their original departure time. Cassie could tell he was fuming as he pulled away from the kerb. He'd rolled up the sleeves of his shirt and the muscles in his forearms seemed particularly tense as he turned the steering wheel.

It always seemed like a very cruel trick that he had such beautiful forearms, Cassie mused, as she stuck a gold patch under each eye to try and combat the dark circles, which were becoming a permanent fixture.

The car was electric, which meant it was deathly silent, which added to the tense atmosphere. Cassie was aware of how loud her breathing was. Was she mouth-breathing?

She couldn't even think of anything to say to lighten the mood because the gloves were well and truly off now. Besides, they were worlds apart with nothing in common, so there really was nothing to talk about.

Until they joined the North Circular, the infamous, always clogged ring road around London. If Cassie had been driving, even though she couldn't actually drive, she'd have headed for Brent Cross and joined the motorway there. Not that Marc would appreciate this nugget of information. Even so, it was impossible to remain silent.

'I've lived in north London my entire life and I have never seen the North Circular completely free of traffic until now,' she said with rising indignation.

'Clearly not completely free of traffic,' Marc said pedantically because there was traffic but it was free-flowing, fast-moving traffic. 'I can assure you that by the time we get to Hanger Lane, it's going to be a complete clusterfuck. Thanks for that.'

'Yes, but—'

Before Cassie could throw caution to the wind and share her preferred route, Marc jabbed a button and a very boring podcast about innovations in finance technology featuring two men – one with a very nasal New York accent – swallowed up the silence. Also, they kept calling it 'fintech', which enraged her for reasons she couldn't even explain.

Cassie had never been so pleased to hear her phone ring. It was eight o'clock and right on cue, her grandmother was calling her as she did every morning, apart from on weekends.

She slipped in her AirPods and took the call. 'Hi, Nan, can't talk right now,' she said.

'So, Dan has been in the wars,' replied her grandmother, Sue, because she always caught up with Cassie at this time, usually as Cassie was walking to the bus stop, and didn't tolerate any deviation from the routine. 'You'll never guess what the silly sod's done.'

'Knowing Dan, he's probably broken several bones while he was playing football,' Cassie said of her uncle, though like Emma, she regarded him as more of an older sibling. Marc actually *huffed* with irritation.

'Torn the ligaments in both thumbs playing five-a-side last night,' Sue announced with some satisfaction. 'He wouldn't be told. I said to him, Cass, I said, you're fifty—'

'Forty-seven, to be fair, Nan.'

'Nearly fifty and you're kicking a ball with a gang of lads half your age. You're going to break your neck.' Sue harrumphed; it was the only word that came close to describing the snort–scoff hybrid that Cassie's grandmother had made her own. 'Has to have an operation, doesn't he? Two plaster casts up to his elbows. Can't even wipe his own arse.'

Cassie felt bad for giggling at her uncle's misfortune. 'Poor Katie.'

'How she hasn't divorced him yet, I don't know. What's that noise? Are you talking to someone?'

'It's a podcast. I'm in a car. On my way to Sussex, remember?'

Marc reached over to turn off the podcast.

'You don't have to do that,' Cassie murmured softly but he shook his head, and now even though she had her AirPods in, every single word of Sue's was audible because, as Cassie's grandfather used to say, she had a voice like a foghorn.

'Well, have a lovely time. We'll miss you on Sunday,' Sue said, because Sunday was the annual end-of-summer family barbecue.

'If Dan's out of action then at least the burgers won't be half raw, half charcoal,' Cassie said. 'I'm amazed we've never got salmonella.'

'Our family have always had cast-iron constitutions. I'd better go, my darling. Lots of love.'

'Lots of love back,' Cassie said as she always did, glancing over at Marc, who was still flaunting his beautiful forearms while his face in profile was positively rigid. 'Do you want to put your podcast back on?' she asked, just as her phone started ringing again. 'Oh, this is work. I have to take this. Sorry.'

Cassie knew that she'd gone out of her way to be annoying when Marc had come to pick her up, but she'd never meant to be *this* annoying on the journey down. After two work calls to head off an impending crisis over a caricature artist booked for an event the following Tuesday, Cassie was all talked out.

She leaned forward to turn Marc's podcast back on but he grabbed her hand. 'What are you doing? You're not to touch anything!' he hissed.

'Sorry! I was just going to—'

'Well, don't.' Marc sucked in a breath, which did amazing things to his cheekbones and once again Cassie marvelled at how such an unpleasant person could be contained in such a pleasant package. 'If you had taken the train, then your incessant chatter would have every unfortunate person in your carriage wanting to throw you out of the window.'

Such an unpleasant person. 'Unlike travelling in your car, where just one person hates me,' Cassie said dryly, though his remark stung a little.

He didn't put the podcast back on, which was a case of cutting off his nose to spite his stupidly good-looking face. Especially as she was now busy in several group chats to discuss Dan's torn thumbs, if Koita had already breakfasted because he was claiming he hadn't, and did Cassie know that rain was predicted for Sunday?

Marc's grip on the steering wheel was currently white-knuckled because Cassie, and she knew that it was her most toxic trait, had keyboard sounds turned *on*. There was something so satisfying about the tapping; it reminded her of the summer she'd taught herself to touch-type with a typewriter and a Pitman textbook she'd found in a charity shop.

He muttered something under his breath that was either 'For fuck's sake' or 'Jesus wept', Cassie couldn't really tell.

By now they were at the Hanger Lane gyratory system, which was busy but hardly a clusterfuck, though Cassie valued her life too much to point that out. When they finally joined the motorway, it seemed to her that they both breathed a sigh of relief. She'd have quite liked a coffee and something to eat but all she had was a packet of Polos in her bag; she offered Marc one, but he brushed her hand away.

Then he put his podcast back on and Cassie continued with her group chats. The Lucy's Naughty Forty chat was in a frenzy. Even though Cassie had sent out itineraries and information sheets, people were incapable of following the most basic of instructions.

Al fresco yoga on Saturday morning was optional. Fancy dress and karaoke on Saturday night was mandatory. Yes, she knew that Anita was allergic to feather pillows and duvets and . . .

> **Cassie:** Heather, honestly, I've told you so many times already. Lucy and Russell are in the cottage, you and Davy have a lovely ensuite room. And we're having fish and chips tonight, not sushi.

She paused. 'Have Heather and Davy paid the deposit?' she asked Marc.

He shook his head. He seemed to be beyond words at this point.

> **Cassie:** Also, Marc is still waiting on the deposit from you and Davy.
> **Heather:** Marc is a billionaire!
> **Cassie:** I think just a multi-millionaire actually.
> **Heather:** So he can afford to swallow two hundred quid!
> **Cassie:** Not really the point. Everyone else has paid the deposit as a token gesture but if you don't want to come, I do understand.

It was always horrible when Cassie could actually feel her blood pressure rising. It seemed to start in her toes and rise up, making her heart beat faster, and, when she pulled out the neck of her hoodie and looked down, mottling the skin on her chest.

She caught Marc's eye in the rear-view mirror. He was smiling now, one of his chilly smiles. He must have thought that Cassie was checking out her own breasts.

'Everything present and correct?' he enquired.

Cassie made a point of looking for a second time. 'Seems to be.'

She was just about to be the bigger person and put her phone away, when it rang again. Both of them sighed.

It was Heather, so Cassie felt entirely within her rights not to take the call. But it was Heather, so she just rang again. And again. It wasn't as if Cassie could turn her phone off altogether.

By now, Heather was ringing for the fourth time.

Cassie had hardly slept. She hadn't had any coffee. No wonder she felt like crying, and all the while she was aware of being trapped in a small, enclosed space with Marc. Could sense his tiny but irritated glances at her, the weight of his disapproval.

'Are you going to get that?' he asked finally, annoyance coating every syllable.

'It's Heather,' Cassie said by way of explanation, but Marc wasn't really an active participant in the group chat, apart from when he was arguing with Cassie. So he hadn't really experienced the full force of Heather's . . . forcefulness.

'Just answer it,' he ordered.

Cassie knew it was going to further enrage him but she put her phone on speaker because this was undoubtedly going to be the kind of conversation that required witnesses.

'Hi Heather, what's up?' Cassie went for her breeziest tone.

'I really must insist that we get the cottage,' Heather said in a tearful voice. 'I can't really do stairs.'

A persuasive argument if only Heather didn't frequently post pictures on Instagram of herself walking, running, doing all kinds of exercise and also wearing high heels when she was #girlsnightout #lovemygirls #wineoclock.

'I'm afraid that's not possible.' Cassie's first boss when she'd moved into event planning after *Skirt* closed had been Penka, a very forthright Bulgarian, whose mantra was 'It's not possible' when dealing with everything from demanding clients to requests that she work overtime.

'Well, I can concede the cottage, but then we have to do sushi tonight,' Heather insisted. 'Iris said she'd prefer sushi to fish and chips. I bet it's not even line-caught fish and Davy can't process carbs late at night.'

Unless the carbs came in a pint glass and then Davy could process them just fine. And what Iris had said was that she wasn't fussed either way and had then apologised to Cassie in their side chat.

Cassie covered the microphone holes on her phone so she could sigh.

'Maybe—'

'No, no!' Marc said sharply. 'Never negotiate with terrorists.'

Cassie pulled a face. 'If you want sushi that badly then maybe you can stop off en route and get some . . .' Marc didn't look angry any more, he just looked disappointed. 'While I have you, Heather, Marc's still waiting on you and Davy to pay the deposit. That's a hundred each.'

'I don't see the point when Marc is paying for everything else. He's bloody loaded *and* I just heard him call me a terrorist, which is very hurtful. Very, very hurtful. Also, I know full well that I was only invited as an afterthought,' Heather said in an angry rush.

'Does this mean you're not coming?' Cassie asked hopefully. 'Because I'm sorry but if that two hundred quid isn't paid, then . . .'

'God, Cassie, I can't believe you're being this tight.' Heather allowed herself a tinkling little laugh. 'Also, did you get my cashew milk?'

Cassie's eyes met with Marc's in the rear-view mirror again.

'Just cut her off,' he mouthed, which was easier said than done.

But not impossible. 'Hang on, Heather. We're just approaching a tunnel.' Cassie did her best impersonation of static noise. 'I'm about to lose reception. I'll see you later. Don't forget to pay Marc.'

'I am *not* happy, Cassie—'

'Sorry, I'm losing you.'

She ended the call and smiled back at Marc. Bonding over a common foe was much better than snapping and snarling at each other.

'The only other time Heather has ever rung me was when she wanted me to plan her wedding,' she revealed as Marc changed lanes with a confident ease that Cassie didn't want to find attractive but did.

'I didn't know you planned weddings too,' he remarked.

'I don't, but Heather wanted me to do it as a favour, plus get her mates' rates from all the vendors.' Cassie shook her head. 'Sushi-gate is nothing compared to that. In the end, I put her in touch with a friend who did plan weddings.'

Marc raised his eyebrows. 'How did that work out?'

'Well, that friend no longer speaks to me,' Cassie said.

'Poor friend.' Though whether that was because Lily had borne the brunt of Heather's bridezilla-ness, or because she no longer wanted Cassie in her life, was a moot point.

At least Marc was in a good mood now. Or rather, he didn't look like he wanted to kill her anymore . . .

'You know, we *are* early. It's not even nine thirty and we're quite near Brighton. Plus, we can't check in for ages, so we could pop into a supermarket and pick up some sushi and cashew milk . . .'

'Absolutely not,' Marc said in a forbidding tone.

'But we're going to have about ninety minutes to kill so—'

'Hey Siri,' Marc drawled. 'Best coffee roastery in Brighton.'

Typical that he couldn't call it a coffee shop like everyone else.

'Here's what I found,' sexy Irish lady Siri announced, and Marc's phone, which was wedged into a holder attached to his dashboard, flashed up with a list of addresses.

'I always say please and thank you to Siri and Alexa,' Cassie said. 'So when AI and the robots take over, I'll have stored up some goodwill.'

'That's not how AI or robots work . . . No, I'm not doing this.' Marc gripped the steering wheel a little tighter. 'So, as we've made such good time despite setting out very late, do you want coffee with a sea view?'

16

Even though it was just a pit stop on the way to somewhere else, Cassie could never go to Brighton, or any coastal town, and not feel a thrill at that first glimpse of the sea.

It made her think of day trips to Southend when she was a kid. Wedged into the middle of the back seat between Dan and Emma, the three of them craning their necks, wanting to be the first to shout, 'I can see the sea and the sea can see me!'

Cassie managed to restrain herself this time but couldn't help the happy sigh at the sight of the pale blue railings along the front, the shingle beach and enticing stretch of sea. The sun was climbing steadily in the sky, chasing away the last of the early-morning chilliness, and glinting off the water.

Marc followed the satnav to the roastery of his choice, which was just off the promenade. Because he was Marc, he found a parking space right outside. And because he was a tech multi-millionaire it took him mere seconds to pay an astronomical parking charge on his phone.

Although she was worried about the time and the online delivery arriving early, Cassie was pleased to stretch her legs, take in a couple of lungfuls of sea air and listen to the caw of the seagulls.

She was also pleased to dive straight for the bathroom as soon as they entered the coffee shop. When she came out, Marc was deep in conversation with one of the baristas about single-origin roasts and the merits of a Latin blend over an Italian blend.

Cassie didn't think she'd ever seen him look so happy. He was obviously going to be a while, whereas she knew exactly what she wanted.

'A three-shot latte with semi-skimmed milk, no foam and one of those pains aux raisin, please.'

Marc was now wanging on about coffee grinders.

It had to be weird to be a multi-millionaire. Weird good, as in you could do a full food shop in Waitrose or M&S and never have to look at the prices. Cassie couldn't imagine such extravagance. Marc probably never had to look at the price of anything he wanted to buy unless it was a private jet or a Picasso.

Still, it must be tiring to have people, like Heather, constantly trying to take advantage. Even if you could afford it. Being a multi-millionaire must mean that rarely did anyone offer to get their round in.

Marc was a lot of bad things. Very bad things. He was now *sniffing* a handful of coffee beans, but he had been very generous when it came to this weekend. He'd saved Cassie hundreds and hundreds of pounds.

She took a twenty-pound note out of her purse to pay for her coffee and pastry, then nodded in Marc's direction. 'And whatever he's having.'

'There's no need,' he said very stiffly.

Treating Marc to a coffee seemed to really annoy him, so it was a win-win. Cassie patted him on the arm and felt his muscles tense at her touch. 'No, it's my treat, princess. You deserve it.'

He looked so offended that Cassie burst out laughing. She accepted the paper bag with her pastry in it from the server and nudged Marc, who was now ignoring her, with her hip. 'I'll be on the nearest free bench on the seafront. Can you be a love and bring me my coffee?'

She didn't wait to hear his icy response but left pretty sharpish after that.

It was five minutes until Marc joined her.

Cassie was on her phone again. It was just one of those mornings. She was now FaceTiming Russell, who was having a wardrobe panic. Or rather, Lucy had nipped out to get a wax and pedicure – she believed they were going away for the weekend, just the two of them – and he was trying to pack a secret bag full of things she'd need.

'It's funny but it looks to me like you're lying on your bed and not packing at all,' Cassie said, as Marc sat down next to her and handed over her coffee. 'Did you spit in it?'

'It did cross my mind, but no,' he murmured, as Russell frowned.

'Who are you talking to?'

Cassie leaned closer to Marc, their shoulders brushing, and held out her phone so Russell could see the two of them. 'Marc's here.'

Russell smiled widely. 'So you haven't murdered each other yet?'

Marc's smile was even wider. 'Again, it did cross my mind, but no.'

'We can get on perfectly fine,' Cassie insisted and she felt Marc's silent laugh, his body shifting against hers, his breath stirring the ends of her hair which had escaped her scarf.

She'd forgotten that underneath her scarf she still had her hair wound round a curling rod, but now Russell was joined by Fleur and Joni, who peered at her curiously.

'How long have you had your eye patches on?' Fleur asked. 'I wouldn't wear them out in public but you do you.'

Cassie's hand flew to her face. She'd forgotten about them too. They hardly even showed in the tiny little square on her phone screen though Marc might have thought to mention it. 'Oh God, what must I look like?'

'We stan a self-care queen. Also, Dad's not packing the secret bag, he's making us do it,' Joni added.

'Delegating,' Russell insisted. He was very smiley but was there something sinister behind his brazen scheme to get the girls to do the legwork? 'So, why I'm ringing is I can't find the list you sent me.'

No, nothing sinister. It was just Russell being Russell. Weaponised incompetence, Lucy called it.

'The list I emailed to you twice. The list that I then sent as several WhatsApp messages. That list?' she asked tartly.

'That's the one,' he said without even a flicker of shame.

'I'll email it again. Also, I'll send it to Fleur and Joni, who seem to be the brains of the operation,' she said as Marc rested his arm along the back of the bench. Cassie could feel his warm touch at her nape. He was still sitting close so he could see her phone screen and if Cassie moved a few more centimetres in his direction, they'd be pressed together, her head on his shoulder . . .

'Earth to Cassie! Are we boring you?'

Cassie blinked. 'No.' She held up her coffee. 'Haven't had enough caffeine yet.'

Russell stretched and it seemed to Cassie that he winced slightly. 'I was saying that I don't know what's happened to our fancy-dress outfits.'

'What's happened is that I have them,' Cassie said. 'I've always had them. On account of you asking me to sort that out for you.'

'Oh, yes. I remember.' He put his arm around Fleur who was snuggled next to him and kissed the top of her head. 'Who are we going as again?'

'It's a surprise,' Cassie said with a delighted grin. 'Just you wait.'

'That sounds ominous,' Russell said, as Marc did lean in close then, so his cheek was pressed against Cassie's and his expensive leather and amber scent was all around her.

'Got to go now, Russ,' he said. 'Cassie gets very crabby when she's not fully caffeinated. We'll see you and Lucy in a bit. Later, brats.'

As Fleur and Joni gasped in mock outrage, he ended the call, plucked Cassie's phone out of her hand and slid it into the pocket of his jeans.

It was Cassie's turn to gasp in entirely real outrage. 'You can't do that!'

'You're welcome to retrieve it if you want me to get the wrong idea,' he said silkily, which was *unexpected*. Almost as if he were flirting. 'Or we can have ten minutes' peace to drink our coffee and enjoy the view.'

Cassie sat back with an aggrieved little snort. She wasn't exactly looking forward to the weekend. Just being near Russell made her feel sad, plus it was quite the busman's holiday. Her to-do lists for each day, but especially for today, were long and involved a lot of heavy lifting. Literally, heavy lifting.

'You're not very good at relaxing, are you?' Marc asked, his fingers brushing the back of Cassie's neck where, according to Castiel, she held all her tension.

Cassie could feel the weight of his gaze on her as she forced herself to take a couple of deep breaths. 'I'm trying,' she muttered.

It was also quite hard to relax when Marc was still sitting so close to her that a casual observer who knew nothing of their long and conflicted history might think they were a couple. But she made no effort to move away from him because even though he was invading Cassie's personal space, he was solid and warm where she felt flimsy and cold.

Cassie sipped her coffee and watched the world go by. In an hour or so the seafront would be busy with pleasure-seekers but now it was home to people walking their dogs, runners and cyclists, a group of middle-aged women emerging from the waves like fierce ancient warriors. They were sitting downwind of the delicious fragrance of freshly baked doughnuts from the stall at the entrance to the pier. Cassie wanted to sniff the air like one of the Bisto kids.

If her hair hadn't still been wanded and wrapped, the slight breeze would have ruffled what Cassie hoped would be loose but structured waves. In an hour or so, it would be far too hot to be wearing a thick hoodie but for now Cassie lifted her face to the sun to get some vitamin D. It was quite peaceful until her phone chimed three times in quick succession.

'And we're done with taking in the view,' Marc said dryly as Cassie turned to him with an imploring expression.

'I need my phone back. It might be something important.'

Marc shrugged. 'And it might be Heather. Again.'

'Do you really want me to retrieve it myself? Surely that counts as sexual harassment?' Cassie didn't even want to entertain the idea of sliding her hand into the pocket of Marc's jeans, so close to his groin, his *cock*. She didn't want to go there. Not ever again.

'Who'd be sexually harassing who?' Marc looked keenly at Cassie, who put her hands to her cheeks which felt as if they was burning. She couldn't even blame it on the sun because she'd slathered her face in SPF 50, as she did every morning. 'You're no fun.'

'There's fun and then there's things that are very much not fun,' Cassie said, as he retrieved his phone and handed it to her.

Cassie made a performance of pulling down the sleeve of her hoodie before taking it like she didn't want to be contaminated. Then an even bigger show of wiping her phone on the thick jersey.

'You really are ridiculous,' Marc said, though it lacked his usual bite, as if he wasn't as annoyed by her alleged ridiculousness as he normally was.

'Whatever.' Cassie held up her very *warm* phone. 'Message from Lydia, the caretaker, we can check in a bit early.' She stood up. 'Which is great. Because it's eleven now and I've staggered our deliveries to start arriving at noon, so I'll still have time to check the rooms first.'

She was already at the kerb and waiting to cross over the road but Marc was still sitting on the bench and absolutely not appreciating the urgency of the situation or that Cassie had a lot of things to do.

'Come on!' she called out with genuine irritation. 'Shake a leg! We haven't got all day.'

17

Half an hour later, Cassie caught her first glimpse of Lullington Cove Manor, which stood high on the cliffs that overlooked the cove. According to her information sheet, which she'd stuck in all the goody bags, the original manor house had burned down in 1875 and some years later, it had been rebuilt in the Arts and Crafts style.

On this glorious late summer's day, the sun shone down on the sandstone, the leaded windows and the gabled roof. It looked impressive without being imposing and elegant without being elitist. Not the kind of place where the owners would expect Cassie to nip round the back to the tradesmen's entrance.

'It's beautiful,' she sighed as they came up the drive, the tyres crunching over the gravel. The front door, painted a muted sage green and framed by a trailing rose, suddenly opened and an elderly but sprightly woman stepped out. 'That must be Lydia.'

It was Lydia, quickly followed by her husband Frank, who was in navy overalls, which Cassie quite coveted, and clutching a toolbox.

Introductions were made, then Lydia ushered them into a wood-panelled hall, which smelled of beeswax and the distinctively spicy scent of the pink and white stocks in a vase on a side table.

'There's a small drawing room on your right then the formal dining room, but the owners have opened up the rest of the ground floor,' Lydia said as they walked through a large arch on the left into a huge open-plan room which incorporated both a lounge and a spacious sit-in kitchen with a walk-in pantry, then a shower room-cum-boot room and a utility room in a side extension.

There were French doors and floor-to-ceiling windows, which took up the entire exterior wall and led out to a terrace with another dining area plus seating around a fire pit. 'Just like *Love Island*,' Cassie felt like saying but she didn't want to lower the tone, as Lydia took them round the side of the house where there was a vegetable garden, herb patch and . . .

'This is Miss Rose's rose garden,' Lydia said reverently, as she fingered the leaves of one of the plants, which was no longer in bloom. In June, they must have been a glorious sight. 'A sprinkler system comes on at four. The only thing we're really precious about are the roses.'

'Was Miss Rose the former owner?' Cassie asked as they walked back along the terrace to the tennis courts and swimming pool, which were situated on the other side of the house. 'Russell – he made the original booking – his grandparents, I think, had a house in the village and he spent summers down here. Apparently, his grandparents knew the owners of the manor.'

Lydia was a very bustling sort of person but now she came to a halt. 'That would be Mr Edward, but he died in the 70s and then we lost Miss Rose a few years back. Her great nephew and his wife live here now, but they're in Australia for six months so we're renting out the house to a few very select guests.'

Cassie straightened up from her slouch and wished that she didn't still have her curling rod in. 'We'll take very good care of the place.'

Marc had been mostly silent up until now, but he put his hand on Cassie's arm for a fleeting second. 'This one will keep everyone in line,' he said. 'She's provided an itinerary, an information sheet and a floorplan.'

It was hard to tell if he was teasing but Lydia nodded. 'It makes my life so much easier when I'm dealing with someone as organised as you.'

'I felt exactly the same way about you.' Cassie allowed herself a little preen, which Marc ignored as he asked Lydia about access to the cove.

There were a few more pointers about the dishwasher, the oven and the grill area on the terrace, then Lydia and Frank took them upstairs to see the bedrooms, which were all as beautifully decorated as the downstairs, each with an ensuite bathroom.

Cassie deposited her goody bags as they went, although Lydia had also provided a pretty tin of homemade biscuits in each room.

'Then there's this last one,' Lydia said, as they came to the end of the corridor. 'It has a lovely view of the lawn.'

'That's you,' Cassie told Marc, who nodded. 'I'm on the second floor.'

Lydia frowned. 'I hope you're going to be all right. The rooms up there have been shut for years; there are plans to renovate them, but I've aired that one out and given it a deep clean.' She gave Cassie a doubtful look. 'Will you be comfortable in a bunk bed?'

Cassie smiled with what she hoped was a lot of enthusiasm. 'I love a bunk bed. I get a choice of top or bottom each night. It's great.'

'You're quite short so I expect you'll fit,' Frank noted sagely. 'There's a loo and a sink next door. You have to give the chain a bit of a yank.'

'I've done my best with that room but the original booking was for the four rooms on this floor plus the cottage,' Lydia said with another frown. 'There's a shower room downstairs.'

'Honestly, it's fine,' Cassie insisted, although, of course, she'd much rather have slept in a pretty room with its own bathroom rather than being on a deserted upper floor with a loo with a dodgy flush. 'I really appreciate that you let us squeeze two more in.'

Lydia looked at her watch. 'Well, we'll let you get settled in and we're in Brighton, so half an hour away if there's an emergency.'

'There won't be an emergency,' Marc said firmly. 'Not on Cassie's watch.'

Again, it was very hard to tell if that was a compliment or a roast.

They watched Lydia and Frank head down the stairs, then Marc walked along the corridor to his room. 'It's not the biggest,' she hurried after him. 'Because everyone else is a couple.'

She glimpsed over his shoulder as he opened the door but all she could really see were dark walls and a huge bed. 'Looks fine,' he said non-committally.

'Here's your goody bag.' Cassie shoved it at Marc, who stared at the stiff grey cardboard bag in bemusement. 'There's a copy of the itinerary and the information sheet in there too, so don't bother me with questions that I've already—'

Marc closed his eyes and groaned. 'God, that bloody itinerary of yours will be imprinted on my brain until the day I die.'

'But in case it isn't, I printed it out and stuck it in the goody bags.'

'Let's see your room. It doesn't sound that great,' he said in a softer voice.

'I'm only going to be there to sleep.' Cassie put a hand on his arm to stop him from heading to the stairs.

'If I were you, I'd stick Heather and Davy in there,' he said, his face settling back into the grim expression from earlier that morning. 'You know it too.'

Cassie shook her head. 'I don't have the strength to cope with Heather kicking off about sleeping in a bunk bed. Can you imagine the hysterics?'

'Worse than sushi-gate.'

'Worse than hen weekend-gate and sushi-gate combined,' Cassie whimpered. 'Do you hate me so much that you'd put me through that?'

Marc tugged gently on her sleeve. 'You keep saying that. I don't—'

The chime of her phone immediately claimed Cassie's attention. 'That's the supermarket delivery. It's being unpacked now. I didn't even hear the van.' She was already scurrying away. 'I'll see you in a bit. I've got so much stuff to sort out.'

Although she often grumbled about it, there was nothing Cassie enjoyed more than having a lot of stuff to sort out, as long as it didn't involve relying on other people who couldn't follow instructions.

The delivery driver left a multitude of carrier bags in the entrance hall and Cassie rolled up the sleeves of her hoodie, all ready to get stuck in as Marc came down the stairs.

'Do you have a system?' he asked, surveying the vast amounts of shopping needed to keep ten people very well fed and watered for a long weekend.

'Oh, I'm fine,' Cassie said as she lifted up two of the bags.

'You can't do this all on your own.' He peered into one of the bags. 'If Russell were here . . . I mean if Russell was . . .'

Cassie took pity on him. 'Even if Russell were here and in full working order, he'd be too busy playing Mine Host to be of any practical help.'

'That's very true.' Marc hefted up some of the heaviest-looking bags. 'But I'm not Russell and we still have the wine merchants' and the butchers' deliveries to come, so for the next hour I'm going to let you boss me around . . .'

Cassie followed him towards the kitchen area with her lighter load. 'I prefer to think of it as taking on a leadership role.'

'As I was saying, I'm happy to be your little bitch for the next hour, but don't let this generous offer go to your head. It's never going to be repeated,' he said as he set the bags down on the marble counter.

'That's a shame,' Cassie said, her mind suddenly going to a strange, dark place where Marc had to do everything she told him to do and . . . 'No! Marc! The red-handled bags are for fridge stuff, the green ones for the freezer. I'd put a good half of that milk in the second fridge in the utility room, so people don't guzzle it down and we've nothing left by Sunday. We'll put the meat in there when it arrives too.'

'To think that you accuse me of micromanaging,' he muttered as he headed for the utility room with a four-litre bottle of milk in each hand.

'No backchat from the little bitch, thank you very much.' Cassie snatched up a tea towel and cracked it like a whip. 'Also, when the champagne arrives you'll have to put some of it in the fridge straight away so it's chilled in time for the welcome drinks.'

'I can't hear you,' Marc shouted, though he could hear her perfectly.

It took just over two hours for the deliveries to arrive and be put away. To get glasses and bowls of snacks ready for their friends' arrival and to make sure that the cottage was absolutely perfect for Lucy and Russell.

Although it was very much outside his remit and below his pay grade, it would have taken her much longer without Marc. She'd tried not to be too bossy but he'd taken her instructions and orders like a champ – though there had been pursed lips, eye-rolling and, yes, a lot of backchat.

It was just after two when Cassie finished lighting the last scented candle and placed it on the low coffee table, which was surrounded by four huge plush velvet sofas in contrasting jewel tones. The vibe of the place from the open-plan living space stretching right down to the kitchen, with its pink Shaker-style cabinetry and Moroccan-tiled splashback, was eclectic but both cosy and stylish.

'What's the point of lighting scented candles when we have the French doors open?' Marc leaned against the arch that led back into the entrance hall.

'I'm creating a vibe.' Cassie assessed said vibe. Ideally, she'd have liked to fill the room with flowers or at least some greenery but she didn't think Lydia would be pleased if she took the kitchen scissors to the garden hedges. 'OK, I think we're done.'

'I can't believe that you do this for a living,' he said and before Cassie could bristle, he continued, 'There are so many different elements to think about. I imagine most of your team aren't as obliging as I am.'

Cassie perched on the arm of the emerald green sofa and rubbed the back of her neck. 'Well if they roll their eyes, then they do it behind my back.' She stretched her arms out in front of her and laced her fingers together until she heard something crack. 'But thank you. It would have taken me twice as long without your help.'

Marc frowned. 'Come on, I'm waiting.'

'Waiting for what?'

'For the sarcastic closing remark that you're building to,' he said with a grin. 'Don't leave me hanging.'

'It was a genuine and sincere thank you. Clearly I need to work on my delivery.' Cassie stood up and walked towards him. 'Though I'm sure you'll say or do something in the next ten minutes that will deserve some sarcasm.' She made sure she bumped him with her hip as she brushed past him, then ducked out of the way of his hand as he tried to grab hold of her. 'I'm going to check the bedrooms one last time.'

'You might want to take that strange contraption out of your hair while you're at it,' Marc reminded her as he watched Cassie take the stairs, one tired step at a time.

18

By three fifteen, as per Cassie's strict instructions, six of the invited guests had arrived.

Digby, Lucy's friend from school, who Cassie had first met at Lucy's hen weekend years before, was a slight, fair-haired man always with a mischievous glint in his eye who worked at Sotheby's in the Rare Books department. His partner, Kwame, was tall, dark and very handsome, and suave where Digby was usually flustered. He also came with a mischievous glint in his eye as a standard feature.

Cassie had also first met Anita, Lucy's friend from university, at the hen and been in awe of the human-rights lawyer who wore all black without looking like a goth and could drink everyone under the table. Anita was still a human-rights lawyer, still preferred a monochrome colour palette but now she had a husband, Azad, who owned several gyms, didn't drink and loved to wear a T-shirt and shorts no matter what the weather. There was also a small daughter who adored the colour pink. 'She's a great disappointment to me,' Anita would always say fondly.

Then there was Iris, a friend from the NCT classes Lucy had attended when she was pregnant with Fleur, and the only one not to be subsequently culled when the baby bubble burst. Iris's humour was as dry as a vodka martini, her auburn curls were vibrant and the volume knob on her broad Glaswegian accent was usually at an eight. She and her partner, Bill, her childhood sweetheart, were both architects, though her real passion was for vintage clothes.

These were Lucy's three best friends, plus partners, and they were good friends of Cassie too. Especially Kwame, a theatrical agent, who worked round the corner from her in Soho. They had a monthly tradition of going to see a play, then a late dim sum supper in Chinatown.

They'd attended each other's birthday parties, summer picnics, anniversary dinners – and not forgetting the raucous night out in honour of Digby finally getting his PhD, which had ended with them singing songs from *Cabaret* in a Hackney dive bar.

There had been many years of many shared joys and some sorrows. As she showed them around the house and to their rooms, Cassie was painfully aware of the chasm that now existed between her and these long-standing friends. She was the guardian of a terrible secret that would mean their little friendship group would never be the same again.

Marc wasn't as thick with the six of them as Cassie was – he was somewhere in the gap between acquaintance and friend. Today he was on his best behaviour, abandoning his usual distanced, diffident stance to help carry luggage (Iris had packed for a whole fortnight), then pour champagne and fetch soft drinks for the non-champagne drinkers.

Cassie clutched a delicate coupe of the ruinously expensive champagne and took tiny sips, the bubbles tickling her nose. OK, her palate was far from refined but she still didn't know why it cost quite so much a bottle.

'If you hold that glass any tighter, it will snap,' Kwame said as he came to join Cassie where she was standing in the archway between lounge and hall. 'Babes, you've done an amazing job. Now stop stressing.'

Cassie looked at her phone. It was 3.45 p.m. 'I'm not stressed,' she managed to force out, though she was gritting her teeth, hard. 'I'm fuming. Lucy and Russell will be here any minute, and Heather and Davy still haven't turned up.'

Heather had been riding Cassie's arse all day, but now she wasn't answering her phone or responding to any increasingly urgent messages.

'Maybe her broomstick got stuck in traffic,' Kwame suggested, his dark eyes dancing because he knew that on the one hand, Cassie thought it was reductive and offensive to refer to women in that way, but on the other hand, Heather really was a witch.

'Let's not even get started on Davy,' she muttered, tensing up as she heard car tyres on the gravel outside.

She tore across the hall to open the front door and almost sagged with relief that it *was* Heather and Davy.

'I hope you remembered my cashew milk,' Heather said as she clambered down from Davy's massive black four-wheel drive that was unnecessary when you lived in very un-rural West Hampstead.

Cassie knew that she should be the bigger person. That she should set the tone for the weekend and be welcoming and rise above. But all she could say as Heather had the audacity to air-kiss in her general direction was a hissed, 'You were meant to be here at three. Lucy and Russell are just behind you and you're going to ruin the surprise.'

'Keep your hair on, Casserella,' Davy said, also going in for a kiss. Cassie stepped back because she knew that it would be far too near her mouth for comfort and with a sly hand on her arse as an added bonus. 'Now go and get a man a drink. I'm gasping.'

'Yes, Cass. Champagne was on the itinerary.' Heather tried to move past Cassie, who was planted firmly in the doorway and not budging.

Instead she turned her head to call out for Marc but as if she'd been emitting a high-pitched distress signal that only he could hear, he was already crossing the hall.

'Marc.' Her voice thrummed with barely suppressed rage. 'Have Heather and Davy paid the two hundred pounds into your account?'

'I haven't checked,' he said, his gaze and tone of voice both even.

'Could you?' Cassie asked with more artificial sweetness than a multipack of Diet Coke.

'We can sort that out later,' Heather said breezily but she wouldn't meet Cassie's eye. Probably because Cassie was sure her retinas were sending laser beams at Heather's face, which was so like Lucy's that it was always a little bit freaky. But where Lucy wore her warmth and her good nature in her ready smile and kind eyes, there was something more pinched, more petulant about Heather. 'Out of the way, Cass, otherwise we really will ruin the surprise. Such a fuss when it's not even Lucy's birthday for another two weeks.'

Cassie felt Marc before he stepped close behind her, a steady hand on her shoulder. 'I've checked my banking app but there hasn't been a payment,' he said easily, because two hundred quid was pocket change.

It was the fucking principle of the thing. 'Then you're not coming in,' Cassie said because she was going to die on this hill, or rather this doorstep, to make Heather and Davy see the error of their tight-fisted, freeloading ways.

'I can't believe you're being like this,' Heather hissed as Davy pulled out his phone.

'Haven't got the bank details, have I?' he said with a helpless air.

'You have. By email and by about fifty WhatsApp messages,' Cassie said, as Marc's hand tightened on her shoulder.

'You holding a grudge is such good entertainment when I'm not the target,' he whispered in her ear.

The grudges she held against Marc, or rather the one massive grudge, didn't matter right now. Even though she and Marc had worked as a team for most of the day, normal service would soon be resumed.

It took long minutes and much huffing and puffing from Davy until he nodded tersely at Cassie and Marc. 'It's gone through now.'

Marc's hand was *still* on Cassie's shoulder, keeping her safe from the collective glare of Heather and Davy, which would otherwise have turned her to dust. 'Yup, received with thanks,' he said, letting go of Cassie so she could take a step back and usher Heather and Davy through the door with a big smile that was as insincere as her greeting.

'*So* lovely to have you here,' she simpered. 'Go through. Help yourself to some champagne.'

The three other couples greeted the late arrivals with varying degrees of friendliness.

'What are the bedrooms like?' Heather asked in lieu of a hello. 'I bet you've all bagged the best ones.'

Cassie didn't have the energy to point out, *again*, that she'd allocated the rooms and it hadn't been a *Real Housewives*-style free-for-all.

'All the rooms are lovely,' Iris said rather sharply with a sharp look at Heather to match. 'Considering that Marc is footing the bill for this beautiful house, I'd be happy to sleep on the floor if I had to.'

This was a lie. Iris had arrived with her own Tempur pillow and a special cooling duvet for her hot flushes. Her words barely glanced off Heather, who'd dumped her handbag on a sideboard, which looked very old and very antique-y to Cassie, and was busy checking the provenance of the champagne while helping herself to a huge handful of spicy nuts.

'So, yes, nuts – did you get my cashew milk?' she asked Cassie again.

'That wasn't possible.' Cassie sighed in relief when her phone chimed from the depths of the pouch pocket of her hoodie. 'OK, that's Russell. They're just driving through the village now. You guys stay in here and wait for my signal.'

'What is your signal?' Anita asked. 'Have you organised a marching band to come stomping down the drive?'

Cassie sighed. 'I couldn't get Marc to sign off on the marching band.'

'I also said no to the Red Arrows doing a flypast,' Marc said, from where he was perched on a window seat with a view of the drive. 'Or somebody could just look out the window and when Lucy and Russell get out of the car, that's the signal.'

'Yes, that would work,' Cassie agreed, as that had been her plan anyway. Though a marching band *would* have been amazing.

She waited anxiously by the arch, until Marc drawled with a complete lack of urgency. 'They're just pulling up outside now.'

Cassie flailed her hands. 'OK! OK! We are now moving to the hall in a timely fashion.'

Once everyone except Davy, who hadn't moved from his comfy spot on the sofa, and Heather, who was looking put upon as she poured herself another glass of champagne, was gathered in the foyer, Cassie opened the front door just enough to see a silver Audi come to a halt and the driver's door open.

'Right, hang on . . . OK, now!' she said, opening the door wide, so everyone could spill out to greet Lucy and Russell.

The collective shout of 'Surprise!' was a bit ragged but Cassie didn't really care because as everyone, minus Heather and Davy, hurried over to greet Lucy and Russell, she realised they'd made a terrible mistake. *She'd* made a terrible mistake.

It was Lucy getting out on the driver's side, even though Lucy never drove long distances because she was scared of going on the motorway. She looked as if she was about to burst into tears – and not happy tears, either. 'What are you all doing here?' she asked sharply, then looked over to Russell. 'Was this your doing?'

Russell smiled sheepishly. 'Guilty as charged.'

Cassie hadn't seen Russell since that morning a couple of weeks earlier when he'd come home from his emergency trip to hospital. He'd looked tired then. But now he looked exhausted and he got out of the car very slowly. She was sure he was thinner but his face puffier. He seemed to have diminished during the past fortnight.

Which was why Lucy wanted to spend this weekend with Russell, just Russell. Because the time they had left was now measured out in months, hopefully lots of months, and weeks and weekends and days, hours, minutes, seconds.

Those tears that were never far away came closer. Marc was standing next to Cassie at the front door. 'We should have persuaded Russell to cancel,' she said but then Lucy mustered up a smile. It wasn't her usual sparkling smile that made the recipient want to bask in its warmth, but it was convincing enough.

'It's so lovely to see everyone,' Lucy said, as she was folded into an Anita and Iris sandwich. 'I can't believe you managed to sneak a surprise past me. Russell is the worst at keeping secrets.'

It was Digby's turn to hug his oldest friend. 'If he'd let the cat out of the bag, Cassie would have ended him.'

Cassie winced at Digby's choice of words but Marc put that steadying hand back on her shoulder. 'Don't exaggerate, Digby,' he said. 'It would have been just a light maiming.'

'It would,' Cassie confirmed as Lucy approached her with arms outstretched.

'I take it you were the brains of the operation?' she asked with a genuine smile now.

'Oh, I helped out here and there,' Cassie said with raised eyebrows and Lucy laughed.

'Thank goodness for that, because if you'd left everything to Russell then I dread to think how we'd survive until

Monday,' she said teasingly, taking Russell's hand as he slowly started up the steps to the house.

'I very much resent that,' he said a little breathlessly. 'But also that's why I threw myself on Cassie's mercy. There's an itinerary.'

'Of course there is,' Lucy said, looking around the hall, the wood panels gleaming in the sun that streamed in through the open door.

'And Marc stepped up at the eleventh hour,' Cassie said with a sideways look at Marc, who shook his head and smiled slyly.

'I can't take any credit for the itinerary.'

'But he can take credit for lots of other things, like choosing the most gorgeous champagne.' This mutual respect and admiration really couldn't last much longer. It was *draining*.

'I'd love a glass. This place is beautiful,' Lucy exclaimed as she walked into the huge living space. She gave a tiny, almost imperceptible flinch when she saw her sister and brother-in-law firmly ensconced on one of the sofas, an almost empty bottle of champagne on the coffee table in front of them and no fucking coaster.

'I can take credit for that,' Russell said, sinking gratefully into the nearest armchair and holding up his hand as Kwame offered him a glass of champagne. 'Not for me, mate, I want to pace myself – but I wouldn't say no to a glass of water if there's one going.'

Once everyone was gathered on the sofas and Lucy had been ceremoniously presented with a glass of champagne and a copy of the itinerary, Cassie allowed herself to breathe out.

It was going to be all right. Even though Lucy and Heather had barely even said hello to each other. Even though Davy kept clicking his fingers at Cassie when he wanted a refill. Even though Russell was still looking absolutely done in, half an hour after he'd first sat down.

'I'd love to see where we're staying,' Lucy said; her eyes were on her husband too.

'In a cottage in the grounds,' Heather said flatly as she ruined that small surprise. 'It looks really poky.'

'It's lovely,' Cassie quickly interjected. 'Its design is based on a Swedish summer house and its fully eco-conscious. Runs entirely on solar power.'

Marc retrieved their bags and Cassie gave Lucy and Russell a brief tour of the downstairs. Then they strolled through the patio doors, past the rose garden and vegetable patch to the cottage, which looked as if it had been transported straight from a Pippi Longstocking novel.

Inside it managed to be both light and airy with its stark design and white-painted walls and floorboards, but also cosy with pops of colour and pattern, including a soft, invitingly plump sofa upholstered in blue and white gingham and a bold yellow and white striped dhurrie rug.

'I thought you'd be more comfy here and you'd want a little privacy,' Cassie said, now it was just the four of them. 'It's all on one level.'

Lucy sank into the sofa and shut her eyes. 'Thank you, it's gorgeous. Not just this cottage. Everything.'

'I'm sorry if you thought this weekend was going to be just you and Russell.' Cassie sat down on a white weather-beaten chair, its padded seat upholstered in a William Morris print.

'We began organising it months ago,' Russell explained, as he sat down on the sofa too so Lucy could rest her head in his lap. 'Once we got the bad news, I didn't want to cancel.'

Lucy raised her head. 'Are you going to do a *Peter's Friends* and tell them all?' The painful-looking furrow between her eyebrows was back.

'No,' Russell said firmly, brushing Lucy's hair back from her face. 'I'm not planning any dramatic confession around the dinner table. Marc would hate that. Too unseemly. For someone who's half French, you have the stiffest upper lip.'

'Someone has to.' Marc was leaning against the front door. He loved to lean on things, his arms folded. 'You lot are far too emotional. Cassie's been on the verge of tears at least ten times today.'

That was unfair. 'Maybe twice,' Cassie said, because that was the other thing that British people did. They made a joke of things even when their hearts were halfway to breaking.

'If you cry, Cass, then I will cry too,' Lucy said, her voice already throbbing. 'I really don't want to cry this weekend.'

'This weekend was meant to be all about celebrating you, but now it's probably going to be my last hurrah with some of the people that I love most.' Russell leaned down to kiss Lucy's forehead. 'I'm sorry I've hijacked your birthday, darling.'

'You haven't. I can't wait to make more memories with you,' Lucy said, which was very sweet. Then she sat up and looked less sad and more . . . furious. 'Who the fuck thought it was a good idea to invite Heather?'

There was no way Cassie was taking that one for the team. 'Nothing to do with me,' she said firmly. 'It's all Russell's fault.'

'The circumstances were beyond my control,' Russell insisted. Even his voice seemed to lack something of its former boominess.

Cassie stood up. 'Well, I'm going to leave you two to settle in and chill for a couple of hours. Don't forget to check out the his 'n' hers goody bags I left on the bed.'

Lucy shot Cassie a look of fond exasperation. 'Even goody bags? We really don't deserve you, Cass.'

'Yet you're stuck with me,' Cassie said, trying to hide her pleased smile. She loved what she did but she also loved being appreciated for what she did. 'We're meeting in the lounge at seven; Anita and Az are going out for fish and chips while we make our way down to the beach.'

'Laden up like pack mules,' Marc added. 'I'll think of something to get you out of lugging duties.'

'I can't remember, is it far to the beach?' Russell asked casually.

'Apparently it's about a five-minute walk. There's steps cut into the cliff and, well, torches for coming back in the dark,' Cassie said brightly, although she wasn't exactly looking forward to either, given her chequered history with challenging sets of stairs.

Lucy and Russell shared a look that spoke volumes. Cassie didn't need a translator.

'We don't have to eat on the beach,' she said quickly. 'We can eat on the terrace. That's fine. Who wants sand everywhere anyway?'

'Do you mind?' Lucy asked. 'We don't want to be the fun police but we're all about conserving Russell's energy rather than pushing through.'

'Don't worry about it for a minute longer,' Marc said smoothly, as he opened the door for Cassie. 'We'll get out of your hair now.'

They walked back to the house in silence. It was only to be expected but Russell's deterioration was still a shock. He couldn't drive. Couldn't manage a five-minute walk down to the beach. How was he going to get through the weekend without people, his friends, realising that something was wrong?

Now Cassie was going to have to tell people that there'd been a change of plans when she wasn't quite sure that she could speak without crying.

She took a deep breath as she stepped through the open patio doors. The group was still camped out on the sofas and looked up as Cassie and Marc approached.

'So, we've made an executive decision to have fish and chips on the patio rather than having to carry everything including all that booze down to the beach,' Marc said in a voice that dared anyone to argue.

'Absolutely fine by us,' Digby said as there were murmurs of agreement.

'Oh, that's a shame,' Heather said sorrowfully because of course she did. 'I was so looking forward to the gentle lap of the waves as we ate.'

'But very much not the end of the world,' Iris said crisply.

Cassie didn't want everyone riding Heather for the whole weekend even if Heather was scaling new heights of absolute fuckery. 'We could have breakfast on the beach tomorrow?' she suggested. 'Let's see how we feel then. So, we'll meet here at seven to sort out the fish and chips order before Anita and Az head to the chippy.'

'Our treat,' Azad insisted. 'As long as you don't take the piss and try to bankrupt us by ordering too many pickled cucumbers.'

Cassie slipped away as Bill lamented the price of fish and chips in poncy southern England and how in his and Iris's native Glasgow, you could buy a fish supper for a family of four and still have change out of twenty quid.

He was drowned out by Heather's plaintive, 'Wouldn't you all prefer to have sushi?'

If Cassie managed to get through the weekend without murdering Heather, it would be a miracle.

19

Now that she'd had a proper look at it, Cassie no longer felt that warmly about her little bunk-bed room.

She'd seen *Gosford Park* several times and it wasn't hard to imagine the lowly scullery maids who'd slept in the room in the olden days. Nursing their reddened, split hands from all that caustic soap, and weeping because the master of the house kept trying to take advantage of them.

It *was* clean at least and although the bunk beds were clearly meant for children (poor children banished to the attics), Cassie usually slept curled into a ball so she would fit.

However, there wasn't a full-length mirror and the very utilitarian bathroom down the corridor only had an antiquated toilet and sink, so she had no choice but to go back downstairs to the shower room-cum-boot room and pray that there was a lock on the door.

There was, and the shower had much better water pressure than Cassie's shower back home. Also, eighteen hours with her hair wound around a bendy curling rod had produced the kind of ringleted waves that were ordinarily impossible to achieve.

Her face was sallow in the unforgiving strip lighting. But for once, she had enough time to do her make-up properly, even using her brushes instead of the tips of her fingers like she usually did.

Then she slipped on one of her favourite dresses. A midnight blue maxi dress with shirred bodice, little puff sleeves and a voluminous skirt because Cassie intended to eat her bodyweight in fried haddock and chips and a tight waistband would spoil her fun.

Cassie didn't have the sort of room where she could just hang out, so once she'd ferried her stuff back up two flights of stairs, she headed for the garden.

It was still sunny and warm, so she slipped off her Birkenstocks to feel the velvety grass beneath her feet. At the edge of the lawn just before it became cliff, there was a wooden bench that looked out to sea.

There was something rare and precious about being able to grab some time when Cassie didn't have to do anything, organise anything, remember anything. She could just *be*.

She was lucky to live in a very green part of London, bookended by Alexandra Park in one direction and Highgate Wood in the other, but even a city kid like herself could appreciate the fresh air of the open countryside. Especially when it came with a faint sea breeze. Cassie knew that if she licked her hand, she'd taste the salt tang on her tongue.

The tide was quite far out but she could see the white-tipped waves as they softly rippled at the shoreline. Tomorrow, she might swim. Or at the very least get her feet wet but now, even with the weekend stretched before her, with a house full of friends, she was gripped with a familiar panic.

She was always going to feel at her most alone among a group of people who had found their person. Whatever life threw at them, they didn't have to deal with it on their own.

Cassie knew that there were no guarantees of a happy ever after. Also, every time she had been an 'us' instead of a solitary 'I', she'd chafed at the ties that bound her to another person. Had felt regret when it ended but also, if she was honest, quite a lot of relief.

Still, it shouldn't be so hard to find your most favourite person and be their favourite person in return. Not when she wanted it so desperately.

Maybe if the other areas of her life were polished to perfection, being a lonely only wouldn't feel so bad. But last time she checked she still had a failed business and an arse-load of related debt. Her domestic bliss was dependent on the whims of her landlords and their late father's cat. It wasn't much to show for thirty-seven years of being alive.

'I don't always want to feel like this,' Cassie said out loud and let the breeze carry her words away. 'Get a grip. Think happy thoughts. You *are* going to have a good weekend.'

At five to seven, the sun was hanging low and though the sky was still blue, it was streaked with delicate trails of sherbet pink and tangerine, which promised a spectacular sunset.

Cassie walked back to the house where everyone, except Lucy and Russell, had reassembled in the lounge to organise dinner.

'Shall we just get a few bags of chips to share?' Anita asked, which was wasn't in the spirit of getting fish and chips.

'I don't really eat chips,' Heather demurred. 'I'll probably just pinch a handful off someone's plate.'

'Not my fucking plate, she won't,' whispered Kwame to Cassie as he came to stand next to her and put an arm round her waist.

Cassie shook her head and hoped that she was banishing the last traces of her bad, sad mood. 'I'm so hangry. If anyone tries to nick my chips, I'll bite their arm off.'

It was left to Iris to be the voice of reason, her Glaswegian accent getting thicker because this was a topic she felt strongly about. 'This is heading into lamb bhuna *Gavin and Stacey* territory. If you want chips, then order your own bloody chips and if there's any left over, I'll turn them into a hash when I make lunch tomorrow. End of discussion.'

Sadly, it wasn't the end of the discussion. The discussion dragged on for several more very long minutes until Lucy and Russell came strolling in. The tense look had gone from Lucy's face as if she'd taken an eraser and a lot of Touche Éclat to it, and Russell seemed to be back to his usual smiley, affable self.

'Shall we order saveloys for the table?' he suggested enthusiastically. 'Who doesn't love a saveloy? Marc?'

'The ghosts of my French ancestors are turning in their graves,' said an amused voice behind Cassie. 'I'll pass on the saveloys. Bad enough I'm eating fish fried in batter.'

'Oh, come on! Mushy peas are exactly the same as pea purée without the delusions of grandeur,' Cassie said over her shoulder and Marc shuddered in a way that suggested he wasn't doing it purely for the drama. Although that could have been because Davy had just made a very off-colour joke about battered sausages.

By the time Anita and Azad returned with four huge bags of tightly wrapped paper parcels that wafted the delicious Friday-night scent of fish and chips in Cassie's direction, the outside table was set with little tealights. The men had taken great delight in making fire in the fire pit and Digby and Kwame had mixed some very strong negronis.

Cassie tried not to *inhale* her large haddock and chips and instead take polite bites, using a knife and fork instead of fingers like she would have at home, but soon she was horsing it down. As so often happened when she was organising an event, she'd forgotten all about lunch and it had been light years since her seafront breakfast.

Heather was on her left and maybe all she'd really needed was some carbs because as she slowly ate a fishcake and a handful of chips, she said, 'OK, I admit this is hitting the spot in a way that a nigiri roll can't.'

'It will be our little secret,' Cassie said. 'Also, I love your jumpsuit. Please tell me it's high street and not completely out of my price range.'

Heather looked down at her slinky emerald-green jumpsuit. Like Lucy, she was tall and slim, which meant that they could wear clothes in an elegant, put-together way that Cassie could never hope to achieve.

'It's Whistles,' Heather said. 'And I know it will be in the sale because whenever I buy anything full price in there it *always* ends up in the sale.'

It was that easy to change the mood. To make a concerted effort to enjoy Heather's company and not treat her like the devil.

Cassie demolished the tail end of her haddock and nodded as Heather described a coat that she'd seen in Liberty, which was going to be the 'fulcrum of my winter wardrobe'.

On her other side, Digby was talking to Russell about some BAFTA-nominated, gritty TV drama that Cassie hadn't seen because she didn't subscribe to Apple TV.

'It's amazing how he can play a total psychopath but also, I totally would,' said Anita of the lead actor.

'Yup. Don't mind if I do,' Digby added with a wolfish grin. 'When's the new series, does anyone know?'

'January, I think,' Anita said. 'Roll on January, right, Russell?'

For someone who'd been so enthusiastic about saveloys for the table, Russell hadn't eaten very much. This was a man who always polished off whatever Cassie couldn't finish when they had lunch at Manzi's. Now he gently pushed away his plate, which was still quite full. 'I don't know,' he said slowly. 'A lot can happen between now and January.'

The chips turned to a claggy paste in Cassie's mouth and for one awful moment, she thought that she was going to be sick. Then came an even awfuller moment as she felt the first tear suddenly descend without warning and land with a splodge on the rim of her plate. Another splodge and another and another . . .

Cassie stood up, scraping back her chair, so everyone turned to her.

'Tartare sauce!' she yelped, tugging at the hem of her dress, which was caught under one of her chair legs.

'Oh, it doesn't matter, Cass,' someone said.

But it did matter.

Cassie ran for the sanctuary of the house but there was no safe haven with an entire wall made of glass.

She pushed open the door of the walk-in pantry and slammed it shut behind her. It was dark inside. She couldn't remember where the light switch was and she didn't care because Russell was dying.

It was only now that Cassie allowed herself to finally confront this horrifying truth. She hadn't even been able to say the word 'cancer' out loud. Had danced around it, even as it cast its long shadow over her.

She rested her arms against a shelf and let the tears come full force, sobbing so hard that she was bent in half.

Russell is dying.

Russell will be dead.

He wouldn't be alive for Lucy's next birthday and he wouldn't be there to see Joni and Fleur graduate and have ridiculous boyfriends and leave home and then return home because they couldn't afford to rent.

He wouldn't be there to cheer on their brilliant careers. Or walk them down the aisle if they got married, or pretend that he didn't mind if they didn't want him to walk them down the aisle because of the patriarchy.

He was never going to see the amazing women that they'd become.

Russell wouldn't even be alive to watch the next season of some stupid TV programme because death was so cruel, so random but also so fucking mundane.

Cassie wasn't just crying but making an unearthly keening noise. She shoved a hand into her mouth to muffle the sound.

Every time she thought that she'd got the sobbing under control, in the seconds it took to take a couple of hiccupy breaths, she was crying all over again.

Time ceased to have any real meaning so she didn't know how long she'd been hiding in the pantry when the door suddenly opened.

Even though it was dark without the light on, Cassie turned around so her back was to the interloper. 'I'm fine,' she tried to say in between the snot and the tears and the hiccups.

'You need to calm down,' said Marc sternly, then turned the light on.

Being annoyed meant that Cassie was able to stop crying long enough to splutter, 'Telling someone to calm down is a fucking stupid way to try and calm someone down.'

She was crying again, as if she'd never stop. Marc sighed and shut the door. He gently but firmly turned Cassie to face him and pulled her, unyielding and unwilling, into his arms.

'Five minutes,' he said in the same stern voice. 'Then I'm cutting you off.'

Cassie tried to hold herself stiff but it was much easier to give in to the impulse to bury her wet, snotty face in the crook of Marc's neck and cry while he stroked her hair and murmured words in French that she could hardly hear and didn't understand.

Eventually her sobs became softer and the gaps in between grew longer and all the while Marc kept stroking the hair back from her hot, swollen face.

Then there were no more tears left, just deep shuddering breaths. Cassie drew back from Marc a little but one of his arms was still around her waist and she was still clinging to him.

The hand that had been in her hair moved to her chin so he could tip her face up and run his eyes over her features as if he were seeing her for the first time.

'I look terrible,' Cassie whispered, trying to hide her face, but Marc wouldn't let her.

'You don't,' he whispered back. 'You never look terrible, not even when you spend the whole day with some odd torture device on your head.'

Cassie managed a weak little laugh. 'My heatless curling rod.'

Marc was still looking down at her. Cassie risked raising her eyes to see that hatefully handsome face that she knew so well, but there was nothing hateful about him tonight. His gaze was concerned, but when Cassie ran her tongue over her dry lips because the crying had leeched all the moisture from her body, he didn't look concerned any more.

He looked as if comfort was the very last thing he wanted to give her. Cassie couldn't even explain why the atmosphere in the small, enclosed space, home to packets of pasta and rice and tins of kidney beans and chopped tomatoes, was now so charged.

Cassie's giddy, gulping breaths sounded deafening. Marc's hand slid, slowly and deliberately, from her waist to her hip and, his eyes never once leaving hers, he pulled Cassie closer.

Then he lowered his head and lightly brushed his lips against hers in a question which was answered by Cassie clutching his arms tight and kissing him back.

It went from nought to oh my God in seconds. From a hesitant kiss to test the temperature to a raging heat as they came together in a messy clash of teeth and tongues. Cassie grabbed handfuls of Marc's shirt to yank him closer still until their bodies were so cleaved to each other that not even a sheet of tissue paper could have come between them.

It wasn't even kissing. It was snogging. Proper, old-fashioned snogging. Cassie hated Marc for what he'd done to her but there had been so many times over the years that she'd thought about how good it had been, before it had all got very bad.

Now here they were, Cassie on tiptoe, her hands in his hair, sharing desperate, needy kisses and Marc's hands were on her arse, almost lifting her off her feet, so he could grind against her. She could feel how hard he was, how much he wanted her.

Eventually Cassie pulled her mouth away to catch her breath. Speaking would have broken the spell so neither of them said a word. Instead they stood there, both panting, eyes fixed on each other's faces.

Cassie didn't know how long they stayed like that. One of them needed to say something. Some bitter little barb to get them back on track. To pretend that the kissing hadn't happened, that it didn't mean anything. She should just leave but she didn't move and instead it was Marc who . . . suddenly dropped to his knees.

He stared up at her with glittering green eyes, his bottom lip caught between his teeth as his hands crept under the skirt of her dress. He traced a path up her thighs, the edge of his nails lightly scoring her skin so that Cassie's knees trembled.

Then his fingers hooked in the waistband of her pants. 'Take them off.'

Marc might have been on his knees in front of her (and that certainly hadn't happened the other time, it had been the other way round) but it still felt like he was very much in control.

Whereas Cassie felt as if she'd lost control the moment that his mouth had landed on hers. Her hands were shaking as she hitched up the voluminous skirt of her dress and tugged down her knickers, then kicked them away. Marc was still staring up at her face even though she was standing there bared to him. She couldn't tear her eyes away from him either and it felt too . . . intimate.

She let go of the scrunched-up navy cotton of her dress with nerveless fingers so her skirt covered him and that was much better. Now she could concentrate on the warm gusts of his breath on her skin, the touch of his hands on her inner thighs.

She gasped when he lifted her up enough that she had to hook her legs over his shoulders so she didn't fall and then his mouth was right *there*. No teasing, no waiting, he simply began to *feast* on her.

Cassie was instantly soaked and twisting to get even closer to him, her arms braced against the shelf behind her, jars rattling . . .

Then Marc suddenly plunged two fingers in her, his mouth still working, sucking on her clit like it was the ripest and juiciest of fruit and she just needed—

The door was abruptly flung open. 'Cassie! There you are!'

It was Heather. Of all the people, in all the pantries in the world, it had to be Heather.

For one agonising split second, their eyes met, Cassie pinned, propped up and panting. Then Heather looked down.

'Is that . . . Marc?' Her tone was positively gleeful.

'No!' Cassie yelped but she didn't know if that was because it was best to deny all plausibility or because Marc was now delicately circling her clit with the tip of his tongue and she couldn't quite believe that this was happening.

'Oh my God, it is!'

Heather was gone as quickly as she'd arrived, pantry door left wide open. Panicked, Cassie tore herself away from Marc, kneeing him in the head so he had no choice but to let go of her and she toppled over, taking several cans of cannellini beans with her.

Marc emerged from under her dress, hair rumpled, eyes glinting. He licked his lips ruminatively, appreciatively, as if he could still taste her.

Cassie couldn't even look at him. It was a much better idea anyway to look for her knickers. Her eyes darted into the corners of the pantry but she couldn't see a small scrap of M&S's finest black cotton anywhere.

'Are you all right, Cass?' Marc was still on his knees, still wanting to look Cassie right in the eye, while she was beyond words. 'I'm sure she won't tell anyone.'

Cassie threw her head back and groaned in a similar way to only a couple of minutes before. 'It's *Heather*! Of course she's going to tell everyone.'

Barefoot, because her Birkenstocks had fallen off as soon as Marc had hoisted her legs over his shoulders, and with her clit feeling like it was about to detonate, Cassie pushed past Marc to run back to the table.

Obviously, she wasn't in her right mind because rather than running towards trouble, it would be a much better idea to flee into the night.

Maybe Marc was right, for once. Maybe Heather wouldn't mention anything . . .

20

As Cassie approached the table, her friends, her dear, dear friends, broke into applause.

It wasn't even sarcastic applause but very good-natured, very enthusiastic clapping accompanied by several wolf whistles.

Cassie was just going to have to style this out – but she'd reckoned without Anita grabbing hold of her wrist, her eyes and mouth three almost perfect circles. 'You and Marc? *You* and *Marc*?'

'We were looking for the tartare sauce,' Cassie insisted as everyone stared at her. She'd had stress dreams very similar to this, but then she'd been naked and at least this time no one was aware that she wasn't wearing pants. Except Marc. He'd been very, very aware that Cassie wasn't wearing any knickers.

As she sat down, her face was so hot with shame that it hurt, and still everyone was staring at her. Cassie put a hand to her hair, which was no longer in artful ringlets, and realised that she must look completely wrecked. Mostly from the crying, but they'd think it was because she'd very recently been in the throes of passion.

'Tartare sauce,' Marc said from behind her. He leaned across Cassie, his arm brushing hers and sending a crop of goosebumps in its wake, to place the jar on the table. It was all Cassie could do not to shiver.

'Where was it then?' Heather asked tartly. 'Under Cassie's dress? Because that's where you were looking for it.'

'He wasn't . . .' Cassie said, though resistance seemed utterly futile.

Marc sat down opposite Cassie and shrugged like this was all too boring for words. 'You always did have an overactive imagination, Heather.'

Heather winked theatrically. 'I saw what I saw.'

Then the teasing started.

'You dirty so-and-sos!'

'In the pantry? Isn't that against health and safety guidelines?'

'I'd say get a room but it sounds like you already did,' Digby hooted. Cassie expected better from him.

Cassie steadfastly ate her chips, which had gone cold because just how bloody long had she been in the sodding pantry?

Across from her, Marc had that muscle banging in his cheek. But he was the one who'd started this. OK, maybe the kissing had been mutual but no one had asked him to get down on his knees and start eating her out. That had been entirely his own decision.

'You are *such* a dark horse,' murmured Kwame, who was sitting on Cassie's other side. He shot her a reproachful look, eyes dancing. 'I can't believe you never said anything. We're meant to be friends.'

'Friends respect other friends' right to privacy,' Cassie muttered, risking a glance upwards to see if everyone was still staring at her.

Of course they were. Then, at the other end of the table, she saw Lucy and Russell clink glasses. Even that wasn't enough for them. They looked over to Cassie and Marc, then they looked at each other and high-fived.

That shared delight, the clinking, the high five, their matching grins, pierced right through Cassie's heart. She hadn't seen either of them look that happy since they'd got here. Actually, it had been weeks – no, months – since either of them had been so carefree.

Cassie forced herself to raise her head and start looking people in the eye. 'So, yeah. I guess the secret's out. Me and Marc. We're . . .' She did a weak jazz-hands gesture. 'We're seeing each other. It's not a big deal.'

'Correction! It's the hugest deal.'

'This is major!'

'Please define what seeing each other means.'

'What the fuck?' Marc mouthed at her from across the table.

Cassie decided that he was the one person she didn't need to look in the eye. Besides, her confession had everyone clamouring for all the gory details. She stumbled through a brief explanation about them growing closer while they were organising the weekend, sure that no one would believe her. But it was all nods and smiles and Iris kept making the same 'aw' noise she made when she was looking at puppy memes. They believed her garbled and woefully inadequate version of events, because they *wanted* to believe it. 'It's really early days and we didn't want to say anything because this weekend is meant to be about Lucy.'

'I don't mind at all!' Lucy blew Cassie an extravagant kiss. 'This is the best birthday present.' She put a hand to her heart. 'I always knew you two would get together.'

This was news to Cassie. And Marc too. 'What was it that gave it away?' he asked with an exquisitely ironic arch of one eyebrow. 'All the arguing we do whenever we're together?'

Nothing could dim Lucy's smile. 'Just the snapping of courtship. Obviously.'

Cassie had hoped that once she'd given the people what they wanted, her torment would be over. But no such luck. Now talk turned to why the hell Cassie was planning to sleep in a bunk bed. Apparently while Cassie had been gazing out to sea and having her scheduled daily existential crisis, there'd been a little tour to see her rooftop eyrie.

'Now we all know that you were going to sneak to Marc's room when everyone had gone to bed,' Anita said, nudging Cassie. 'So silly. You might as well move your stuff over.'

'Then you won't have to get up to no good in the pantry,' Davy grinned. 'I bet you've traumatised all the dried goods in there.'

The teasing was never going to stop and meanwhile Marc was glaring at her, Heather was smirking but Lucy and Russell still looked thrilled, so that made everything worth it.

Everyone was too full to even think about a pudding. It had been a long day and Cassie had packed the schedule for tomorrow so as soon as dinner was finished, people made noises about having an early night.

'If you told my younger self, who didn't get to the clubs until after midnight, that twenty years on, being in bed by nine thirty was the dream, she'd have decided to die young and leave a beautiful corpse,' Iris said with a dramatic swoon.

As people drifted off, Marc was waiting to corner Cassie as she walked to the kitchen with a stack of plates. 'You and

I will be having a talk,' he said harshly. 'Just as well we're sharing a room, isn't it?'

'Look, about that . . .' she began but he was already walking away with quick, angry strides.

'Later,' he threw over his shoulder.

Cassie decided later could be much later. So late in fact that everyone would be asleep and she could slip away by cover of darkness. She might never see her friends again, but that would be a small price to pay for not having to deal with Marc's fury. Still, technically, he'd started it . . .

She lingered for a long time clearing the table but when she finally brought in a bin bag full of fish and chip wrappers and related debris, she found Azad and Bill already loading the dishwasher.

'Oh, you don't have to do that! There's very specific instructions,' Cassie said officiously.

Azad waved the information pack at her. 'We'll figure it out.'

'We have a couple of degrees between us,' Bill added.

Cassie was fully prepared to stand her ground until they got fed up and left her to it. She could easily spin out loading the dishwasher for half an hour but Lucy came up behind her and put her arms around her waist.

'Come on, my lovely girl, let's go and get your stuff,' she said, her voice expectant. She clearly wanted all the gossip. As Cassie let herself be reluctantly led up the stairs, Lucy's face was still wreathed in smiles.

'I always hoped this day might come and now that it's here, you know, it just makes sense,' Lucy said, when actually none of it made sense.

'It's very early, very *very* early and who even knows if—'

'Marc is good people,' Lucy insisted. 'You know that he's paying for Russell to have these complementary therapies as part of his palliative care? Massage, acupressure, reiki, whatever we need. And yes, we might have got some of them on the NHS if we didn't mind waiting for two years, or paid for it ourselves, but Marc has sorted it all and it's one less thing to worry about.'

'He is generous,' Cassie agreed, their voices quieter as they came to the first floor where Anita and Iris, who were in rooms next to each other, had their doors open. 'But it's easy to be generous when you're very rich.'

'That's not fair and it's not strictly true,' Lucy insisted. 'Marc expresses his love through gifts, whereas you're all about the acts of service.'

'You're not going on about love languages *again*, are you?' Cassie groaned, because Lucy's love language was physical touch – and banging on about the five different love languages.

Lucy refused to read the room. 'They just sum people up so well and what's really interesting is that words of affirmation are how you and Marc both receive love. Which is a really positive thing for your relationship. You both know how to validate each other.'

'Calm down, Gwyneth Paltrow. No one's talking about love. Again, for the hundredth time, it's a very new thing.'

'Is it, though?' Lucy stopped halfway up to the second floor so Cassie would get the full force of her most sceptical look. 'Me and Russell always thought something happened between you at our wedding.'

'Nothing happened,' Cassie said crisply as she started up the last flight of stairs. She didn't even feel that bad for lying. 'We were just two people meeting for the first time.'

'Still, you've always had this weird tension together. I just never knew it was sexual tension. Sorry!' Lucy added hastily, as Cassie gave her a glare that implied such lame jokes demeaned both of them. 'I'm just glad that you've finally realised that his bark is worse than his bite.'

The biting, those marks that Marc had left on her the night of the wedding, hadn't been so bad. It was the imminent barking Cassie was dreading. She opened the door of the infamous bunk-bed room.

Lucy shuddered. 'To think you were going to sleep in here! Let's get you packed and delivered to lover boy.'

Cassie stuffed her washbag into her holdall. 'Please don't call him that.'

It only took a minute to get her things together then there was no point in putting it off any longer, but as Cassie headed to the door, Lucy barred her way.

'Joking aside, I need to say something to you,' she said softly, taking hold of Cassie's hand. 'I love you very much.'

Cassie was sure she was all cried out but apparently not. 'I love you too.'

'You are such a good friend to the four of us,' Lucy continued. 'I worry sometimes that I don't show up for you in the same way that you constantly show up for me. You always have done.'

'It's not a competition,' Cassie told her gently. 'Friendship isn't transactional.'

'I know that things have been quite hard for you these past few years and you haven't been that happy, but if Marc can make you happy, then I want you to really go for it. You deserve to be happy,' Lucy persisted. 'So please, don't overthink things.'

'But surely happiness should come from within rather than relying on another person for it?' Cassie pondered.

'Did you just hear me tell you not to overthink things?'

'Also, what happened to only having conversations that pass the Bechdel test?' Cassie grumbled but she pulled Lucy in for a quick, heartfelt hug.

Cassie could have done without Lucy knocking quite so loudly on Marc's door. When he opened it, she shoved Cassie at him, so he had to put his hands out – on her. 'Please guys, do everything that I wouldn't do!' Lucy practically chortled as Cassie shut the door behind her.

21

Marc stepped away from Cassie instantly as if he couldn't bear to touch her. Cassie gently dropped her bags on the floor. They were both silent as they heard Lucy say something to either Anita or Iris, then the sound of a door closing and Lucy's footsteps becoming fainter until they couldn't be heard at all.

One quick glance at Marc's frigid face was enough to know that he was still angry with her. Why did Cassie find his disapproval, and the things it did to his cheekbones, so sexy? What was wrong with her?

It was a big room. Not the biggest the manor had to offer but big enough for a huge bed, which would have looked tempting at any time. The walls and ceiling were painted a grey so dark it was almost charcoal and the bed and its quilt and its many cushions and pillows were dressed in dark blue and black. There was a dark-blue velvet bench at the bottom of the bed and matching armchairs in a little seating area, with an occasional table between them.

That was where Marc sat now, legs crossed, arms folded, face like granite. Cassie remained standing by the door, because she'd already decided that she wouldn't be staying long. Their positions made her feel like a naughty schoolgirl hauled up in front of the headmaster for snogging boys when she should have been in a maths lesson.

Like Marc was suddenly going to put Cassie over his knee and spank her.

Where were these thoughts coming from? They were coming from fifteen minutes in the walk-in pantry, that's where. It had also been months since anyone had touched Cassie with any kind of erotic intent. Not since she'd hooked up with the least offensive of her ex-boyfriends because they were both horny and still single one Saturday night.

'What the fuck are you playing at?' Marc had obviously decided that he'd given Cassie the silent treatment for long enough. 'What happened earlier, it was the heat of the moment. Emotions were heightened. It wasn't meant to give you ideas.'

Cassie made the universal scoffing sound for 'Are you on crack?' Then she treated herself to an extravagant eye-roll. 'Oh, please, don't flatter yourself. Like I begged you to go down on me? I don't think so!'

The look Marc gave her was no longer angry, but more cool, considered. 'Well, you certainly didn't object. Quite the opposite.'

This was all going very off-message, very fast.

Also, there was a very simple explanation as to exactly what Cassie had been playing at. 'They looked so happy, Lucy and Russell, when they thought we'd got together.' She shrugged. 'So I said what I said.'

'But we're not together,' Marc said witheringly. 'God, we're already the keepers of one huge, horrible secret.'

Cassie couldn't help but take offence at the notion that Marc considered pretending to be her boyfriend as yet another horrible secret.

'OK, fine,' she snapped. 'You can be the one to tell them tomorrow that we've broken up already. Because you're an arse. I'm sure it won't come as that much of a shock.'

She picked up her bags. It *was* fine. In fact, she was relieved she'd be spending the night scrunched up on a too-small bunk bed with a base made of cheap plywood, but before she could leave, Marc was on his feet so he could stand between Cassie and the door.

'I want Lucy and Russell to be happy,' he said quietly, as if he was tempting fate even saying the words out loud. 'Of course I want that.'

'I don't know if you looked at them while everyone was teasing us but they even high-fived each other. So, it just popped out,' Cassie explained, matching Marc's change of energy and dialling down the belligerence. 'It wasn't planned. It was a spur-of-the-moment thing.'

'But this . . .' Marc gestured at the two of them, him barring her exit, Cassie still in flight mode. 'I mean, how long can we do this for? What if he goes into remission?' he added wistfully. 'For years, decades. It could happen. It does happen.'

Cassie sighed a little longingly herself as she let her bags drop again and stepped into the room properly so she could perch on the end of the bed. They were clearly going to have to chat this out, so she might as well be comfortable. 'If there's an outside chance that Russell goes into remission and we have to keep acting like love's young dream, then it would be a small price to pay, wouldn't it? So, can't we just suck it up for the time being . . . ?'

She blushed at her turn of phrase. Then Cassie also couldn't help but look at Marc. Their eyes met and there it was again: that skin-itching tension.

He pulled something out of the back pocket of his jeans. A scrap of black cotton. 'I think these belong to you.'

Part of Cassie was grateful that Marc had retrieved her knickers before anyone else could find them, and another part of her felt hot and heavy as she remembered how they came to be in his possession. 'Yeah. Well. Obviously.' Her voice was very husky and it was very hard suddenly to remember how to breathe.

'What happened in that pantry, what I did, it wasn't planned either . . .' Marc said, fingers stroking the small bundle of black cotton.

'Like you said, heat of the moment,' Cassie said in a choked voice, though she was trying hard to feign detachment. She turned her face to stare blindly at the wall.

'Look at me, Cassie.'

It was more of a plea than an order. Forcing herself to meet Marc's eyes felt as hard as running a marathon or solving quadratic equations. His stare was dark and fathomless.

'Did you come?' He made each word sound like a promise.

She shook her head. 'Heather was a bit of a mood-killer.'

He pushed himself away from the door. 'Do you want to pick up where we left off?'

The air in the room felt as thick as treacle. Cassie still couldn't look away as Marc slowly approached the bed. There were times when she hated how arrogant he was. But now, as he prowled towards her with that little half-smile, it made her feel as if she was about to come to the boil.

'Do you, Cass?' he asked her again.

He came to a stop as Cassie wriggled back on the bed. Then she slowly, ever so slowly, raised the hem of her long dress.

First she treated him to the sight of her ankles.

Then, in a tempting whisper of cotton along her shins, she uncovered her knees.

Marc's eyes were fixed on her, his tongue swiping at his bottom lip. Considering that he'd been married to a woman who'd walked for Victoria's Secret, Marc's enthusiastic reaction to the slow exposé of Cassie's very unremarkable legs was . . . *pleasing*. She rewarded him by taking even more of her own sweet time, so that empires rose and fell, tectonic plates shifted position and took whole continents with them, as Cassie delighted in the tickle of the material against her skin as she leisurely and unhurriedly bared her thighs.

With each centimetre that she revealed, Marc took a step closer to her. Then, just before she got to the good part, Cassie stopped and leaned back on her elbows.

'Get on your knees,' she said in a raspy voice that didn't even sound as if it belonged to her.

Immediately, obediently, Marc dropped to his knees, so close that when Cassie stretched out one leg, her foot came to rest on his chest. She was sure she could feel his heart beating, positively thundering away, beneath her toes.

Marc bent his head to kiss the top of her foot, his lips hot against her skin. 'I want you so much,' he murmured reluctantly as if the words had been pulled out of him under duress. 'I know you want me too.'

It was as if the time that had lapsed since he'd been on his knees before her in the pantry had melted away and Cassie was right back to that here and now when she'd been all sensation. Her nipples were hard, her breathing heavy, a deep, dark need uncurling and unfurling.

But Cassie was also feeling something else. Something that wasn't so urgent because it had been sixteen years in the making.

Triumph trumped her own treacherous desire every time.

'Look at me,' she commanded and Marc tore his gaze away from her still quite unremarkable legs so he could look her in the eye. 'Poor Marc. Do you want me to put you out of your misery?'

'How are you going to do that? Because I've got some ideas of my own.' Marc smiled. It was a good smile, dirty and flirty, full of promise of what he could do with that wicked mouth of his. He was so certain that he had Cassie all worked out. But he didn't know the half of it. The half of her.

'You have no idea what I want to do to you,' Cassie said with a smile of her own. His eyes dropped down to her breasts, which to be fair were positively heaving, then back to her legs, one foot still resting against his chest because her core strength from all the yoga was impressive. What a pity that Marc was never going to benefit from *exactly* what she could do with that core strength when she really put her mind to it. 'But it probably contravenes the UN's policies on torture.'

Oh, his eyes lit up at that, like Cassie was all ready to don a shiny PVC catsuit. 'I'm not really into pain but—'

'Enough!' she snapped because he was derailing everything again. She flexed her foot with enough force that it was clear she was pushing him away. That . . .

'It *was* just the heat of the moment. And now I've come to my senses,' she enunciated each word with relish as Marc sat back on his heels to put some distance between them.

'Me having sex with you again? Dream on. It's *never* going to happen.'

Marc put his hands up like Cassie had just arrested him. His smile was now that condescending twist of his lips that made her want to flex her foot again so she could kick him in the teeth. 'OK, yeah, whatever you say,' he said, like he didn't believe a word of it.

It also made Cassie want to repeat her vow to never have sex with him again. Fiercely. And very loudly. But she wasn't going to give him that kind of satisfaction – or any other kind of satisfaction, come to that.

Pretending to be a couple and having to share a room was always going to be hideously awkward. Cassie had just made the situation even worse but it was totally worth it. It didn't matter what had happened in that pantry; they were still sworn enemies and she needed to remember that.

As Marc stood up – without even wincing, which made Cassie even more annoyed – she raised her arms above her head in a lazy stretch like she didn't have a care in the world. She even managed a condescending smile of her own. 'Just as well that it's a big bed,' she said. 'We'll put some pillows down the middle and I'm sure we can manage not to kill each other for a weekend.'

Marc looked up at the ceiling, like he was hanging on to his sanity or his temper by one very frayed thread. But when he looked at Cassie, his face was expressionless. 'I wouldn't be so sure. The weekend is still young. Now, do you want the bathroom first?'

When she emerged from the bathroom in a black lace-edged camisole and sleep shorts, Marc was sitting in the armchair, the miniature bottle of whiskey from his goody bag empty on the table next to him. Like she'd driven him to drink. Then he stood up and, without a word, but with narrowed eyes, he walked to the bathroom.

While he was in there, Cassie did seriously think about doing a runner but then she sat down on the bed. Its mattress was firm, its pillows numerous and even if things were awkward, at least they'd be awkward on sheets that had to be at least 600 thread count.

'I'm a duvet-hogger,' Cassie warned Marc when he came out of the bathroom in just a pair of black boxer shorts. It was best to lay all her cards on the table. 'I can't sleep unless I'm wrapped up like a burrito.'

She tried to avert her eyes but she could see that he had a really good body for his age. Or just a good body. Period. End of. Not open for discussion.

He was lean, thanks to running a couple of marathons a year, but he clearly did a lot of strength training too, because his muscles were beautifully defined. The room was lit only by Cassie's bedside lamp so her ogling and subsequent blushes went unnoticed as Marc put his phone on charge then walked towards the bed.

'I don't like to have the covers on me at all,' he said, eyes narrowing again as he caught sight of the decorative scatter cushions stacked down the middle of the bed. 'Are you ready to turn out the light?'

Cassie waited until he'd got into bed then plunged the room into darkness. Right on cue, before she could do any breath work or meditative exercises to try and relax her mind, the panic arrived.

It wasn't even her usual existential dread or her grief about Russell; it was a panic that could be summarised in ten words, the letters six feet high and in lurid neon.

WHY, CASS, WHY? WHAT THE HELL IS WRONG WITH YOU?

The pantry had been bad enough. But pretending they were a couple, even if it was for the best of reasons, was sheer fucking madness. As was goading Marc and scoring cheap points when they needed to be a team, a united front. Fat chance of that now.

What was even worse, maybe the worst thing of all, was that he'd asked if she'd come and she hadn't. And now, lying next to him, even with a duvet tucked tightly around her, Cassie wanted to come more than ever.

She tried not to squirm with longing. She didn't even realise how restless she was, how insistent her wriggling, until his hand landed hard on her hip.

'Go to sleep, Cassie,' he said sharply.

It was a warning; an order, which Cassie decided it was best to obey.

LUCY'S NAUGHTY FORTY BIRTHDAY WEEKEND EXTRAVAGANZA!

ITINERARY

SATURDAY

8.00 a.m. Breakfast buffet. Some beautiful pastries are being delivered, plus there's the usual cereal, fruit, toast and toppings.

9.30 a.m. A lovely lady called Astrid will be leading an al fresco yoga session on the lawn. (Hope you remembered your yoga mats!) If that's not your thing, then Az has planned a clifftop run. And if that's not your thing either, feel free to chill.

11.00 a.m. A swim in the pool/on the beach (tbc) for those who want to.

12.30 p.m. Lunch. Iris and Bill are making a light picky-bits lunch. There will definitely be a charcuterie board.

2.00 p.m. Tennis tournament. One knockout set per round. Winners play winners, until we have our ultimate tennis champions. (I know this is a lot of exercise for one day, but Lucy is one of those annoyingly sporty types.)

3.00 p.m. Masseur, Rob, arriving. Half-hour sessions in the morning room, so as soon as you're knocked out of the tennis tournament, go and find him. Last massage at 5.00 p.m. reserved for Lucy.

7.00 p.m. FILM FANCY DRESS KARAOKE BARBECUE SPECTACULAR

What it says on the tin. Come in your finest film-inspired fancy dress. We're firing up the barbie and once we've eaten, we're firing up the karaoke machine until the wee small hours (or until the neighbours complain).

Please note: Participation in both the fancy dress and karaoke is MANDATORY.

Also please note: I bagsy 'Cruel Summer' by Taylor Swift.

22

Cassie was woken up by – what else? – the chime of her phone alerting her to a message that the breakfast boxes stuffed full of viennoisserie would be arriving within half an hour.

She uncurled herself from the duvet and that was all it took for the memories of the previous night to come flooding back, and she wished that she was still asleep. Actually she wished she could be in a coma for the rest of the weekend.

Marc.

Marc!

Marc eating her out in a walk-in pantry.

Marc, her arch-nemesis, now fake boyfriend.

Marc, who'd still been DTF until Cassie had rejected him in the meanest, most spiteful way possible.

Marc who was currently asleep, his back to her, his breathing deep and even.

It had all really happened and sadly, wasn't just a fever dream.

Cassie made a great effort to be quiet as she tiptoed across the room. She really didn't want to wake Marc up. They needed to talk, although she didn't have a bloody clue where to start, but she really wanted to schedule the conversation for after she'd had a fortifying cup of coffee.

In the bathroom, Cassie pulled on a swimsuit and over that, her yoga gear: high-waisted sports leggings and an open-backed yoga top with the words 'Nama-Slay' printed on the front. Last year her little brother Ryan had really leaned into buying her presents with the word 'Slay' emblazoned on them. Yet, this year, 'Slay' had apparently been cancelled and if Cassie dared to use the word in his presence, he'd mock her with an absolutely brutal, 'OK, Boomer.'

Cassie braided her hair into two plaits and pinned them up. She looked fresh-faced and wholesome in the bathroom mirror. Appearances could be very misleading.

Marc was still asleep but Cassie only let herself sigh in relief once she'd left his room – their room – and was halfway down the stairs.

Perfect timing as there was the crunch of gravel outside and Cassie opened the front door to see a smiling woman with matching braids unloading boxes from the back of her pink van.

'We're both working the Heidi look,' she said. 'If you take these, then I'll grab the rest.'

The biggest box contained Lucy's birthday cake, which Cassie stashed in the fridge in the utility room. She arranged the breakfast pastries on a couple of platters, cut up fruit and poured granola into a big glass bowl, and was waiting for the kettle to boil when Marc suddenly appeared through the arch at the other end of the room and made her jump.

'You should have woken me up,' he said, walking towards her and running a hand through his hair, which was still tousled from sleep – or maybe still tousled from all the tugging that Cassie had done in the pantry. 'Are you all right?'

Now that was a loaded question. Also, Marc was a lot less absolutely fucking livid than she'd expected him to be. 'I'm trying to decide if I should make toast or let people do that themselves,' Cassie prevaricated. Although, to be fair, her 'all right-ness' was currently dependent on delivering a successful breakfast buffet. 'Should I decant jam and butter into little dishes? What do you think?'

'I think that this isn't a hotel and no one will judge you if they have to make their own toast or spread jam straight from the jar,' Marc said.

This was good. They were speaking to each other politely. In fact, in quite a friendly way. Then Marc looked at Cassie and she looked back at him. It seemed as if The Complete Works of Shakespeare were contained in that one shared look.

The kettle boiling was a welcome distraction. Cassie reached for a mug from the cupboard directly in front of her – there was no point asking Marc if he wanted one – and the jar of coffee that she'd included in the supermarket order.

'I got your yoga mat out of the car,' Marc said. 'It's by the front door and also, I don't want to start another fight, I really don't, but how can you drink that muck?'

Cassie paused from dropping a heaped teaspoon of delicious freeze-dried coffee granules into a mug. 'I like what I like and also, that thing,' she gestured at the coffee machine, which was taking up a hell of a lot of counter space, 'terrifies me. I bet you bought a bag of fancy coffee beans from your new best friends at that roastery we went to yesterday.'

'Of course I didn't.' Marc grinned and held up a small brown paper sack that he'd been hiding behind his back.

Then as Cassie sipped her coffee, which had taken her mere seconds to prepare, she watched Marc fuss and faff about with grinding beans and warming milk and tending to the gurgling, hissing machine like it was a fractious newborn. On the one hand, it was actually quite sexy to see someone, Marc, do something that they so obviously enjoyed, and do it well. On the other hand, it was also very irritating, because, Jesus, it was only coffee.

All Marc had to show for all that effort was a tiny cup of espresso. 'The first of many,' he protested when Cassie pointed that out. 'I'm just getting started. Is that all you're having for breakfast?'

Cassie had half turned away from him because although she was an adult woman who owned her sexuality, she didn't want to eat a banana in front of him. Not after last night. 'I can't exercise on a full stomach.' She nibbled the end of the banana in the least coquettish way she knew how.

'Me neither. It seems a pity that you've laid on this lavish breakfast banquet and you're just having a banana and all I'm going to have is at least another two cups of coffee.'

Cassie wished they could be like this all the time. Chatty, smiley.

Maybe they could, but first she had something to say.

'I'm sorry about last night,' she said, making sure to look Marc straight in the eye. 'I behaved like a right twat.'

'Which particular bit of last night are you apologising for?' Marc asked lightly as his face said something else.

'The last bit,' Cassie explained, her chin tilting upwards because yes, she was apologising, but she hadn't been entirely in the wrong. 'I'm not going to have sex with you, it would be a really bad idea, but I could have told you that in a much nicer way.'

Marc folded his arms. 'And the whole fake-dating debacle?'

'I'm not apologising for that. It felt like the right thing to do at the time.' Cassie paused to ponder. 'It still does, unless you really can't face it.'

It was Marc's turn to consider things. 'I'm sure we can muddle through.' He was still looking intently at Cassie. 'Do you want me to apologise for what happened in the pantry? Because I could say sorry, but I don't think I am.'

'Well, OK, that's very honest of you,' Cassie said, finally looking away again because she was hot just thinking about what had happened only a few metres away from where they were standing now. His fingers in her, his mouth on her. If Heather hadn't interrupted them . . .

'But I am sorry for trying to chance my luck later,' he said and unlike Cassie, he didn't seem even remotely embarrassed. 'You're right. Fucking would just complicate things. There are already too many secrets.'

Cassie needed this conversation to end sooner rather than later. She could process and pore over what Marc had just said when she was on her own. 'Can you keep another secret?' she asked with a flutter of her lashes. She hadn't meant to sound quite so flirty but then again, they were meant to be seeing each other.

Marc didn't call her out on the flirting. Instead he faked surprise, a hand to his chest. 'You're asking me if I can keep a secret? Right now, I feel like I have a PhD in the art of keeping secrets.'

'This is just a little secret in the grand scheme of all the other secrets we're keeping.'

'Well, that's all right then.'

Cassie opened a corner cupboard, pulled out a saucepan and lifted its lid to reveal the surprise. 'I can't breakfast now but I'm hiding this for later. It's a cruffin with pistachio cream inside,' she explained.

'A cruffin?' Marc asked in the same way that Lady Bracknell might enquire about a handbag.

'Half croissant, half muffin, though maybe it's more like a flaky doughnut,' Cassie mused.

'You do remember that I'm half French and I consider that . . . that . . . that bastardisation of one of our greatest national dishes to be a hate crime.'

When Marc's arm brushed against Cassie's as he peered down at the cruffin, everything in her seemed to melt.

'So, would you pop one in there for me too?' he continued as if everything between them was fine. It wasn't fine though. After last night, being this near to him felt like an itch that Cassie couldn't and shouldn't scratch. It would leave terrible scars. But she still leaned into him, so her hip bumped against his thigh. 'I'm trying to keep this light, Cass.'

'I know. So am I,' she said.

Marc tucked a stray tendril of her hair that hadn't made it into a plait behind her ear. 'Then again, we do have to act like convincing lovers,' he said, his thumb caressing the tender patch of skin behind her ear.

Cassie curved her body closer to his. As if they were magnet and metal and couldn't keep apart. 'As long as we both know that it's not real . . .'

'We will have to kiss sometimes. They'll be expecting that,' he whispered against her lips and—

'Look at you lovebirds! Isn't that a sight for sore eyes?'

They sprang apart as Russell and Lucy came towards them. Cassie didn't know whether to be mad or relieved at the interruption but she decided to be relieved because the boom was back in Russell's voice, his face relaxed, his expression teasing.

'Sleep well, did you?' he asked, Lucy beaming behind him.

'Very well,' Marc said, refusing to be drawn. 'The two of you look like you had a good night's sleep too.'

'Yeah, we did,' Lucy said with some surprise, as she hoisted herself up on one of the stools on the other side of the kitchen island.

'But I'm still not up to a run, or even a gentle jog.' Russell's light faded a little. 'I miss running. I also miss not lying to my friends.'

'I have no problem lying to your friends. Let's just keep it simple and stick with the pulled-muscle story,' Marc said, as he fiddled with the coffee machine. 'Do you want a coffee?'

'A latte, please,' Lucy said. 'And no wanging on from you about how in France only small children drink milky coffee.'

'I'm glad it's not just me he plays the coffee snob with,' Cassie muttered as she hunted for a butter dish in the cupboard nearest to her.

'What you drink can only loosely be described as coffee,' Marc said with that supercilious curl of his upper lip, which this morning no longer had the power to rile Cassie into a teeth-grinding, fist-clenching irritation.

Especially as both Lucy and Russell were looking at them with fond amusement as if Cassie and Marc were putting on a show just for them. Which actually they were. Cassie needed to remember that.

They were only doing this, whatever the fuck *this* was, for Lucy and Russell.

Later, Cassie would have to remind Marc that even if they were pretending to be in the first giddy flush of dating, swatting her on the arse with a tea towel was strictly forbidden. But not now because Kwame and Digby with their yoga mats, followed by Iris still in her flamboyant flamingo-adorned satin pyjamas, had surfaced.

Marc was in his element as he took people's coffee orders and accepted their fulsome compliments for his hard work in keeping them caffeinated.

It was only when Heather and Davy made it downstairs that the flaky pastries and the freshly brewed coffee weren't good enough.

'I have bacon and berries for breakfast at the weekend,' Heather said, instead of a breezy 'Good morning'. 'Crisp but not done to a crisp.'

'And I'll have a fry-up,' Davy said, clicking his fingers in Cassie's direction.

All Cassie's good intentions to be kinder to Heather had been abandoned at the exact moment the previous evening when Heather had caught Cassie and Marc in a compromising position.

She could cook some bacon, it would take five minutes. But instead Cassie stared at Heather in a way that she hadn't stared at anyone since she was thirteen and challenged

Tamara Stirling to a fight over a spotty boy whose name she couldn't even remember now.

'Does Cassie look like a line cook?' Anita enquired sharply before Cassie could fully regress to her aggy teenage self and tell Heather that she was going to fuck her up.

'I was only saying.' Heather gave a little laugh. 'Goodness.'

'No fry-up, then?' Davy stuck his chest out. 'But I'm a growing boy.'

'If you want a fry-up, you'll have to make it yourself,' Marc said coldly. Cassie noticed that he wasn't offering to make Heather or Davy a cup of coffee either.

After much debate and talk about how white sugar and refined flour were carcinogens, Heather selected a pain au chocolat and performatively left the chocolat on the side of her plate, with a shiver of revulsion.

Meanwhile Davy ate two croissants – one cheese, one plain – a pain aux raisins and was just zeroing in on a sourdough pretzel when Azad asked if he was planning to run on a full stomach.

'I've run on a fuller stomach than this,' Davy declared and demolished the pretzel in three bites. The running club left shortly after that.

'Heather keeps a carb-free home,' Lucy whispered to Cassie as they rolled their yoga mats out on the lawn where Astrid, a serene, graceful woman in her seventies, with beautiful, long white hair coiled in a bun, had arrived for their yoga class. 'I can't believe we share DNA.'

'Did you all drink a lot last night?' Astrid asked as Anita retrieved an empty champagne bottle that had rolled from the patio to the lawn.

'Not excessively,' Iris decided. 'But quite comprehensively.'

'Feeling a little fragile this morning,' Digby added with a delicate shudder. 'Can you be gentle with us?'

'I'll avoid Sirsasana li Padmasana then. That's a tripod headstand with lotus legs pose,' Astrid explained with a smile. Her back was as straight as a ruler as she sat cross-legged. 'Let's be kind to ourselves. Lots of stretching to get the blood flowing and we'll finish with a short meditation.'

Cassie needed all the stretching out she could get. There had been a lot of driving yesterday, stuck in a car for hours, then a lot of running around. She tried to iron out the kinks in her lower back and felt her hamstrings protest as she went into downward dog.

The class finished with them all starfished on their mats as they listened to the sounds of the earth. Astrid said that once, when she'd really got deep into her meditation, she'd been able to hear the grass growing; 'but that was at a Peruvian ayahuasca retreat so I might simply have been off my gourd.'

Cassie could quite easily have fallen asleep if left to her own devices, but Lucy and Iris were determined to swim in the sea.

'Could we have a little dip in the pool instead? The pool that is heated to exactly twenty-eight degrees?' Cassie asked as Lucy took the weak hand she proffered and yanked Cassie to her feet.

'But it's hot, properly hot for an August bank holiday weekend and the sea won't be that cold,' Lucy insisted. 'Can I list the benefits of open-air swimming?'

'Please don't,' Anita said because she wasn't keen either. Heather had already hurried off after issuing a warning that there was probably raw sewage floating about and she could do without a dose of E. coli.

'Now, dearest, sweetest Cassie, don't shout at us but . . .' Kwame trailed off and made a winsome face, which had Cassie instantly suspicious.

'Why? What have you done?' she asked, hands on her hips.

'We haven't *quite* sorted out our fancy-dress costumes,' Digby said.

'Which means you haven't even begun to sort out your fancy-dress costumes,' Lucy said, because she and Digby went way back.

'Just a few things left to get so we're going to push off to Brighton.' Kwame tried another winsome smile. ''Cause the fancy dress is mandatory but the tennis isn't, right?'

'To translate: they're going to Brighton for the day, will have a nice lunch while they're there and will definitely miss the tennis.' Lucy didn't seem too cross about it, although this now meant that there'd be an odd number of couples for the tennis tournament. The logistics of it were already making Cassie's head hurt.

'They'd better be some bloody amazing costumes,' she muttered.

'Oh, they will be,' Digby assured her. He was already backing away. 'We'll see you later this afternoon.'

'Ladies.' Kwame bowed his head like a visiting dignitary then took his leave too.

'Honestly, they've had the itinerary and their information pack for weeks,' Cassie said. 'I sometimes wonder why I even bother.'

'But I'm very glad that you do bother. So, are we swimming now? In the sea? You'll be glad that you did, Cass.' Lucy struck a muscleman pose. 'It's so invigorating!'

Cassie had already been far too invigorated during the last twenty-four hours.

But it was meant to be Lucy's special weekend and Lucy was right about the temperature. It was mid-morning but the sun already felt quite fierce. This was going to be Cassie's last chance to have a dip in the sea this year so she shoved her Birkenstocks on. Then she and Anita trailed behind Lucy and Iris, who were properly prepared with dryrobes and goggles.

'Because they're wild-swimming wankers,' Anita muttered to Cassie as they approached the steps that led down to the beach.

Going down them, especially in Birkenstocks, was perilous. Cassie was relieved they hadn't tried to do this in the dark with a lot of glassware.

However, once they were on the beach with the sun beating down on them, the water rippling enticingly and sand that sank beneath their toes, rather than the shingles and pebbles that mostly dominated this stretch of coastline, a heated swimming pool couldn't begin to compare.

There were few things nicer than the English seaside when the weather was obliging; it made Cassie think of the summer holidays of her childhood. A bucket and spade for building elaborate sandcastles, sandwiches from home that were always a little bit crunchy thanks to her own sandy hands, and the smell of sun cream as her grandmother slathered her up like she was buttering a chicken for the Sunday roast.

The Proustian rush made Cassie feel quite giddy as she pulled off her yoga gear, then the four of them held hands and ran towards the sea.

It looked so blue, so light-dappled, like they were in the Mediterranean.

'Woo-hoo!' screamed Iris, as they plunged into the water.

'Fuck me! That's fucking cold!' Anita yelped because they weren't anywhere near the Mediterranean. They were up to their waists in the English Channel and it was bloody freezing.

Cassie tried to retreat but Lucy refused to let go of her hand. 'Come on! Don't be such a baby!' she insisted. 'Total immersion.'

Cassie tried to pull away with every fibre of her being. Turned out her fibres were as puny as the rest of her. 'No further! I don't want to get my hair wet.'

The water was up to Cassie's neck. Her nipples now resembled frozen peas. She was going to have to do a wee just to warm herself up, like shipwreck survivors did when they were treading water in cruel seas and praying for a life-boat. She'd seen a Netflix documentary about it.

'Just give it five minutes,' called Iris, who was experiencing a similar mutiny from Anita.

'Is that how long it takes to develop hypothermia?' Anita asked glumly.

'Try breaststroke,' Lucy advised as she finally let go of Cassie's hand.

The thing was that she was in the sea now. She might as well make the best of it. So with her face still scrunched up with extreme displeasure and her head lifted up so her hair didn't get wet, Cassie swam a few metres.

It wasn't *that* bad. It wasn't that good either, but she slowly swam over to where Lucy and Iris were frolicking, diving down, kicking up their legs then spluttering to the surface.

'You'll soon warm up,' Iris said. Cassie had never realised it before but there was something of the games mistress about her. 'You think this is cold? This is nothing.'

'I'm swimming. I'm swimming,' Cassie said, lifting her head even higher because she didn't want to get sea water in her mouth, just in case Heather's dire warnings about raw sewage proved correct. 'But if you splash me, I'll kill you.'

Anita had already gone back to the beach and was sitting there forlornly. Cassie swam to the wooden groyne that marked the boundary of the cove. By the time she swam back, she'd warmed up.

It would have been quite nice to float on her back and stare up at the wispy clouds floating across the blue, blue sky, but Cassie didn't have hair-washing then the subsequent hair-drying and tonging on today's to-do list. So she swam to the groyne again, trying to keep up with Lucy and Iris who were powering along like they were going for gold. Eventually, even they decided it was time to call it quits.

'Energising though, isn't it?' Lucy asked as she strode out of the sea like Ursula Andress in *Dr. No*. 'I'll get you swimming in the Hampstead Ladies' Pond one day.'

Lucy never would. Emma had swum in the Hampstead Ladies' Pond once, got into difficulties and they'd had to send a rowing boat out to rescue her. Also, there had been fronds, Emma had reported. Fronds that had wrapped around her ankles in a very unpleasant manner.

Still, Cassie made vague noises of enthusiasm before collapsing onto the sand. There was a shout from above and she raised her head to see some distant figures running past. Three of them: Azad, Bill and Marc, who waved. Cassie waved back, though it was probably a collective wave and not just for her. Who knew what had happened to Davy? He was probably incapacitated after scarfing down all those pastries.

It would have been nice to stay on the beach, gently baking, and maybe even messaging one of the men to fetch them some ice cream, but they couldn't muster up a single tube of sunblock between them. Cassie's swimming costume was still damp so struggling back into her yoga gear was a workout in itself.

The walk back up the steps wasn't just a workout. It was much worse than that. More like an ultra-marathon. Even Lucy was red-faced and breathing hard by the time they reached the top.

'I need water and more coffee and I really hope there are some pastries left,' she panted.

Once they were back at the house, Cassie realised there was nothing pressing on her to-do list. She could have another coffee, eat her pistachio cruffin and chat nonsense with her friends.

Azad and Bill were back from their run but Marc had carried on. 'He tried to be polite about it but I could tell our little ten-kilometre loop had barely touched the sides for him,' Azad said.

Davy came strolling in not long after that. 'I stopped to have a slash behind a tree and then I couldn't find you,' he said, although Bill had already told them that Davy had lagged so far behind that in the end they'd abandoned him. To be fair, Davy didn't seem to mind. 'Where's Heather?'

Heather had commandeered the morning room where she was FaceTiming loudly with her real friends.

Iris and Bill started preparing their picky-bits lunch and refusing all offers of help. Cassie knew she should have a shower and change out of her still-damp yoga gear but Russell was on the sofa opposite telling a story she'd heard many times before, about meeting Sean Connery in a curry house, and she wanted to fix this moment in her mind, so she wouldn't forget it. The way that Russell always rubbed his hands together as he approached his punchline and shook with silent laughter after.

Then Marc stepped through the patio doors. He was hot, sweaty, even his hair was wet. He lifted the hem of his black running top to wipe his face and Cassie had to look away from that delicious strip of tanned skin, the muscles clearly delineated without looking ridiculously ripped. The dip on either side of his hips . . . that little trail of hair that disappeared into the waistband of his black running shorts.

'Seen something you like?' Lucy was perched on the arm of Cassie's sofa and when Cassie forced herself to look at her friend – and anyway, Marc had pulled down his T-shirt now and was filling up his water bottle – she was grinning. 'Also, is that a love bite on your neck?'

Cassie wished that she could tell Lucy everything. That was what you were meant to do with best friends. Tell them that you were seeing a man that you'd never liked in a whole new light. And oh, yes, actually I first shagged him sixteen years ago and now I'm pretending to fake date him to make you and your dying husband happy.

How could she tell Lucy any of that? Instead, she shrugged. 'I burned myself on my hot brush last week,' she said, which was the God's honest truth, but Lucy clearly didn't think so because she hooted with laughter.

23

After a long, lazy lunch featuring the promised charcuterie board, three different salads, an open rustic heirloom tomato tart and a long, lazy digestive period, it was time for tennis.

Cassie was still in her yoga gear, not that she had tennis whites. She needn't have worried on that score, though, because apart from Heather, who wanted them all to know her tennis dress was from Lululemon, everyone else was in shorts and T-shirts as they assembled by the tennis court.

'Shall we play in our couples then?' Bill suggested. He pointed his racket at Russell, who looked the part in white Fred Perry and navy shorts but was sitting on the wooden bench in front of the court. 'We let you skip the run but you are playing tennis, aren't you?'

'He's not. Still got that pulled muscle from our London Marathon training,' Marc said smoothly. 'Just as well. I live in fear of his backhand.'

'Still?' Azad frowned. 'Are you sure it's only a pulled muscle? I know a great guy who specialises in sports medicine, if you want his details.'

'Um, that would be great,' Russell said without any of his usual bluster, because keeping the truth from your friends for the greater good was all very well, but in reality, it felt kind of awful.

'You can umpire,' Marc continued in his high-handed way, which usually made Cassie seethe. 'I can double up and partner Cassie, then Lucy.'

That was very kind of him. He kept being very kind and it kept being . . . very disconcerting.

But Cassie hadn't brought a sports bra with her, plus she hadn't been to the sort of school where you played tennis in summer, so she seized the opportunity: 'I'm going to sit this out too. I have stuff to sort out quite soon. The massage guy,' she added vaguely.

'You can be ball girl,' Heather decided, as she tapped the heel of her trainer with a racket.

'Bet you'd love to get your hands on my balls, eh, Casserella?' Davy said with a snigger.

'In your dreams,' Cassie said as she sat down next to Russell. 'Also, I think that counts as sexual harassment.'

'It does,' Anita agreed. 'I'm happy to represent you pro bono, Cass. So, who's playing first?'

Anita and Azad, and Heather and Davy, who was still muttering about how you couldn't say anything any more because people were so woke, were drawn to play the first set.

'I hope this isn't going to take forever,' Cassie said to Russell. 'The massage guy has just messaged to say he's going to be early.'

'I reckon about half an hour a set.' Russell took a coin out of his pocket. 'Heads to serve. Heads or ta—'

'HEADS!' Davy shouted before Russell could even finish his sentence. Then he wanted best out of three when the coin landed tail side up.

It set the mood for the game. Though it was less a game and more of a slaughter. Anita and Azad were clearly the better players, effortlessly breaking Heather and Davy's serve and winning the first three games without summoning up a single bead of sweat between them.

The more points they won, the more appallingly Davy behaved. He was all over the court, making it impossible for Heather to take a shot, then he'd scream at her when they both missed the ball.

'What the fuck are you doing?' he shouted after he'd skidded for the ball, even though it was heading in Heather's direction. She'd looked ready to smash it back over the net, but couldn't because Davy was in the way. 'A child could have hit that. For fuck's sake!'

Heather wasn't the sort of woman who was going to take that kind of abuse lightly. 'Not my fault,' she snapped back after Davy couldn't get his serve over the net and blamed her for distracting him. 'God knows you've had plenty of practice shooting blanks.'

'That's a bit close to the bone,' Cassie murmured. Even though Davy argued every point they lost, the set was over in twenty minutes with Anita and Azad winning six games to one, and only because they'd let Heather and Davy win a game to be sporting. It was very unlike Anita. She was the reason why Monopoly wasn't on the itinerary.

'Fuck this!' Davy flung his racket down the length of the garden and stormed off, while Heather rolled her eyes.

'I've never wanted him more,' she said in a deadpan fashion. But she wiped away a tear with an impatient hand in a way that tugged on Cassie's heartstrings – even if she hadn't forgiven Heather for the previous night.

'The massage guy is here!' Cassie stood up. 'You can have the first session, if you want?'

Heather nodded tersely. 'He's going to have his work cut out for him.'

Poor Rob, the masseur. He was young, fair-haired and very smiley. His smile started to slip as Heather interrogated him about his technique, which was mostly Swedish, but he could go harder if needed.

'Much harder,' Heather insisted as she toed off her trainers. Cassie was glad to leave them to it.

She stopped off in the kitchen to grab some cold drinks, then went back to the court, where Iris and Bill were facing off against Lucy and Marc.

'This is a bit more like it,' Russell said, leaning forward, his elbows on his knees. 'Both couples evenly matched, both fiercely competitive. Why *are* all our friends so competitive?'

'Beats me.' Cassie sat cross-legged on the bench. 'Life's too short to get so invested in whacking a ball over a net.' Then she thought about what she'd just said and winced. 'I'm so sorry, Russell.'

'Nothing to apologise for. It is short. Far too short.' Russell patted Cassie on the back. 'I would give anything for a bit more time.'

'But good time,' Cassie said softly. 'Not managing to snatch a couple of extra months but feeling so wretched, you wish you hadn't bothered.'

'That's the rub of it. It doesn't benefit anyone.' Russell looked and sounded so lost that Cassie felt frightened to touch him, in case he shattered. But when she put her arm around him, rested her head on his shoulder, he felt reassuringly solid, as if he wasn't going anywhere. 'Thank you for under-standing. I know this must be hard for you.'

'There's nothing to thank me for,' Cassie insisted past the lump in her throat. 'I get it. You know I do.'

'Russell, was that in or out?' Iris shouted because even if Russell was planning to bow out early, life was still going on. The sun was still shining, the birds were still chirping in the beech trees that bordered the near side of the garden, and a ball was still being hit over a net and landing too close to the baseline to call.

'In,' Russell said with great confidence. 'Definitely in.'

'Are you sure?' Bill asked.

Russell nodded. 'Quite sure.' He turned to Cassie with a ghost of a grin. 'Haven't got a clue but obviously I'm going to find in favour of my wife.'

'Obviously,' Cassie said, as she opened a can of Diet Coke.

She settled back to watch the rest of the set. It was four games all. Lucy played tennis twice a week in spring and summer and still got a regular game in during the colder months. She could handle all her shots with ease and Marc let her. Unlike Davy, he was effusive in his praise.

'Oh! Great shot,' he said, clapping his palm against his racket when Lucy just nudged the ball over the net after a fast-paced rally. And when Bill served an ace, Marc let out an appreciative whistle.

In much the same way that she'd got a secret thrill from watching him dick about with the coffee machine, Cassie felt the same frisson as she watched Marc play a game he clearly enjoyed and was good at. Also, the way his biceps bulged as he clutched his racket and the way his T-shirt rode up when he was serving were very pleasing to watch.

'Cass? You've got something on your face,' Russell pointed out.

She managed to stop looking at Marc, who was in the crouch position, waiting for Bill to serve, his thigh muscles taut and . . . 'What?' She touched her right cheek. 'Where?'

Russell delicately dabbed the corner of his mouth. 'A little bit of drool.'

'Oh, piss off, no I haven't,' she huffed half in jest, half in mortification. If they were meant to be convincing their friends that they were genuinely attracted to each other, then Cassie was clearly doing a bang-up job.

'Marc is a really good bloke,' Russell said softly. 'One of the best. I'm glad you've finally realised that.'

'Russ, we're just getting to know each other . . .'

'Technically, you've known each other for sixteen years.' Russell shrank back from Cassie's exasperated look because no one liked a pedant. 'Yes, he was a bit of a prick back then, all part of the agent provocateur image, but he definitely improves on acquaintance.'

It was a fair point. But Marc had really only improved on acquaintance in the last twenty-four hours. Before then, he'd given every indication that he disliked Cassie as much as she disliked him. Or thought she did . . .

'Fantastic shot, my love!' Russell shouted as Lucy did one of those tricky sleights of hand which made it look as if the ball she'd just hit would be out, but actually it was in. Cassie was relieved that this disconcerting conversation was over.

After a nail-biting last game, Marc and Lucy won seven games to six and after a short break, with Iris being dispatched to have her massage, Anita and Azad and Lucy and Marc squared up to play the set that would determine the tournament winners.

Cassie made a valiant effort not to sit in a heart-eyed daze as she admired how firm Marc's arse was in his shorts. Instead she admired his serve, and his grin every time he and Lucy won a point, which was often.

Anita and Azad crumbled under the combined firing power of Lucy and Marc. The set was over in just under thirty minutes.

Because the four of them were adults, they shook hands and hugged each other at the net, then walked off court to be met by Cassie.

'I have trophies for the winners,' she said, handing Lucy and Marc the little silver-plated trophies she'd had engraved.

'She thinks of everything,' Lucy said, giving Cassie a sweaty hug. 'You always go above and beyond.'

'Don't I get a hug too?' Marc asked and as their four friends looked on approvingly, Cassie allowed herself to be drawn into the hard heat of his body. She wondered briefly how it would feel to be skin to skin when he was breathing hard and had a faint sheen of sweat, which might have been repellent on another man, but on Marc it seemed very arousing.

Marc tightened his hold on her waist and when he kissed the top of her head so she could smell that fresh sweat mixed with the subtle richness of his aftershave, she felt . . .

'Cass, you're drooling again,' Russell pointed out, which she absolutely wasn't but she pulled herself free of Marc, who was now smirking. Of course he was. They all were.

'I hate each and every one of you,' Cassie said, which just delighted them even further. The only solution was to cling to the authority that the itinerary gave her. 'Iris should be finishing up in the next five minutes so Anita, it's time for your massage. Lucy, you're booked in after Anita. You get a full hour, though quite frankly, neither of you deserve a massage.'

'Well, I'm ready for a disco nap,' Russell said, touching the side of his head in a farewell salute.

Lucy and Anita were already heading to the house and Azad was back on the court – he and Marc planned to play a couple more sets after Marc had finished standing a little too close to Cassie for comfort.

'What are you planning to do for the rest of the afternoon?' he asked. He hadn't seemed to move but his leg was brushing hers and his hand was burning hot at the small of her back, fingertips just making contact with the curve of her arse.

'The karaoke system should be here soon,' Cassie said thickly as his hand slipped down not even a centimetre but still it made her catch her breath.

'I can sort that out,' Marc said easily, at odds with the intense look he was giving her.

Cassie tried to wrest back some control. 'That would be great because I really want a bath.'

They were facing the tennis court where Azad was knocking balls over the net and couldn't see Marc's hand dipping ever so slightly under the waistband of her leggings so his fingertips grazed her bare skin.

'So soft,' he murmured almost to himself. 'Is that an invitation, Cass?'

Their lie, their big lie, which Marc had been so furious about, was now charged with sexual tension.

She moved away from his hand. 'Not an invitation,' she said firmly. 'I don't have a bath at home so I'd really like one now. I'll be done in about an hour.'

Marc nodded, his face now aloof so it was impossible to know what he was thinking. But then, did Cassie ever really know what he was thinking?

'An hour then,' he confirmed.

'Then we should probably have a proper talk about how we're going to do this. You know, set some boundaries,' Cassie said in a low voice, although the thought filled her with a leaden dread.

'Can't wait,' Marc replied, his attention on a stray ball that had settled at the bottom of the grass verge just outside the tennis court.

Like he didn't have a care in the world.

24

Despite the worry that was nibbling at the edge of her nerves, Cassie could only sigh rapturously as she slowly lowered herself into a bath that was a couple of degrees hotter than bearable.

It was a proper, deep roll-top bath and Anita had given Cassie the little bottle of fancy bubble bath from her goody bag. There was no point in having a bath without bubbles.

Cassie could feel the tension slowly ebbing away as she submerged herself up to her neck and leaned her head back. She focused on the silken water against her skin, the steady in and out of her breathing.

It was all working perfectly until Cassie heard footsteps in the corridor outside. Why was Marc coming back to the room even though it hadn't even been twenty minutes, let alone an hour?

The footsteps faded away and Cassie's heartbeat returned to normal as she faced the unwelcome truth that she had half hoped it was Marc.

She'd told one lie. A lie to make her two dear friends happy during their darkest hours and now it was going to lead to hopefully (because she wanted Russell to be around and shining his light for as long as possible) months of deception and subterfuge.

Cassie knew that if she indicated she was willing, Marc would happily, and skilfully, fuck her. Which was oddly validating, but in the cold light of day, and even in the sun-flecked late-afternoon light of the bathroom, having sex with someone who didn't like you wasn't good for your self-esteem or your self-worth. Cassie deserved better than that.

It was different for men, though. They could quite happily fuck about and keep their emotions in check.

Even though they'd been getting on quite well over the last couple of days, was that only because Marc had wanted to sleep with Cassie? Had he just been buttering her up when he'd been so helpful around the house? Just like he'd been friendly a couple of weeks ago to get her onside, so they could perform an intervention on Russell and bully him into having treatment that he didn't want.

That made Marc look very bad; bordering on evil. He wasn't evil. Annoying, yes. Arrogant, also yes. Autocratic, again very much yes – and also, wasn't autocratic the same as arrogant?

The bath was no longer fulfilling its relaxing remit. Cassie hauled herself out of its now cooling depths and as she roughly, almost angrily, towelled herself off, she was no clearer in her mind about what to say to Marc when he arrived for their chat.

She'd probably start by drawing an outline of her body and pointing to the places that he could touch and the places that were completely out of bounds. Then she'd play the rest of the conversation by ear.

It was another half an hour or so before there was a gentle knock at the door and, it seemed to Cassie's oversensitive ears, a voice that sounded positively indecent enquired, 'Are you decent?'

'Very decent.' Cassie's stomach churned as the door slowly opened.

Marc stood on the threshold, his expression dumbfounded for just a moment, before he schooled his features into something less surprised. 'I was not expecting . . .' he gestured at Cassie, who was sitting cross-legged on the bed, '. . . this.'

Cassie had used the time wisely. She was now transformed into Mrs Mia Wallace from *Pulp Fiction*. It was the lowest effort fancy dress imaginable but still highly effective. A white tailored shirt, black cropped flares and the *pièce de résistance*, her hair pinned up and hidden away under a sharp, dark-brown bobbed wig. Her make-up was more dramatic than usual, and she'd forgone her bronzer so the deep wine red of her lipstick really stood out.

Now she was about to apply the finishing touch: Chanel's Vamp polish on her nails.

'This old thing,' Cassie said breezily. 'Literally, this old thing. All I had to buy was the wig.'

'I'd have hardly recognised you,' Marc admitted, as he shut the door. Even that decisive sound of wood on wood had Cassie's heart skittering. 'The karaoke system's been delivered and it's all ready to go. Talking of which, I need to hit the shower. I smell pretty ripe.'

He tugged his T-shirt over his head and though Cassie wasn't going to have sex with him, she could still appreciate the way his abdominal muscles rippled.

It wasn't even six and Cassie didn't need to be downstairs for a little while, so as Marc took a garment bag out of the wardrobe, she tried to relax her posture as she said, 'If you're not too long, then maybe we could have that chat before we go downstairs.'

She'd been aiming for a studied nonchalance but it sounded as if her vocal cords were tied up in knots. No wonder Marc frowned.

'I don't need long,' he said.

He was as good as his word. Twenty minutes later, after Cassie had employed a second coat on her nails then a clear top coat, he emerged from the bathroom in a sharply tailored black suit and snowy white shirt.

Marc was what Cassie's nan would grudgingly call a 'handsome bastard' before launching into a lecture about the dangers of men who were blessed with more than their fair share of good looks. 'They don't have to try so hard and they know it. Far better to aim for a bloke who's more homely looking. Less likely to break your heart.'

There was no way that Marc was going to break her heart but even so, he was very pleasing to the eye in jeans and a T-shirt, or even running gear, but in an impeccably cut evening suit, he was absolutely devastating. Cassie was reeling from a dizzy sense of déjà vu.

He'd been wearing a black suit and white shirt on the night that they'd first met, and that had not ended well. So she tried to hide her admiration and also her discomfort with a casual, 'That's a bit fancy for a barbecue, isn't it? Also, it's meant to be fancy dress.'

'It *is* fancy dress,' Marc said indignantly, shrugging off his jacket and placing it over the back of one of the armchairs. 'We're going as John Travolta and Uma Thurman in *Pulp Fiction*.'

'I said *I* was going as Uma. We didn't have any discussion about what you were going as.'

Even if their friends didn't believe that they were a couple, even if last night had never happened, there'd be no doubting it now when they turned up in their complementary fancy-dress outfits. It felt like even more lying.

'I thought it was implied, and John Travolta was an easy look to pull together. I don't know why you're getting so worked up about this,' Marc added – although if he'd really known Cassie, then he'd know that she could get worked up about anything.

She watched as Marc sat down to pull on black socks. God, he even put his socks on elegantly. 'You've completely fudged the whole fancy-dress thing,' Cassie said, because she'd been not letting things lie since the day she was born. 'Your hair's all wrong too. John Travolta had shoulder-length black hair pulled back in a ponytail. Have you got a wig?'

'I have not,' Marc said evenly.

'Or a bootlace tie?'

'Nope.'

'Then you're not in fancy dress. You're just wearing a white shirt and a black suit.'

'Cassie, really, does this matter?' Marc asked in the same even tone, crossing his legs, and Cassie was sure that he wanted to sigh in a long-suffering way, but he managed to restrain himself.

Of course it wasn't important. But it was easier to bitch about his complete lack of a fancy-dress costume than any of the things that were really bothering her, which were much harder to articulate. To say the words out loud. To ask the difficult questions when Cassie knew that she wouldn't like the answers.

'I just want everything to be perfect,' she said weakly.

'Nothing is ever perfect.' Marc let Cassie digest that – although it wasn't news to her – then leaned forward. 'So, this chat. Shall I go first?'

Her muscles immediately tensed up. Even her toes, nail polish gleaming, were suddenly rigid. Cassie nodded.

'I want to clear something up. A couple of weeks ago, I liked that we were getting on better, swapping "banter"' – he accompanied his air quotes with a self-deprecating smile – 'in the chat, maybe becoming friends. Because we haven't ever managed a friendship, have we?'

'Well, there is a history . . . when we first met . . .'

'Let's not go there just yet,' Marc said and Cassie mar- velled at how he could sound so calm, so in control, when her heart was going like the clappers. 'When I came to see you at your office, the coffee and cake, none of that had an ulterior motive. I was just hoping we were in a better place. It wasn't some evil master plan to get you onside.'

His gaze was steady, but that tell-tale muscle was pound- ing away just above his jawline and it made Cassie dread what might be coming next. 'When I talked about us staging an intervention, persuading Russell to have treatment, I had the best intentions. I really did. Because if it was me, if I had everything that Russell had, so many people who love him, I'd fight. I'd throw everything at it and I just really wanted – still want – him to do the same. I need you to know that.'

Whatever resentments Cassie had been harbouring about their argument in Soho Square, she decided to let them go.

To have them hover in the stillness of the room, along with the dust motes, then dissipate to nothing.

'I get it,' Cassie said, because now she did.

'I've known Russell since we were both seven. I can barely remember a time when he wasn't in my life. He's so much more than a friend.' Marc swallowed hard, as if he was having to force each word out. 'I don't know much about having a family but that's what he and Lucy feel like. If . . . when he goes, nothing will be the same. I won't be the same.'

Cassie had never known Marc allow himself to be so vulnerable and it was only fair that she return the favour. 'The reason why I've accepted what Russell wants, why I got so angry with you, is because I've been here before.' She wiggled up the bed to grab her now mostly empty, mostly flat can of Diet Coke, because her mouth had gone horribly dry. 'My grandfather had an aggressive cancer with a really short prognosis which he refused to accept. He wanted all the treatment. The chemo, the radiotherapy, we even went private to get a second opinion. We all chipped in but my gran still had to take out a loan and forked out thousands of pounds for an experimental therapy, which didn't really help. It just made him suffer for longer.'

Cassie would never be able to talk about this without her voice thickening, having to squeeze the words past the sobs that were bubbling up.

'I'm sorry,' Marc said. 'That must have been hard.'

'It was the most horrific thing that has ever happened to me.' Cassie sniffed the tears away and didn't even care about the snotty, phlegmy sound she made. 'He maybe squeezed out an extra month, but it was a terrible month, and the

months before that were fucking terrible too. The side-
effects from the treatment, the infections, being in hospital
more often than not. He was in pain and he wasn't at peace
because he was so determined to keep fighting.'

She took another swig of flat Coke. Marc was silent and
respectful of the fact that Cassie wasn't finished but that
it would take her a little while to speak her truth. 'I have
so many great memories of him but they've been tainted
by his last months. Marc, he was tormented, emotionally,
physically . . .'

As clearly as if it had happened only hours earlier, Cassie
could recall the last time that she'd spoken to her grandfather while he was still aware of what was going on. He
was in a wheelchair, hunched in on himself in pain. A once
robust, imposing man now shrunk in body and spirit, they
were waiting to see his consultant and Cassie had asked
if there was anything she could do. Did he need water?
Would he be more comfortable if she slipped the cushion they'd brought with them behind his back? Should she
ask the receptionist how much longer the wait would be?
'You've always had such a kind heart, Cass,' he'd said in the
laboured croak which was how he talked now. Then, in the
most despairing voice, 'I just don't know what to do with
myself. I can't bear it.'

'It was the absolute worst,' she now told Marc. 'There were
times when I wished that he would just *die*. I felt as if I was losing my mind. I was twenty-eight. Twice as old as Joni and Fleur
but I could hardly cope. I wouldn't want them to go through
any of that. So do you understand now where I'm coming
from? Why Russell has chosen to just have palliative care?'

Marc didn't argue that it had been ten years ago and treatments had improved. Or that he knew the best doctor at the best hospital and it would all be different. He simply nodded. 'Thank you for sharing that with me.'

Cassie tipped her head back and blinked rapidly. 'I'm not going to cry. I'm not going to cry.'

She heard Marc stand up, then he was sitting down next to her. 'Do you need a hug?' he asked uncertainly.

'If you touch me I *will* cry and I really don't want to have to redo my make-up,' Cassie said with another emphatic sniff.

Marc *was* touching her. His thigh, his arm pressed against hers, but instead of Cassie finding his nearness secretly arousing, now it was secretly comforting.

'You're all right.' He made it a statement, not a question.

'I am,' Cassie confirmed. 'It just still gets to me. He was only sixty-three. I know it's a cliché, but it's no age to go, is it?'

Marc didn't point out that Russell was only forty-four, which was even crueller. Instead he said, with some surprise, 'Your grandfather was sixty-three and you were twenty-eight? I think you got your maths wrong . . .'

That made Cassie grin, tears now retreating into the distance. It was another reminder that although they'd known each other for years, they didn't really know anything about each other. Not the important stuff.

She hit him with the headline, which always made people gasp: 'My mum had me when she was fifteen.'

Marc didn't gasp but he let out a long, low whistle. 'That must have been . . . tough.'

'Quite confusing sometimes.' Cassie leaned back on her elbows and wondered how much to tell him.

She'd grown up with a sense that she hadn't been entirely wanted and that everyone had just made the best of the situation.

She was sure there must have been conversations about abortion and then, after she was born and Alison had immediately decided that motherhood wasn't for her, adoption. Her grandparents had still been in their mid-thirties, although with three children of their own they'd decided that they were done with babies. But as her very prosaic grandfather had said, 'One more puppy on the pile wasn't going to make much difference.' Her grandmother Sue had sounded a bit more sentimental when she'd told Cassie that 'as soon as they put you in my arms, I knew you weren't going anywhere'.

It had helped that Cassie had apparently been a very placid baby, and even if Alison had checked out and ten-year-old Dan was indifferent, then eight-year-old Emma was absolutely besotted with her new niece. As if Cassie was a Tiny Tears doll come to life solely for her own pleasure.

Most of Cassie's earliest memories were of her special and tender relationship with Emma, who'd lift Cassie out of her cot so they could sleep together, despite Sue's dire warnings about the dangers of smothering. Emma had kept a notebook to list Cassie's early milestones, from first steps to first words to first ice cream. Emma's friends were similarly obsessed and always popping round 'to have a go with the baby'.

It had been a happy childhood but an odd one. Now, Cassie shrugged. 'It took a village and all that. Alison, my mum, got married to this amazing guy when I was twenty and then they had Ryan, who we all adore. I think it made her re-evaluate a lot of things. She's never really been a mother to me but we have a much better relationship now.' She sighed. 'Families are really complicated.'

'Your dad?' Marc asked.

Cassie shrugged again. 'Got shipped off to family in Ireland. I've connected with some cousins through Facebook but I've never been in contact with him. Can't really see the point now anyway.'

It had used to hurt but now it didn't. Not really. A year ago, she and Kwame had been to see a revival of Arthur Miller's *Death of a Salesman*. When Willy Loman had said that he 'still felt kind of temporary about myself', it had been like a small incendiary device going off in her head. It was almost exactly how Cassie felt about herself but she'd never been able to find the right words to express it.

'It does sound like you have a lot of love in your life, though,' Marc said gently, which was also true.

'I've never been in any doubt about that.' Cassie sat up straight. Now they seemed to be even closer and it felt right to rest her arm on his shoulder. 'What about you? Were you raised by a village?'

Marc's laugh was entirely without humour. 'By staff, mostly. It's quite hard to talk about my formative years without reverting to stereotypes. French father, who was a charming but largely absent presence. Would much rather spend time with his latest girlfriend. English mother, who coped with his infidelities by presenting a very chilly exterior to the world.' He shrugged. 'It was quite a relief to be packed off to boarding school at the age of seven.'

'That must have been . . . tough.' Cassie echoed his own words.

'Not at all.' Marc flashed his teeth in an approximation of a smile. 'I learned how to completely repress all my emotions at a formative age. Probably why I'm so successful at establishing and maintaining meaningful relationships.'

Cassie immediately thought of Marc's eight-month marriage. From the way Marc's lips tightened, she wondered if he was thinking about it too.

'You don't think that you're lovable?' she asked, because in all her panic and ongoing existential crisis, Cassie never blamed anything about her situation on her lovability, but rather on a series of unfortunate circumstances.

Marc raised an eyebrow. 'That's what the evidence suggests.'

Cassie shook his arm. 'You don't give yourself enough credit. I've got to know you better these last few weeks and I . . .' Where to even start?

He smiled. Not a tenth-generation smile like before but one of his smirky, sly smiles that nobody could love, although lately it had been having quite a . . . *stimulating* effect on Cassie.

'These last few weeks you've wanted to plunge a knife into my back.'

'Of course I haven't!' Cassie snapped reflexively. 'Not your back. I wanted to look you in the eye when I stabbed you through the heart.'

She hadn't meant for things to get so dark. But Mark laughed as if he was genuinely delighted. 'I'm keeping you away from all sharp utensils.'

Cassie made a show of checking the time on her imaginary watch. 'I haven't wanted to kill you for approximately the last twenty hours. And during those twenty hours there have been moments when I quite liked you.'

Now his smile needed to come with a parental advisory warning. 'I bet you did.'

'I'm not talking about *that*.' Although they really needed to talk about *that*. 'You've changed for the better over the years. For one thing, you're not calling yourself a disruptor any more.'

'And you used to be a real people-pleaser,' Marc remembered, which was fair. He knew better than anyone just how much of a people-pleaser she'd been. 'Though even then, but especially now, you have a very low tolerance for suffering fools.'

They lapsed into silence, charged, not with sexual tension, but with all the things they couldn't say or hadn't quite worked out. Cassie's arm still rested on his shoulder, their bodies touching, so close that she could see that he was a week away from a haircut.

If they were silent then they couldn't talk about the fucking massive elephant in the room.

As usual, Cassie was rescued by the chime of her phone. One, two, three times.

Three plaintive messages from Russell, which made her grin, and when she showed them to Marc, he smiled too.

Russell: Have you got our fancy-dress costumes?
Russell: Should I be terrified?
Russell: Because I am terrified.

'OK, looks like I'm needed elsewhere.' Cassie patted Marc's thigh, all that hard muscle. So hard. 'Good chat.'

It had been a good chat. Not the chat that Cassie had been expecting and dreading. She still needed to talk to Marc about boundaries and wrong touching. But that could wait. She'd need a couple of drinks first.

Cassie stood up and stretched, noting the way that Marc's eyes were suddenly fixed on the pale sliver of belly now exposed.

'Should he be terrified?' he asked as Cassie retrieved a taped-up carrier bag from a shelf in the wardrobe.

'Oh yes. He should be very, very afraid.'

'It's odd but when you're being evil and it's not directed at me, it's actually quite . . .'

Cassie raised her eyebrows. 'Quite what?'

But Marc shook his head, eyes gleaming. 'I've already said too much. If I say anything else, it will only encourage you.'

25

Cassie knocked on the door of Lucy and Russell's cottage then left their costumes on the step and ran away before they answered.

She couldn't wait to see them properly kitted out. Just the thought made her snort with laughter as she came through the patio doors into the kitchen.

'Are you going to share the joke?' asked Marc, stepping out from behind the open fridge door and almost giving her a heart attack.

'You'll find out soon enough, unless Lucy and Russell bottle out of the fancy dress,' Cassie said with another small but very unattractive snort. 'What are you doing in the fridge?'

'Do I need permission to open the fridge?' She deserved the arch look that he was giving her but as Cassie glanced down at her phone and the very long – even by her standards – to-do list, she knew that she was about to become – again, even by her standards – very bossy.

'I've got a lot to do and I don't need you getting in my way,' she said.

'Which is why we should divide and conquer. I'll sort out everything booze- and barbecue-related and you can do the other stuff,' he said smoothly. 'Then I'll set up the karaoke after we've eaten.'

Cassie frowned. 'When you say "everything booze-related", are you including glasses, ice, soft drinks? And the barbecue – Lydia and Frank left very specific instructions and a user's manual . . .'

'It's lucky that I can read then, isn't it?'

Cassie ignored the sarcasm. 'Are you going to marinate the meat? Is there a separate space for the vegetarian stuff?'

'What I'm going to do is stay in my lane, and you can stay in yours.' Marc kicked the fridge door shut with the back of his foot. 'It's a barbecue. It's karaoke. Neither of which is rocket science.'

'If you say so,' Cassie muttered because even relinquishing a little bit of control, especially to Marc, made her feel dangerously adrift. Like the person she'd once been, instead of the person she now was.

'I do say so,' Marc said firmly. 'Now, out of my way. I've things to do, places to be.'

Cassie huffed like a furious little dragon. Not just at his peremptory tone but Marc physically moving her out of the way, his hands on her hips, when he could have just gone around her, instead of through her.

Soon, though, she was too busy to worry about Marc or how she could still feel the imprint of his fingers on her hips. She organised condiments and bread, dips and crisps and carried them out to the table on the terrace where they'd eaten the night before. Back and forth she went, each time loaded up like a little pack mule.

Cassie was quite insistent that this time, she didn't need any help. Everyone had mucked in on previous occasions, apart from Heather and Davy who just expected to be waited on hand and foot.

'Just take a seat by the fire pit – you're to do nothing but enjoy yourselves,' she said to Anita and Azad, who were the first to put in an appearance, dressed quite fabulously as Morticia and Gomez from *The Addams Family*. In all the time that she'd known Anita, Cassie had never seen her looking quite so slinky and glamorous as she did in a black fishtail gown with plunging neckline and a wig which gave her long, black starlet waves. While Azad, well, he was dressed in a dinner jacket – Cassie suspected that was going to be an overriding theme of the fancy dress.

She was right: the next couple to arrive were Iris and Bill, Iris in a beautiful sparkling gold flapper dress with delicate beadwork and Bill wearing – big surprise – his best suit and bow tie. 'We're Daisy and Jay from *The Great Gatsby*,' he said. 'Because madam had to justify the ridiculous amount of money she spent on yet another vintage dress.'

'It's from the 1920s,' Iris said in a reverent whisper. Then she did a pleased little shimmy so the beads reflected in the glow of the fire. 'Please note, we're referencing the 1970s adaptation of *The Great Gatsby*, starring Mia Farrow and Robert Redford. Not more recent, inferior versions.'

'Noted,' Cassie said, as she put down a bowl of nuts, then turned and did a double take at the sight of Heather and Davy.

Heather looked stunning as Barbie in a figure-hugging, hot-pink jumpsuit, which showed off every toned inch of her tall, slim body, and a big blonde bouffant wig. And Davy? Davy was just Ken.

'Wow! You look amazing,' Cassie said and Heather preened like a cossetted, pampered Siamese.

'You look . . . nice too,' Heather said after a long pause. She took a seat next to Anita. 'I'll have a gin and tonic, Cass. Heavy on the gin.'

'She's been knocking them back all afternoon. The old lush,' Davy said, stroking his bare chest. Cassie wasn't one to body-shame, but if she'd been Davy, she'd definitely have done up some of the buttons on the distressed denim waistcoat. 'A bottle of lager, Casserella, and make it quick, I'm gasping.'

'Marc's sorting out the drinks,' Cassie said. Davy's eyes lit up when he looked across the terrace to see Marc, and now Azad and Bill, all gathered around the grill.

'They don't have a bloody clue what they're doing,' he said, already heading in that direction. 'Hey, Marco! You're going to need a bigger boat!'

'He's really grinding my gears today,' Heather hissed. 'He's clearly not going to get me my drink either. Not when he can bore on about barbecues instead.' She stood up and wobbled alarmingly in her very high, hot-pink open-toe stilettos. Heather had many faults but when she committed to a look, she really committed. 'I'll just get it myself. Unless you were planning on being helpful, Cass.'

'I will,' Cass said with great patience. 'I just need to unload the dishwasher first. I'm out of bowls.'

'Don't bother,' Heather snapped and teetered off in search of a gin and tonic herself.

Cassie had just finished taking a stack of plates from the dishwasher to the table when Digby and Kwame appeared, with a great flourish, on the terrace. Cassie couldn't resist eyeing them up and down, then saying, 'Really? You had to go all the way to Brighton for *that*?'

They were wearing red Adidas tracksuits and black curly bubble wigs in homage to Wes Anderson's *The Royal Tenenbaums.*

'Would you believe that we couldn't get red Adidas tracksuits anywhere in London?' Digby made his eyes go especially wide.

'No, I would not believe that,' Cassie said, but she couldn't pretend to be annoyed with them for a moment longer. 'You both look brilliant, you know you do. Plus, you get extra points for not simply turning up in your dinner jackets and claiming to be James Bond.'

'That was our plan B,' Kwame admitted. 'Now what can we do to help?'

'Well, the men have gathered around the barbecue because it takes at least three of them to grill some sausages, but apart from that, everything is under control,' Cassie said.

Digby and Kwame decided to join the women, who were not remotely interested in making fire, and Cassie headed back to the kitchen.

She was just adding olives to a simple Greek salad when she heard Lucy and Russell approaching. As they covered the short distance from the cottage to the terrace, they were singing lustily, or rather yodelling. Though it was proving quite difficult to yodel when they were laughing so hard.

Cassie ran to the terrace, already giggling herself, to see her two friends decked out as Maria and a random von Trapp male child, from *The Sound of Music.* It was Lucy's favourite film in the whole world and a Boxing Day tradition that she'd serve fondue and expect everyone to sit through the entire three hours.

Lucy caught sight of Cassie and held out her arms. 'Babes! Best fancy-dress costume ever!'

There was no point in being modest. Cassie had absolutely excelled herself when she'd found a selection of dirndls on a German fashion website. Obviously, she'd gone for a party dirndl in a glittery silver, which Lucy evidently loved from the way she was twirling in it.

'I'm not quite so pleased,' Russell said and Cassie had to turn away. She couldn't even look at him as tears streamed down her face. This time they were tears of sheer joy. 'Really, Cass? Really?'

Cassie had tried so hard to find a costume that remotely resembled anything that Christopher Plummer had worn in the film. Eventually she'd found a seller on Etsy who could make romper suits – even for a grown man, as it turned out – from a very similar fabric to the brocade curtains that Maria von Trapp had repurposed as children's play outfits.

'I can't even look at you,' Cassie spluttered. She put a hand to her ribs. 'Oh God, it hurts.'

Russell had accessorised his ensemble with a white T-shirt and trainers, which just made it even funnier. 'I look like a prize plum,' he said, pulling on the short legs of his outfit.

'It was nearly pleather lederhosen,' Cassie managed to say as she carefully wiped under her eyes. Her fingertips carried the black smudges of what was left of her mascara.

'I'd have preferred lederhosen.' Russell couldn't stay angry for long. Not that Cassie had believed he was genuinely cross. Besides, he loved to be the centre of attention. He also loved to barbecue and now that their big reveal was over, it was clear where his priorities lay.

'I'm sure Marc has got a pair of barbecue tongs with your name on,' Cassie said when she saw him casting eager looks in that direction.

'He'd better have.' Russell puffed out his chest, which, there were no two ways about it, was not as broad as it used to be. 'I am the grill master, after all.'

Lucy wandered after him to get a drink and Cassie went back into the kitchen to find Russell something to sit on, only to discover that Marc had beaten her to it. 'Davy keeps pestering me to chuck lighter fuel on the barbecue,' he said conversationally. 'I might knock him out by hitting him over the head with this stool.'

'I don't think anyone would blame you if you did,' Cassie told him and he winked at her. Winking wasn't a very Marc thing – but then he'd been doing a lot of not very Marc things this weekend.

'Well, I hope the defence calls you as a witness. The champagne I put in the fridge should be chilled by now, but I also just mixed some Aperol Spritzes for Iris and Kwame, if you don't mind taking them over.'

'Of course.'

'You're an angel,' Marc said and what with that and the winking, Cassie wondered just how much he'd had to drink himself. Now he hefted up the stool, then stepped out onto the terrace. 'Russell! Sit down. You shouldn't be standing with that pulled muscle.'

Cassie retreated to the shower room to repair her make-up. Without her usual bronzer, she looked pale and with the streaked mascara, she was serving raccoon realness. There wasn't time for a full repair job. She wetted a cotton bud under the tap to remove the worst of the damage, then went heavy with the concealer, powder and yet more mascara.

She still had quite a lot to do. Make a dressing for the salads for one thing, but Cassie spent long minutes gazing at herself in the mirror over the sink. It was disconcerting to not quite recognise her own reflection. The wig, the dramatic make-up. Generally, Cassie was happy with the way she looked. Like so many other women, she felt that now she was well into her thirties, she'd settled into her face.

But now she wondered if other people thought that she was pretty.

No, not other people.

Marc.

He wanted to have sex with her, so he must do. Though thinking someone was pretty and thinking someone was hot were different things.

There was a small footstool in the shower room, which Cassie climbed on so she could pull up her shirt and look at her body in the mirror above the sink. To scrutinise her breasts, the indentation of her waist, the gentle but definite curve to her belly.

Marc hadn't seemed to mind how she looked last night even though he'd been married to a model, which she really needed to stop obsessing about. But he'd only seen her legs. There were other parts of her that had aged over the years. Cassie hoisted her breasts up to where she thought they'd been sixteen years ago when they'd been higher, firmer.

Then she realised what she was doing and jumped down from the stool. Who cared what Marc thought about her face? Her body? And the inner changes that maybe weren't visible but were even more significant?

Cassie cared, even though she wished that she didn't.

Time to nip this in the bud and to absolutely not have sex with him because she still couldn't have sex with someone, with Marc, and have it mean nothing. She'd never really been the kind of person who could have casual sex. Cassie wasn't a casual person. When she'd had sex with Marc, it had meant something and it would mean something now. Especially now, when she was seeing glimpses of a person that he'd never let her see before. Or maybe she just hadn't been looking at him hard enough.

There was a sudden knock at the door. 'Cass? Are you in there?'

Pep talk over, Cassie unlocked the door to find Iris waiting for her. 'Marc made you and Kwame Aperol spritzes. They're on the counter by the fridge.'

'Great, but never mind that.' Iris's auburn curls bounced as she shook her head. 'You have to come. It's all kicking off. Don't you have some kind of special events-planning training for when this stuff happens?'

With Iris leading her by the wrist, Cassie was coming whether she liked it or not. 'Kicking off in a good way?' she asked futilely as she grabbed a bowl of cheesy puffs en route to wherever they were going.

'In a very bad way,' Iris hissed, sounding very dour. 'Heather . . .'

It was impressive how one woman's name said out loud could make Cassie's heart sink so low. They rounded the corner of the terrace to the fire pit, where Lucy and Heather were having an argument. Both of them standing up and jabbing fingers at each other but not making full body contact. Yet.

'There's champagne nicely chilled in the fridge if anyone wants a refill,' Cassie chirped in a feeble attempt to distract them, then wished she hadn't when Heather glanced over at her, her face positively malevolent. Still, she tried again. 'Come on, let's not ruin the night before it's even begun.'

'But that's what you do, Heather, isn't it?' Lucy shouted, her face red. 'You ruin things. I wish you'd never come.'

Cassie put a gentle hand on Lucy's arm. 'Don't say things you'll regret,' she warned in a quiet voice.

'Oh, fuck off, Cassie. Who asked you?' Heather demanded but Cassie wasn't the target of her rage. Heather turned back to her sister and jabbed her finger again.

'Yeah, because you're perfect Lucy, with your perfect husband and your perfect kids and your perfect life and it's always about you . . .'

Lucy jabbed right back. 'That's funny because every time we get together, it always ends up being about *you*. You always have to be the centre of attention. You can't bear for anyone else to be happy . . .'

'I wish you knew what it was like to have things not go your way—'

Heather wasn't able to finish her sentence, thank God, because as she stepped forward to completely invade her sister's personal space, she managed to turn her ankle in her perilously high Barbie heels.

She let out a little gasp and then, inevitably, the tears came.

It was always easier to cope with a crying Heather than any of the other iterations of Heather. 'Come on, let's get you inside,' Cassie said, putting her arm around the weeping woman.

Heather, docile now, let herself be led back into the house where Cassie had to kneel on the floor like a supplicant to get Heather out of her heels. Her ankle was already swelling up like a pufferfish.

'I'm just so miserable, Cass,' Heather sobbed, as she limped through the open-plan living room. 'No one really knows what's going on in my life.'

Cassie knew that hurt people hurt people but there were also lots of hurt people who didn't lash out at anyone within range. She wasn't going to get into that now. Instead she made soothing noises. 'I don't think we ever really know what anyone else is going through.'

'I know I put a brave face on it, but I'm suffering on the inside. Have you any idea what it's like to be married to Davy? To see his face when I wake up, mouth open, the morning breath . . .'

It certainly painted an ugly picture, though Heather was usually the smuggest of all marrieds. She'd once said when Cassie had been optimistic about a new boyfriend, 'Get real,

Cass – relationships don't actually count unless the man loves you enough to marry you.'

Now, Cassie refused to be drawn in. Even if she did think that being married to Davy must be a source of near permanent irritation. She shouldered open the door of the morning room. 'Why don't you lie down on the sofa here where you can be a bit more private? I'll tuck this throw around you and let's prop your foot up on this cushion.'

Heather was uncharacteristically compliant. Cassie left to find a bag of frozen peas for Heather's ankle, a glass of water and a couple of Nurofen. She'd only been gone five minutes, but when she returned Heather was crying again. It really was like the hen weekend. A frightening thought.

She paused from fussing around Heather, who seemed to be liking the fussing a little too much. 'Hang on, I'll be right back . . .'

This time she came back with a bucket she'd found in the utility room.

'If you're going to puke . . .'

Heather gasped in outrage. 'I would never!'

That was a lie. 'If you're going to puke,' Cassie repeated, making sure to enunciate each word so there could be no misunderstandings, 'then I am begging you to puke in this bucket.'

Cassie stayed, stroking her Barbie wig, until Heather fell asleep.

Everyone, but especially Lucy, seemed quite subdued when Cassie returned to the fire pit with a bottle of champagne. 'No sad faces,' she said a little desperately. 'Have some champagne and let's think happy thoughts. I've got a couple more things to do then I'll be back.'

As she left them, she heard Lucy ask, 'Do I really make everything about me? I don't, do I?'

'Sweetheart, it's your fucking fortieth birthday weekend, everything is *meant* to be about you,' Iris said fiercely. 'Pay her no mind.'

As Cassie bobbed back and forth with salad dressings and more cutlery, and she'd forgotten napkins, Lucy looked more and more cheerful. Especially once the men had finished grilling meat, though why it took four of them to cook a few burgers and sausages, Cassie didn't know.

She was rummaging in a cupboard for a serving platter when she felt a light touch on her back. She knew it was Marc before she even turned around to see him looking at her with a faintly exasperated expression. Though it seemed softer, more forgiving than the exasperation she usually roused in him.

'Come and eat,' he said, holding out his hand.

'I will. I just—'

'Do what you're told for once,' he snapped without any real fierceness, so Cassie *allowed* Marc to take her hand. That was the only reason.

'But we need at least one more platter,' she said as he pulled her out to the table where everyone was now gathered.

'I think we can survive without at least one more platter,' he replied implacably. 'Now, what do you want to eat?'

He held out a chair for Cassie to sit down, though she was quite capable of pulling out a chair herself. Then she remembered that they were meant to be playing a part. 'I'll have a burger, please,' she said. Then, mindful of the many other barbecues she'd attended that summer, 'I don't mind if it's a bit rare but if it's actually raw in the middle, then I'll pass.'

'I'm offended by that implied criticism of my impeccable grilling skills,' Russell said as Marc took a plate then a brioche bun and built Cassie a burger, asking her at every stage of its construction what she liked by way of pickles, sauces and sides.

Again, he was just pretending to be a devoted boyfriend but he did put together a great burger.

Even though it wasn't real, there was something lovely about Marc sitting next to her, his arm round the back of her chair. Or maybe it was just that she'd really needed to eat, and she'd needed a glass of something alcoholic to drink even more than that.

With Heather asleep elsewhere and Davy neutralised without her – and also because he and Azad were having a very boring, very in-depth conversation about cricket – it was the perfect evening.

It was another warm, balmy night, the faintest of breezes wafting gently in from the sea. The heavenly scent of clusters of night-blooming jasmine in the wooden planters that lined the terrace competing with the equally heavenly scent of fried onions. Then there was that warm contentment that came from delicious food, the company of friends and getting pleasantly buzzed.

Once they were finished eating, Marc rested his hand on Cassie's knee and she was tipsy enough to just live in the moment. That a handsome, sexy man, as unpredictable and as unreliable as the bank holiday weekend weather (rain was still forecast for tomorrow), had his hand on her knee. To everyone else, he must seem a little besotted with Cassie, which wasn't the truth but he did want her and for tonight that was enough.

Except she absolutely wasn't going to sleep with him.

26

They decided to move into the huge lounge for the karaoke. By general consensus, it was agreed that it was better to do a quick clear-up now before they all got too incapacitated, rather than leave it until the morning, when they all planned to be very hungover.

Cassie tried to stand up but Marc tightened the arm he still had around her shoulder. 'I need to make sure people are rinsing the plates before they go in the dishwasher,' Cassie pleaded, but when she tried to explain how hard it was to budge streaked-on ketchup, Marc kissed the words out of her mouth.

Her gasp was swallowed up by his soft, lingering kisses. Over the ringing in her ears, Cassie could hear Anita giggling. She could tell from the way Marc's hand tensed on her leg that he was holding back.

The thought of what he could do when he really let himself go made her shiver. But it, the kisses, the hand on her leg, it was all just pretend.

'You're cold,' Marc said, standing up and pulling Cassie to her feet. He put his arm around her again as they followed the sound of laughter and chatter to the kitchen.

The clean-up was very much in progress, with Lucy supervising. She was currently more Captain von Trapp than Maria as she issued orders and wiped down surfaces as if the kitchen were her battleship. Cassie wouldn't have been surprised if Lucy had whipped a whistle out of the bodice of her dirndl and given them all a call sign.

Marc pushed Cassie gently down on one of the sofas in the living room. 'Sit here and do not lift a finger while I finish setting up the karaoke.'

'Sir! Yes, sir!' Cassie saluted Marc, unprepared for his wolfish grin.

'You've never called me sir before,' he drawled. 'We should revisit this later.'

He held Cassie's gaze and she knew that her cheeks were stained with red. 'There will be no later,' she muttered but Marc turned away as if he hadn't heard her.

Cassie was saved from the inevitable five minutes of analysing every single one of Marc's words, non-verbal cues and micro-expressions by a FaceTime call from Fleur, Joni and her brother Ryan, who was there for a sleepover, supervised by Russell's parents.

'We need to see Mum and Dad's fancy-dress costumes,' Joni announced without preamble. 'They keep ignoring our calls. Rude!'

'Do you want to speak to them or shall I just take a picture?'

'Both!' Fleur squealed.

The three of them were in full and very heavy make-up so no doubt they'd spent the day watching YouTube beauty tutorials and uploading clips of themselves dancing to TikTok.

'I'll go and find them but I will also be filming them during the karaoke.'

'That's why you're our favourite,' Fleur said.

Lucy and Russell were huddled over the laptop that came with the karaoke system so they could scroll through the catalogue of songs. They looked up as Cassie approached.

'I have two people who want to talk to you,' she said, turning her phone round so Fleur and Joni could see their parents in full Tyrolean garb.

A lot of whooping issued forth from her phone. 'Are we allowed no dignity?' Russell scowled, taking Cassie's phone. 'You horrible children, why aren't you in bed?'

When Lucy panned down so they could get a good look at their fancy-dress outfits, the response was enthusiastic and very high-pitched.

It was quite some time before Cassie got her phone back. By then, everyone was gathered on the sofas, glasses in hands, and there was an expectant, very giggly atmosphere as Marc ran through the karaoke protocol.

Typically, he kept it brief. 'You pick your song. You pick up a microphone. The words appear on the laptop screen. You sing. Any questions?'

'On the itinerary, Cassie said that participation is mandatory,' Azad said. He paused to cough dramatically. 'Except I've got a sore throat.'

'Mandatory as in you will be singing,' Lucy said sternly. 'No ifs. No buts. No wriggling out of it.'

Lucy *really* loved karaoke. Cassie did too. She'd once been told by a music teacher that she had near perfect pitch and for two years after that, she would sing wherever she went in the hope that she'd be discovered by a pop mogul and whisked away to a life of stardom. There had been much flouncing and door-slamming when her grandparents had refused to let her audition for *Pop Idol.* So it wasn't a surprise that on any night out that involved booking a private room at Lucky Voice, Cassie would end up hogging the mic. It wasn't one of her most endearing traits.

Now she tried to play it cool as she waited to look through the catalogue. Her showstopper was always 'Total Eclipse of the Heart' and she and Lucy did a rousing duet to 'I Know Him So Well', but hopefully she'd have a chance to do more than two songs. A lot more.

'Just one thing, guys,' Russell announced, clinking his glass to get everyone's attention. 'We'll be singing in our couples, so you might want to think about choosing a duet. Cassie and Marc have already called dibs on "Islands in the Stream".'

Cassie and Marc had done no such thing. Or rather Cassie hadn't, and from the sudden panicked look in Marc's eyes as he checked the wireless microphones, he hadn't either.

Russell raised his glass in a silent salute to Cassie because he was a shit-stirring bastard. When Cassie raised her middle finger he just laughed. She didn't want to be sad, not tonight, but if this weekend was about making memories then Cassie wanted to carry this memory of Russell in his von Trapp brocade-curtain romper suit, absolutely in his element as he joked with Azad and Anita, in her heart for a long, long time.

She was startled out of her reverie by Marc sitting down next to her with a heavy thud and a heavy face. 'I do not sing,' he hissed at her.

This wasn't a surprise. Everything he did, he did with such control, such ease. He might not call himself a disruptor any more but Marc was cool and karaoke was not cool.

'It won't be so bad,' she said, patting his arm. 'Yes, you're going to look like a bit of a prat but—'

'When I say I don't sing, I mean I can't sing,' Marc confessed with a grimace. 'You *have* to get me out of this.'

On the contrary, Cassie was now even more excited about the karaoke. Maybe if she heard Marc murdering the Dolly Parton and Kenny Rogers classic, all these complicated feelings that she didn't even understand herself would disappear. She positively yearned for The Ick.

'You'll be fine. Have some more booze,' she said helpfully.

'There is not enough booze in the world.'

Marc didn't even crack a smile when Cassie nudged him playfully. 'I don't mind doing a lot of the heavy lifting. Maybe you can just talk-sing?' Another thought occurred to her. 'You do know how to do the Electric Slide, don't you? Like in the David Beckham documentary?'

He gave her a long, hard look. 'You're speaking. Words are coming out of your mouth but I haven't got a clue what you're banging on about.'

Oh yes, The Ick was imminent.

But first, Iris and Bill did a passable and very entertaining 'Anything You Can Do'. What they lacked in hitting the right notes in the right order, they made up for with hammy theatrics.

Then Davy kicked it solo as everyone agreed they didn't have the heart to wake up Heather. That was the official party line. It turned out that Davy was a bit of a dark horse, with a pleasing baritone that he used to great effect to serenade each of them in turn with a rendition of 'Fly Me to the Moon'.

The real star turn was Kwame. Cassie might have almost perfect pitch but Kwame was classically trained. He'd been a chorister, had done a degree in singing at the Royal College of Music and two years in the chorus at the English National Opera until he decided that he'd prefer to be well paid, rather than poor but singing his heart out every night.

His performance of 'I Dreamed a Dream' sent chills running down Cassie's spine. Even Digby chiming in occasionally with very pitchy harmonies couldn't ruin the magic. 'Oh my God,' Marc said faintly as Kwame hit and held the last exquisite note.

It was an impossible act to follow. Anita and Azad didn't even try but mugged their way through 'Don't Go Breaking My Heart' and Lucy and Russell attempted 'I Got You Babe', but abandoned it halfway through because they were laughing too hard to sing. Cassie tried to film them, but her giggles made her hands shake – the incongruity of their *Sound of Music* outfits and Lucy getting annoyed because Russell wasn't taking it seriously was too much. Then Cassie wasn't giggling any more and had to swallow down a sob as she carried on filming, not wanting to miss a second of her friends, arm in arm, heads touching as they sang the final refrain.

Another memory for the vaults . . .

'I swear, Cass, if you get me out of this, I'll give you anything you want,' Marc muttered in her ear, as Kwame beckoned them to the microphones with an evil smile. 'I'll let you keep my credit card. Buy you a yacht . . .'

'I don't have any use for a yacht.' Cassie got to her feet as Marc shrank back on the sofa. 'Don't be such a baby. And don't forget the Electric Slide.' She yanked him up with a groan.

'You're going to pay for this,' he said softly as they took the mics from Kwame, but he made it sound more like a promise than a threat.

As the opening notes rang out, Cassie was already grooving. Then she stopped and glared at Marc as he missed his cue.

'You have to sing Kenny's part,' she snapped at him.

He came in late and off key until it was time for them to sing together. The only way to get Marc to sing on cue was to pinch his arm and he was absolutely harshing Cassie's mellow, which didn't return until she got to sing the second verse solo.

It was one of her favourite songs. At every wedding she'd ever been to, and Cassie had been to a lot of weddings, the night usually ended with a big circle of guests surrounding the bride and groom as they all sang 'Islands in the Stream'. Even Marc couldn't ruin that.

Fortunately by the second chorus, he'd loosened up a bit or got the hang of where he was meant to come in. Although it could have been Cassie's eyes promising him untold pain.

He talk-sang rather than sang, but by the end, he was even following Cassie's lead as she bumped her hips against his, arms aloft. It was more of an Electric Shuffle than the Electric Slide, but Marc had made the effort, which was all Cassie wanted. By the last chorus, he was even smiling and leaning in close as they kind of harmonised with each other.

She'd never thought of Marc as cute but he was being cute, his grin endearing, his eyes on her, as they sang the closing notes.

The Ick, alas, was nowhere to be found.

Cassie took a bow to the smattering of applause and was just about to put Marc out of his misery and pull him back to their sofa, when Russell held out his hand.

'Not so fast,' he said. 'We're not done with you yet!'

'Russ, no . . .' Marc said, his arms round Cassie's waist as if she were a human shield.

Cassie took pity on him. 'Come on, hasn't Marc suffered enough?'

There was a chorus of 'no's, which Cassie didn't really mind. She was always up for a second song but Russell and Lucy had other plans.

'Dance for us,' Lucy called out, clapping her hands as the song from the *Pulp Fiction* twist contest, Chuck Berry's 'You Never Can Tell' started. 'Come on, dance!'

Everyone took up the chant. 'Dance! Dance! Dance!'

It was textbook bullying. Just as well that Cassie liked to dance almost as much as she liked to sing. Marc was standing still and frozen in the middle of the room.

'Do you know how to twist?' Cassie shouted over the music, as she swivelled on one hip. 'Just follow my lead.'

Marc didn't follow her lead. Not even when Cassie did one of her favourite moves, holding her nose and twisting right down to the floor, like she was going underwater. Or the most famous bit of the dance from the movie when Uma Thurman and John Travolta dragged their hands across their faces, fingers scissored.

'I can't do this,' Marc mouthed and Cassie shrugged help-lessly because the clapping and the chanting wasn't abating. 'But I can do *this*.'

This was suddenly taking Cassie in his arms and holding her close as he finally started to move.

'I've had nightmares that are quite similar to this, except I'm naked,' he said in her ear.

'You've had nightmares about me?' Cassie pouted.

'Those aren't nightmares and in those dreams, we're both naked,' he purred, his hand tightening on her hip.

Before Cassie could react because no, he did not just say that, Marc twirled her away from him.

Then she was back in his arms and they were dancing so close together that it felt too intimate, even with every-one watching. Then Marc twirled her again and again, until Cassie felt quite dizzy.

'Just hold me and dance,' she said when she was back in his arms, but the song was coming to an end and it was time for a big finish.

Cassie clutched on to Marc's arm, his shoulder, as he extravagantly dipped her, then held her like that and, despite the awkward angle, Cassie knew that she was safe. That he wasn't going to let her come to any harm. Not when he could swoop down and claim her lips as the music faded away and she couldn't hear anything except the pounding of her heart.

Then she was upright again, still holding on to Marc, who didn't seem inclined to let go of Cassie either. 'That's quite enough of that now,' he said sharply, which was at odds with the way he looked down at her. 'We're not performing monkeys.'

After that, predictably, the karaoke was the domain of the hardcore. Cassie, Lucy, Kwame and Iris singing showtunes until Cassie, who was really quite drunk by now, realised that she still hadn't sung the song she'd bagsied when she was writing the itinerary.

'We have to do "Cruel Summer",' she insisted as she scrolled through the catalogue. 'Why haven't they got "Cruel Summer"? What kind of two-bit karaoke system is this?'

'We could do "Shake It Off"?' Iris suggested but Cassie shook her head.

'But it's not Taylor's Version! This is a disaster.' She pulled out her phone. 'We'll sing along to "All Too Well" instead. All ten minutes and thirteen seconds of it.'

It was the quickest way to clear the room. As the four of them, drunk and swaying, gathered around Cassie's phone, everyone else decided to head back outside.

It was a wise decision because there was a lot of very loud singing. A lot of passion when they got to the bridge. If Cassie hadn't been holding her phone with one hand, then she'd definitely have done a double fist of pure emotion.

Wrung out from their performance, the four of them joined the others on the terrace where there was more champagne. More singing. A heated debate was raging as to whether they should fire up the barbecue again as there were a lot of sausages left and singing had made everyone ravenous, when Heather emerged from the house.

She was wobbling from side to side because she was still drunk. How on earth could she *still* be drunk?

'Hello, fuckers!' she shouted, which got everyone's attention. 'I want to sing a song too.'

'Oh my God,' Lucy muttered under her breath. She and Cassie were sitting on the low wall that divided the terrace from the rest of the garden.

Cassie patted her hand. 'I should probably have checked on her. Maybe if we ignore her?'

'That never, ever works. Why is she so determined to spoil everything?' Lucy looked imploringly at Davy, who was standing nearby with a bottle of beer and what looked like zero fucks. 'Davy, please . . .'

'All right,' he muttered, putting down his bottle with a beleaguered air. 'Now, now, Heatherette. You've had a few too many sherbets . . .'

'Oh fuck off, Davy!' Heather started humming 'The Stripper' and nearly fell over as she attempted a bump and grind. 'Look! I've still got it.'

She snatched off her wig and threw it at her advancing husband.

'Come on, old girl, let's get you to bed,' he said, like he'd had a lot of practice dealing with drunk Heather and being sworn at.

'I'm not going to bed. I'm going to show everyone that I'm still a powerful and sexual woman.' Another bump and grind had Heather putting all her weight on her bad ankle.

It seemed to happen in slow motion. Heather's shriek of pain, the way she went down like a sack of spuds, then burst into tears.

'This is the worst fucking party I've ever been to,' she sobbed. 'I wish we'd never come. My real friends are much more fun.'

Lucy buried her face in Cassie's shoulder, the force of her own sobs shaking her body. 'I wish she'd never come too.'

'She's going to feel bloody awful in the morning,' Davy said cheerfully as he and Azad got Heather to her feet and led her, still crying, from the terrace.

There was a hushed silence now, everyone embarrassed and not quite sure what to do. Cassie put her arms around Lucy and stroked her back as her friend quietly wept. Yes, Heather was an absolute menace and had ruined Lucy's hen weekend, Joni's fifth birthday and Lucy and Russell's tenth anniversary, but Cassie knew what these tears were really about.

'I can't bear it, Cass,' Lucy whispered. 'I don't know how to get through each day when my heart is fucking broken.'

Cassie rocked her like a small child. 'I'm so sorry. It's so unfair.'

Digby sat down on Lucy's other side and leaned against her, his hand on her shoulder. Digby was the person who'd known Lucy the longest and although he didn't know the real reason for Lucy weeping so desperately, his presence seemed to calm her.

'It's not like you to be a maudlin drunk,' he murmured.

Lucy shuddered a couple of times, then sat up straight. 'Sorry.'

'Nothing to apologise for,' Digby said, brushing Lucy's page-boy Maria von Trapp wig back from her tear-streaked face.

Then Iris was kneeling in front of Lucy with some damp kitchen roll and Cassie shuffled along the wall to make room for Russell.

Even when Kwame and Davy returned and opened two more bottles of champagne, the mood was subdued. Subdued but in ridiculous fancy dress.

Cassie was relieved to see Marc walking towards her from the other end of the terrace. With their unofficial leaders, Lucy and Russell, out of action, sitting quietly with their arms around each other, Marc was the most grown-up person there. The designated adult.

He sat down next to Cassie and bent down to take off his shoes, then this socks. Which was random. And really weird. 'We need to change the mood,' he murmured for her ears alone.

It was a nice thought. 'I think the only thing that will change the vibe is a direct hit from an overhead missile.'

'Do you trust me?' Marc asked, which was a loaded question.

Cassie decided to go with a half-truth. 'Maybe.'

Marc let that register. Then he sighed as he shrugged off his suit jacket. 'I was hoping for more enthusiasm but maybe will have to do. Take off your shoes.'

She was intrigued to know where Marc was going with all this cryptic vagueness. She toed off her ballet flats and when Marc stood up and offered her his hand, Cassie let him pull her up.

He didn't give her any time for doubt, but started running, so Cassie had to run too even though they seemed to be heading straight for the swimming pool.

Correction, they were jumping *into* the swimming pool. Cassie screamed, half in shocked delight and half in horror because she really didn't want to get her wig, and the hair underneath the wig, wet.

Her scream when they actually hit the water, which felt cold rather than heated to a temperate however many degrees, was even louder. They'd gone in at the deep end and Cassie was completely submerged, her feet scraping the bottom of the pool, until Marc, still holding her hand, pulled her spluttering to the surface.

'What the fuck, Marc?' Cassie gasped and he let go of her hand to smooth his wet hair back. He looked supremely pleased with himself. Cassie couldn't let him get away with that. She brought her arms down hard to splash him in his stupid handsome face but he grinned and splashed her right back.

'Are you two completely mad?' Kwame was standing at the edge of the pool and already toeing off his trainers. 'And room for a little one?'

Kwame didn't jump but cannonballed into the pool, sending an arc of water through the air, which splashed the others who had followed him and were now taking off their shoes and generally seemed delighted by the distraction.

Digby was next, Anita, Bill and then, accompanied by wolf whistles and whooping, Azad took off his trousers and jacket. 'It's my best suit. It's my only suit!'

He jumped in and was promptly pushed under the water by his loving wife.

Iris was hesitant, despite her love of wild swimming – and swimming didn't come much wilder than this. 'I love the gay abandon, guys, but I'm wearing vintage,' she said. 'You have to respect the vintage.'

'Off! Off! Off!' Cassie shouted.

'Oh well, if you insist.' She very carefully took off the dress, draped it on a pool chair, did a little shimmy in her slip and finally jumped in.

Only Lucy and Russell were left on the edge, both of them hesitant. They shared an anxious glance, which made Cassie wonder if this had actually been a really bad idea. Then Marc swam up behind Cassie and put his arms around her waist, holding her up as they both trod water.

'Come on!' he shouted encouragingly.

'Yes! Last one in is a rotten egg!' Digby clapped his hands. 'Don't be such pussies!'

The look that Lucy and Russell now shared was conspiratorial. Then they didn't even take off their footwear, but jumped in holding hands.

An impromptu singalong to 'Sweet Caroline' was inevitable, then 'Can't Take My Eyes Off You'. Yes, it was incredibly cheesy but lovely too, even with the smell of chlorine and the chafing of wet clothes.

A fitting end to the evening's activities. To go out with a splash and a 'na na na na na na na na na' rather than a whimper.

Then it was time to squelch back to their rooms.

27

Cassie could feel Marc's eyes on her as she went up the stairs ahead of him.

Despite all the pep talks she'd given herself throughout the day, as soon as Marc shut the door behind him, Cassie knew they were going to have sex.

Knew it because she felt like she might die if they didn't.

She paused on her way to the bathroom. 'I need a shower,' she said, her eyes on Marc, who looked like he had a fever. He was breathing hard, his face flushed as he watched Cassie unbutton her shirt. Her skin was already so sensitised that she wanted to scream at the drag of wet cotton across it. 'If you . . . I mean . . . you can come too if you like.'

Cassie barely had time to step under the spray in the walk-in shower before Marc joined her. She briefly wondered if this might be too awkward, too much too soon. Being naked together, showering together, but the doubts flew right out of her mind in the time it took Mark to push her against the wall so she had the cold tiles against her front and him hot and hard behind her.

She expected him to turn her around then and kiss her just the right side of forceful, but he did something much better. He picked up Cassie's bottle of shampoo from the recessed shelf and when he was sure that her hair was wet, he began to rub in the shampoo. Massaging her scalp with fingers that didn't miss a spot, then rinsing until her hair squeaked.

'Conditioner?' he asked because he was a man of the world.

'Just the ends,' Cassie said, her back still to him.

Marc's touch was gentle as he separated out the strands until he was sure that the conditioner had been rinsed out. Then he gathered her hair up in a loose ponytail, wound it around his fist and tugged hard. It made Cassie's knees weak and she had to put her hands flat against the wall.

'Spread your legs,' he whispered in her ear, biting down on the lobe. His hand drifted to her pussy, which was as wet as the rest of her. 'This needs some attention too.'

Cassie couldn't bear it any longer. She wriggled around in his arms so she could touch him too, her hands moulding to the damp planes of his chest. 'I can think of something else that needs attention.'

Marc's cock was already hard against her belly. When she dragged his head down for a kiss, she could feel it quiver between them. Cassie put her hands on his shoulders and thought he'd hoist her up in his arms, slam her back against the wall, take her like that, but he shook his head, even though she hadn't yet run her plans by him.

'That's not going to happen,' he said sharply.

It was one of the most confusing rejections Cassie had ever had. Both of them naked, his erection prodding at her but . . . 'You don't want to have sex with me?'

'I very much want to have sex with you, but not in a shower,' Marc said, leaning down to steal another kiss. 'One of those things that sounds good in theory. In reality, too slippery.'

'Slippery is good,' Cassie said, as she rubbed shower gel on her breasts. Not because they needed a good clean but she liked the way Marc went immediately non-verbal and moistened his lips with a flash of tongue.

'I prefer a little friction myself,' he said, once Cassie had moved on to washing her arms. 'But if you like slippery, I'm sure we can come up with something.'

'Something's already up,' Cassie pointed out, grazing the tip of his cock with one soapy hand.

'Enough of the double entendres. It's like sharing a shower with Davy, which is one hell of a buzzkill.' Marc turned her around again, so she couldn't put her hands on him any more. 'I'm sure you're clean enough.'

Cassie wanted to say something about getting very dirty but fair warning, she really didn't want to kill the pleasing buzz, which was making her nerve endings sing. 'I'm done here. Do you have any objections to having sex on the bed?'

'No objections at all,' he said with a half-smile. 'Let's pick up where we left things last night. Go and lie on the bed, eyes closed, legs spread, and wait for me.'

Someone telling Cassie what to do, especially when that someone was an older white man with a public-school accent, made her hackles rise. Like Koita when he saw the two chihuahuas that lived further down the crescent.

But in this context, and with the way that Marc tugged on her hair again as she brushed past him, smiling when it made her gasp, being told exactly what to do was unbearably, suddenly-quite-hard-to-breathe hot.

She wrapped herself in a thick white towel, left the bathroom and walked over to the bed, her feet leaving damp tracks on the plush carpet. She switched off the big light – this was absolutely not a big light moment – and turned on the lamps on either side of the bed. Then, as instructed, Cassie lay down, took a deep breath to give herself some courage, untucked the towel and parted her thighs.

Her body was warm from the shower and the change in temperature to the still air of the room instantly made her nipples pucker, her skin feel tight, even as Cassie felt as if she was coming to a slow simmer.

She heard the shower turn off, her ears straining for the sound of his movements, for the bathroom door to open, the soft thud of his footsteps bringing Marc closer to her, but there was nothing.

Just the anticipation. The mere thought of what Marc was going to do made Cassie tilt her hips, take deep, shuddering breaths, and she knew that if she put her hand between her legs, she'd be slick with need.

Maybe she was just impatient but she was sure that Marc was making her wait much longer than was strictly necessary.

Then the bathroom door opened. Cassie was lying widthways across the bed so as soon as Marc stepped out, he'd be looking directly at the pulsing damp heart of her.

'Oh God, what a beautiful sight you are,' he murmured as if he was talking to himself.

Her eyes still tightly shut, Cassie sensed the displacement of air as he stalked closer to her. Then he stopped and she was sure she could feel the heat coming off him, his eyes taking in every damp, pliant inch of her.

She sucked in a gasp when he suddenly took hold of her ankles and slowly and deliberately pulled her to the edge of the bed. Then he parted her legs even further and she felt him lean down to run the tip of a finger between the lips of her pussy, to delve, then dip into her.

He hummed slightly when he felt how wet she was. But when Cassie arched her hips again to get more than that light touch, he took his hand away. She opened her eyes to see him suck the finger into his mouth, a hint of teeth, another flash of tongue.

'I can't wait much longer,' Cassie admitted with an edge of desperation. 'I thought you'd be on your knees by now.'

'I didn't tell you to open your eyes,' Marc said sternly, the sternness doing as much for her as the heat of his gaze, the anticipation of what was to come. 'Maybe I should make you wait a bit more.'

She pouted. 'Why would you do that? That's just mean.'

Marc's smile was positively feral. 'When you know that you're about to get exactly what you want, then it doesn't hurt to savour the anticipation.' Just as Cassie was about to protest in the strongest possible terms, he did drop to his knees, dragging her closer still so she could drape her legs over his shoulders.

Then he got straight to business and took Cassie right back to where she'd been over twenty-four hours earlier. One finger inside her, then two, his mouth sucking hard on her clit. It didn't take any time at all before Cassie was gasping and grinding against his mouth. She couldn't remember the last time she'd come so quickly.

She barely had ten seconds to bask in the afterglow before Marc pulled her down so they were both on the floor, Cassie on top of him as she kissed the taste of herself from his mouth. Somehow the towel she'd been lying on was caught between them, so she lifted herself up, Marc groaning as her pelvis ground against him, tugged it free and threw it behind her.

And there they were. Both of them naked. Nothing and nowhere to hide.

'Look at you,' he murmured, his tone and his gaze reverent. 'Still so fucking sexy. All this time, Cass, and I still think about how you felt, how you looked, how you tasted. Your mouth, your breasts, your cunt.'

'I never think about you,' Cassie said, as she leaned forward so her breasts were brushing his face, but when Marc tried to mouth one, she pulled away.

'You never think about me?' He sounded . . . not peeved. Maybe a little offended.

Cassie shook her head as she moved back and straddled his thighs. Then she rubbed the back of her hand against his cock. He was so hard that it had to hurt. 'Not once have I thought about all those pretty things you said to me in French,' she said, relishing the way his dick throbbed at her words. 'About how you told me exactly what to do when you fucked my throat. I wonder if you still taste the same.'

Then she bent her head and took his cock in her mouth. She could still remember what he'd taught her. She'd picked up a few new tricks since then too.

She could tell that he was trying to keep still and when his hands crept up to tangle in her hair, he didn't push her head down. To reward him for learning some manners, Cassie took him as deep as she could, gagging a little but she didn't mind that and Marc certainly didn't. Because every time she spluttered, his cock jerked in approval and soon he had her hair clutched in a loose ponytail so he could see exactly what she looked like as she sucked him off, her mouth stretched tight around his dick.

When Marc threw his head back and his grip on her hair became more frantic, Cassie pulled her mouth free and tightened her grip on the base of his shaft. 'Don't you dare,' she hissed, because he wasn't going to come in her mouth, not when she wanted to lift herself up, then sink slowly down on his cock.

Cassie could feel him pulsing against the walls of her pussy and, like him, now that she'd got exactly what she wanted, she wanted to savour it. To draw out the moment. Marc tried to grab her hips to get her to move so he could control the pace – he still loved to be in control – but Cassie pinned his arms above his head, both of them panting as she took him in a little deeper.

They both knew that he could easily free himself if he wanted to, but it seemed like he didn't want to. His hands flexed in her grip as he watched her through heavy-lidded eyes.

Cassie forced herself to go as slow as thick honey dripping off a spoon, relishing every single groan she wrenched out of him as she squeezed around his cock again and again because she'd done so much bloody yoga in the last sixteen years.

Then, when she couldn't bear it any longer because tormenting Marc was just tormenting herself, Cassie leaned forward so she could get some friction on her clit. Then she was moving faster and faster and he was looking up at her like she was a goddess or something.

'*Tu es si belle. Ta chatte est si bonne. Je veux que tu jouisses sur ma bite.*' Cassie still didn't know what he was saying but she knew it was something filthy and then she was coming even harder than she'd done a few minutes before. Arching her back and tossing her head and it was only the bruising grip of his hands on her hips that kept him inside her.

Because Marc was still hard, and biting his lip to stop himself from coming even as her walls kept fluttering around him.

'Can you take one more?' he asked.

What he was asking was quite impossible. She wasn't twenty-one any more but she found herself nodding. 'Can you give me one more?'

He pulled out of her and had her on her back so quickly that Cassie could only blink up at him as he lowered his head to suck one aching nipple into the moist heat of his mouth, his fingers tugging at its twin.

'I don't actually need any more foreplay,' Cassie said, spreading her legs.

'Good.' He was back deep inside her with one strong thrust.

Neither of them were going to last long. Not when Marc was fucking her hard and fast and Cassie had one hand on her clit, the other hand digging into his back.

She wanted this to last, wanted a few more X-rated memories that she wouldn't forget, but she was coming far too quickly again and then Marc pulled out and it took just a couple of strokes of his hand before he painted her belly with sticky white ribbons of cum.

He rolled off her and they both lay there on their backs, staring up at the ceiling, breathing hard, not touching until Marc took Cassie's hand. She threaded her fingers through his and they stayed like that. Cassie knew that she'd suffer for this tomorrow with aching muscles, carpet burns and a metric ton of regret but for now, she was perfectly content.

28

Cassie had never even imagined that she would have sex with Marc again.

She certainly would never have entertained the idea that the aftermath of the sex would be so . . . civilised.

They got up from the floor, wincing as aches in their sixteen-years-older bodies made themselves known. Cassie retrieved her towel and tucked it around her again as she hurried to the bathroom.

'I'm just going to . . .' It wasn't necessary to finish the sentence, just shut the door behind her.

Then she had another shower. Washing all traces of Marc from her skin and when she emerged in the same black lace-edged camisole and sleep shorts as the previous night, this time he gave her an appreciative look.

If Cassie had been a more forgiving woman, maybe she wouldn't have pretended to be shocked to see Marc sitting on the edge of the bed in boxer trunks.

But she was someone who still bore a grudge so she did a double take, hand on her heart. 'Wow! You're still here,' she gasped. 'That's unexpected.'

'I guess I deserve that,' he said evenly, although Cassie liked to think that he looked maybe a little ashamed. 'Do you feel better for getting that out of your system?'

'Not sure.' After everything that had happened between them in the last few hours, it felt like a cheap shot. Had it made things awkward again? Or maybe it was the sex that had made things awkward.

But when Marc came out of the bathroom to find Cassie already in bed, he seemed relaxed and shot her an easy smile. As soon as he got into bed too, under the covers this time, he curled himself around her and that felt . . . nice. Very, very nice.

The energy between them was still so intense that Cassie regretted her earlier words. She didn't want to sever this connection. Not now. Not when he was running his fingers through her still damp hair.

'I can't even feel happy for five minutes without remembering that some day soon, Russell won't be here. Then the happiness disappears,' Marc suddenly said, his breath ghosting across the back of her neck.

That wasn't why she shivered.

'I feel like all the colour will be gone from the world,' Cassie said. She wasn't usually so articulate or poetic, but when she was with Russell, it was like being enveloped in a glow of golden energy. 'I try to tell myself that he'll live on in our memories but Russell . . . he's just one of those people who's *so* good at living.'

'People will say he lived life fully but that's not much of a comfort.' Marc tucked his arm around Cassie's waist. 'It's just a meaningless platitude.'

'But if you look at what Russell's going to leave behind, it's a lot more than most people achieve,' Cassie said, because she'd been trying to take some comfort from what Russell's

legacy would be. 'His work: the books and the TV pro-
grammes and the podcasts. He left his mark on the world.
And I see so much of Russell in Fleur and Joni, so that's
some kind of comfort too.'

'It just seems so unfair that some people live to a hundred
and some people die very young or in the absolute prime of
their lives,' Marc sighed. 'Does that sound too fanciful?'

'Not at all. My first job was at a funeral director's and
I had those same feelings all the time. It also makes you
think about your own mortality.' This was the kind of conversation that you could only have in the dark. It was the
conversation that Cassie had been desperate to have ever
since she'd found out about Russell's diagnosis but she'd
never imagined that Marc would be her confidante. 'If I die
tomorrow . . .'

'You are not going to die tomorrow.' Marc's loose embrace
tightened.

'Hopefully I'm not but you just don't know. Lucy and I
have a friend, Esme, from our *Skirt* days. She was at a hen
party, had an accident while she was getting out of a taxi and
a week later, she was having brain surgery.'

'Did your friend die?'

'No, except she can't make a fist with her left hand any
more,' Cassie mused. 'But her whole life changed in the split
second it took one angry cyclist to come out of nowhere and
knock her to the ground. People die all the time. Without
warning.'

Marc kissed the delicate patch of skin just below her ear.
'You are *not* going to die anytime soon. You're going to live
to be a very old, very imperious lady.'

'I'd love that,' Cassie said wistfully, though she couldn't imagine a time when she'd finally have zero fucks to give. That the fuck well would have truly run dry. 'But *if* I did die quite soon, then I'd have absolutely nothing to show for it.' It was strange saying the words out loud, having thought them for so long. 'I don't have a partner and no prospects on the horizon, which means I'm probably not going to have kids . . .'

'Do you want children?'

'Maybe. Maybe not. But I want that to be my own decision. Not a decision forced on me by circumstance and the absolute fuckwits I get matched with on the apps.'

Cassie felt rather than heard the low rumble of Marc's laughter. 'I hate the apps.'

'You're on the apps?' If Marc was on the apps and they'd never been matched even when they'd been in the same room, then that was proof of what Cassie knew for certain: they were absolutely incompatible, even if she was currently in his arms.

Unless Marc was only on that special app for very rich and/or very famous people.

'All I really want is to be someone's favourite person. It shouldn't be that hard.'

Marc pressed a kiss to Cassie's shoulder. 'It really shouldn't.'

'But it is, so I'm a certified spinster of the parish. I've never been anywhere. I've never done anything.' She huffed in frustration at her sad little life. 'The one thing I've ever achieved, starting my own business, I managed to fuck up.'

'You didn't fuck it up,' Marc said, lightly pinching Cassie's hip in admonishment. 'The pandemic happened. I know I'm going to sound like some mawkish, inspirational quote on Instagram accompanied by a picture of a tree or a waterfall, but you've achieved the most important thing in life. You love and you're loved. You've got that village, Cass.'

'You're loved too,' Cassie said immediately, reflexively.

'It's sweet that you think that but no, not really.' Marc said it lightly as if he weren't bothered at all, because he always talked a good game.

Cassie tried hard to think of who might love Marc – the caring, generous, strangely perceptive Marc, not the iconoclastic disruptor with a perma-sneer. 'Lucy and Russell?'

'Thank God for Lucy and Russell,' Marc said.

'Did you love your wife?' As soon as the words were out there in the world, Cassie wished that they weren't.

There was a silence that dragged on and was about two seconds away from becoming excruciating instead of merely awkward, when Marc said, 'I wanted to. I mean, I really fucking tried.'

'And did she love you?' Cassie already knew the answer but maybe she'd been wrong. Maybe those five minutes in the guest bathroom of his Battersea penthouse apartment with the wraparound views had just been Camille playing a part, rather than baring her soul to three people she didn't know.

'I'm not stupid. I knew that she was marrying me for my money,' he said slowly. 'But I hoped that wasn't the only reason. It turned out that it was. Her old flame or new husband, whatever you want to call him, has an art gallery in his one-hundred-room chateau just off the Bois de Boulogne. I can't compete with that.'

'Why would you want to? I mean, it's so tacky.' Cassie
snorted even though someone who loved absolutely irredeemable reality TV shows and was secretly partial to a Bombay
Bad Boy Pot Noodle wasn't the best judge of what was tacky
or not. It had to be painful for Marc to dredge this up, but
there was one last thing that Cassie had to know. 'Were you
sad when it ended?'

Marc rolled onto his back so Cassie felt suddenly bereft
and quite cold without the weight and heat of him pressed
against her. She'd probably gone too far with the deeply personal and invasive questions.

'Sad. Angry. Full of doubt, which I compounded by making a couple of bad business decisions and losing a lot of
money.'

Cassie 'hmm'ed sympathetically. She could relate to that.
She was sure that while she'd lost thousands, Marc could well
have lost millions. Still, it was all relative.

'Losing the money didn't really matter. That wasn't
important.' Spoken like someone who still had an obscene
amount of money. Marc rested his hand on Cassie's belly
because he still had her unspoken permission to touch her
where he wanted. 'But losing someone who I really tried to
love . . . The failure to love and be loved back, it was fucking
devastating.'

She'd never heard Marc sound so raw, so honest. Maybe
now was the time to talk about what had happened sixteen
years ago and see if they could move past it.

'I know that we're hardly even friends, more like sworn
enemies, but I'm so sorry that happened to you. You didn't
deserve that,' Cassie said as Marc rolled over again so his

back was to her. She reached out her hand in a comforting gesture but her fingers had barely grazed his skin when he flinched away from her touch.

'It's late. Instead of all these true confessions, we should try and get some sleep.'

Cassie retreated to her side of the bed and rolled herself up in the duvet. She felt stung by his sudden withdrawal, though it shouldn't have come as a surprise. They *were* sworn enemies, even though they'd currently suspended hostilities. Despite the fact they couldn't keep their hands off each other, despite the fact that they were already grieving for someone they both loved very much, too much had happened in the past for them to ever really be at peace with each other.

God, he'd never once apologised or even come close to saying sorry and just like that . . . Cassie was angry with Marc all over again. If only she could be one of those people who let things go, instead of poking and prodding so the wound never really healed.

Next to her, Marc was silent. He might have been asleep or, like Cassie, he might have been wide awake and ready for a long night of staring up at the ceiling for hours.

LUCY'S NAUGHTY FORTY BIRTHDAY WEEKEND EXTRAVAGANZA!

ITINERARY

SUNDAY

I'm aware that it's been a pretty action-packed weekend so you'll be pleased to know that today is all about the chill.

10.00 a.m.-ish Breakfast is a help-yourself kind of deal. Then the morning is your own (please see enclosed information sheet for details of some lovely local walks).

3.00 p.m. Sunday roast, courtesy of Digby and Kwame who'll have been slaving away for hours (yes, Iris, they're doing a veggie option too).

5.00 p.m. A screening of one of Lucy's favourite films, title tbc (she's promised that it won't be *The Sound of Music*).

Evening: Fingers crossed we'll have a mountain of leftovers to snack on, booze still to be drunk and we can generally just hang out in a freeform, organic way.

29

When Cassie woke up, she was alone and disorientated for a few blissfully ignorant moments, then it all came rushing back like a tidal wave of icy, dirty water.

She'd drunk too much. Her head felt as if it was stuffed full of cotton-wool balls and she was hideously dry-mouthed. But the hangover from too much champagne, then switching to red wine at some point in the evening, was nothing to the emotional hangover. Heather. Lucy. The fighting. The tears.

But mostly, those two deep conversations with Marc. She hadn't just laid her soul bare, she'd laid her body bare too. Despite all the good reasons not to, she'd had sex with Marc.

Fuck me once, shame on you. Fuck me twice, shame on me.

Now she was sore and aching and she couldn't even blame it on all the booze. She'd been on her knees for ages last night as she'd ridden Marc slowly, then he'd fucked her into the floor. Cassie was too old to be fucked into the floor. No wonder her back was killing her.

While Cassie was taking this scenic tour of all of yesterday's most horrific highlights, she couldn't forget the way Marc had recoiled from her touch once the afterglow had worn off. He might not have disappeared while she was cleaning her teeth, but he'd definitely reverted to type.

It was just about sex for him. But it was so much more than that for Cassie because of her stupid, fallible heart. No matter how much she thought she'd grown as a person, underneath the semi-sophisticated surface that had been buffeted and made glossy by all those premium beauty products, she was still that naïve, hopeful twenty-one-year-old that had been seduced then discarded. Even after sixteen years of the condescending, knowing smirk on Marc's face when he looked her way, all he had to do was throw her a few small crumbs of comfort and off came her knickers again.

Worse than that, Cassie had told him things, including her most secret fears, and now she wished that she could take them all back.

Cassie couldn't bear to replay her latest idiocies over and over again. A brief look at her phone to discover it was nearly ten o'clock had her stumbling out of bed with several muttered swear words. It was amazing how late you could sleep when you'd had too much to drink, and three orgasms. She really had to stop thinking about the sex except when she was telling Marc that they would no longer be having it. It was a one off-thing. Never to be repeated.

When Cassie emerged from a very perfunctory and very quick shower – she didn't want Marc to come back to the room and find her naked and think she was raring for another go – she gave herself a long, hard look in the mirror.

Her reflection, ashen and red-eyed, frowned back at her. She'd gone to bed with her hair damp and now it was frizzy and sticking up in odd and random places. Her head was too tender to even contemplate her usual bad-hair-day plaits, so she settled for a loose ponytail.

When she drew back the curtains it was to a day that was as grey as her mood. The sky bulged with the promise of rain to come. It felt as if summer was now over and a cold, damp autumn had already arrived.

As she came downstairs, in a clean pair of joggers and her beloved oversized hoodie, the house was quiet and still, although there were tempting aromas of bacon and coffee. Cassie followed her nose to the kitchen where Lucy was pouring boiling water into a mug.

'Great timing. Do you want a coffee?'

'Yes please.' The words felt lumpy in Cassie's mouth. She hauled herself up on a stool, then slumped over the kitchen island. 'I can't believe I slept so late.'

'Marc said not to wake you.' Lucy held up the jar of instant coffee. 'He also gave me very detailed instructions for the coffee machine, which I've already forgotten. Your usual?'

Lucy knew exactly how Cassie liked her coffee. Two teaspoons of coffee. Then one third semi-skimmed milk to two thirds boiling water.

'Nectar of the gods.' Cassie closed her eyes as she took the first appreciative sip. 'Has he gone for a run?'

'Marc? Yes. I don't know how he can run with a sore head,' Lucy said as she opened the fridge.

So at least this time, although technically he'd done a runner again, he was planning to come back. 'He's got a sore head?'

'Hangover or sleep-deprived or both.' Lucy closed the fridge door and turned to Cassie with her wickedest smile. 'I can't imagine why he'd be sleep-deprived but Iris said you were both being quite *loud* last night.'

Hands that were hot from holding a mug of coffee didn't do much to cool down Cassie's face. 'Just don't,' she warned. 'And no, I won't be taking any questions at this time.' She held up a warning finger as Lucy opened her mouth. 'Or at any other time. Where is everyone?'

'Iris and Bill have taken their breakfast back to bed, and Anita and Az and Digby and Kwame have gone into Brighton for brunch, then to a supermarket. They need some fancy extra ingredients for lunch today and somehow we've run out of food. There are hardly any crisps left,' she added with a real note of panic to her voice.

'And I'm here,' said a very small voice from behind Cassie, who swivelled round on the stool to see Heather curled into a tiny ball in the corner of the nearest sofa. She was still wearing her pyjamas and looked even rougher than Cassie felt. 'But not for long.'

Cassie waited for an apology for the way Heather had behaved the previous night, or even a thank you for making sure that she didn't choke on her own vomit, but she'd have a bloody long wait. Whatever. Even though she never failed to surprise Cassie with just how self-involved and gaslighty she could be, Cassie was used to Heather after all this time.

'Oh, I didn't see you there,' Cassie said breezily.

'For now,' Heather insisted.

Cassie and Lucy managed to roll their eyes in near perfect unison. 'Heather and Davy have to go home early. Some kind of domestic emergency, apparently,' Lucy explained. 'Davy is packing.'

'I don't know why you're saying it like that, as if it's just an excuse,' Heather said in an injured tone. 'It's hardly my fault that the washing machine's leaking.'

'I thought you said it was the boiler!' Lucy snapped back.

'That does sound like a pain. Hopefully if there's any damage, your insurance will sort it out,' Cassie said soothingly because she couldn't bear to be witness to another argument between the two of them and, quite frankly, Heather and Davy going home early was the best news she'd had in ages. Cassie was even tempted to help them pack.

There was no need for such drastic action. 'OK, car's loaded up. Ah, ladies.' Davy stuck his head round the arch at the other end of the long room. 'We'll be off now. Unless . . . did you want to get dressed?'

Heather uncurled herself and glared at her husband. 'If I'd wanted to get dressed, I'd have got dressed. These are silk. It's not like I'm wearing some ratty pyjamas and an old dressing gown. No offence, Cassie.'

'None taken,' Cassie said, as she and Lucy shared another incredulous look at the sheer nerve. Cassie was pretty sure that Heather had never seen her in ratty pyjamas and an old dressing gown, but she let the diss go unchecked. Just sign her up for a sainthood.

To make sure that Heather was actually leaving the premises, Cassie and Lucy waved them off from the front steps, then walked back into the house arm in arm.

'You weren't tempted to tell her about Russell?' Cassie asked softly.

Lucy shook her head. 'No. Because she'd find a way to make it all about her, probably by telling as many people as possible.' She assumed a haughty face. 'Oh, it just slipped out and they were going to know eventually. God, Lucy, why are you being like this?'

Even without Lucy's uncanny impersonation, Cassie could imagine it only too well. 'Is Russell all right after yesterday? It was quite full-on.'

'He's fine. Tired. I made him take a sleeping pill last night.'

They were back in their previous positions, Cassie on her stool, Lucy standing on the other side of the kitchen island. Cassie reached across the marble worktop to take her friend's hand. 'And how are you?'

'I'm fine,' Lucy was quick to say.

'Really?'

'On the surface I'm fine but my heart, Cass . . . my heart is very, very heavy,' Lucy said in her squeaky, gravelly voice.

'You never have to pretend that you're fine with me. You can be as unfine as you need to be.'

'I know.'

Neither of them said anything but they held hands until Cassie's stomach, barely satisfied with a mug of coffee, rumbled in protest.

Lucy broke free with a laugh. 'You need feeding.'

Cassie rubbed her tummy. 'Is there anything left to eat? I feel like all I've done since I got here is stuff my face.'

'I can do you an egg mcmuffin/French toast hybrid with one rasher of bacon, one egg, a stale croissant and a shit ton of butter.' Lucy opened the fridge again. 'And some tomato on the side to be healthy.'

'That might keep me going until Digby and Kwame's Sunday roast. Because we both know that when they said it will be ready by three . . .'

'We'll be lucky if we sit down to eat at five . . .'

'I thought six,' Cassie grinned. 'Care to place a small bet?'

Cassie wolfed down her delicious breakfast and had another mug of coffee while they FaceTimed the girls and Ryan who were planning to go out for bubble tea, then spend the day binging a Netflix K-drama. A very pale Iris and an even paler Bill came down with their breakfast plates and said that they were going to drive to the Sussex Downs for some fresh air 'because Nurofen hasn't touched the sides of the hangover'.

Then Marc and Russell appeared like two apparitions on the terrace.

Even though she'd been expecting it, Cassie still gave a nervous start when Marc tapped on the patio door. As Lucy hurried to open it, Cassie assumed a neutral expression, bland as a bowl of unseasoned porridge.

'Good morning – or should that be good afternoon?' Russell sounded chipper but despite the sleeping pill, he looked tired. It could be the weak light from outside but there was a grey tinge to his face, and as Cassie went to hug him, he drew back a little. 'Gently, please.'

Cassie drew back too. 'I could pat you on the arm, if you'd prefer,' she said, trying to make light of it, but suddenly her heart felt very heavy too.

'A pat would be lovely and anyway, I don't want Marc offering to fight me for putting my hands on his woman,' Russell said, with a sly glance at Marc, which was more like the old Russell; the Russell that Cassie was already missing.

'Hardly,' Marc said. He was in his running gear, pink-cheeked and glowing. Compared to Russell, he was rude with good health. 'Cassie is very much her own woman and it wouldn't be a fair fight. We both know I've always been able to take you.' He smelled of the outdoors, of wet grass and sea salt, when he put a stiff arm round Cassie and brushed his lips against her cheek. Today Cassie couldn't find her motivation to play the other half of a blissfully happy couple. She held herself very still and made no attempt to lean into the kiss or the man, who gave her a curious look.

'What's wrong?' he hissed in her ear as Lucy and Russell's attention was on each other.

The limpness of Cassie's smile barely raised the corners of her lips. 'Nothing. I'm good,' she assured him.

Marc stepped away from her. Now his face was blank too. As if hiding your true feelings was a big trend for autumn. He ran a hand through his hair. 'I'm going to hit the shower and Russ, you can explain your ridiculous scheme to your wife and see what she thinks about it.'

Cassie inwardly sighed with relief as Marc headed out of the room and, glad of the distraction, turned to Russell, who took Lucy's hand and placed it over his heart.

'No. No. Whatever it is, the answer's no,' Lucy said as sharply as her voice allowed.

'But sweetheart, angel, my darling girl . . .' It was Russell at his most ingratiating. There hadn't been quite so many endearments but that was how he'd roped Cassie into organising this weekend in the first place.

Cassie slid down from the stool. 'I'll leave you two alone.'

Lucy's hand shot out to wrap around Cassie's wrist in a strong grip. 'Don't go anywhere. I have a feeling that I'm going to need back-up.'

'It's nothing bad. I slept well. I feel great,' Russell said but his exuberance was tattered at the edges. 'I want to go down to the beach.'

That didn't seem so dreadful. Lucy nodded as if she was thinking the same thing. 'Oh! OK! Yeah, we can go to the beach. I can drive us down to the village and where do we go from there, Cass?'

Cassie tried to remember what Lydia had said. 'I think there's a little path – it's not a long walk. I can look it up.'

'No, I want to go down to *this* beach.' Russell gestured to the garden outside the windows. 'I have so many happy childhood memories of the cove. And it's just down a few steps. It's not going to be too arduous.'

'I don't think you're remembering the steps too well,' Lucy said, sending a pleading look at Cassie. 'There's a lot of them and they're very narrow and very steep. Going down them was bad enough, but . . .'

'Going back up was really hard-going.' Cassie took her cue. 'Also, it looks like it's going to rain.'

'I'll take it slowly,' Russell insisted. 'The forecast says it's not going to rain for another couple of hours. We won't be that long.'

'I don't think it's a very good idea,' Lucy said, stroking Russell's cheek. 'You overdid it yesterday.'

'There's a bench at the bottom of the garden just before the cliff edge. Maybe you could look down at the cove?' Cassie suggested, but Russell wasn't having any of it.

'Let's be honest with each other: this is probably going to be my last chance to walk on a beach. Have a paddle, feel the sand between my toes. If that's the case, then I want it to be this beach.'

Yes, Russell was easy-going and affable but he was also one of the most determined people Cassie knew. His whole career was testimony to that. He was a person who made things happen, usually by getting other people to bend to his very charming will. Now he would not be swayed and Lucy, given the circumstances, let herself be convinced.

30

By the time Marc came back downstairs, Cassie had stress-drunk a third coffee and had a bad case of the jitters. Not just because she hated arguing with Russell but also at the sight of Marc in jeans and a soft black V-neck cashmere sweater over a white T-shirt, looking as stupidly handsome as ever. Then she thought of the difficult, confronting conversation that they absolutely had to have today, and her heart started properly thudding. She couldn't even blame it on an excess of caffeine.

'Have you managed to talk some sense into this fool?' Marc said, glancing at Lucy, who was biting her thumbnail, then Cassie, who wouldn't meet his eyes. 'No, of course you haven't.'

'It's fine,' Russell said airily. 'Christ, it's not like I'm an invalid.'

There were so many things that Cassie knew Lucy wanted to say. She wanted to say them too. Like, remember the night you spent in A&E because you couldn't breathe?

'We have a deal, Russ,' Lucy said, her voice vibrating with emotion. 'You are not taking off your shoes and socks and going for a little paddle.'

'Because it's going to rain and the sea will be absolutely baltic,' Cassie added, but Russell waved their concerns away.

'Yes, yes. So you keep saying.' He might have agreed in principle but Russell's mouth was set in an obstinate line. He looked just like Joni when she was intent on getting her own way.

Ten minutes later, they set off as if they were planning to scale a small but challenging mountain in treacherous conditions. Russell, protesting all the way, had been bundled into a thick jumper. Lucy had gone back to the cottage to get his puffer, while Cassie packed water, a banana and a chocolate bar in case Russell had a sudden sugar craving. She'd also found a waxed waterproof coat hanging up in the boot room and Marc had unearthed a deckchair from one of the outhouses.

'Ridiculous and so unnecessary,' Russell insisted as they made their way across the garden to the cliff steps.

Cassie was beginning to think that Russell was right and they were being overly dramatic. It was windy rather than breezy but the wind was at their backs, so descending the steep steps was a brisk business.

Once they were on the beach, Cassie hoped this wasn't going to take very long. It wasn't the benign, balmy scene it had been the day before. The sea was choppy and grey, and sharp gusts of wind rolled off the waves and scoured their faces.

Marc marched on ahead. He stopped a couple of metres away from the water's edge then wrestled with the deckchair until he had it open. 'Sit on that,' he ordered tersely. 'Cass and I will be huddling against the cliff face and trying not to get hypothermia.'

'It's not cold. It's just bracing,' Russell said, but a moment later, he was sinking gratefully into the deckchair.

It was hardly comfortable, sheltering at the foot of a bloody cliff and sitting on sand, which Cassie was sure would somehow manage to circumvent both her joggers and her knickers so that she'd be finding it in *crevices* for days.

It was also unbearably uncomfortable sitting next to Marc, who was gazing out at some point in the middle distance as if Cassie wasn't even there. Or wasn't worthy of his attention, anyway.

The only other thing to look at was Lucy and Russell. Lucy was sitting on the ground next to Russell's deckchair, her head resting on his thigh, his hand on her shoulder. Despite the wind, the frenetic waves, there was a stillness to the two of them.

Their love was palpable. A living, breathing thing. What Cassie and Marc were doing made a mockery of it.

Which made things easier.

'I'm not having sex with you again,' Cassie said, which wasn't how she'd planned to start this but it was as good a place as any.

Now she had the full weight of Marc's regard. 'I wasn't aware that I'd asked you to.'

It was his coldest, most cutting voice, which made things even simpler. 'Last night was a huge mistake,' Cassie persisted. 'Anyway, I know what you're thinking because I've been frozen out by you before.'

'Please enlighten me as to exactly what I'm thinking then,' Marc said tightly, his eyes as chilly as the sea.

'You needn't worry that I think we're now having the love affair of the century. Or that I'm going to make demands on you. I know what having sex with you means. It means absolutely nothing. Believe me, I learned that lesson the first time round.' It was easy, it turned out, to say these things, but much harder to ignore the small but powerful part of Cassie that wished they *were* having the love affair of the century. In another world. In another time.

'Why do you have to keep bringing up things that happened years ago?' Marc had the nerve to ask. 'Let the past belong in the past.'

'I'm bringing it up because we have never, ever talked about it and yet it's the entire reason why we hate each other.' Cassie was so angry, she could hardly get the words out. All weekend she'd let herself be lulled into complacency, into imagining they were *friends* because what? Marc had fostered that false sense of intimacy that he did so well.

But the way he'd gone silent on her last night, then physically recoiled when she'd touched him, had reminded Cassie of who he really was. She was cross with herself that she'd even needed reminding.

'We're different people now. I thought we were agreed on that,' he said dismissively like this whole conversation was boring, beneath him.

'Not that different,' Cassie said bitterly. 'You still think I'm only good for one thing and I'm fine with that—'

'You certainly don't sound fine with it—'

'Sixteen years ago, yes, it was consensual and yes, I do believe that if I'd asked you to stop, you would have, but even at the time and especially afterwards, I felt compromised.' Cassie had had years to think about this, to select each word with care as if she was picking the smoothest, roundest pebbles from the beach.

'How did I compromise you?' Marc demanded, looking at Cassie as if he were seeing her for the first time and not much liking the view. 'You said that you wanted it too.'

'Compromised because you picked me up like you were separating the weakest antelope from the rest of the herd. You said the next day that you chose me because you thought I was some cheap little tart who'd only been invited by accident . . .'

'I never said that! I can't remember exactly what I said because it was sixteen fucking years ago, but I definitely didn't say that . . .'

Cassie shut her eyes and she was transported back to that terrace and a Marc who was as scathing as the Marc of today. 'You said that you picked me because I'd been shoved on a back table, that I was some work colleague of Lucy, who'd be dumped soon enough. You don't get much more dismissive than that!'

'We were both adults, both free agents. It wasn't a big deal,' Marc insisted woodenly.

'Not to you, it wasn't,' Cassie said bitterly. 'I mean, you were so determined that you were going to cop off that you'd even done a recce first. Planned a route back into the hotel so no one would see us. I was just *there*. A piece of fluff to be brushed aside when you'd got what you wanted. And I could have put the whole thing down to experience but . . .'

She had to pause to take a deep breath because she'd rehearsed this confrontation countless times over the years but it was still hard work to finally speak her truth.

'But what?' Marc snapped. 'You got off. You know you did.'

'I did, and then you sneaked away without even saying goodbye. Have you any idea how that made me feel? Or how you made me feel the next day too? You made me feel *horrible*, like I just wasn't good enough. Exactly the way that you made me feel last night.'

'How you feel is on you . . .' Marc began haltingly, colour dotted along his cheekbones.

'Do not even fucking go there,' Cassie warned him, knowing that her own face was red with fury. 'So, I'm not doing this any more. I thought perhaps we could be some comfort to each other, be on the same team, but we can't when we don't even like each other and we never will.'

Even though he was sitting next to her, Marc had never looked so remote. 'So you keep saying. You hate me. Yes, I've got the message.'

'That has been our entire vibe ever since the morning after the wedding and it's ridiculous to think that's ever going to change, even if, even if . . .'

'Even if we keep fucking,' Marc supplied coldly and deliberately.

'It's just fucking and it complicates everything so we're not going to do it again,' Cassie vowed. She looked over to Lucy and Russell and her heart plummeted. They were at the water's edge, barefooted, even though they'd promised they wouldn't. 'For Christ's sake. Look at them!'

Marc glanced over at their friends. 'You're not even thinking about them.'

'Fuck you! All I do is think about them.' Cassie gave Marc an almighty shove, which barely unseated him. 'We have to tell them that we're over. That we're not compatible, we never were, we were just fooling ourselves and that we've decided to call it quits. No hard feelings.'

That sounded sensible. Doable. Workable. Even though the feelings were actually very hard.

'Nope, that's not happening,' Marc said like his opinion was the last word. Which it wasn't.

'They'll be fine,' Cassie insisted, bracing her hands behind herself as the first move in hoisting herself up off the sinking sand so she could go over to Lucy and Russell to ask them what the hell they were playing at and to put their shoes and socks back on.

She'd barely lifted her arse up before she was pulled off balance by Marc grabbing her arm and dragging her closer, his hand at the back of her head, pulling her to him in a mocking parody of a lover's embrace. Cassie wriggled desperately to free herself but Marc's hold tightened.

'You were the one who said we were dating,' he reminded her grimly. 'You were the one who boxed us into a corner—'

'Which I wouldn't have had to do if you hadn't gone down on me in the bloody pantry and—'

'And you were the one who said that it had made Lucy and Russell happy, so if you think I'm going to do anything that will make them unhappy, then, darling, you're living in a dream world.' Marc slowed his words down to a sarcastic drawl.

'I can't do this any more,' Cassie said, hating the pleading, desperate note in her voice and hating that, even now, with Marc this close, she wanted to kiss him. Wanted to press her fingers to his forehead and smooth away his frown.

'Tough, we're doing it, we're committed. Or so help me, Cass, you didn't like the way I treated you sixteen years ago, but I can be a lot nastier than that, believe me,' he snarled.

It should have been ridiculous. The theatrics of a pantomime villain, but Marc's face, his tone, was so utterly forbidding that it sent a chill through Cassie that had nothing to do with the wind that had picked up in the time they'd been arguing and now had a ferocious bite to it.

She managed to wrest herself out of his tight grip. 'I *really* don't like you,' she shouted over the tandem crash of waves and wind.

Marc moved away as if he couldn't bear to be near Cassie. 'And I don't care,' he hissed.

She'd thought that their argument on the terrace all those years ago had been vicious, but this felt even worse. Then Cassie looked up to see Lucy and Russell walking towards them, her arm around him, their steps slow and laboured, shoes in their hands.

'I've been calling you,' Lucy said, once she was closer. 'Can you . . . I couldn't work out how to fold the deckchair.'

Cassie scrambled to her feet. 'Yes! Of course!' She picked up the carrier bag she'd brought. 'There's a towel in there. I thought we'd agreed no paddling.'

'I know,' Russell said, his voice strained, his breathing heavy. 'Can you shout at us when we're warm and dry inside, please?'

'Oh, there will be shouting,' Marc promised. 'Some quite choice swear words too.' He took Russell's arm, as he was trying to bend down to dry his feet. 'Here, brace yourself on me.'

Cassie couldn't fold the deckchair either and struggled back up the beach with it. At least Russell could sit down now, and didn't even protest about it, as Lucy dried his feet with the towel. Then she put his socks and shoes back on.

'I feel like a child,' he said almost to himself.

'I was aiming more for Jesus and Mary Magdalene and the whole washing the feet thing,' Lucy said with desperate good cheer. 'Once an ex-convent schoolgirl, and all that.'

'That's kind of weird, Lucy,' Marc said, echoing Cassie's own thoughts, though she didn't want to be on the same page as him. She didn't want to be on the same *anything* as him. 'But let's save our energy for the climb.'

Once Russell was upright again and already leaning heavily on Lucy, Marc folded the deckchair with annoying ease then brandished it at Cassie, like he was a matador and she was a very, very angry bull.

'We're going to do this slowly and one step at a time,' Marc said calmly. 'Lucy and I will be next to you and anytime you need to stop, just say.'

Lucy looked up at the imposing cliff face and the many, many steps. 'We'll do this in no time,' she said but the anguished look she gave Cassie said just the opposite.

The wind that had been such a help on the way down was in their faces and beating them back on the way up. The steps were also so narrow that it was impossible for Lucy and Marc to take Russell's weight.

Instead Marc went in front and Lucy went behind and it seemed to Cassie, bringing up the rear with the very heavy and cumbersome deckchair, that they were trying to lift Russell from one step to the next.

Cassie could smell the rain in the air as Russell finally admitted defeat and sat down heavily on a step about halfway up the cliff.

'I just need to catch my breath,' he said.

'Use your puffer.' Lucy was already delving in the carrier bag.

'I don't actually need it,' Russell insisted but Lucy held it out to him.

'It can't hurt,' she said, worry etched into her features, into the tense set of her shoulders.

Cassie leaned on the deckchair and tried to ignore the panic that was rising up in her. She looked up at the steps they still had to climb, then back to Russell, who was sweating but shivering despite the thick jumper Lucy had made him wear and the waterproof coat that Cassie had foisted on him before they started the climb.

What would happen if Russell really couldn't go any further? Even with the best will in the world, and even if they summoned up the superhuman strength that people found in desperate times when they could suddenly lift buses off someone trapped beneath the wheels, it still seemed hopeless.

Could they call 999 and have Russell airlifted to safety? Or what if he took a sudden turn for the even worse? What if . . .

'OK, let's do this,' Russell said in a firmer, much less wheezy voice. 'I can do this.'

'You can do it,' Marc affirmed. Russell stood up and they continued their perilous climb once more.

It was slow and Russell had to keep stopping, but he didn't sit down again and though Cassie hadn't wanted to keep looking up at the distance they still had to go, suddenly, there were only five steps left.

Three more steps and there was the lawn laid out temptingly before them.

Two . . .

. . . and thank God, one.

It was Cassie who went sprawling as she misjudged the depth of the final step and fell over the deckchair that she was trying to lift up.

'Are you all right, Cass?' Lucy called out as she and Marc hurried Russell over to the bench.

'I'm good!' Cassie called back, though she'd trapped two fingers in the deckchair's wooden frame and banged her knee. 'Don't worry about me!' Even though she wanted to lie down on the grass and cry for Russell and Lucy and yes, cry for herself because that argument with Marc had been utterly necessary but so cruel and just once, just one measly time in her entire life, she wanted to know what it was like to love someone and have them love her back. Without caveats or confusion.

But it wasn't going to be Marc. Even if she was tormented by the past. By the maybe-things-could-have-been-different if what had happened sixteen years ago hadn't just been an opportunistic and predatory one-night stand in a hotel room. Anyway, for it to be a one-night stand, Marc would have to have stayed for the whole night, instead of asking Cassie to get him a glass of water so he could do a runner.

If he had stayed, then perhaps . . .

'You don't look all right,' said Marc, suddenly standing in front of Cassie because she'd been motionless at the cliff edge, paralysed by coulda woulda shoulda.

'I'm fine.' They were the words that would be engraved on her tombstone, in a font that implied just the opposite. Maybe Copperplate or something similarly Gothic.

'Go and help Lucy and Russell then,' Marc ordered brusquely, all but snatching the deckchair from her. 'I'll put this away.'

'I don't need you to tell me what to do,' Cassie snapped, but he'd already stalked away from her, so she headed to where Lucy and Russell were still sitting on the bench. Her knee was throbbing but Cassie forced herself not to show it and plastered a smile on her face.

Cassie left them at the cottage ten minutes later. Lucy was running Russell a hot bath and Cassie fancied the same. She didn't care what Marc said about keeping this, this . . . charade going; she was going to move her stuff to the room that Heather and Davy had vacated.

She was halfway across the lawn when she felt the first pinpricks of rain. By the time she limped up to the patio doors, it had progressed to a deluge of slanting sheets of water and her hair was wet, her hoodie soaked, as she rapped impatiently on the glass.

Iris opened the door, and Anita was ready with a towel. Digby and Kwame had made a start on lunch and there was already a delicious aroma of garlic and herbs wafting around the kitchen.

Cassie had thought she wanted to be on her own to lick her metaphorical wounds but she was pleased to be cocooned in the warmth of the busy kitchen and the attention of her friends. A mug of tea was placed in front of her along with a fudgy chocolate brownie bought in Brighton, while Azad tended to her non-metaphorical wounds with ice for her knee and antiseptic wipes and plasters for her fingers.

Marc was nowhere to be seen and Cassie was quite happy to stay where she was, listening to the easy conversation around her and occasionally holding up her plastered fingers forlornly whenever Kwame and Digby asked for volunteers to peel vegetables or make a quick roux for a Sunday roast that clearly had as many side dishes as Christmas dinner.

The rain had set in for the day; the garden was a green blur as Cassie sat on the window seat and chased raindrops as they trickled down the glass.

Then she saw a dark form coming towards the house. Indistinct at first, then taking shape as Lucy and Russell, under a gigantic golfing umbrella, came nearer. Cassie jumped up, wincing as her tender knee twinged, to open the patio doors. She steeled herself to smile, to act as if the sight of Russell's grey face was nothing out of the ordinary, except . . .

'Oh my goodness, something smells good!' Russell exclaimed, as he stamped his feet on the coir mat. 'I'm starving.'

He wasn't grey but pink from their race across the lawn. Although Cassie was still sure that he was thinner, frailer, with each passing day, their friends didn't seem to notice.

'Had a bath, he's much better,' Lucy whispered in her ear as she gave Cassie a quick squeeze.

'I'm glad.' Cassie *was* glad but it was getting harder and harder to reconcile this version of Russell, now leaning over Digby to investigate what was bubbling away in the pans on the range, with the other, less vigorous version who was becoming more and more familiar.

There would be a day, maybe quite soon, when Russell wasn't going to bounce back. Before, all those weeks ago, when Cassie had first been told that Russell was dying, it had seemed impossible to comprehend. Not Russell, when he was always fizzing with energy, with life; but now his diagnosis, the terrible prognosis, was becoming only too believable.

31

It was the kind of Sunday Cassie could never have imagined when she was younger and wondering who she might be when she grew up.

A country house. Engaging, interesting friends. Flicking through the *Sunday Times* and the *Observer* supplements (her grandparents had taken the *Sunday Mirror*). The frequent pop of the champagne cork because, incredibly, they still hadn't drunk all of it.

Then there was a quite legendary Sunday roast served only two hours late, which featured a leg of lamb studded with rosemary and garlic, a beetroot Wellington as a veggie option, sausages and chicken drumsticks left over from the barbecue and a mouth-watering array of side dishes. Goose-fat potatoes, cauliflower cheese, red cabbage, honey-glazed carrots and parsnips, green beans with flaked almonds, and the plumpest, crispest Yorkshire puddings.

They were all settled in the cosy living room and no one wanted to change location to the formal dining room. Digby and Kwame arranged the dishes on the kitchen island and everyone grabbed a plate and helped themselves, then found a spot on one of the sofas.

It all looked delicious but Cassie had no appetite. Not even for a Yorkshire pudding soaked in gravy. She was worried, desperately worried, about Russell. But she also wished – how she wished! – that she'd never pretended she and Marc were together. They never had been and they never, ever would be. That was why her mouth was dry, her stomach felt as if it was lined with hopping frogs and the food, lovingly crafted by Digby and Kwame, who weren't bashful about receiving compliments, might just as well have been Turkey Twizzlers and oven chips.

Marc, who'd been absent all afternoon, appeared just before the food was served, to much good natured-teasing. 'I don't cook,' he'd protested. 'Couldn't tell one end of a potato peeler from another. But I can open another bottle of champagne, if anyone needs a refill.'

He was charming and seemingly in good spirits. Not even a little bit destroyed by anything that had happened earlier.

Cassie was quite adamant that she wasn't going to play the devoted girlfriend any more but as she took a plate, Marc was suddenly next to her, his arm sliding firmly around her waist so she was anchored to him. 'You go and sit down, darling,' he said, kissing the top of her head. 'I know *exactly* what you like.'

She could hardly fling herself away and cry, 'Get your filthy hands off me!' – or she could, but of course she didn't want to make a scene. Fake dating was one thing, but fake dating as that one couple who lived for the drama was quite another very, very annoying thing.

So she could only nod in agreement and Marc's grip on her softened and became more caressing, his thumb resting comfortably in the dip of her waist. That was torture itself but when Cassie purposely chose a seat in the corner of one of the sofas, Iris and Bill taking up the rest of the space, Marc soon appeared with two plates and an ingratiating smile on his face.

'Bill, do you mind if I turf you out? You and Iris must be so bored of always sitting next to each other . . .'

'So bored,' Iris agreed happily.

'. . . and I don't get to sit next to Cassie nearly enough,' he continued smoothly, smile still in place but his eyes flashing a warning at Cassie.

'I don't want to stand or sit in the way of you two lovebirds,' Bill said, damn him, getting up to offer his seat to Marc.

It was a big sofa. They didn't even have to touch each other, but Marc sat down so close to Cassie that there was no escape. She had the sofa arm on one side and his hard thigh pressed against hers on the other.

'You're ridiculous,' Cassie whispered as quietly as she could, given how enraged she was. She was even more indignant because being so close to him that her breath ruffled his hair, close enough that she could bite down on his earlobe if she fancied that instead of a roast potato, still felt intoxicating. 'I already told you that I'm not doing this.'

'Yes, you fucking are,' he whispered. Then he sat back with a grin that Cassie didn't like and didn't trust. 'Come on, Cass, clear that plate. You need to keep your strength up.'

'Can you keep it down tonight?' Iris asked wearily. 'Surely you're not going to be doing it two nights on the trot?'

'Once a week is industry standard,' Digby added. 'Unless it's a birthday.'

'What can I say?' Marc shrugged. 'We're in that infatuated stage. Can't keep our hands off each other.'

'Not that the infatuated stage lasts forever,' Cassie said.

'Oh, please! Everyone can see how perfect you are for each other,' Anita scoffed. 'Even stirs my sceptical and wizened old heart.'

To pay her back for speaking truth to power, once Marc was finished eating, he put a hand on Cassie's knee – not even the injured one, so she could flinch away – and an arm around her shoulders.

Cassie expected one of her cynical, always-with-the-mocking friends to make gagging noises, but the gagging noises never came. Digby and Anita, on the sofa opposite, even shared an indulgent look and nudged each other. Only Lucy didn't seem to be buying what Marc was trying so hard to sell. She stared at the two of them like they were a particularly thorny cryptic crossword clue that she couldn't quite figure out.

'You're laying it on way too thick,' Cassie muttered.

'Just keep smiling.' Marc turned his head to kiss Cassie's cheek, his lips scalding her skin. Then there was a gentle tug on her ponytail.

It was as if there were a trip-wire connected to her clit and every time Marc gave her ponytail a tiny jerk, she could feel it pulsating away between her legs.

From the smug smile on his face, Marc knew that too.

After dinner, there was still no escape. Cassie knew that if she fled to the room she was sharing with Marc, he'd come to find her. He was in that kind of mood; relentless, tormenting. Cassie supposed it was effective when he was tech entrepreneuring but to be the sole target of Marc's manipulations made her feel like a small, unprofitable company that he was planning to asset-strip. Not in a fun, sexytimes way either.

They all agreed to a small window to digest dinner before pudding. Anita wanted to play Monopoly, though she was banned from playing Monopoly after an incident on a similar Sunday afternoon in 2019 when Bill had landed on free parking. He'd been awarded the pot of money accrued through parking fines, Super Tax and various other penalties. Anita, who was almost bankrupt apart from one house on Old Kent Road and one on Whitechapel Road, had upended the entire board in a fit of pique.

'Cluedo? Let's play Cluedo,' she cajoled in the face of zero enthusiasm.

'It's a literal case of love the player, hate the game,' Russell said, ever the voice of reason. What were they going to do without him as their eternal referee? Always able to mediate squabbles without ever making anyone feel that they were the guilty party. 'We're watching a film. But first we'll spend at least twenty minutes arguing about which film. Then we'll serve pudding before we watch it.'

Choosing a film only took five minutes. 'It's a rainy evening so I want something in black and white, funny, romantic, not heavy,' Lucy said.

'*Bringing Up Baby*,' Iris said immediately. 'Cary Grant. Katharine Hepburn. A leopard. What more could anyone need?'

Cassie couldn't sit, pinned between Marc and the sofa arm, for an hour and forty-two minutes. Not with him constantly touching her and tugging on her bloody ponytail, as everyone looked on in fond amusement.

'I've got a headache,' Cassie heard herself announce. 'I think I'm going to bow out of the movie. I should probably have a nap.'

'I'll join you,' Marc said immediately.

'I don't think poor Cass is going to have much of a nap if that happens,' Kwame said with a wink.

It wasn't a lie about the headache. Her head was throbbing almost as much as her knee. 'I'll take a couple of Nurofen and sort out pudding, then see how I feel before the film starts.'

'Oh, don't go,' Lucy said, her face pulled into a frown. 'Why don't you sit quietly and I'll sort out pudding? What is pudding, by the way? Though I don't know how anyone can still be hungry . . .'

Bill shrugged. 'I mean, I could manage something sweet.'

Lucy couldn't sort out pudding because pudding was the birthday cake that had been delivered yesterday morning with their breakfast boxes and stashed in the fridge in the utility room. It was a surprise.

Cassie tried again. 'I'm happy to do pudding, as long as someone else can make coffee.'

Marc's hand tightened on Cassie's knee. 'Well, coffee is my thing.'

'The perfect team,' Russell said with a grin, as Marc stood up then held his hand out to Cassie, who had no choice but to let him pull her up.

Then, determined to make her suffer even more, he wouldn't let Cassie walk to the kitchen unmolested but put his arm round her waist again.

As soon as the kitchen island was between them and their audience, Cassie pulled away from his touch.

'Cassie,' he said, his voice low and urgent. 'Come on . . .'

She ignored him and dived for the sanctuary of the utility room, sure that he would come after her, even after she slammed the door shut. Cassie paused, heard Marc call out, 'So, who wants what?' and allowed herself to breathe out. To wriggle her shoulders as if she could shake off her demons that easily. Then gather herself.

She was able to gather herself to the halfway point, which was as good as it was going to get. Cassie carefully removed the cake from its box. It was another Lucy favourite: a lemon and elderflower cake, roughly and rustically covered with buttercream on the sides and 'Happy Birthday, Lucy!' iced in a loopy cursive on the top.

Cassie had already secreted a cake stand, candles and matches in the utility room on Friday because she was *that* organised. Now she waited with one ear pressed against the door until she heard the coffee machine gurgle into action yet again.

She lit the four candles she'd placed on the cake – forty would have been overkill – nudged open the door and slowly walked back into the kitchen.

Marc was staring at the coffee machine like it was about to impart the meaning of life, but as Cassie walked past him, he shifted his gaze to her, then sighed.

For someone who loved singing, Cassie couldn't muster up a passable 'Happy Birthday', but luckily Kwame was the first to see her coming with her precious flaming cargo held aloft and did the honours, the others quickly joining in.

'Oh my goodness!' Lucy exclaimed, her face flushed with delight. 'It's not even my actual birthday for another two weeks.'

'You don't have to have any cake if you feel that strongly about it,' Digby said as Cassie placed the cake on the coffee table in front of Lucy.

'But you must make a wish,' Iris said firmly. 'It's bad luck if you don't.'

The delight was instantly wiped from Lucy's face and she gripped Russell's hand tightly as she leaned forward to blow out the candles.

Cassie knew exactly what Lucy was wishing for because she'd wished, daily, for the same thing ever since that awful Friday evening at the beginning of July.

She bit her bottom lip as Lucy and Russell's friends, blissfully unaware of what lay ahead, cheered as the flame of each candle was extinguished.

There was a flurry of activity as the cake was whisked away to be cut and plated. The coffee was ready. Another bottle of champagne was opened. Cassie's headache had upgraded itself to thumping.

She'd had more than enough coffee for one day, and couldn't face any more alcohol, so she poured herself a glass of water and gulped down the tablets. Then she approached the sofas where everyone was now assembled, looking expectantly at the big TV as Azad tried to log in to his BBC iPlayer account.

'Sorry to be such a baby . . .' Cassie pulled what she hoped was a suitably contrite face. 'I think I need to sleep this headache off.'

'But it's our last night together,' Lucy protested. She looked absolutely devastated. As if her whole happiness depended on Cassie being in the same room as her. 'We'll all budge up, you and Marc can have a sofa to yourself. I'm sure he won't mind if you want to stretch out.'

'How could I mind that?' Marc asked in a silky voice, as Digby obligingly joined Lucy and Russell on their sofa. 'You can use my lap as a footrest.'

Was this agony ever going to end? After the day they'd had, that moment on the cliff steps when Cassie had thought all hope was lost, there was no way that she could refuse Lucy anything. Cassie tucked herself into the smallest space that she could at the other end of the sofa.

Marc patted his thighs. 'Ready for a foot rub?'

Cassie shook her aching head. 'I'm good, thanks.'

'Oh, come on, Cass,' Russell protested from the sofa next to her. 'Never look a gift massage in the mouth.'

'And be quick, film's about to start.' Lucy pointed the remote at Cassie as if she could bend Cassie to her will by pressing the red button.

'I don't bite,' Marc muttered, looking for all the world as if he were the one suffering here.

With a sigh, Cassie uncurled herself and wriggled around so she could stretch out her legs, then lift them up so her feet rested in Marc's lap.

His hands immediately settled around her ankles and Cassie was tempted to tell Marc that she was suffering with a nasty fungal infection.

'I wouldn't,' she said, as Lucy pressed play and the RKO Pictures ident appeared on the screen: a flashing radio tower and Morse-code beeps. 'My feet are dirty. Horribly, horribly dirty.'

Marc lifted up Cassie's right foot. 'Looks pretty clean to me. I'll make a note to wash my hands afterwards.'

If Cassie had been in agony before, now she was experiencing torture. Exquisite torture. Marc was so good with his hands. She knew that only too well. But as he gently stroked the bony upper part of her foot, which probably had a proper name but it had been a long, long time since Cassie had done

GCSE biology, his touch was comforting. Which was hard to
bear when it was an entirely false kind of comfort, solely for
the benefit of their audience.

Considering that *Bringing Up Baby* was meant to be one of
Lucy's favourite films, she continually kept glancing over at
Cassie and Marc as if the two of them were far more capti-
vating than the screwball antics of Grant and Hepburn.

Cassie barely looked at the obnoxiously large TV screen.
She lasted for half the movie, but when Iris asked for an
interval because she needed a wee and a willing person to
mix negronis, Cassie made her escape.

'Let me go,' she hissed at Marc as the lights, which had
been dimmed, brightened.

'Everything will be better if you stay,' he said in a quiet
voice. He turned to look at her, his face not set in tight, angry
lines, but soft and pleading.

He was a much better actor than she was. Cassie yanked
her feet free, swung her legs round and stood up so quickly
that the room spun. 'Guys, this headache, it's not getting any
better.' Cassie pressed her fingertips to one aching temple.
'I'm going to bail and get an early night.'

'Are you sure?' Lucy pouted. Cassie loved Lucy and she
had a free pass right now, but also Cassie kind of wanted to
kill her best friend. Just a little.

'Quite sure,' Cassie said, having to climb over first Marc's
legs, then Russell's on the sofa at a right angle to theirs,
because neither of them even attempted to let Cassie squeeze
past.

She was almost out of the room when Marc didn't just
catch up with Cassie but body-blocked her from slipping

through the archway. His hands were on her again, on her shoulders.

'Don't go,' he said quietly, his eyes intent on her face so that if anyone was looking at them, and Cassie could guarantee that they definitely had some fascinated spectators, they'd think that Marc was the very definition of the devoted boyfriend.

If only they knew the ugly truth.

'Please leave me alone,' Cassie begged just as quietly. 'I told you, I can't do this any more.'

'But you have to,' Marc said, his hand on her shoulder. 'Christ, is being with me that much of an ordeal?'

'Yes! You don't like me but you'd still fuck me and it's messing me up. Last night . . .' Cassie tailed off as she realised they still had an audience.

'I don't know why you keep saying that,' Marc said, his eyes now blazing and not bothering to keep his voice down.

'Because it's the fucking truth! Why are you still touching me?' Cassie had gone from a whisper to a scream in eleven words. But it worked because Marc took his hands off her pretty damn quickly, his arms falling to his sides.

'Cass, please . . .' he said. 'Let's go somewhere quiet and talk about this.'

'Let's not,' Cassie said flatly, free at last to head for the stairs. 'And don't you dare come after me.'

Marc didn't come after her. It seemed as if Cassie's words had finally penetrated his thick skull. But she still ran up the stairs like the hounds of hell were at her heels.

Once she was inside their – no, *his* – room with the door firmly shut, Cassie didn't waste any time. She packed her bags, and was just about to flee to the sad little attic room with its flimsy bunk beds and spooky vibes, when she again remembered that there was now an empty room on this floor.

If Cassie was going to be miserable, then she could be miserable in a king-size bed with pocket-sprung mattress and ensuite bathroom.

Davy and Heather had left the house that morning under something of a cloud, so it was no surprise that it looked as if a major weather event had occurred in their room. As Cassie surveyed the mess – the pillows and duvet scattered on the floor, the sheet half pulled off the mattress, dirty plates and cups on the bedside tables – she wondered if she should petition the Met Office to name their next storm after Heather.

The bathroom was just as bad. Damp towels in a heap on the floor. A tap still running. Dear God, no! Someone hadn't flushed. It was a yellow warning, rather than a brown, but Cassie still retched as she wrapped loo paper round her fingers then pulled the chain.

Cassie was completely in the mood for some very angry cleaning. There was a linen cupboard further down the corridor and, muttering furiously under her breath, she collected clean towels and fresh bedding. No way was she going to sleep on a sheet that had known the touch of Heather and Davy. Especially if, contrary to all the evidence, they were still into each other enough to have sex.

Ugh! It was a thought too awful to contemplate.

It was only slightly cathartic to wrestle with a fitted sheet instead of wrestling with her many demons. She yanked each corner into place, swearing if any of them threatened to make a bid for freedom. Next, she was unnecessarily rough with pillows and pillowcases.

Then it was time for the big guns. One king-size duvet and one king-size duvet cover. She sat down on the bed, the duvet draped over her knees, and inserted her hands into the duvet cover until she was gripping the top two corners, which she fitted over the duvet. Then with a firm hold on the top edges of both duvet and cover, she'd stand up, give them both a good shake and the two of them would be in perfect harmony. Place on bed, another good shake. Job done.

It wasn't rocket science. Cassie had been making her own bed since she was ten and she changed her bedding once a week because she wasn't an animal. That meant in her lifetime, she'd probably fitted duvets and duvet covers together more than one thousand four hundred times.

But this evening she kept losing the top corners of the duvet, or they wouldn't fit neatly into the top corners of the cover. It was as if she'd lost the use of her opposable thumbs. Cassie's swearing and muttering intensified with each attempt until she finally succeeded and stood up to shake the recalcitrant bedding into order.

Something wasn't right. The duvet was lumpen and wouldn't lie flat in its silky-smooth Egyptian-cotton cover.

Cassie's shaking became more frenetic, her attempts more frantic, until she realised that hello, hi, she was the problem, it was her.

She'd put the duvet cover in widthways and not lengthways. Like she was some kind of rank amateur when it came to making a bed.

'Oh for fucking fuck's fucking sake!'

Cassie wrenched the two apart, heard an ominous ripping sound and then threw the duvet in one direction and the cover in the other and why was she crying? It wasn't worth crying over a spilt, or split, duvet cover.

But still she cried. Collapsing back on the bed so she could curl herself into the smallest ball and cry like her heart was breaking.

Because it was. Breaking for Russell and Lucy. For all their friends downstairs who didn't know that this weekend was as much a goodbye as it was a celebration.

But mostly Cassie cried because her heart was breaking on her own behalf, which made her feel so guilty that she cried even harder. She hadn't closed herself off to the possibility of love but she'd started to prepare for the possibility of no love. Had told herself that it would be a relief when there came a time that she could delete all the apps and never have to go on another blind date with a man whose profile had managed to hide the fact that he was a total sociopath.

Yet somehow, this weekend she'd willingly fallen into bed with a man who hated her. A man who'd treated her so terribly in the past. Using her all those years ago, then making it obvious every time they were in the same space that Cassie was beneath him in every way. She wasn't cool enough, or clever enough, or pretty enough.

But when Cassie really had been beneath Marc, his body pressing down on hers, his mouth and his hands and his cock giving her so much pleasure, there was nowhere else that she'd rather be.

All those long, long nights of The Fear, when she'd wondered what was wrong with her that she couldn't find someone to love. Until these last three days when a man that she thought she'd hated had turned her life upside down. Even though it hadn't been real, to Cassie's indiscriminate heart, it had felt real.

She wanted to hate him but she also wanted to mean something to him. This weekend, Marc had let her see a side of him that she'd only had glimpses of before. A man who was kind, thoughtful, indulgent, funny. The sort of man it wouldn't be that hard to fall in love with if there was even an outside chance that he might love Cassie back.

But there wasn't and he didn't. It was all just hopeless.

32

Cassie continued to cry until she cried herself to sleep. An exhausted, comatose kind of sleep so that when her phone beeped imperiously, she had to struggle her way towards a thick-headed, swollen-eyed wakefulness.

She squinted at her phone in the now darkness of the room, the illuminated screen making her eyes water. Outside, it was still storming, the rain and the wind lashing at the windows.

She had a voice note from Lucy. Not unprecedented. But uncommon. Usually they messaged each other constantly throughout the day, unless the message proved to be so convoluted that they ended up calling.

But tonight, she'd sent a voice note. So it couldn't be that urgent and Cassie could just go back to sleep, perchance to have some really unpleasant nightmares. But she was a millennial (an elderly millennial, Ryan said when he was trying to wind her up) and Cassie couldn't ignore an electronic summons.

She switched on the bedside lamp then pressed play on Lucy's message.

'I'm going to have to speak quietly because Russell doesn't know I'm doing this – I'm in the bathroom, because he says that I shouldn't meddle. But I'm not meddling.'

Lucy sighed as if everything she wanted to say was in that frustrated exhalation of breath.

'It's obvious that things with you and Marc aren't good. He was trying to pretend that everything was fine but he's a terrible actor and you, when you're in a sulk, there is no hiding it.'

Cassie couldn't take offence because it was true. Despite her best efforts this weekend, she had the worst poker face.

'I know there's history between you,' Lucy continued in a breathless rush. 'Russell and I have *always* been convinced that something happened at our wedding. But ever since then, you've always been lowkey hostile with each other and it's so frustrating to see. Because both of you are such good people.

'Marc can come across as a bit of a dick sometimes but Cass, he can be so lovely too. Just think about it. Why would Russell and I love Marc so much, if he was a terrible person? He's far from terrible. He has been so loyal to Russell, such a good friend to the four of us. I know, beyond a shadow of a doubt, that if you let him, he would love you in the way that you deserve to be loved.'

Lucy sounded close to tears and it was like a knife wound to the gut. The very last thing that Cassie had wanted to do was to cause Lucy any more upset and worry.

'Life is unfair and it's so fucking brief, gone in an instant, and all we can really do is cling on to love with both hands if it happens to come our way.

'Marc could make you so happy, Cass. You just have to let him. I need you to do that for me. Because I only ever want what's best for you and I'm trying not to be angry with you but *I told you*! I told you, Cass, not to overthink things.

'I've got to go. I love you even though you're an utter twat.'

Cassie could hardly make sense of what she'd just heard. How much had Lucy had to drink anyway? She needed time to process, to think . . .

Or maybe she should take Lucy's advice and not think but just feel . . .

Cassie tried to listen to her heart, but her heart was battered and bruised and wasn't convinced that Marc even liked her, much less would ever decide that he loved her. Did she even like Marc? Could she love him? Would she let herself love him if the circumstances were different?

Besides, she wasn't *unhappy*. Not really. But then, she could be happier.

This probably counted as overthinking.

Cassie wondered briefly what the difference was between simply thinking and overthinking. Then, as if her body was acting independently of her busy, busy brain, she stood up and walked towards the door.

She even opened the door and stepped out into the corridor to see . . . Marc coming towards her.

Her brain wanted her to retreat, to back away slowly, but Cassie kept moving forwards until she and Marc met halfway.

They both stopped, a ruler's distance and sixteen difficult years between them.

Cassie had been staring at her feet but now she lifted her puffy face so she could look at him. If nothing else, she loved to look at him, even when he was sneering at her.

Except he wasn't sneering at her. His expression was grave, as if he'd just received news that had smashed his world into dust.

Eventually one of them would speak but Cassie was sure it wasn't going to be her. She didn't know where to start. What to say. None of the words that she thought of – I, you, we – was the right one.

'I'm sorry.'

That was a good place to begin, except Cassie hadn't made a sound.

Marc took a step closer to her and held out his hands, palms upwards, as if he was doing penance.

'I'm sorry,' he said again. 'I'm so sorry. I'm a fucking idiot.'

'No, you're not.' Marc was many things, but not that. Cassie wasn't exactly perfect either. 'I'm an utter twat,' she said, 'if it makes you feel any better.'

'You're not and it doesn't,' Marc assured her. 'You've been crying. Did I make you cry?'

There was no point trying to hide her red, blotchy face. Cassie shrugged. 'I had a lot of things to cry about.' She didn't sound too far away from yet more tears.

'Before, earlier, downstairs . . . Christ, why is it so hard to get my words out?' Marc took a deep breath. His shoulders dropped as if he was making a concerted effort to find some inner calm. 'I wasn't trying to hurt you or goad you. I am so sick of always fighting with you. I don't want to do that any more. I was trying to make up, to remind you of how good we can be.'

Marc looked and sounded so sincere: his brow was furrowed, his hair in disarray as if he'd been tugging on it.

'But we're not together,' Cassie said. 'That was just pretend.' All the old feelings of rejection, of not being good enough, rose up in her again like mercury in an old-fashioned thermometer when the patient had a raging fever. 'You don't even like me.'

'No . . . !'

Just as Marc was about to deny what Cassie knew to be true, the door just behind him opened and Iris stuck her very annoyed face out.

'Some of us are trying to get some sleep. You have a room. You have *two* rooms. Can you go into one of them and shut the door behind you?'

Marc turned to her with a flat smile. 'Will do.'

'We're so sorry. Of course we will,' Cassie echoed.

'Whatever you're arguing about, it can't be that important,' Iris continued. 'Apologise, have some of that noisy sex you love so much, then I don't want to hear another peep from you until the morning.'

Completely unsolicited relationship advice given, Iris retreated, leaving Marc shuffling his feet and Cassie holding her hands to her inevitably flushed cheeks. She'd spent so much of this weekend with a burning hot face that it was a miracle she had any skin left.

'Our . . . my room?' Marc gestured down the corridor but Cassie shook her head. There were already too many memories trapped between those four walls.

'Let's go into the other room,' she muttered.

Marc indicated that Cassie could lead the way. She could feel the back of her neck tingling as he walked behind her to her new room. Then he shut the door as Cassie wondered where best to sit to have this argument.

It was probably going to be an argument.

It was a pretty room, its walls painted an eau-de-Nil green, accented in the delicate chintz fabric of the padded headboard and the bucket armchairs, one of which Cassie sat on.

Marc stayed where he was, leaning on the door as if he didn't have the strength to stay upright. 'Why is the duvet on the floor?' he asked. 'And the duvet cover?'

'I had problems putting them together.' When Cassie smiled, it felt as if she'd only recently learned how to use her facial muscles. 'I don't suppose you're an expert in making beds?'

His smile was just as tentative. 'I'm painfully aware of how this sounds but I can't remember ever having to insert a duvet into a duvet cover. I've always had a cleaner.'

Cassie couldn't help a tiny and appalled 'Wow'.

'Yeah, I know.' Marc gave a shaky grin and Cassie didn't know what he had to be so nervous about – although she was feeling nervous, too. She'd stopped trying to operate on sheer instinct and was back to overthinking, which meant that she felt increasingly anxious.

She pulled her legs up so she could rest her chin on her knees and worry at her bottom lip. She could throw caution to the wind and tell Marc what was in her heart. What was the worst thing that could happen? He'd reject her, and people had been rejecting Cassie all her life. She'd get over it in time. She always did.

'I don't hate you, Cass. You always insist that I do but I don't. I never have,' Marc said suddenly.

'Well, you certainly don't like me very much,' Cassie said dully. 'Every time our paths cross, you sneer at me and always have some sarcastic little remark all good to go.'

'That's just self-defence.' Marc pushed away from the door and walked over to the bed and sat on the end of it. 'Because you always look at me like you wish I was dead. Now I understand why.'

Cassie really needed Marc to show his workings. 'Why is that then?'

'I can tell you why but first I have to apologise.' Marc stared at the floor, then at the wall to the left of where Cassie was sitting, where a set of four bucolic prints by Eric Ravilious was hung. Everywhere but at Cassie.

'I don't even know what you're sorry for,' she said, although she knew what she *wanted* him to be sorry for.

He didn't breathe in so much as shudder. 'I'm sorry about what happened sixteen years ago. I'm sorry that I made you feel . . . what was it you said? I made you feel horrible and I'm so sorry for that. I haven't even got anything to say in my defence. Back then, I thought I was the king of the world, untouchable. I was deep into my fuckboy era and proud of it.

'So at weddings and parties, I'd hook up with someone, a distant relative or casual acquaintance who'd be taken out of rotation soon enough, and we'd both have a good time and then I'd never have to see them again. I wasn't built for relationships.'

That sounded reasonable enough but it wasn't at all how Cassie had remembered it. 'I felt so used afterwards. When you didn't come back.'

Marc nodded. 'I get that and believe me, the absolutely withering look on your face as you told me to fuck off back to San Francisco the next morning is etched into my cortex.

I often relive that moment when I'm wallowing in self-loathing. I shiver just thinking about it.'

'I was really hurt . . .' Cassie couldn't explain it any better than that – and also she wasn't going to apologise for it, because Marc had deserved it.

'I've thought about that night a lot – hard not to when I get back to London a few years later and you haven't been taken out of rotation, you're someone I have to see all the time.' Marc's smile was positively mournful. 'Why couldn't you have been a distant second cousin?'

'I'm sorry the stroppy girl who told you to fuck off was still hanging around.' Cassie was aiming for a little bit of light humour but Marc shook his head.

'That stroppy girl has become one hell of a woman. Everyone else could see it, except me,' he said gravely, then stood up to take a few short steps so he could get down on his knees in front of her. She shifted back nervously in the chair.

'What are you doing?'

'Apologising. Grovelling. I don't even know.' Marc took hold of Cassie's cold hands. She let him even as suspicion was writ large over every centimetre of her face. 'That night, Cass. I always thought that it wasn't that bad. Not really. I got you off twice and yeah, skipping out on you was a dick move but I never imagined . . . when you said today on the beach that you felt compromised . . . I'm so ashamed of myself. I really and truly am sorry for making you feel like that. No wonder you hate me.'

Cassie had been waiting sixteen years to tell Marc exactly how he'd made her feel that night. To confront him, to finally say her piece, that was all she'd ever wanted. But now that

Marc was down on his knees, she realised that she'd also wanted – no, needed – an apology. If her heart and shoulders hadn't been so heavy with all her other burdens, then Cassie was sure she'd feel the lightening of relief. Also, there was one point of order.

'I don't hate you!' she protested. 'My feelings about you have always been . . .' she tried to find the right word, a collection of letters and syllables that would perfectly describe how seeing Marc could make her feel both swoony and rageful. All Cassie could come up with was . . . 'complicated. Everything would be easier if I did simply hate you.'

'You really don't hate me?' Marc asked quietly, one of her hands still in his, his eyes on her face, his features solemn.

'No,' Cassie admitted, because it was the truth. A truth that she'd hidden even from herself. 'But I'd think back to that night and even though it was in the past, every time I saw you after that and caught the way you looked at me, I remembered how you made me feel. Inadequate. Not good enough. Or pretty enough. Or posh enough.' She choked out a tiny, self-deprecating laugh as Marc scrunched up his face as if he was in pain.

'Posh enough?' he echoed in disbelief. 'What has that got to do with anything?'

'Everything,' Cassie said because even if that night had never happened, there was always going to be a huge divide between them. 'Look, I've done all right for myself, but I'm still a girl from a council estate with five GCSEs and a Level 3 Diploma in Business Administration.'

'You're that and you're so much more,' Marc said, giving her hand a little shake. 'It's easy to be successful when you come from wealth, we both know that, but you're entirely self-made. More than good enough, so pretty that all I want to do is look at you until it starts to get creepy, and you have more class in your little finger than the two duchesses I know.'

His words, the sincerity and conviction oozing from every syllable, and the rapt way he was gazing at her, suffused Cassie with a Ready Brek glow, which heated up her cheeks yet again and made her duck her head away from his scrutiny.

'You don't know any duchesses,' she muttered.

'I do; also a countess and a marchioness. I'm an irredeemable posh boy who's had everything in life handed to him. No wonder you hate me.' It was Marc's turn for a self-deprecating laugh and to avert his eyes.

'Not everything,' Cassie reminded him gently. 'I had my village and that's a privilege too. And I've already said that I don't hate you. Although there have been times when I've really hated your stupid handsome face. Usually when you're smirking.' She ran the tip of one finger along one of the cheekbones that made his stupid face so handsome.

'Now that you've said that, all I want to do is smirk.' Marc covered Cassie's hand as she cupped his cheek. 'And every time you've ever given me your best bitch goddess glare, it's always felt like a declaration of war.' His hand moved to Cassie's chin to hold her still while his eyes burned into her. 'Then at my engagement party you actually touched me, wished me well for my future. That was one hell of a headfuck.'

'I did mean it. I wanted you to be happy,' Cassie insisted, though if Marc had been happy with Camille then he wouldn't be here now.

'Camille didn't love me and I didn't love her and after two minutes with you on that balcony, we were doomed. I let myself remember that night, what we did, how good it was.' Marc took hold of Cassie's hands again, his eyes never leaving her face. 'For weeks afterwards I couldn't get you out of my head. I'd just celebrated my engagement but I couldn't stop thinking about you.'

'I've thought about you a lot too.' Cassie shifted on the chair as she debated her next confession. The one that made her want to press her legs tight together – or maybe do the opposite. 'That night. It wasn't completely awful. Like you said, you did get me off twice. I have very fond memories of the . . . getting me off.'

'You have no idea how many times I've fucked my own fist while I remembered how you tasted, how you felt,' Marc said softly, so that Cassie wasn't so much shifting in her chair as squirming. 'These last two days have been magical, more than I ever dreamed of, and also – don't take this the wrong way, but also . . .'

'Also, fucking terrifying?' Cassie suggested, because they finally seemed to be in sync with each other. 'Is that why you gave me such serious cold shoulder last night? Even though we were sharing a bed, it still felt like you'd sneaked out while I was in the bathroom.'

'Look at it from my point of view,' Marc said. 'I'd been honest with you, made myself vulnerable in a way that I rarely do, then you reminded me that you hated me.'

'Because that's always been my default position. That we don't like each other. This weekend, like you said, I'd forced you into a corner . . .' Cassie tailed off, then rallied.

'Reminding myself, and you, that we didn't like each other was a get-out clause. I thought that you'd want to get out of that corner soon enough.'

'I've grown very fond of this corner. I think I'd like to stay in it for as long as I can.' Marc lifted Cassie's cold hand to his mouth to press a warm kiss to her knuckles. 'Wasn't there even a small part of you that thought we should give this a proper chance?'

'No,' Cassie said flatly, because she hadn't allowed herself that fantasy. 'I've given you the highlights about Alison, my mum, who from the moment I was born didn't want anything to do with me.' It would always hurt. 'So it won't come as any surprise that I have a pathological fear of being rejected. I don't even know why I paid for a year of therapy when I already knew that.'

'I've been in therapy for years to work through my feelings about being sent to boarding school at seven and having my marriage end after eight months in the most public and painful way imaginable.' Marc sat back on his heels but instead of withdrawing completely from Cassie, he rested a hand on her knee. 'Always better to absent yourself first before the other person has a chance to obliterate you from their life.'

Cassie nodded. Her heart was thrumming at a rate that felt positively alarming. 'There are going to be some really dark days ahead for both of us,' she said and Marc's thumb was already there to brush away the tear that was about to begin its slow descent. 'We both want to be there for Russell and Lucy and the girls and I think . . . I would like it if we could be there for each other too. So, that is, I mean, maybe we could agree that we'll stick this out . . . together.'

'Together is good,' he said, his tone utterly sincere, as if each word was a solemn vow.

Cassie had come this far. She could manage to go a little bit further. 'I did wonder if this was only about the sex for you.'

'Don't get me wrong, the sex was great, but it's so much more than that,' Marc said quickly.

'Really?' She couldn't help the doubtful tone to her voice.

'Yes, really. I want to show you something,' Marc said, piquing Cassie's interest, though she was immediately worried that it could be something bad. Though things had already been bad – they couldn't get worse, surely. 'And I need to get up because my knees are killing me.'

He rose with a grimace and a small groan, then held out his hand to Cassie, who let him pull her out of the chair then lead her to the bed.

'Sit down,' he said and when Cassie sat on the edge of the bed with an anxious glance up at him, he sat down next to her. Then he took out his phone. 'Russell sent me this message about half an hour ago. Here.'

At first the words blurred in front of her eyes, then they became sharper, more in focus.

> **Russell:** I doubt I'll be here for your wedding but I'm going to tell Lucy to play this video on a big screen when they do the speeches. Why are you screwing this up? This woman is the best thing that's ever happened to you. Don't be such a fucking idiot.

'Oh God,' Cassie murmured, pressing play on the attached video clip.

It was the two of them singing 'Islands in the Stream' and bumping hips because Marc hadn't got the hang of the Electric Slide and kept going in the wrong direction. Cassie hadn't even noticed at the time because she was too busy laughing when she wasn't telling him off, but now she could see the way Marc was looking at her as she was singing: tender, amused, soft. It was a mirror for the expression on her own face as Marc was serenading her.

'I don't think anyone's ever looked at me like that before,' Marc said. 'And I'm pretty certain that I've never looked at anyone like that either. You always find a way to get under my skin, don't you?'

Cassie looked up from the screen where the two of them were now captured twirling to Chuck Berry shortly before they ended their performance with an extravagant dip and kiss. 'In a bad way or a good way?'

'Honestly? It's a bit of both.' Marc fell back on the bed and after a moment of hesitation, Cassie let herself fall too, then rolled on her side so she wouldn't miss the mix of emotions that played across his face. Hope mixed in with quite a lot of fear.

She could relate to that.

'There was no video but Lucy just sent me a voice note. Summary was that you were actually a very lovely man and I needed to stop overthinking and being an utter twat.'

'I still say that you're not a twat, but you're the noisiest thinker I've ever come across.' Marc tapped a finger to the side of Cassie's head. 'Always so much going on in here.'

'I'm sure there are going to be times when I'll still hate your pretty face,' Cassie said. 'But Lucy's right. You are kind of lovely and now you've let me in, I don't want to find the way out.'

'Would it be the worst thing in the world to keep this going?' Marc asked, as he turned on his side so they were face to face.

'Because of Lucy and Russell?' If that was the only reason, it was still a good reason, even if—

'And because maybe, and everything in me is cringing as I use this hackneyed phrase, there's a chance we could be each other's person.'

Cassie wriggled closer to him. 'It's amazing that even when you're saying something romantic, you have to be an arse about it.'

'It's a gift, what can I say?' Marc managed to sound flippant even as he put his arm around Cassie's waist and pulled her closer still.

He flinched when Cassie put her ice cold hands on either side of his face. 'You're doing that thing where you use sarcasm to deflect your feelings,' she told him gently.

'Yeah, that's more of a curse than a gift.' He sounded so sad that she softly brushed her mouth against his to take some of the hurt away.

'Well, I don't mind keeping this going if you don't.' Cassie kissed him again, her lips as light as a butterfly. 'You are quite good in bed so there's that.'

'I try.' They were back to being flippant, their default position. But then he kissed Cassie's forehead, her swollen eyelids, the tip of her nose and she couldn't remember a time when she'd been made to feel so safe, so cherished.

Like she really was someone's favourite person.

33

They kissed for what felt like whole centuries, arms wrapped around each other, legs entwined. Fairly chaste kisses until Marc dipped his tongue into Cassie's mouth and that was all it took for that hot, heavy feeling to take over.

'Before, when I said I wasn't going to have sex with you ever again . . . Maybe I was a bit hasty,' she murmured against Marc's lips.

Cassie felt rather than saw his smile. 'You keep saying that you're not going to have sex with me then you go back on your word.'

'I know. I'm the queen of mixed messages,' she murmured but then they were kissing again, bodies straining closer still.

Cassie wouldn't have minded just kissing. Kissing without end. Marc's hand cupped the back of her head, his thumb caressing her neck. Then his kisses, his caresses, stopped and he pulled back from Cassie.

What now?

She didn't even realise she'd said it out loud until Marc frowned. 'You have a huge knot here,' he said, his fingers gentle on her nape again.

'Oh, yeah. I carry all my tension in my neck and shoulders.' Cassie reached for him so they could kiss again but Marc was still frowning, still using his mouth for speaking.

'Why didn't you have a massage yesterday?' he asked.

The sudden gear-change threw Cassie. She wasn't feeling so deliciously heady any more. The massages. Yesterday afternoon. That all felt like a world away. 'I never planned to have one otherwise I wouldn't have been able to fit everyone else in and I wanted Lucy to have a full hour.'

'The thing is, Cass, you're so good at taking care of people but who takes care of you?' Marc asked softly.

His question unexpectedly made her eyes smart. 'I can take care of myself,' she said.

'You can,' Marc agreed. 'But I think that sometimes you need to let someone else take care of you. Like now, for instance.'

'But I can—'

He was already shifting away from her to stand up. 'Before, I didn't force the issue when I offered to give you a foot massage because I thought there was a good chance you might kick me in the face, but you're having a massage now whether you like it or not,' he said very sternly. He paused at the bathroom door. 'You'll have to lose the hoodie.'

He was gone for all of half a minute and when he returned with a large towel, Cassie was sitting up. Still in her hoodie but with a knowing smile on her face.

'There are easier ways to get me naked,' she said. 'Like, you could just ask me.'

'This isn't about me getting you naked.' Marc sounded outraged at the suggestion. 'I'm trying to do something nice for you. I'm still very much in grovel mode. I'd take advantage of it if I were you. I can't guarantee how long it will last.'

It was very sweet of him. And what had Russell said earlier? That she shouldn't look a gift massage in the mouth. Besides, Marc was very good with his hands.

She stood up and pulled off her hoodie, pleased that she was wearing a pretty black lace bralette. She pinged the waistband of her joggers. 'Should I take these off as well?' Her tone was a lot more flirtatious than she'd intended.

'It's up to you,' Marc said in an offhand manner as he retrieved the duvet from the floor then laid it on the bed. 'They might interrupt my flow.'

Cassie nodded. 'OK.' It was quite hard to take off joggers with elasticated cuffs in an alluring way but Marc seemed more interested in spreading the towel over the duvet. He barely glanced at Cassie, who was pleased that this was one of the very rare occasions when she was wearing a matching set of underwear.

He set something down on the bedside table, then pulled off his black cashmere sweater, his feet already bare. As always, he looked just as elegant in jeans and a white T-shirt as he did in one of his bespoke suits.

'Aren't you going to take off your clothes?' Cassie asked. Things were now a little stilted between them. Maybe it was the imbalance of being half naked while he was fully dressed. 'You wouldn't want to get them messy.'

'Lie down, Cass,' Marc said, his voice laced with amusement. 'It's going to be quite hard to do this with you standing up.'

Cassie put one knee on the bed, a hand on her hip, so she was posed prettily. Marc was now making a valiant attempt to keep his eyes on her face but his eyes drifted down and he pursed his lips in a silent whistle.

'On my tummy?'

He grunted in assent and turned away as she lay down on the towel, wriggling to get comfortable.

Marc sat down on the bottom of the bed, so Cassie had to look over her shoulder. He tapped her on the arse with the flat of his hand. Not hard enough to hurt, but the shock of the contact, the sharp sound in the soft quiet of the room, that edge to him, the fizzing anticipation that this was probably going to be a lot more than just a massage, made her suck in her breath.

'Eyes front, arms by your side,' he snapped, which was at odds with the gentle way he stroked down the back of her leg, pausing to press an entirely superfluous kiss to a random spot on her calf.

Cassie heard the faint click of something being opened. Then something wet and thick being drizzled down one leg, then the other. The scent of figs reached her as Marc's hands began to work the expensive body oil, which Cassie asked for every birthday and Christmas, into her skin.

He took her right foot in his hands and worked his thumbs along her instep, his touch too firm, too sure, to be ticklish. Laughing was the last thing on Cassie's mind. It was all she could do to stifle her groans as Marc moved on to her left foot and worked his palm against her heel.

He travelled up her calves, kneading muscles that were always tense.

Cassie tried to stay silent. She didn't want to give Marc the satisfaction that he'd take from every moan that he dragged out of her. His hands smoothed up her thighs, then in between them so he could part her legs. She was starting to hate her very expensive and favourite pair of knickers. Just as Cassie was sure that his fingertips were about to slip under the black lace, his hands suddenly swept back down to her knees.

Marc was a horrible, terrible tease. He kept coming closer and closer to her aching pussy, and every time she willed his fingers inside her, he'd divert his course.

'You are *so* mean,' she groaned and he slapped her on the arse again. Harder this time, not that Cassie cared. Not when his hands were smoothing over her buttocks, dipping just beneath her waistband . . .

She did moan, but in frustration, when she felt him shift on the bed and then more oil tracing along the taut line of her spine.

'I'm just going to unclip this,' he murmured, not waiting for permission, which Cassie would happily have given, to unfasten her bra. 'That's better.'

He worked all her sorest spots. The small of her back. The grooves under her shoulder blades. Then her shoulders, where she carried all her heaviest loads, and finally the permanent knot at the back of her neck.

By the time he was finished, Cassie felt as limp as a pan of noodles that had been cooked for too long.

'You can turn over,' Marc said hoarsely.

Cassie rolled over slowly, her movements muted and sluggish. Then she sat up slightly, aware of Marc's eyes on the sway of her breasts, as she tugged off her knickers and dropped them on the floor.

Marc sighed heavily as he pulled his T-shirt over his head. Then he tipped more oil onto his hands and let it drizzle drop by drop onto her breasts, her belly. 'You are so fucking hot,' he muttered as he shaped Cassie's breasts, his thumbs rubbing against her tightly budded nipples. She arched her back, offering herself to him, but he moved up to her collarbones, tracing the hollows with his thumbs.

Then back to her breasts, down her belly, to the top of her pubic bone . . . and he actually had the nerve to smile when Cassie parted her legs so he could see how pink and glistening and desperate she was.

'I'm in charge,' he murmured, picking up Cassie's arm to rotate her wrist, manipulate the fleshy mound of her thumb.

Cassie had been relaxed but now she was as taut as a violin bow.

She flexed her fingers and as Marc let go of her, she seized him round the wrist and dragged his hand down to her cunt. He barely struggled. A token protest at best as he obeyed Cassie's silent instructions. She pressed his hand through the sticky folds of her pussy, two of his fingers slipping inside her, his thumb pressing against her clit.

She kept tight hold of Marc's wrist as she fucked herself on his hand, not quite believing that she was doing this but also not really giving a shit. Then he crooked his fingers in just the right way so that they brushed against the good place with every thrust of his hand, until Cassie went rigid, every muscle that'd he worked so hard on tightening as she ground against his fingers, his thumb, his hand.

'Oh God,' she whispered, trapping his hand between her thighs, his movements soft now, keeping her at a three rather than letting her drop down to zero.

'See, I can take care of you,' Marc said in a rather unsteady voice. 'If you let me.'

'It's my turn to take care of you.' Her voice was hoarse even though she'd hardly made a sound. 'If you want, or you could just fuck me.'

'I'm good to go and yes, I'd love to fuck you,' Marc said.

He was sitting on the edge of the bed, one hand still gently on Cassie, in her. Her pussy clung to his fingers as he slowly disengaged. Eyes never leaving Cassie's flushed face, he sucked the fingers into his mouth. Then he stood up to impatiently lose his jeans and boxer trunks.

'I want to taste you too,' Cassie whispered and she sat up so she could lean forward and suck the tip of his cock into her mouth, her tongue tracing the vein that pulsed along the underside of his shaft.

'Cass, if you keep doing that, then it's game over and if I don't get inside you, then I'll lose my mind.' He gathered her hair up so he could slowly pull her mouth off him. As revenge for all the teasing, just before she let go, Cassie held him lightly with her teeth. Then she took pity on him, kissing the head of his dick then lying back down.

'Payback's a bitch,' she said, spreading her legs and pulling him down so he was on top of her.

Marc took the still sticky hand that had been inside her and wrapped it around his cock, so he could rub the head along her slit, catching her clit on the upstroke as Cassie curled her fingers in his hair, tracing the delicate curve of his ears, the tense set of his jaw because he was gritting his teeth.

'Kiss me,' she breathed against his lips and as Marc slipped his tongue inside her mouth, he slipped his cock inside her, his length, his girth dragging against her swollen, still-sensitive walls. She pulled away from his mouth long enough to say, 'Don't move, just kiss me.'

He'd fucked her hard and fast last night but now Cassie wanted the weight of Marc's body on her, anchoring her, his mouth slowly and sensually moving on hers, one hand tangled in her hair, his other hand clutching hers.

Cassie wrapped her legs tight around his hips as her pussy gripped his cock. Marc groaned into her mouth as she fluttered around him.

'This is some tantric shit,' he mumbled after what felt like hours and Cassie laughed softly which made him groan even more.

The base of his cock was rubbing against her clit in just the right spot and Cassie could feel the need in her becoming more urgent.

'OK, you can move now,' she whispered.

He kissed her very slowly, very deeply then shifted back a little, closing his eyes in what looked like pain as Cassie tightened her legs.

'Cass, I have to pull out now,' he said like he was in a thousand agonies. 'I don't have any protection. I never expected this. Any of this. I'm clean and I haven't been with . . . but . . . I would never . . .'

'I'm good, I'm safe.' Cassie moved her hands down to his hips. 'You can come inside me if you want.'

He did want. Of course he wanted. He managed five really good thrusts and then Cassie could feel him spurting inside her, which set off a series of tiny dynamite charges.

Marc rested his forehead on Cassie's shoulder and she stroked the back of his neck. When he tried to withdraw, she refused to let him go.

'Can we just stay like this?' she asked.

'Aren't I too heavy for you?' Neither of them was able to speak in anything louder than a whisper. 'You can't be comfortable.'

'I don't care.' Cassie kissed along his cheekbone. 'Let's be still for a while. I want to hold you.'

'A few adjustments, that's all.'

He rolled onto his side, taking Cassie with him, so they were still pressed together, still joined. She hooked her leg over his and sighed as his arms closed around her.

He kissed her mouth again, as soft as a feather. 'I wish we could stay like this forever.'

'Oh God, me too.'

They fell asleep like that, the half-moon peeking in at the window the only witness to the start of something that had taken sixteen long years to begin.

Something precious.

LUCY'S NAUGHTY FORTY BIRTHDAY
WEEKEND EXTRAVAGANZA!

ITINERARY

MONDAY

10.00 a.m. AND NO LATER! Breakfast. I'm hoping that there is still food left, otherwise we'll have to go foraging in the nearby countryside or, more likely, send someone on a mercy dash to the nearest shop.

Noon: We need to have vacated the premises.

I hope this has been a weekend for the ages and that we've yes, lived, loved and laughed.

Now, can you all do one? Haven't you got homes to go to?

34

When they woke up, the sun was shining and they were holding hands. That had to be a good sign, Cassie thought and when she came out of the bathroom mid-tooth-clean, even though all his things were in the room down the corridor, Marc was sitting on the edge of the bed. Rumpled and bleary-eyed and back in jeans and T-shirt.

There were so many things she wanted to say to him. Everything might be different now that it was morning.

She settled for a quiet but heartfelt, 'I'm glad you're still here.'

Marc nodded. 'I'm glad that I'm here too.' He paused as if, like her, he was searching for the right words. 'I want you to know that I meant everything I said last night,' he told her, his face focused and serious. 'We're heading towards real heartache in the next few months, but you and I, we're a team, aren't we?'

'I'm not going anywhere,' she said, wishing she didn't still have toothpaste foam around her mouth, which rather spoiled the solemnity of the moment. 'If there are hard times ahead, then I want us to go through them together. It's so odd . . .'

'What? Us?' Marc frowned. 'I don't think the idea of us is that odd.'

'Not us.' Though it *was* odd that suddenly the two of them were an us. 'Odd that when I think about the future, I feel devastated about Russell but now . . . *hopeful* too. Is that wrong? It feels wrong.'

'I know exactly what you mean. But it also feels right, doesn't it?' He looked hesitant, which was so unlike him, until Cassie nodded.

There was a small silence, not charged but thoughtful. Then Cassie glanced at the clock on the bedside table to see that it was half past nine. 'I need to organise breakfast.'

Marc had followed her gaze to the clock and must have come to the same conclusion. He stood up. 'I really wish I could have you all to myself today. Spend a few hours spoiling you absolutely rotten.'

'I don't need to be spoiled,' Cassie said because these new old feelings for Marc weren't about his bank balance but who he was. His money still felt like something that came between them.

'Oh, Cassie, you do. For once in your life, you really do need to be spoiled,' Marc drawled, then he caught the mutinous expression on her face. 'But let's start with me taking you out to dinner. This week.'

This week. Cassie thought about the coming week. Everyone back from their summer holidays. The start of the autumn season. London Fashion Week just around the corner. Her diary was horrific and . . . 'Yeah, this week,' she said firmly. 'I'd love that.'

Marc stood up and stretched lazily. 'Right now, I need a shower then breakfast.'

Cassie held up her hand then went back into the bathroom to spit and rinse again. 'If there's any food left.'

'There's food left,' Marc said, leaning in the bathroom doorway. 'I stashed bacon and eggs and bread in the salad drawer of the spare fridge in the utility room.'

'Oh! I'm impressed. Even I hadn't thought to do that. If you ever fancy a career change to event planning . . .'

Now that her mouth was minty fresh, Cassie was ready for a kiss, but Marc fended her off with one arm and insulting ease. 'I need to brush my teeth and I need a lot more than one kiss.' He took a step backwards. 'I'll see you downstairs where we'll run the gamut of lots of nosy questions and really bad jokes.'

Marc was right. Cassie came down the stairs to find that Anita and Azad were at the front door, bags packed, as they had to be back in London for lunch with their extended family.

'We've had the best weekend,' Anita said, holding out her arms for a goodbye hug. 'Thank you for not waking us up last night with your noisy shagging. How did you manage to keep it down?'

'I'm not even going to dignify that remark with a response,' Cassie said, squeezing Anita hard enough that she squeaked. Last night hadn't been about scratching a sixteen-year itch with some very enthusiastic, noisy shagging. Last night had been about . . . making love. Not that she was going to share that with the group. 'Although I did Amazon Prime a ball gag for Marc, which turned up yesterday while you were out.'

Azad gasped in genuine shock. 'Really?'

'No! Of course not!' Cassie hugged him too, then pushed him out of the open door. 'Honestly, what are you like?'

Iris and Bill and Digby and Kwame were already in the kitchen with a sorry pile of random food foraged from the fridge.

Bill's eyes lit up as Cassie walked through the open-plan lounge towards them. 'Thank you for not—'

'Not another word if it's about anything to do with what I may or may not choose to do with another consenting adult,' she said grandly.

'All we were going to say is that we slept well last night and so we thank you for not being at it like very loud rabbits,' Digby added. Then his face dropped. 'How do you feel about some cold carrots and parsnips and a chicken drumstick split between two for breakfast?'

'Not good,' Cassie said. 'Just as well that Marc planned for this. I hope you're going to thank him when he comes down and not treat him to any more salty remarks.'

'Wouldn't dream of it,' Iris said, her face a picture of innocence.

Cassie was retrieving all the ingredients needed for a decent breakfast from the fridge in the utility room when she heard someone behind her.

She turned to see Lucy standing in the doorway. 'Do you hate me?' she asked tentatively. 'Was I overstepping?'

'I could never hate you,' Cassie said, nudging the fridge door shut with her hip. 'And you stepped just enough. The video Russell sent Marc didn't hurt either.'

'A video?' Lucy put her hands on her hips. 'And he told me not to meddle!'

'I'm glad you meddled rather than knocking our heads together,' Cassie said as Lucy relieved her of the carton of eggs, which was about to fall.

'So the meddling was . . . successful?' Lucy blocked Cassie's exit from the utility room. 'Please say it was successful.'

'If by successful you mean that we established that neither one of us hates the other and that actually we like each other a lot, then yes,' Cassie said, which barely explained the difficult conversation of the previous night and its very encouraging conclusion.

'Only like?' Lucy sounded very disappointed.

'More than like. I think we might be on the cusp of something that feels really special.' If Cassie hadn't had her arms full of perishables, she'd have held her thumbs for luck like the Fossil sisters in *Ballet Shoes*.

'I like really special. Really special is great.' Lucy clasped her hands together in mild rapture.

Cassie nodded. 'Yeah, it is great.' She could have been on her merry way but she paused. 'Luce, I'm so sorry if me and Marc and all our drama has used up a lot of your emotional bandwidth these last few days. I know that you've got so much on your plate without us . . .'

'No! Oh my goodness, no! If I wasn't holding these eggs, I'd smack you,' Lucy exclaimed. 'You have no idea how lovely it's been to think about something that isn't Russell's illness. It's usually all that we talk about – until this weekend, when all we've talked about is you and Marc.'

Of course Cassie was pleased that she and Marc had provided a welcome distraction and some entertainment, even if there had been times this weekend when she'd thought she was losing her mind. 'I dread to think what you and Russell have been saying about us.'

'Not just me and Russell. Everybody has been talking about it!' Lucy smiled very smugly. 'Did you not wonder why we all went silent whenever you entered a room? What was strange was that everyone seemed so surprised. But I wasn't surprised. I know you'll deny it but you two have always had this weird kind of chemistry.'

Cassie was sick of keeping secrets and also, even though she was grateful for it, Lucy *had* called her a twat. 'That's probably because we slept together the night of your wedding,' she said, as she slipped past her friend. 'Did I never mention it?'

'What? No!' Lucy tried to grab hold of Cassie but she evaded her grasp. 'Oh, I knew it! I mean, I had my suspicions, but yes, it all makes sense now. I need details.'

'I've said enough. Now you and Russell will have plenty to talk about on the drive home. Think of it as an early birthday present,' Cassie insisted, lowering her voice as they stepped back into the kitchen. 'But Marc and I, we're good.'

At the sound of her voice, Marc looked over from where he was now stationed with Russell in front of his beloved coffee machine. He smiled at her. A sweet smile that Cassie hadn't known he had in his repertoire. Just because he'd heard her voice.

'Good is perfect,' Lucy whispered. She walked over to Russell and slipped her arm around him. 'OK, so who's having bacon and eggs? Iris, I forget, are you a vegetarian who will eat eggs?'

35

Even though they were all on a clock, it was a long and leisurely breakfast. Going back for more toast until there was no bread left. Lingering over a last cup of coffee until it was time to bring their bags downstairs. To make sure that there were no champagne flutes floating in the swimming pool. And yes, to check three times that the barbecue hadn't miraculously turned itself on overnight.

Iris and Bill left first, then Digby and Kwame, who'd managed to book a room in a very eclectic boutique hotel in Brighton to prolong the weekend one more night.

Then it was just Cassie and Marc, Lucy and Russell left standing on the drive, about to get into their respective cars and head back to London to whatever lay ahead, both good and bad.

But the bad seemed a long way away from the sound of birdsong and the faint lap of the waves as they danced along the shoreline. Marc was loading the last of their bags into the car and Cassie lifted her face towards the sun and watched a plane leave a vapour trail as it drifted across the clear blue sky.

'I don't want this to be over,' she said, her words sounding like a sigh.

'Me neither.' Lucy pulled out her phone from her slouchy denim tote bag. 'It's not even eleven thirty. What time do we have to leave?'

'Noon. Midday.' They should get going. It was a long drive. Bank holiday traffic. Savita had already messaged to say that they'd run out of Dreamies and could she pick some up on the way home. Koita had clearly been mainlining them the whole weekend. So many good reasons to get on the road. 'But I mean, if we were still here at twelve fifteen, I don't think that they'd charge us for an extra day.'

'Seems a pity to waste a sea view,' Russell said as he leaned against the side of his car. 'Shall we just take a few minutes?'

Marc closed the boot. He was wearing shades so it was hard to know exactly what he was thinking, though his lips thinned so Cassie imagined that he was probably thinking about what a nightmare the bloody Hanger Lane gyratory system would be if they dawdled.

Then he smiled. 'I think we can spare the time, as long as you're not planning on doing anything crazy like abseiling down the cliff face.'

Russell shrugged. 'Well, now that you mention it . . .'

There was no abseiling. Just a slow amble around the house and across the lawn until they came to the bench on the cliff's edge. Russell sat down with a grateful 'Ooof'. Marc indicated that Lucy should sit down next to him, but she shook her head.

'We're about to spend hours sitting next to each other,' she said, shaking her head. 'You take the bench. I know the ground will be too hard for those old bones of yours.'

'You're all heart, Luce,' Marc said but he sat down next to his best friend, nudging Russell with his elbow and they both smiled, their body language relaxed and comfortable.

Lucy perched on the arm of the bench next to Russell, and Cassie kicked off her Birkenstocks so she could feel the grass, lush and green after the previous day's rain, tickle the soles of her feet. She was wearing jeans and what she called her Frida Kahlo top, a loose-fitting black cheesecloth smock with puff sleeves and colourful embroidery. Nothing that would stain as she sat down on the grass and rested her back against Marc's legs. Immediately his hand stroked her hair, which she was wearing loose, twisting a strand of it around his finger.

Then the four of them were silent. Each lost in their own thoughts but still very much four people who'd always be bound together after years and years of sharing each other's joys and sorrows, of in-jokes and the long, convoluted story of the time that Russell and Marc had run the London marathon and Lucy, eight months pregnant with Fleur, who was mostly resting on her bladder, had managed to wangle her way into the famous green Cabmen's Shelter at Temple to use the loo.

Sometimes you didn't need words to express your love for someone. It was Russell's hand resting briefly on Cassie's shoulder as she shifted position. It was Lucy leaning against Russell's side as she watched two seagulls circle overhead. It was Marc not mentioning the bank holiday traffic, which had to be killing him, and the way he smiled faintly when Cassie licked the back of her hand to confirm that yes, her skin tasted of salt because that faint sea breeze was still fulfilling its remit.

Cassie's heart was full. It had been a weekend like no other. She felt as if she'd experienced every emotion and probably even some that only the Germans had words for. But it was now, these few precious, peaceful minutes, that she knew she'd come back to over and over again.

Though it was hot, the sun fierce without the benefit of the shade from the graceful trees that bordered the garden, after yesterday's storm, there was also a suggestion of crispness in the air.

It felt like the last day of summer. Swallows ready to fly south for the winter and new school uniform hanging up on the wardrobe door.

It was both an ending and a beginning.

There was a sadness that had already seeped deep into her bones at the thought of living the rest of her life without Russell, her beloved friend Russell, in it.

Yet now there was also a giddy sensation, a heightened sense of exhilaration at the thought of this new, unexpected *thing* with Marc. But to call it a thing made it seem ordinary, maybe even fleeting, when it felt like it was *extra*ordinary and maybe, after such a long time coming, built to last. She was even excited at the prospect of spending three hours in a car with him – longer if the Hanger Lane gyratory system did them dirty.

The joy wouldn't cancel out the grief, and vice versa. They were two opposing states of being that Cassie would get used to but she didn't want to think about anything except right now, this garden, these three people who had her heart. She wished she could capture this moment, freeze it in time.

Then a sharp breeze ruffled the leaves on the trees and Cassie shivered. Marc combed his fingers through her hair again.

'We should go,' Russell said reluctantly. 'I don't want to, but . . .'

'I know.' Marc's hand tightened in Cassie's hair, then relaxed. 'But it's not goodbye. Not yet.'

'Not for ages,' Lucy said tightly but she was getting to her feet. 'Cass, shall we do one last sweep to make sure we haven't forgotten anything.'

Cassie knew for certain that she hadn't forgotten a single thing but she also knew, without needing to be told, that Lucy wanted Russell and Marc to have a few minutes alone, just the two of them.

Then there was no putting off the inevitable. The four of them gathered on the drive again, ready to say their good-byes.

'What did we ever do to deserve friends like you?' Russell asked, throwing his hands up.

'Clearly something very bad,' Marc said.

'Maybe to deserve you but Cassie is an angel,' Lucy insisted, her arm tight around her friend. 'Honestly, thank you both for this weekend. You've given me memories that are going to last a lifetime.'

It seemed to Cassie that everything, even the most innocuous words, were now shot through with grief. A lifetime could last for decades or it could be so suddenly and cruelly cut short.

'It was a great weekend,' Cassie said firmly. 'Even the shit bits – no names but I'm thinking of Heather and Davy – were all right because they made the good bits even better.'

'You do know that Heather will find a way to make my funeral all about her,' Russell said.

Cassie felt foreboding flicker through her. 'Don't, please,' she begged.

Russell held out his arms and drew the three of them in so they stood in a circle, arms around each other. 'I have to laugh about it because I'm out of other options and we all know I'm right about Heather.'

'She'll rock up in full widow's weeds,' Lucy said, as if Heather's funeral behaviour was something she and Russell had already discussed.

'Yup, black lace mantilla, and she'll howl all the way through the service,' Marc added.

'Crying so hard but not hard enough to make her mascara run,' Cassie noted and the four of them took a moment to contemplate Heather allowed to run amok at the wake.

'But anyway, enough of that – it's been the most heavenly weekend,' Lucy said. 'Just, thank you both. We love you so much.'

'Beyond words,' Russell agreed. 'And it makes . . . things a little more bearable knowing that . . . Marc, you'll be there to look after my girls.'

This time Marc didn't counter with a sarcastic reply. 'You know I will.'

Russell pulled the three of them in even closer. 'And Cassie, she's also one of my girls. You have to look after her too.'

Cassie blinked back tears as Marc kissed the top of her head.

'Always,' he said.

Acknowledgements

Thank you to my biggest cheerleader, my agent, Becky Ritchie, and Euan Thorneycroft, for being my surrogate Becky, as well as Harmony Leung, Alexandra McNicoll, Jack Sargeant, Gosia Jezierska, Lucy Joyce and all at A. M. Heath.

At Hodder, thanks to Jo Dickinson and Lucy Stewart for silk pursing this sow's ear, Charlea Charlton, marketing maven, Kallie Townsend, publicist extraordinaire, Amber Burlinson for a beautiful copy edit, and the whole Hodder Fiction team. I'm also beyond grateful to Sofia Hericson and Jo Myler for my gorgeous cover.

To Sarah Bailey for the coffee klatches, Eileen Coulter (and god-dog, Eric) for pizza evenings, Cari Rosen for yenta-ing.

To the reviewers' group chat, my girls, Nina Pottell, Fran Brown and Sarah Shaffi. #youhadonejob

And to Anna Carey, Jane Casey, Harriet Evans, Cress McLaughlin, Laura Wood, Fiona Gibson, Holly Bourne, and I know I've forgotten so many people, but it is such a joy to have the friendship and generous support of other writers who understand what a ridiculous and lonely job this can be.

Finally, a huge thank you to Roy Koita, who was the successful bidder in the Book Aid For Ukraine auction, organised by Hayley Steed. Roy, it was a delight to name a character after you and I hope you enjoy reading about your namesake as much as I enjoyed writing him. Sorry you had to wait so long!